HER SCREAM

~~~ TWISTED THREADS ~~~
REDO
SHERYLL O'BRIEN

This is a work of fiction. All characters in this book are the product of an overactive imagination. Any businesses, organizations, places, events, and incidents are used fictionally. Any resemblance to a real person, living or dead, is a tremendous coincidence.

ISBN 978-1-939351-34-0

Printed in United States of America

Mom,

Here's your **big-ass** book.
Enjoy!

ACKNOWLEDGMENT

Helena,
Thank you for letting me use your name,

And tramping you up a bit.

A heartfelt thank you to my team:

Andria Flores ~ Editor extraordinaire.
Nancy Pendleton ~ Goddess of the publishing world.
Jessica Champion ~ Web designer and manager.
25 Hours Consulting

Special thanks to:
Jessica Champion ~ Cover design

And to:
Os Flores, Arlington PD ~ Procedural Consultant
And Andria's Good Cop!

For a complete list of Sheryll O'Brien's books,

Please visit pullingthreadsnovella.com

I wish you'd reconsider.
Thanksgiving

The roads were slick, too slick for anyone to be on them. Jenna Farnsworth wasn't traveling that night; she was inside where it was safe and warm, but the people she loved most in the world were on the roads. The worried woman, the one nearing a full-on panic attack, paced the enclosed front porch of her second-floor apartment. On every third pass by the front windows she stopped to peer out. Tiny ice pellets tapped gently against the glass, and beams from the streetlights across the way cast a shimmery glow over the icy scene. "Beautiful," she whispered. "Dangerous," she reminded.

Jenna's parents, Teddy and Maxine, were making their way to Philly for a late Thanksgiving dinner and sleepover at her place. The next day they were heading north to spend the winter with her aged grandparents. Jenna asked her parents—begged them—not to come...

"Mom, it's really bad here. Please don't come."

"We'll take it slow, Jenna. Besides, your father's Land Rover is really good in snow."

"It isn't snowing in Philly, Mom. It's a sheet of ice out there. Please don't come."

"If we don't see you tonight, we won't see you until the Farnsworths of Oneida kick us out in the spring. It's Thanksgiving, Jenna, and you've done the turkey."

"Mom, I wish you'd reconsider."

Teddy Farnsworth was behind the wheel of the Land Rover when it slid off a creek overpass only ten miles from his home in Malvern, Pennsylvania. His wife, Maxine, died instantly in the crash, Teddy, soon after. His last act on earth was taking hold of his beloved's hand and choking a final, "I love you."

The Women

North I-476 to I-81.

She wipes away big tears that suddenly blur her vision. Tears brought on by the last words she would ever share with her mother. "It's really bad here. Please don't come. Mom, I wish you'd reconsider." For weeks, those words have looped incessantly, fraying her nerves, and shredding what remains of her heart. She forbids this new set of tears from falling, "No. Not again." Jenna pulls a ragged breath, straightens in her seat, cracks open a window, breathes in cold, crisp air, and forces herself to pay attention to the conditions of the road. "Snowy, but no ice," she relaxes into her whispered words, then immediately scolds herself, "Pay attention! There's no ice, but it's slippery." She focuses on the road for a minute, then follows a memory...

"This is a great apartment," the prospective subletter enthused. "It's close to campus, just the right size, and you're leaving all of the—"

"Everything. I'm leaving everything. There are 18 months left on my lease."

"Eighteen months? You're subletting for all of that time? You're not—"

"Coming back. No. I'm not coming back."

In the few short weeks between Thanksgiving and New Year, the bereaved woman left her Philly apartment, withdrew from her graduate studies at Drexel University, enrolled in a graduate program at Styles University, sublet a place to live in Syracuse, packed her few belongings, and left her home state of Pennsylvania. Oh, and she buried her parents, Theodore and Maxine Farnsworth, during that time, too.

In a feeble attempt to lessen the loneliness, Jenna talks to herself. "Styles University has one of the best Library Science grad programs in the country, I'm subletting from my best friend, Mary, while she's doing a study abroad, I've already met Keith Moreno, Mary's **really** cute boyfriend and owner of the house I'll live in, and if things go well, Mary said I can move into the second-floor apartment when he's finished renovating. She even joked that she'd leave Keith to himself downstairs and move in with me upstairs. Most of all, I'll be minutes away from my only living relatives." A wide smile conquers as she thinks of her elderlies, "Grams and Gramps." She pulls a deep inhale then lets it usher away tiny bits of torment that still linger. "Oneida Lake. My most favorite place. The one that holds the happiest moments of my life." She welcomes snippet-memories of canoe rides with her dad, campfire confessions with her mom, long walks along the shoreline with her grandfather, and short walks to Eileen's General Store with her grandmother. Her mind easily shifts to fun-filled days of swimming and picnicking with 'the McLaughlin Boy' as her grandparents called him. "Mac," she whispers on a sigh, then quickly enjoys a laugh when she struggles to remember his real first name, "Bobby. It's Bobby." She exhales her next words, "Might have forgotten his name, but there's no way I'd forget him..."

"Mac. Stop! Mac, really. I don't want to get .... wet!" she spit the last word with a mouthful of lake water. The sopping young woman threw herself chest to chest against the athletic young man and tried mightily to drag him beneath the water's surface. "There's **no** way you're not going under, McLaughlin!" Panting hard from her unsuccessful efforts, she resorted to splashing the fair-haired trickster.

"Huh. I'd forgotten how cute Mac was, even with the one-blue-one-brown-eye thing. Small thing to overlook on someone that cute— but it always freaked me out." Jenna pushes those thoughts aside, her smile fading with them. Reality grips, and she reminds herself why she is heading north, "Because of that day in November." She tears at the memory of the conversation she had to have, the one that still bangs incessantly...

"Grams, is Gramps there? .... Yes, of course I remember I already called to wish you Happy Thanksgiving .... Grams, can I talk to Gramps?" She heard the budding concern in his voice when he took the receiver, "Jenna. Is everything alright?" She couldn't speak for several minutes. By the time she did, he already knew.

Jenna shelves her thoughts and pulls her wayward Subaru back under control on the slippery road. "Get your shit together, Jenna! Before any life changes can take root, you've got to get to Syracuse, and you've got to get there in one piece."

I only want to rape you.

The slumbering woman is woken by the crushing weight of a man as her scream fills the space between them—as it brands them, bonds them. The terrified victim thrashes about wildly, and her assailant pushes down mightily. She feels a muscle rip across her lower back. The heat of the injury travels up her spine and around to her hips.

"Stop moving," he demands, his large hand easily covering her mouth and nose.

Can't … breathe … do what he says.

He stays pressed on top of her, his hand still silencing her, his hard, evil thing digging into her leg. **"Don't move,"** he warns again.

Want … to … live … do what he says.

"You need to obey me."

She closes her eyes and silently recites the rape victim's chant. *No. No. No.*

"Open your eyes," he loosens his hand a bit.

I need to obey.

The man uses his free hand to move away bangs that partially cover her cobalt-blue eyes. He runs his thumb down her cheek as though caressing her, then fingers her blonde hair as he moves it off her shoulder. He feels the slowing of her breaths beneath him. The experienced rapist recognizes the signs. *She's coming around. She'll take what's coming.* **"I don't want to hurt you. I only want to rape you."**

The words confuse her. She furrows her brow.

"What's your name?"

"Jenna," she whispers.

"Beautiful name for a beautiful woman. Jenna, this can be a rape or a murder. You can get over one of those two events. I suggest you not fight this." He pushes himself up, straddles her waist, and pulls a knife from an ankle strap before he releases himself through the fly of his jeans. **"Don't scream,"** he rasps. He takes his hand completely away from her mouth and waits.

She makes no sound.

He fists a measure of her long-sleeve, winter-warm nightgown in one hand and slices through it.

She gasps when the cold blade touches her skin, shivers when the bitter cold air buds her nipples and raises goosebumps on her arms and legs. She tries to get her arms out from under his knees.

He presses down, then skims the knife across her left breast, drawing blood. He warns her with his eyes.

Ski-mask, undershirt, jeans, dark eyes, chapped lips, minty breath, and a gold wedding band on his knife wielding hand. She closes her eyes and brands those things to memory. She will wish she hadn't, one day. Big tears begin wetting her lashes as they take to their journey.

One by one, they slide across and down her cheeks, some pooling in her ears, others finding her pillow. "Please, I've never," she sobs. She can tell he is smiling beneath the wool mask.

"A virgin. My lucky night," he laughs. He cuts the strap of her undies, moves the flimsy cloth to the side, and pushes in, in, in, in. He slows, raises his chest off hers, and brushes away hair from her face. "Beautiful, Jenna. Your first time. You should..." He kisses her.

The victim hasn't moved since her rapist left, though she is desperate to. She tried several times, but the muscles in her lower back are torn to shit, as is her vagina. She stopped crying some time ago, but is racked with an uncontrollable shaking that began the second he got off her. She shudders at the memory of the scratchy kiss he pressed to her lips and his parting words…

"Maybe we'll meet again, someday." Then he leaned really close and whispered, "Maybe we already know one another, Jenna."

Don't call the police.

Blankets could warm her and return a bit of her stolen dignity, but they are heaped at the end of the bed. She is desperate to take hold of them, to cover what he has done, what she has become, but she can't move. The sound of a wounded animal reverberates deep as she pulls her nightgown together along the sliced edges. She's heard that woeful sound once before—on a day of ice covered roads when no one should have been driving. *Don't go there,* she warns. Beams of light coming from the side driveway travel across the walls and ceiling of her bedroom. They may have woken her or perhaps released her from a stupor. "Keith," she whispers as a set of tears spring forth. "Keith," she whispers again.

The exhausted man parks his Jeep on the driveway at 10 Oren Street. He drags his ass from the warmth inside, feels the immediate sting of snow that whips and swirls against his face and finds its way into the collar of his jacket, causing a shiver. He trudges through knee-high frozen fluff that's lighted from behind by his Jeep. He slips and slides the last few steps to the back porch, climbs the snow-covered stairs, leans against the railing, and quickly taps the toe of his boots on the side of the house. The tall, dark-haired man pulls the storm door toward him and notices the inside door is partially open. He pushes it wide and calls out, "Jenna!" He sees small puddles of water just inside the entranceway and wet patches on the carpet as he moves through. "Jenna!" he calls again. He hears what sounds like moaning coming from the direction of her room. He pushes open her bedroom door, a guttural sound escapes— maybe his, maybe hers—as he steps inside.

"Ccccold," she stutters.

Keith grabs hold of the twisted covers at the foot of the bed and lays them across the shivering, bloody woman. He grabs a throw from her reading chair and lays it on top then inches toward the head of the bed. She stares vacantly past him.

"Jenna. Jenna. Can you hear me?"

She squeezes her eyes shut and nods, opens them seconds later, and gently shakes her head. A tear slides down her cheek, then off to the side when another pushes it along.

"I'll get help." He takes his cell from his pocket.

"No. No. No." she whispers.

"No, what?"

"Don't call the police."

"What? I have to call. You need help. You've been ……. you need help."

"Not yet, please."

Keith sits on the floor next to the bed, presses his back tight against the wall, starts to dial 9-1-1 several times, stops himself before pressing send, not sure why. When Jenna reaches her hand over the side of the bed, he takes hold of her trembling fingertips and listens to her chants, "No. No. No." From time to time she sobs through pitiful moans; other times she bears her pain in silence.

"Keith. Keith."

He startles at the sound of his name, scrambles from the floor, loses his breath at the sight of her, "I'm sorry ……. I didn't hear you. Can I help you?"

"I need to use the bathroom."

"Oh. Oh. Okay. What should I do?"

"If you can help me sit up."

He moves the covers the rest of the way off of her, trying not to look. He reaches to pull her nightgown together, but stops when she flinches at his approach. "Your nightgown. Let me pull it together ……. you'll be warmer."

She nods. She tears. She tries to move. She winces in pain.

"Your back?"

"Yes."

"Can you roll onto your side? Away from me?"

She tries. She rolls.

"I'm going to inch onto the bed next to you. Okay, lean back against me." He steadies her, supports her weight, and helps ease her into a sitting position. "Jenna, I think we should call for help."

"Not. Yet." She pants through painful spasms.

"Okay. How are you doing? Can you get up?"

She inches across the bed, edges her legs over the side, and places her feet onto the floor. She grimaces through each movement, shedding plenty of tears, but she prevails. The trembling, swaying woman leans against the man she barely knows, and as soon as she can, she seeks shelter inside the bathroom. She closes the door behind her, flips the lock, presses her back against the sturdy wood, and breathes—she just breathes.

Keith is sitting on the hallway floor when Jenna opens the bathroom door. She's wearing an ankle length terrycloth robe. Her stick-straight, waist-length blonde hair is pulled back in a sleek ponytail. Her checks are shower-pink flush, and her bangs fringe her cobalt-blue eyes, which are darkly circled.

"You showered. Are you supposed to?"

"I had to get him off."

"Are you going to report this?"

"I don't know."

"What about the evidence?"

"I don't care."

"How's your back?"

She moans, "Awful. The shower helped a bit, but I could use some help to the couch."

"Lean in. You must be hungry. I can make you something, maybe some tea and toast."

"Please."

He settles her in front of a crackling fire in the den and busies himself in the kitchen across the hall. When he returns, she starts talking. "I didn't hear him." She takes the cup of tea he prepared and holds it in both hands, a welcome bit of tactile comfort. "I couldn't breathe. He held his hand over my mouth and nose."

"Jenna, you don't have to."

She speaks as though she's at the far end of a fog. Her words are quiet, flat, almost robotic in delivery. "Stop moving. You need to obey me. Open your eyes. What's your name? Beautiful name for a beautiful woman. This can be a rape or a murder. You can get over one of those two events. I suggest you not fight this. Don't scream. A virgin. My lucky night. Maybe we'll meet again, someday."

Several minutes of silence pass. Keith moves to the fireplace and sits on the raised hearth, "Jenna, I think we should call someone, if not the police, then someone else."

"I only know you." A memory attacks. "Maybe we already know one another, Jenna." She zones out—comes back again several minutes later. "I only know you," she sips her tea, tears when she finds it has grown cold. She settles the cup on the end table, "I need to rest."

"You can use my room."

"Can I stay here? The fire feels nice."

"Sure. I'll go get a pillow and blanket."

"Not mine, okay?"

"Okay. Anything else?"

"My computer."

Keith puts a small backpack on the couch near her, "I grabbed a sweater and a pair of stretchy black pants from your laundry basket. They're inside with the computer. Can you manage?"

"Yes."

"Okay. I'm staying home today, so you can rest." He closes the door behind him.

Jenna inches her legs into the tight material and pulls it to her knees, slips off one shoulder of her robe and gasps at the sight of a blood-stained piece of gauze she taped to her breast after her shower. She closes her eyes as she eases her robe off and pulls a baby blue sweater over her head. She winces through the process of getting herself to a standing position, and fears she may pass out from pain when pulling up the leggings. She pants through the endeavor, and is winded and weeping when she settles back onto the couch. Sleep rescues her before her tears have time to dry.

Syracuse Police Department

Detective Matthew Cambridge enters the station in a **very** unusual way. "Good morning, Diane," the chipper greeting given to the woman he meets at the stairs leading inside.

She falters a step, then stops cold when he opens the door for her.

"After you, Ms. Earls."

"Seriously?"

"Yeah."

"You're in a good mood."

"It'll last five minutes. I suggest you take advantage."

The administrative assistant continues the back and forth, "Married life looks good on you, Detective."

"Yeah." He follows her to her office, grabs his mail, and heads to the break room for coffee. "Empty. The room and the fucking pot." He heads to his office, peers through the window of a connecting office, and repeats, "Empty." He checks the police call log, "Quiet night."

Detective Raymond Chase, a mountainous Black man, who prefers Fedoras to wool caps, and trench coats to jackets, spends a few minutes with Diane Earls in spirited conversation.

"Wasn't born yesterday, Diane."

"Hand to God, Detective. He said good morning, held the door open for me, and said his good mood would last five minutes."

"Don't suppose I'm still in the window."

The administrative assistant hands off a stack of mail with a smile, "Sorry Detective, the Good Mood Ship set sail hours ago. He's back to his surly self."

"I'll be in the break room." Ray grabs his call log and heads that way, meeting his partner in the hallway, "Cambridge."

"Working half days now?"

"Don't report to you, Matt. Saw the log, another quiet 24."
"Yeah."
"Anything happen along the Lakes?"
"Not that I've heard."

Destroying evidence.

Jenna startles awake the next morning, the nightmare fresh on her lips, "No. No. No."

Keith moves away from the fireplace, "I'm sorry, Jenna, I didn't mean to disturb you. I just came in to stoke the fire."

"Keith, where?"

"You're in the den."

"What time is it?"

"A little after five."

She looks through the open window shades. The dark sky offers no hint, "AM or PM?"

"AM. You slept straight through yesterday. You must have needed the rest."

"Yes."

"Are you hungry?"

"Yes, and I need to pee," she yelps when she moves to get up, "my back. I forgot."

"Let me help." He is slow moving toward her. His eyes fix on a pinkish stain on her sweater.

She follows his eyes and covers her breast with her hand, "He cut me."

"Should we call?"

"No."

Keith walks Jenna down the hall. She glances at her closed bedroom door to the left of them, then steps through the open door on the right.

"Are you going to shower?"

"Maybe later. I really need something to eat and drink."

"I'll wait for you."

With her face scrubbed clean and hair brushed through, Jenna joins Keith in the hallway. She shakes her head at his offered hand, "I'll take it slow, thanks."

"What would you like for breakfast?"

"Any lasagna left from the other night?"

"Seriously?"

She nods. "I guess my appetite isn't in sync with the time of day."

He readies their plates and joins her at the table. She notices a plastic garbage bag set near the counter and an empty bathroom basket nearby.

He follows her line of sight. "You threw away your nightgown when you showered, yesterday."

"Yes."

"I found it in the bathroom trash. I put it into a bag in case you want to report this. It's evidence."

"I don't. Can you help me remove the bed linens and blankets? I don't want them."

"I'll handle it, Jenna. Don't. Move."

Jenna begins to tremble, the shake quickly morphs to a full-on panic attack. "He said…he said… 'Don't. Move.'"

Keith pushes back from the table and reaches out to her.

"Don't. Touch. Me."

He jumps back. "Jenna. You need help. We need help."

"No. No. No."

Syracuse Police Department

"Fuckin way to start the day," Detective Chase grouses as he pulls onto the parking lot a little past noon.

His partner, Matthew Cambridge, is leaning against a railing at the top of the stairs. "Did the brass assign new working hours for the Sexual Assault unit, Old Man?"

"You stalking me?"

"Nope. Are you working noon to eight now?"

"Just blowing through some personal time, Cambridge. I'm here until six unless there's a call. You?"

"Caitlyn's working late, so I'll be here until she's done." Cambridge is still working when the call comes in.

10 Oren Street

Police strobe lights catch falling and blowing snow in their beams coloring the lacey flakes a whimsical blue. The image is not in sync with the events that took place inside the lovely home. The first officer to arrive knocks on the front door.

"In here," Keith calls out. He is sitting on the couch next to Jenna holding onto the frigid fingertips of her trembling hand.

The officer steps into the living room.

Keith starts to get up.

Jenna tightens her fingers around his.

Keith addresses the officer, "I called 9-1-1. I'm the one who found her."

"Step aside, Officer." The order comes from a man in a blue tweed sport coat, white button-down shirt, faded jeans, and Sperry boots. He enters the room, ignores Keith, and moves into the line of sight of the victim.

She makes no notice of him.

"Vacant," he assesses quietly. "What's her name?"

She whispers, "No. No. No."

Keith answers, "Jenna. Jenna Farnsworth."

"Ms. Farnsworth, I'm Detective Cambridge." Before he says another word, a female paramedic enters the room. The detective whispers, "Her name's Jenna," to the approaching woman.

"When was the assault?"

"Not recent, from the looks of things."

"I found her. Two nights ago."

"Why the delay?" the detective and paramedic ask in unison.

"I wouldn't let him call."

Cambridge takes control. "Men, outside. Marilyn, if you need your partner, he'll be in the bus." He points to Keith, "You come with me." The men are entering the kitchen when the detective pushes in, "Why the wait, Mister—"

"Moreno. Keith Moreno." He grabs a glass from the counter, fills it with water, and takes a long pull. He offers a meek smile when Jenna walks past with the paramedic.

The detective steps to the counter, taps the window above the sink, and waves the first responding officer back inside. "Officer Parks, my partner is delayed in getting here. Stick around while Mr. Moreno and I talk."

"Yes, sir."

The detective points to a chair at the kitchen table, "Have a seat, Mr. Moreno."

Keith doesn't move, "I'll stand." He grabs a Sherpa-lined corduroy jacket from the back of a chair and tugs it on. "How about we shut the back door. Jenna's been freezing since the..."

Cambridge nods to the young officer, "Shut the door." He addresses Keith, "Take a seat, Mr. Moreno, either here or at the station."

He takes a seat.

"You called 9-1-1 at 10:10 PM."

"Yes."

"To report a rape."

"Yes."

"That happened two nights ago."

"Yes."

"Why the delay in reporting it?"

"Jenna refused to let me call."

"Why?"

"I'm not sure, but she got really upset every time I suggested it." Keith runs his hand through his hair, "More than upset, she became panicked."

The detective notices a shake in Keith's hand, and a noticeable stain on the cuff of his

23

jacket. "Mr. Moreno, where were you when your roommate was being raped?"

"I don't know."

The door to the den opens. Keith can see Jenna sitting on the couch, he can tell she's been crying.

The paramedic stops in the hall outside the kitchen, "Detective, a minute please."

Cambridge follows her down the hallway past two good sized bedrooms. "What's up, Marilyn?"

"I'm going to take Jenna to UU for a physical workup. She's already showered, so I'm not sure if SART will do a rape kit."

"Fuckin A."

Marilyn stays on script, "She wrenched her back during the rape, and she has a pretty deep slice to her left breast. She's been tending to it, but it needs a couple stitches."

"Okay. I'll swing by the hospital when I'm done."

"Jenna wants Keith to meet her at UU. She just moved here, and he's the only person she knows, other than her elderly grandparents."

"Not sure about Moreno, Marilyn. He says he doesn't know where he was when his roommate was being raped. There's a stain on the cuff of his jacket that looks like blood, and you're telling me the victim's breast is cut."

"Your call, Detective. Jenna will be with the sexual assault response team for at least four hours. If you decide not to bring Keith to UU, call Kathy Kimball. She's on tonight."

The EMT heads back to the den.

The detective heads back to the kitchen after a quick stop at the rape room. He is **not** happy when he returns. "Mr. Moreno, was Ms. Farnsworth raped in the bedroom across from the bathroom?"

"Yes."

"Was she raped on the bed?"

"Yes."

"Where is the bed linen?"

Keith points to a plastic garbage bag.

"Fuckin A! Officer Parks do not leave this room. Do not take your eyes off that bag. When the forensic team gets here, tell them the evidence has been in plastic." He addresses Keith, "How long has it been bagged?"

"Less than 24 hours."

"Officer, make sure you tell the techs that. Come on Moreno, we're going for a ride."

Can you roll onto your back?

For the second time in two nights, Edith Cunningham is pulled from the warmth of her bed before her usual midnight bathroom shuffle. The elderly woman lives in a sweeping Victorian across the street and down a bit from Keith Moreno's place, where evening activity is becoming routine. As much as she can, she hurries through her bathroom business, then shuffles to the bedroom window, the one reflecting pulsing blue light. "Police and an ambulance are at Keith's." She tsk, tsk, tsks as she wipes breath fog from the windowpane. She nods in affirmation, "So, that was a scream I heard." The haze of sleep or perhaps the ravages of old age leave her unsure when the scream happened, but it doesn't dull the terror of it.

Heading to UU
Marilyn McGinn places a call en route to the hospital. She tenses when she hears the all too familiar refrain on the other end of the line.

"Syracuse Rape Crisis Center, this is Josephine Mayer."

"Hey, Joey, I'm glad you answered. I'm bringing a survivor to UU. ETA ten minutes. Can you handle this case start to finish?"

The Director of SRCC doesn't handle cases anymore, but she agrees, "Sure." The wife of Paramedic McGinn knows why she's being called in on this case. "REDO?" Joey asks. She presses the phone tight against her ear, but can't hear the EMT's answer over the blare of sirens, even so, Joey knows in her gut— REDO is back.

Upstate University Hospital
Jenna Farnsworth is admitted to UU and taken to one of four private exam rooms located just outside the Emergency department. Sexual Assault Response Team member, Kathy Kimball, introduces herself, takes Jenna's vitals, and does a physical exam.

"I'm going to administer an NSAID for your back pain, and then clean, stitch, and dress the injury to your left breast." The physician's assistant announces her every approach, gains permission for every touch. She is just finishing the wound dressing when there's a knock. "If it isn't Josephine Mayer on the other side of that door, leave. If it is Josephine, come on in."

Jenna is curled in the fetal position and beginning to feel some relief in her lower back when a pretty African American woman with sparkling green eyes and smattering of freckles on her cheeks enters the room. Joey takes a seat near the bed and in the direct line of vision of the patient. "Hi, Jenna, I'm Joey." She pauses. She assesses. She continues. "Your EMT, Marilyn McGinn, asked me to work with PA Kimball on your case. Kathy and I are part of a sexual assault response team that provides medical care and emotional support. Jenna .... I'm a rape crisis counselor."

Jenna tears at the words.

Joey places her hand, palm up, on Jenna's gurney. The young woman waits many seconds before taking hold. Joey folds her fingers around Jenna's, then gets down to business. "Kathy is finished with your medical exam, and when you are ready she will move on to the sexual assault exam. I understand you've already showered."

"I shouldn't have. He said I shouldn't have."

"He?"

"Keith. My roommate."

"The man who found you?"

"Yes."

"We still might get evidence of the assault. We'd like to do a Rape Kit."

"Even though I showered?"

"Yes. Do you consent to this procedure?"

"Yes."

"Okay. I'll be here with you the entire time. Kathy and I will explain things as we move through the process, but if you have any questions or need a break, just let me know."

Jenna closes her eyes.

Kathy Kimball takes over. "Jenna can you roll onto your back?"

*Open doors, wet floors,
and hinky feelings.*

"Nice of you to join us, Detective Chase."

"I live to serve, Detective Cambridge."

"Chase, this is Keith Moreno. His roommate, Jenna Farnsworth, was raped in Mr. Moreno's home two nights ago. Since that time, Ms. Farnsworth and Mr. Moreno have occupied the crime scene, and one or both individuals compromised evidence. They removed it from the victim's body, and from the assault location, a bed in one of the bedrooms, and they bagged it all up."

"In paper?"

"Nope, plastic."

Chase takes a seat.

Cambridge pushes in, "Mr. Moreno, you said you don't know where you were at the time of the rape?"

"That's right."

"How is that, Mr. Moreno?"

"I don't know what time Jenna was attacked, Detective Cambridge."

"Let me rephrase my question, Mr. Moreno. Where were you on the evening of January 8th?"

"At Styles University. I headed there after dinner, so I got there a little after five. I went to the computer lab to work on a project, then headed over to Turner."

"The campus music school," the detective clarifies.

"Yes, Turner Theater to be exact. Zach Taylor, a friend of mine, is performing his capstone cello solo next week and is freaking out. I threw a little moral support his way by listening in on his practice."

"His rehearsal," the detective corrects.

Keith shrugs. *What an ass.*

"So, this Zach Taylor, he's the next Yo-Yo Ma?"

Keith shrugs. *A real ass.*

"What time did you get to Turner Theater?"

"After seven. Zach's **practice** began at seven, and he was already doing his thing when I got there."

"Did anyone see you?"

"Whoever was in the auditorium. I didn't think to buffer the door before it closed behind me, and it slammed pretty loud. I got a few angry eyes for the interruption."

"What time did you leave the auditorium?"

"Not sure, but Zach was still playing. He finished his song and had started it again."

"His piece."

"What?"

"He finished his piece and had started it again."

"Whatever."

"Then what?"

"I went back to the lab at Hadley Hall and graded a few term papers."

"Are you a professor, Mr. Moreno?"

"A TA, a teacher's assistant. I'm also a PhD candidate."

"Congratulations," the detective says dismissively.

What a dick.

"Let's clarify. You were grading term papers in a lab at Hadley Hall in January? Isn't the University on winter break?"

"The term papers are from the winter semester, Detective. Anyway, I left when I finished my work, probably around eleven-thirty. I was supposed to meet up with Zach at DJ's On the Hill. I thought better about it and came home."

"Thought better about it?"

"DJ's **On the Hill**. There was over a foot of snow when I started home. There was no way I was bothering with The Hill."

"What time did you arrive home?"

"Not sure exactly. Detective, let me cut to the chase. I pulled onto the driveway, trudged through snow to the back porch, and pulled open the storm door. That's when I noticed the inside door was open a bit. I got a hinky feeling in my gut, pushed the door completely open, called out to Jenna, then noticed wet puddles on the entranceway floor and wet patches on the rug leading down the hall. I heard a moan coming from Jenna's room right before I rushed inside." Keith hangs his head, "Jenna was sprawled on the bed partially naked and bloody. She stuttered the word 'cold' so I pulled up the blankets that were at the foot of her bed, grabbed another blanket from her reading chair, and took my cell out to call 9-1-1. She insisted I not make the call."

"Why?"

"I don't know."

"Then what?"

"I sat on the floor next to the bed holding onto Jenna's hand. She chanted, the word 'No' over and over. After a while, she said she needed to use the bathroom and needed some help because her back hurt. I got up to help." He shakes his head slowly. "She had moved the blankets off the top part of herself, blood was smeared across her chest from a cut on her breast."

"Was it still bleeding?"

"I'm not sure. I tried not to look. I pulled her nightgown together and—"

"Pulled her nightgown together?"

"It was cut, like down the middle. We got her onto her feet and to the bathroom. I told her she needed help, but again she refused. She went into the bathroom and when she came out she was wearing her bathrobe and it was obvious she'd showered."

Detective Chase joins in, "You said you headed to Styles University around five after having dinner. Where'd you eat?"

"At home, with Jenna."

"Where did you go when you got to SU?"

"Hadley Hall. It's where the engineering and computer science department is located."

"Anyone see you there?"

"There were a few people, most had left, probably because of the snow. It was coming down at a steady pace. But there were some people working in the computer lab."

"You said you arrived at Turner a little past seven, and people will verify this because you slammed the door, and Mr. Taylor was already playing."

"Yes."

"And you left while your friend was still playing?"

"Yes."

"How long were you inside Turner Theater?"

Keith shrugs.

"Venture a guess, Mr. Moreno," Cambridge pushes in.

"Ten, maybe fifteen, minutes."

"Then you headed back to Hadley Hall to grade a few term papers. That task kept you at the computer science department until eleven-thirty?"

"Yes."

"Anyone see you during that period of time?"

"I didn't see anyone. The place was pretty much cleared out because—"

"—of the storm," Cambridge smirks and finishes Keith's sentence.

What a dick. What a fucking dick.

The interview is interrupted by a knock on the glass. Detective Chase heads to the hall, Detective Cambridge continues pushing in with

33

the person of interest. Chase is back in the room within minutes, and he catches the next line of questioning by his partner.

"Then, instead of heading to DJ's On the Hill to meet up with your friend, you blew it off and went straight home."

"Yes."

"But you're uncertain about your arrival time."

"Yes."

"How far from your house is Hadley Hall, Mr. Moreno?"

There is a pause, a long pause, "A couple miles."

"Before we go on, Mr. Moreno, is there anything you want to add to your statement, something that might help establish your timeline?"

"No."

"According to your statement, Mr. Moreno, you returned home, parked your Jeep on the side driveway, walked to the back porch, where you opened the storm door, found the inside door open, got a hinky feeling in your gut, entered the house, and called out to your roommate."

"Yes."

"Tell me about the puddles on the entranceway and the wet patches on the rug leading down the hall."

"I'm particular about the hardwood floors. I busted my ass putting them in, and I insist people take their boots off and leave them on a mat by the back door. It's probably why I noticed the puddles; they were out of place and looked like they might have come from someone's boots. Same for the wet patches on the carpet."

"So the puddles on your hardwood floors replaced the hinky feeling in your gut."

"No, Detective, I noticed the door open, the wet floors, and immediately called out to Jenna. I have a question for you, Detective Cambridge. Are you an asshole with everyone, or am I the lucky one?" The detective smiles at his partner, who offered a poorly squelched laugh. "I'm an asshole with everyone, Mr. Moreno. Isn't that right, Chase?"

"Established as fact, Cambridge."

"Back to me asking the questions, Mr. Moreno. You thought you heard a moan from Jenna's room, so you pushed open the door and saw your roommate sprawled on the bed, partially naked and bloody."

"Yes."

"You covered her with blankets from the foot of the bed, grabbed another blanket from her reading chair, and began a call to 9-1-1."

"Yes."

"Were the lights on?"

"What?"

"Were the lights in Jenna's bedroom on when you pushed open the door?"

Keith pauses.

Cambridge pushes. "You opened the bedroom door and saw Jenna sprawled on the bed partially naked and bloody. How did you see that? And how did you know the blankets were twisted at the foot of the bed and that there was a throw on Jenna's reading chair?"

"I turned on the lights."

"When did you turn on the lights? You didn't mention anything about turning on lights during your previous 'cut to the chase' presentation, Mr. Moreno."

Keith gets a bit hot under the collar. "I could see Jenna when I opened the door, and I knew about the throw on her reading chair."

"Are there lights in the hallway?"

"Yes."

"Were they on when you pushed open your roommates door?"

"No. I don't think so. I don't remember. Am I under arrest?"

"Not yet."

Keith Moreno leaves the interview room and takes a cab to UU hospital.

STDs and Plan Bs.

Keith Moreno wasn't the only one who headed to UU from SPD. Within seconds of entering the Emergency department, Keith learns pretty quickly that people do not like Matt Cambridge. An ED duty nurse doesn't even try to hide her annoyance when the detective approaches.

"Cambridge."

"Sheila."

Nurse Hannen bristles at the familiarity.

"How's Coach?"

"Maybe you should ask him yourself, Matt."

The woman goes back to doing whatever she was doing and talks to the air around her, "SART is finishing up with the patient. PA Kimball can fill you in on the medical exam and evidence retrieval—and a head's up, Joey Mayer is the SRCC liaison." The nurse's comment lands the way she intended, like a kick to the detective's gluteus maximus.

Cambridge lets out a maximus growl.

The nurse snickers.

Keith takes it all in from a seat in the waiting area.

PA Kimball is the first to exit the exam room, followed closely by Jenna and Joey. Two of the three enter a small lounge across the hall.

Joey approaches Cambridge, "Is that Keith Moreno?"

"Where?" He spins toward the waiting area. "Yeah. Why?"

"Jenna wants him with her."

Cambridge shakes his head. "Not a good idea. He's lawyering up." The detective thinks a minute, "On second thought, bring him in. Let's see how Ms. Farnsworth reacts now that she's had some time away from him."

The rape counselor waves Keith forward, "Ms. Farnsworth has asked that you join her."

The detective lets them pass and watches Jenna from the doorway as Keith enters the room. She is already seated on a small couch, her feet swung onto the cushions next to her, her arms folded across her abdomen, her hands clutching the scrubs she's changed into.

"Jenna," he chokes from across the room.

The others watch Jenna's facial expressions change from toughing it out to tearing up.

Joey addresses her newest client, "Jenna, do you consent to having Mr. Moreno in attendance during this conversation?"

"Yes."

"Detective Cambridge," Kathy Kimball begins, "Jenna has given an account of the events. Her testimony was witnessed in its entirety and recorded in full by SRCC counselor Joey Mayer and myself. The patient willingly submitted to a medical and sexual assault exam. She has received an intramuscular injection of

Toradol for an injury to her back. The medication will not affect her memory recall. She has been tested for STDs and given Plan B to prevent pregnancy. She has been discharged from UU and has requested that she be taken to 10 Oren Street."

"Forensics is still working the scene. No one will be allowed in for a few hours."

"I can take you to Grams and Gramps," Keith offers.

Jenna nods, but somewhere deep inside her head she screams. *No. No. No.*

Detective Cambridge drives Jenna and Keith to 10 Oren with information for Jenna and a warning for Keith. "CSI is finished inside. Officer Parks will stay on scene until you head to Oneida, Ms. Farnsworth. Stay close to home, Mr. Moreno." The detective spins his Land Rover around, pulls to the side of the road, and watches Keith help Jenna to the passenger side of the Jeep. He settles her in, goes to the driver's side, starts the engine, hops back out and begins clearing a blanket of snow from its roof. Before Cambridge drives away, he takes a good daytime look at the residential street. A curtain in the front window of a Victorian across from the Moreno home moves aside. He chuckles at the vision of an old lady, "We've got a looky-loo. Could be a witness."

Beauty and the Beast.

Caitlyn English slaps angrily at the buzzing alarm clock, inches herself across the bed to snuggle close to her husband, and moans into his pillow when she realizes he's not there. "Oh, Matt. Not another one," she quietly laments.

Newlywed Caitlyn English is a rank-and-file member of the Onondaga County lifer's club—and she is damned proud of it. The thirty-four year old was born and raised in Syracuse, New York; attended Styles University; graduated summa cum laude from the University's College of Law; found employment at the only place to which she applied, and planted roots in the community she never once considered leaving. Caitlyn lives in a sprawling brick home in the upscale wooded community of Fayetteville, though she spends little time there. She works sunup to sundown in the Sexual Crimes Division at the Onondaga County District Attorney's office where she made Assistant District Attorney in record time. Her claim to fame was the successful prosecution of every sexual assault case Detective Matt Cambridge brought her way. The arresting and prosecuting duo became known throughout Upstate NY as:

The Counselor and **That** Cop

There are many ways to characterize Caitlyn English: accomplished, brilliant, conscientious, dogged, earnest, fearless—all apt descriptions, but the most commonly used word when referring to Ms. English begins with G: gorgeous. Caitlyn English is Grace Kelly gorgeous, a dated reference perhaps, but the actress-turned-princess and the lawyer-turned-wife are doppelgangers—blonde, blue-eyed, and perfectly curvy. Like the actress, Ms. English has a penchant for cashmere sweaters, wool pencil skirts, and cultured pearls. She carries herself with poise, offers a quick smile, and is universally well-liked, unless you find yourself on the other side of a legal battle, that is. ADA English is tough as nails and sharp as a saber. Defense attorneys prepare clients for stints in prison as soon as she is assigned as prosecuting counsel.

Matt Cambridge is the polar opposite of his new wife. He bangs through life with wrecking ball precision, rarely smiles, and is universally disliked. The detective's brusque, disrespectful manner is tolerated because he is great at his job. And when the social scene demands his attendance, he gets by on his Jeffrey Dean Morgan movie star looks. Still, when Matt Cambridge snagged Caitlyn English as his matrimonial mate, the whole of Syracuse law enforcement was rendered mute. Even now, months after their elopement, few people can explain the romance between The Counselor and **That** Cop.

"Tough night?" she asks when Matt crawls into bed and she snuggles against his chest.

"...and morning. A rape on Oren. Joey Mayer caught the case. She's gonna start with the whole REDO shit."

"Is the victim a repeat?"

"Nope. She's new to town."

"Well, that's the first telltale sign of REDO, Matt."

"I know." The husband pulls his wife beneath him and kisses her deep. When he pulls his lips away, she pulls a shaky breath.

"And that's the first telltale sign of great sex ahead," she purrs into his neck.

Oren

Keith is sitting on the floor by the back door of the second-floor apartment when Jenna walks out of the bathroom. Her hair is in a high ponytail, and her bangs fringe her eyes, which are red and puffy from crying. She's wearing a pair of Drexel University sweatpants, a long-sleeve navy T-shirt, and pair of rag socks. Her movements are as slow as molasses.

"Thanks for letting me shower up here. I just couldn't go back into your place."

"I brought you a coffee," Keith points to a travel mug on the counter.

Jenna nods and smiles. Sort of.

"I'm a suspect, you know?" The words cross the room as though they'd been carried by a speeding bullet.

Jenna slumps back against the wall and lowers herself along it. Her eyes fix on the space in front of her, then move about as though they are seeing the rape play out on a slow loop. Her face registers fear, confusion, repulsion, and pain. She pushes back the tears that threaten. "You?" she wipes the lone traitor that finds her cheek.

"Cambridge is riding me pretty hard, but once he starts checking my alibi, he'll have to look for the guy who…" Keith stops when Jenna surrenders to her emotions. He wants to move near her—hold her—give her support. He does none of those things.

"Keith. Say these words: 'I don't want to hurt you. I only want to rape you.'"

"What the fuck, Jenna! He said that?"

"Say it, please."

"I don't want to hurt you. I only want to rape you," Keith struggles through.

"Again. Say it again, but with menace—no, say it with seduction."

Keith forces himself to go there, hates himself for going there. "I don't want to hurt you. I only want to rape you."

The silent voice in Jenna's head screams, *No. No. No.*

From R to R.

Joey disconnects from leaving her fourth voicemail message and tosses her cell onto the bed. She is sprawled across the foot of it, her chest cushioned by a pillow resting against her wife's legs. "Marilyn."

"Mmm."

"What was it about Jenna's rape that made you think it was REDO?"

Marilyn pulls a shaky breath in, then lets it shake back out. "You know."

"Yes, but indulge me."

"Jenna kept mumbling, 'I don't want to hurt you. I only want to rape you.'"

"Anything else?"

"Everything else, Joey. The cut on her breast, the kiss goodbye, the suggestion he'd see her again."

Joey nods. The SRCC counselor surmised all that as soon as Marilyn asked her to handle **this** rape, and she heard Jenna say all of that during her sexual assault exam at UU. That's not why the wife, asked the question. She is gauging a situation, looking for signs of distress in Marilyn—a two-time victim of the rapist Joey named REDO.

SPD

The detective is late getting to the station. He spent an hour sexing his wife and four times that amount of time resting his bones. He is trying to sneak by Diane's office, but is pulled up short by her call.

He pokes his head in, "Make it fast. I'm getting a late start today, Diane."

"Back to your old self, I see."

"What do you want?"

She points to a sealed evidence envelope.

"Thanks." He hustles down the hall, bangs into his office, and knocks on his partner's closed office door. "Not here." He opens the large, yellow envelope and gets to work. Inside the package he finds information from two sources, CSI and SART. He starts with forensics.

DNA present on victim's nightgown and bedding. Scheduled for analysis.

"DNA present. Maybe you didn't kill the evidence, Mr. Moreno." The detective moves on, "SART checklist: complete. Collection of vaginal and pubic area samples: check. Signed and witnessed consent forms: check. Detailed summaries made during the medical and sexual assault exams: check. Handwritten notes by PA Kathy Kimball and SRCC counselor Joey Mayer: check. Audio cassette: check. And ...." He removes a piece of paper with the word REDO written in black sharpie. "Here we go,"

Cambridge mutters in concert with a knock on his door. "Great," he snarls when Joey Mayer walks in.

"Have you listened to the tape or read the notes, yet?"

"Nope."

"Let me get you from R to R, Detective. First R, Jenna Farnsworth was RAPED. Second R, the rapist is REDO. There is a serial rapist in our community."

"I know," the detective interrupts. "Sit down and shut up, Joey."

She wants to smack the detective almost as much as she wants to hear what he has to say. She postpones the smacking for the listening.

"You know who I am, right?" the detective begins.

"Yeah, you're **That** Cop and your wife is The Counselor. Been wondering how you managed to snag Caitlyn English. Gotta tell you, Cambridge, I figured if you ever ended up with a wife she'd be of the Mail Order variety."

Cambridge laughs, "Me too. Let's leave our wives out of this."

Joey nods, "For now, but don't forget, REDO's reign of terror is personal."

"I know." Cambridge pauses. "Joey, you missed the mark when I asked you if you knew who I was."

"How so?"

"I'm the detective who has a near-perfect arrest record with this department. The only case that keeps it from being perfect is REDO."

"—and Mendez."

Cambridge practically growls, "We had that asshole dead to rights."

"Only because you guys never found his alibi witness. You and English got the conviction, Cambridge, but it was kicked to the curb when his alibi came forward."

"Yeah, almost a year later. That fuckup put some heat on Chase and me, but Mendez was Caitlyn's first big case. When it blew up in her face, it almost sidelined her from moving up the ranks at the DA's office."

"There's that, Detective, but the **real** issue, the one that matters to women in Syracuse, is that it put Mendez back on the streets—right before this whole rape and repeat shit started. Are you guys sure he's not REDO?"

"Yes, but we'll check him out. Right now, I need to rule out Moreno. He was the last person with Jenna before the rape and the first person with her after the rape, and he belongs to the Onondaga County lifer's club. He could be good for all of the rapes. You need to stay out of this, Joey. Do your job, and let me do mine. Now, get out." The detective waits until Mayer is down the hall before heading in that direction. "Time to pull some threads on Keith Moreno's statement."

I'm the nosey neighbor.

The night Edith Cunningham heard Her Scream, she pulled her rocker to the front window and turned it so she has a perfect view of Keith's place. She was on vigil when the emergency people arrived, watched the ambulance leave with the girl, and was still watching when the man in a sport coat took Keith away. And she didn't miss a beat when Keith and the new girl returned home and headed around back. She left her lookout to do some light housekeeping, but she's been back in her rocker for more than an hour, now.

"Time for some tea." Before Edith leaves her perch, she sees one of those boxy cars pull to the snowy curb out front. "Looks like the car that took Keith away." She watches the familiar man in a tweed sport coat get out of the car and sprint to her porch. The hunched woman, frail in body, not in spirit, pulls open the front door. "Come on in," she says before any introductions even take place.

"Ma'am, you shouldn't just open the door."

"And you should be wearing an overcoat. Now that we've bossed one another, what's your name, and what happened to that sweet girl living with Keith?"

"Name's Matt Cambridge. I'm a detective with SPD, ma'am."

"Name's Edith Cunningham. I'm the nosey neighbor. I've got things to say, so come on in. What's your name?"

"Matt Cambridge," he repeats with a smile. The detective eyes the rocking chair near the front window facing the Moreno house, and notices the curtains pulled aside and tucked behind a healthy potted plant so they won't fall forward and obstruct her view. "You said you have things to say, ma'am."

"Prefer Edith or Mrs. Cunningham, Detective."

"Mrs. Cunningham, looks like you've been watching the events at the Moreno place."

"Ever since I heard that awful scream."

"We should sit and talk, Mrs. Cunningham."

"Kitchen's good for sitting, talking, and drinking tea. Will you have a cup?"

"Lead the way," Cambridge smiles.

"Do you want to ask questions, or should I just prattle, Detective."

"I'll listen a while."

"Mind if I make tea while you listen?"

"No, ma'am."

"I was asleep until something woke me. I wasn't sure what it was at first, but after living with it a spell, I'd say it was a scream. A terrifying one at that."

"What time was that?"

"Didn't look at the clock I'm afraid, but I retired around 8 PM, so after that and before my midnight bathroom visit," she hands him his cup and sets hers down, "You best let me say my piece, so I'm not to forget some."

"Yes, ma'am."

"The noise got me from bed. I went to the window overlooking Oren. Didn't think much then, Detective, but I could have gone to the window overlooking Gage, but I think my mind knew the scream came from Oren. There are only the three houses up here past the bend, so not much to see. And with the wind blowing the snow pretty bad at the time, I couldn't see much, anyway. The Fletcher's house was dark. That's the blue Victorian across the way. Stan and Helen are in Florida at some retirement village or such. As I say, I looked to Keith's place and saw his boxy car wasn't in the driveway, but both girls' cars were there. Mary's and the new girl's. Sorry to say I can't remember the new girl's name at the moment." Edith stops, "You might as well ask your questions now."

"You said the Fletcher's house was dark. How about Mr. Moreno's house?"

"There were low lights on inside, but it looked as though the back porch light was out."

"Is that unusual?"

"Keith's good about putting it on, but he left around suppertime, so maybe the new girl forgot to put it on."

"Tell me about the low lights that were on in the Moreno house."

"Looked like a lamp, or maybe a hall light, or a bathroom light was left on. Nothing bright, but enough to make your way. Maybe the new girl left them on being as she's in a strange place and all."

"Had the street been plowed?"

Edith begins shaking her head, "Now see, it's good you asked because I forgot to tell you that it hadn't been plowed. I know because I could see tire tracks in the road."

"Near the Moreno place?"

"No, at the Fletcher's. Now, that's odd, isn't it? There was a car parked at Stan's and Helen's. A boxy kind of car like yours and Keith's."

"What color was this boxy car?"

"Dark, black or gray maybe."

"But the Fletchers are away, right?"

"Yes, until spring."

"Did you notice any footprints at the Fletcher's or heading toward Keith's house?"

"Don't think I would have, what with my eyesight not being what it once was. But the car at the Fletcher's was cleaned off. The cars parked on Keith's driveway, Mary's and..."

"Jenna," the detective helps out.

"Yes, Jenna. Their cars were covered in snow. Did I tell you I went back to bed?"

"When was that, Mrs. Cunningham?"

"I stayed a spell at the window, then went back to bed. I got up again when the blue lights came."

"When the police arrived?"

"Yes, and the ambulance."

"The emergency personnel came last night, ma'am."

"Yes." Edith pauses a minute, "You should probably ask me if the street was plowed."
"We just discussed that, ma'am."
"So we did."

Cheating boyfriends
and Gilmore Girls.

Jenna and Keith are getting into the Jeep when they hear Cambridge shout their names. Jenna freezes in place, "I can't deal with him right now, Keith."

"Get in the Jeep. I'll be right back."

"I thought you were taking Ms. Farnsworth to Oneida Lake," the detective says on approach.

"She wanted to shower first."

"Inside your place?"

"No. Upstairs. It's still under construction, but Jenna didn't want to be downstairs."

"Any chance you were hanging out upstairs sometime between the hours of 7:30 and 11:30 the night of the rape, Mr. Moreno?"

Keith pauses. "I'm not answering any questions without a lawyer." He turns when he hears Jenna move behind him.

"Why do you consider Keith a suspect?" she demands of the detective.

"SPD won't rule your roommate out until we verify his alibi, Ms. Farnsworth. Tell me, have you ruled him out?"

Jenna doesn't answer the detective's question. She's too busy listening to the *No. No. No.* scream in her head.

The detective gives up on getting an answer. "Ms. Farnsworth, I've reviewed the information from UU SART. I'd like to talk to you. Have you slept at all since—"

"No," she interrupts.

"I'd like you to come to the station sometime in the next few days." He hands her his card. "Call, and we'll arrange a time."

She and Keith start toward the Jeep.

The detective calls from behind, "Mr. Moreno, was Oren plowed when you arrived home?"

"Yes, but it was filling back in."

"Any cars at the Fletcher's?"

"Just Stan's and Helen's."

"Where will you be staying Ms. Farnsworth?"

"22 Shore Road, out in Cleveland. My grandparents' place is a half-mile from Eileen's General Store. It's the sage green lakefront house."

The Lake

Grams is thrilled to see Jenna standing on the back porch. She's not thrilled to see the man with her.

"Grams," Jenna bends low when the tiny woman opens the door and her arms. "Grams," she repeats this time on a sigh. Jenna straightens slowly, her sore back tightening in protest of her movements. She makes introductions. "This is Keith Moreno, my landlord. You probably already know he's Mary's boyfriend."

Grace Farnsworth smiles at the young man and remembers Mary's words about him…

"Keith and I had an awful fight. He became really upset when he found out I applied for and accepted a study-abroad program in Paris without his input. He said it wasn't my decision to make because we are in a relationship, and we should have discussed it as a couple."

Grace Farnsworth shook her head at the tears Mary shed during the next part of their conversation. "We talked for hours—well, I talked for hours, and he pretended to listen. When I got up this morning, Keith was already gone, and when I came home ……. he was there with another woman. I went to my bedroom and stayed there until the woman left. I thought he'd apologize and beg my forgiveness, but instead, he got really angry at **me** and acted as though it was **my** fault he was unfaithful. I never saw him so pissed and unreasonable."

Grams sneaks a look at Jenna's guest trying to square what she heard about the angry, cheating Keith with the nice looking man standing on her porch. "Come on in, you two. Tell me what brings you to Oneida."

"I've had some back luck with a broken pipe," Keith begins. "It happened overnight, and we can't stay at the house until it's fixed and the water is back on," his mistruth delivered pleasantly and effortlessly.

"Grams, would it be too much trouble if we grabbed some shut-eye? We won't bother you for much else, I promise."

"No bother, Jenna. Show Keith to the room in the loft, and you can take the small bedroom."

There really wasn't much needed by way of showing Keith to his quarters. Jenna points to a stationary ladder leaning against the wall between the living room and kitchen and says, "Go up."

Before Jenna closes her bedroom door, Grams calls out to her, "The McLaughlin Boy bought his parents' place next door. He just moved in and plans on living here year-round. Bert and Betty moved to Florida. Did I mention that?"

"I don't think so."

"Mac finished his time in the Army and is looking to set roots. He's a very handsome young man, Jenna. He looks like the diner owner on the *Gilmore Girls*. My, my, you and Mary loved that show. I could barely get you away from the T.V. and out of the bungalow that summer you two visited. The two of you watched every single rerun, not that I minded. I took quite a liking to the story. You know, Jenna, every time Mac is back in these parts, he stops by and asks about you."

"Grams, I hadn't thought about Mac in years, but he crept into my mind on the drive north."

"Maybe you'll catch up with him now that you're local."

Jenna smiles at Grams then steps into the small bedroom. "There's no way I'm seeing Mac. Not now." Her hand finds her breast as she yawns and closes the door. Grateful to be alone, she thinks about crawling into bed, remembers why she won't, slumps against the wood barrier, and slides the length of it, eventually finding floor with her ass. She touches her left breast again, "An ugly reminder of what he did, what he took." Jenna wraps her arms tight around her bent knees and sobs. "How did I get here?" The broken woman pulls a blanket from a nearby seaman's chest and curls into a ball on the floor?

Keith waits until the old lady is out of earshot, "Who the fuck is Mac?"

Not a guess, unfortunately.

When Detective Matt Cambridge is processing a case, he spends some time at SPD, but most of his time is spent on one of his drive-abouts. The gumshoe takes his Land Rover onto an interstate, puts his foot to the floor and his mind to the facts of a case. No one at SPD objects to his absence—could be because of his success rate solving violent sexual assaults—could be because he's an asshole. Today, Cambridge takes a drive before heading to the station. On his circuitous route, he focuses on Aldo Mendez, "The one who got away…"

"What the hell is going on, Detective Cambridge." The ADA asked, arms folded across her chest, toes tapping rapidly on the floor.

"Sonia Perez is what's going on. She's the hooker Aldo Mendez said he was with the night Joanie Newton was raped."

"I know who Sonia Perez supposedly is, Detective, though you assured me that she did not exist. In fact, I built my prosecutorial case against Mr. Mendez around your assurance that she was a figment of the defendant's imagination. Need I remind you, the State of NY v Aldo Mendez was **my** case, my first solo case. The conviction of Mr. Mendez for the crime of digital rape—a very difficult premise for any jury to understand, let alone convict on—will be overturned, and he will be on the streets in a matter of days if Ms.

Perez can satisfactorily corroborate his story that he was in Brownsville at the time of Ms. Newton's attack, and not in Syracuse where Ms. Newton was being attacked."

"This is what I can tell you, Ms. English. Ms. Perez showed up at the station, today, and told Diane Earls she wanted to talk to the detectives who put Aldo Mendez in jail for a rape he didn't commit. Detective Chase spent a couple of hours taking her statement."

"And?"

"It's got legs. She said she met Mendez in Brownsville, not on the streets where she usually meets her men, but at a slum hotel that rents rooms by the hour. She'd just finished a John, had taken a shower, and was leaving the room when she bumped into Aldo in the corridor. He liked what he saw, made a few moves, asked her to his room, and kept her there for the rest of the night. Apparently, the star-crossed 'lovers' exchanged phone numbers so they could continue their romance. The hooker was Aldo's alibi, and we chased his alibi, **even** after an eye witness put Aldo outside Joanie Newton's townhouse the night of the assault. I went to the Brownsville section of East Brooklyn looking for Aldo's hooker and came back with nothing more than a few offers from the ladies of the evening. At the end of the day, Ms. English, no one at SPD **or** in the public defender's office could ever reach Sonia Perez, in person or by phone."

Cambridge is pretty torqued from his road trip when he parks his Rover at the station. He stops by Diane's empty office, grabs his mail, goes directly to the break room, and taps on the doorframe, "Chase, I need some background on Jenna Farnsworth. This is what I've got so far: born in Malvern and lived in Philly before moving here in early January. Her parents were killed in an MVA on Thanksgiving Day, sending her north to be near her paternal grandparents, Emmett and Grace Farnsworth. They live at Oneida Lake."

"This is looking good for REDO."

"Yeah. I want you to dig deep on Keith Moreno. He owns the crime scene, is a lifer of Syracuse, was the one who found the victim, didn't call it in, and fucked with the evidence. He said he only did what Ms. Farnsworth asked or told him to do, but there's more to his story. Find a thread for us to pull. Looks like breaktime's over, Old Man."

"Asshole," the sixty-year-old replies while his partner is still in earshot.

Cambridge snaps, "I do the leg work, you do the desk work. Get what I need, Chase, and stay out of my way." The detective drops his mail onto his desk and his ass onto his chair. He boots his system and does what he always does when he gets to the station: searches for rapes in the Finger Lakes region. Matt Cambridge no longer thinks of Onondaga as the only county he serves. A spike in rapes at or near colleges and universities throughout Upstate NY has broadened his territory. "SPD brass gets a call for help, and they send Matt Cambridge." The detective's frequent assists allows him access to police department data bases, and he uses that privilege daily. "Nothing yet. Guess I can concentrate on Farnsworth and Moreno."

The Lake

Jenna made it to bed at some point and slept the night through. She is startled awake by a man's voice, and lurches forward, painfully stretching the muscle in her back before realizing where she is and that she is alone. She scooches herself up, leans back against the headboard, and listens.

"Heard you finished your stint in the Army."

"A month ago."

"Mac," Jenna whispers. "The boy I wanted to be my first." Her eyes fill when she remembers how she lost her virginity.

"How long have you known Jenna?" Mac asks.

"She moved into my place last week, but I met her a couple years ago when she visited Mary. How about you?"

"Since we were kids. Jenna came here every summer, a few times she brought Mary along."

"We're all **very** fond of Mary, Keith." Gramps pushes in. "Are the two of you still an item?"

"Of course they're still an item. And what's with the tone, Gramps?"

"We're taking a break while Mary's in Paris. We'll see how things are when she returns."

"What the hell? Taking a break?"

There's a soft tap on her bedroom door, "Jenna, dear. Are you awake? Mac's paid us a visit. You should come say hello."

Jenna clutches her abdomen and slips under the covers. The words, *No. No. No.* banging in her head.

Hadley Hall

Detective Cambridge makes a trip to Styles University not sure he'll find anyone on a Sunday—he finds the perfect one. He introduces himself to the administrative assistant at the front office. He can't help but notice the bat of her eyes, her sexy little smile, and pair of budded nipples pressing tight against her satiny blouse. The surly detective would normally cut through this bullshit and give her a taste of who he really is, but he needs information, so he gives her a once over and a dimpled grin.

"Miss Verde?"

"Helena, please."

"Helena, I'd like to talk to anyone who might have been in the computer labs January 8th around 5 PM."

"I was here, and I think Keith Moreno was in one of the labs. As for students, he'd have a better idea who was still around."

"There were students in the labs?"

"Not sure of that, Detective, but there were students roaming The Hall near that time. Most of the faculty and staff were gone because of the snow, but the students, especially those living on campus were still milling about."

"And you, Helena? What time did you leave Hadley Hall?"

The vixen with short blonde hair and chestnut brown eyes, blushes—deeply. "Around seven."

"Can anyone verify that?"

"Keith Moreno. He walked me to my car and brushed it off on his way to Turner Theater." The woman blushes again before asking, "Is Keith in some sort of trouble, Detective?"

"How well do you know Mr. Moreno?"

She blushes. She flushes. She turns a guilty shade of rojo.

"Interesting way to answer my question, Ms. Verde." He walks away.

Cambridge finds a seat in the far right corner of the auditorium, kicks back and enjoys Zach Taylor's impersonation of Yo-Yo Ma. "Impressive." He gives his head a good shake. "Shit. I shouldn't know one way or the other. Shit. Caitlyn's classical crap is taking hold." He's enjoying the performance and thinking about getting tickets for Caitlyn when the door near him slams shut. The smattering of audience members jump and shush the intruder.

Zach plays through the commotion.

Nipple-vixen turns and leaves when she sees the detective.

Cambridge ponders. "Here to talk to someone, Ms. Verde? Wasn't me, that's for damned sure." He joins in with applause for the cellist, waits while the musician cases his instrument, stops for advice from a gray-haired, bespectacled man in the front row, and leaves through a side door. The detective moves swiftly down the aisle and exits the auditorium. It takes a few minutes for him to weave his way through a labyrinth of short connecting halls backstage eventually ending his journey at a packed solarium. Tucked in a back corner, deep in conversation he finds what he knew he'd find. He approaches the assistant and the musician with a 'got-cha' smile, "Nice to see you again, Ms. Verde. I assume you told Mr. Taylor who I am, and now he knows why I'm here, so let's just jump right in." He is met with silence. "Mr. Taylor, where were you September 8th between the hours of seven and midnight?"

"At Turner, and then making my way home."

"What time did you leave the SU campus?"

"Around ten."

"Were you alone?"

"Yes."

"Did you see Keith Moreno between the hours of seven and midnight?"

"Yes."

"When, and be specific."

"He showed up at my rehearsal sometime after seven and left a short time later."

"You were playing while he was in the auditorium, is that correct?"

"Yes."

"The same piece you were just playing?"

"Yes."

"Bach's Cello Suite No. 1 – Prelude?"

Zach raises a brow and tilts his head, "Very good guess, Detective."

"Not a guess, unfortunately."

Zach smirks.

"You were playing that piece when Keith arrived at the auditorium **and** when he left?"

"Yes."

"Prelude is less than five minutes, is that correct?"

Zach glances at Helena and shakes his head, "Look, Detective, I'm not involved in whatever this shit is. My whole future will be decided on the performance stage next week. I don't know anything about the other night. I definitely don't know why I'm being asked to confirm timelines and shit."

Cambridge enjoys the blush that spreads cheek to cheek on Ms. Verde's face, "Mr. Taylor, you can leave. Ms. Verde, you can come to the station tomorrow afternoon for questioning."

"Do I need a lawyer?"

"If you think you need one, you'd better bring one."

REDO

Her Scream, the virgin's scream, it seduces him, owns him. The powerful sound easily triumphs over the others who clamor for his attention. He lingers in bed, welcomes the cacophony of rape sounds. The scream. The breathless pant. The whimper of fear. The moan of acceptance. The ripping of pussy silk. The tearful goodbye. He smiles at the slow recall—it excites him, fuels him. The ramrod between his legs hardens and twitches with need. "Not now." He pushes from bed.

REDO opens a chest of drawers, digs deep and removes a white cotton T-shirt. He traces the outline of a crimson stain, presses the soft fabric against his face and breathes in. He hardens even more. "My sweat—her blood—our bond. My control—her submission." Unwelcome words flash: *like father, like son.* A memory buds, "No." The memory nudges, "No." The memory takes hold. "No." The memory wins…

"Get in our room."

The boy shook his head, "Please, I don't want to."

"You'll lay under my bed and learn how you keep your woman in line."

The boy shook his head, "No, Daddy, please."

"Get your ass in that room, or it'll be you who bears the brunt of this evening."

The boy inched into the room, slid under the bed, and swallowed the tears that threatened. He held his breath when he saw his mother's feet turn the corner, watched in horror as his father's booted feet moved toward her, listened in anguish to Her Scream when she was thrown hard onto the mattress. The boy covered his ears, desperate to muffle the pleas that filled the room. He shook his head in rhythm with her repeated cry of NO, released tears of sympathy at her pain and fear. The boy hated the rape sounds back then; he much preferred the whispered apologies that signaled the end of his father's brutality and his mother's suffering.

Almost by accident, REDO learned he could silence the haunt of his mother's screams—with their screams, the college coed's screams. He closes his eyes and wills memories of the sounds **he** ordained. He waits. "Yes. Yes. There they are." He puts the bloody trophy back into the drawer, strokes his erection, and heads for a shower.

A tale of three women.

Marilyn skims Joey's shoulder as she moves through the kitchen. She can't help but notice the enormous mug of black coffee in Joey's hands and the dark circles under her eyes—both, telltale signs. "I kept you up last night." It could have been a question. It wasn't.

"The nightmares were bad, Marilyn." It could have been a question. It wasn't.

"Yeah."

"I wanted to wake you. I needed to wake you."

"Joey, we've hashed this out a hundred times. I need to work through the nightmares start to finish if I'm to get a reprieve."

"I know, but it's hard, Marilyn. You were thrashing so violently, I thought you might hurt yourself, or…"

"You?"

"I had to leave our bed. I don't know how you can handle it. His words—you repeat them over and over."

"They're only words, Joey. It's the intent behind his parting words that we should be concentrating on. REDO is going to rape Jenna again. You need to tell her that her rapist gets off on paying a second visit to his victim," the survivor of REDO's rapes angrily reminds, though she needn't.

"I will, when the time is right."

"When the time is right? She needs to know now."

The SRCC director gets up and starts pacing. "Jenna hasn't reached out for counseling, Marilyn. She's still reeling from the attack, not to mention she's new to the area and doesn't have a support system in place. She shouldn't have more shit dumped on her. And there's time. REDO waits almost a year before his second attack."

"Assuming we know about all of his rapes."

Joey nods, then shakes her head, "I can't say anything to Jenna. If Cambridge found out I told a rape survivor that she's part of a repeat offender program, he'd kill me. If she comes in for counseling and the topic comes up, I'll tell her about REDO. Right now, I'd rather help you."

Marilyn pushes past, "Not now, Joey."

The Lake

Grams and Gramps make it to Jenna's bedroom door seconds after Keith lands with a thud from the loft ladder. His hand reaches for the doorknob, but stops when Gramps shouts, "No!"

"Sir, she needs our help," Keith pleads.

"Step aside, young man."

Jenna pulls open the door with one hand, and wipes the last of morning's sleep, and a few errant tears from her eyes with the other. "Keith is only trying to help, Gramps." Her words do little to diffuse the tension.

She addresses her grandparents, "I need to tell you something. Let's sit in the kitchen. Grams, you might want to put on a pot of coffee." With that, Jenna heads to the bathroom and sequesters herself in the tiny space until the smell of coffee beckons. Everyone is seated at the table when she returns. She doesn't join them, "What I'm about to tell you will upset you greatly. Before I begin, I need two things. Don't touch me. Don't repeat this."

Grams and Gramps take hold of one another's hand.

"Keith and I are not here because of a broken pipe at his place. He lied to you because I asked him to. We are here because of a crime that occurred at his home. A rape. My rape."

"Oh, Jenna," her grandparents whisper, their pastel-blue, age-clouded eyes filling with tears.

Gramps addresses the other man in the room, "Can you tell us?"

Jenna nods, takes space across the room, and gets pulled into her own thoughts...

"Stop moving" ……. "You need to obey me" ……. "Open your eyes." The man brushed away bangs that partially covered her cobalt-blue eyes, ran his thumb down her cheek as though caressing her. "I don't want to hurt you. I only want to rape you."

He pressed down, ran the knife across her left breast, drawing blood. He warned her with his eyes as he cut the strap of her undies, moved the flimsy cloth to the side and pushed in, in, in, in. He stopped, but stayed in. "Jenna. Look at me. It's okay if you enjoy this—it's your first time. Jenna. Let me bring you to…"

Jenna is startled by a touch on her shoulder, "Don't!" she spins.

"I'm sorry. You were so far away, off somewhere else. You didn't hear your grandmother ask if she could hug you."

Jenna looks at her Grams; the elderly woman is barely holding on. As much as Jenna wants to deny the request, she just can't. She nods and walks to the old woman. They embrace. The hug feels good—until it doesn't. She frees herself when the words *No. No. No.* start banging in her head. "I'll be back in a few minutes. I need to do something." From behind the safety of her closed bedroom door at her favorite place in all the world, Jenna makes **the call.**

Fayetteville
The detective's got his hands full of woman and is very tempted to ignore his ringing cell. He thinks better of it and steps from the shower. "Cambridge," he snarls.

"It's Jenna Farnsworth. I'd like to get this over with."

"I'll be at the station in an hour." He tosses his cell onto the bath mat, steps back into the shower and continues where he left off, "Against the wall and spread 'em. We've got twenty minutes, Counselor."

"Don't know about you, Officer, but I'm not going to need that much time."

*Maybe we already
know one another.*

Detective Chase has been at the station for more than an hour when Detective Cambridge breezes in.

"Thought you were on night shift, Old Man?"

"Beat you in, Hot Shot."

"Yeah, why?"

"Thinking about REDO."

"What about him?"

"Don't know. I guess I'm just looking for a thread."

"If I can't find one, you won't," Cambridge scoffs.

"You're an asshole, Cambridge."

"General consensus, Old Man."

Chase offers a laugh, stops when there's a knock on the doorjamb. "Excuse me, Detectives, Jenna Farnsworth is here," Diane announces.

"Come on, Old Man." The lead detective pulls up short when he sees Joey Mayer in the conference room with Jenna Farnsworth. "Fuckin A." He damn near pulls the door from its hinges, "You're not staying, Joey."

"Then I'm not staying, Detective," Jenna gets up from her seat. She squares off with the man, "I don't know what your problem is, or why you think it's okay to be so damned rude. The only person in this room who has any reason to be rude, is me. So I will be. If you want my statement, if you want my cooperation, you will do things my way or not at all. Joey stays or we both leave."

Cambridge releases his seethe, "Please take a seat, Ms. Farnsworth. You, too, Mayer." The moment calms as the detective fiddles with a tripod and attached video camera. He speaks over his shoulder, "It's SOP to video a victim's recall and..."

"Survivor," Joey interrupts.

Cambridge clenches his jaw, "It's SOP to video a survivor's recall, and then we'll discuss the events point by point and prepare a statement for your signature."

Jenna nods.

"I'll document the opening sequence of the video, and then you can begin when you're ready Ms. Farnsworth."

"Before we begin, Detective, would you please introduce the other man in the room?"

The other man in the room doesn't wait, "Detective Raymond Chase, Ms. Farnsworth. I would have introduced myself, but Detective Cambridge was in the middle of a hissy fit."

Three people in the room snicker.

"Are you done?" Cambridge asks.

The rape survivor begins to tremble, a flashback pushes free, "**Are you done?**" She shakes her head, shoots pleading eyes Joey's way, "I don't think I can."

"Try to relax, Jenna."

She unravels at a memory. "Try to relax." She begins pulling rapid, shallow breaths, and stammers, "Oh, God, I shouldn't have. How could I have?" She pushes from her chair. "I shouldn't have come." The words hit hard. She falls back onto her seat and buries her face into her hands.

The room stays silent as Jenna works through whatever grips her. After many minutes, she pushes through her emotional pain.

"Jenna, we can come back another time."

"No. Let's get this over with."

Cambridge presses a button on a remote and begins speaking, "Detective Matthew Cambridge, Detective Raymond Chase, Jenna Farnsworth, and SRCC counselor, Josephine Mayer are present for ...."

Jenna spaces through the rest of the opening sequence, and only returns to the here and now when she hears, "Excuse me, Ms. Farnsworth, you can begin."

She smiles at the nice detective and pulls a shaky breath. "Keith Moreno and I had dinner. He headed to Styles University around five not expecting to be back until late. He was meeting a friend at a place called DJs something or other. It was the first time I'd been left alone at Oren. I moved here at the beginning of January from Philly and didn't know anyone to hang out with, so I decided to spend the night reading in my room. I reviewed my syllabus and worked through the first few chapters of my coursework, then turned in at a little past nine."

Those are the last words Jenna speaks with any inflection. From that point on she retells her experience as though she's watching a movie reel and narrating what the audience is seeing. The thing is Jenna is the only one seeing the horror of that night.

"I was woken in the middle of a scream. I was silenced by a hand covering my mouth and nose. I couldn't breathe and was really struggling. He pressed me down using his full weight. He demanded I stop moving, and when I did, he removed his hand from my face." Jenna's eyes are in constant movement as the events are released from her memory. "He stayed pressed on top of me; his erection was digging into my thigh. He warned me not to move. I could no longer move because I'd wrenched my back in the struggle. I closed my eyes. He told me to open them. He tightened his hand over my mouth until I obeyed him."

She closes her eyes tight and continues with her story. "Things changed when I opened my eyes ……. For a moment it felt like he was seducing me ……. He raised himself up, unzipped his jeans ……. He pulled a knife and ran it across my breast drawing blood ……. I asked him not to because I am, because I was, a virgin ……. He cut away my panties and ……."

There is silence in the room for a full minute as Jenna struggles to say the word.

"And he raped me, vaginally. As horrible as the event was, it got worse. He acted as though it wasn't a rape. When he climaxed, he whispered my name, and when he got off of me he pressed a kiss to my lips and suggested we'd meet again someday, and that we might already know one another." She sits with those words banging in her head for several minutes.

"Is that the end of your statement, Ms. Farnsworth? Is there anything you'd like to add?"

She begins hyperventilating, swivels her seat and puts her head between her knees. His words torment. **"Look at me. It's okay if you enjoy this ……. it's your first time. Jenna. Let me bring you to ……. Maybe we'll meet again, someday. Maybe we already know one another, Jenna."** She dry heaves over a basket. "Maybe we already know one another." Jenna sits up and stares at the detectives, first one then the other. "Do I know him? Do you think I know him? I just moved here, the only guy I know is ……. "

Silence fills the room.

Jenna pushes to her feet and paces a bit, her arms in constant motion, her hands attempting to shake away nervous energy. When she stops, she addresses Cambridge. "It isn't Keith. It can't be Keith. Can it?"

Joey and Jenna take a minute outside the conference room while Cambridge and Chase prepare for the interview. When the counselor and the survivor return, the dislikable detective points to seats on one side of the table. Jenna and Joey sit, the men take seats across from them and Cambridge begins. "Ms. Farnsworth,

Detective Chase and I will ask you to confirm, deny, or correct some things you just said. Sometimes a yes or no answer is appropriate. If we need more we'll ask."

Jenna nods.

"On the night of September 8th you went to your bedroom after Keith Moreno left 10 Oren Street."

"Keith left around five. I went to my room closer to six. I cleaned up after dinner, folded some laundry, and sort of just putzed around."

"And you went to bed for the night around nine."

"Yes."

"What time do you think you fell asleep?"

"I tossed and turned a bit, but probably within a half hour or so."

"What time do you think you were woken?"

"I have no idea."

"But you were woken from sleep."

"Yes, a deep sleep."

"Can you describe your assailant?"

Jenna closes her eyes, tight. "He wore a black ski-mask, a white undershirt, and jeans. His eyes were dark. His lips were chapped. His breath was minty, and he wore a gold wedding band. He might be left-handed."

"Why is that?" Detective Chase asks.

"Because the wedding band was on the hand that held the knife."

Both detectives jot that information down.

"Can you estimate a height?"

Jenna closes her eyes again, "I'm 5 '7" so I'd say he's at least 6'. He left his boots on. Huh, I just remembered that."

"You saw them? Can you describe them?"

"No, they dug into my legs and banged against them. I have bruises on my shins. They came from his boots."

"What about a coat, shirt, sweater, sweatshirt?"

"What?"

"You said he wore an undershirt."

"Yes. I didn't see any other shirt or a coat."

"It's winter."

She shrugs.

The men jot some more notes.

Cambridge starts again, "Did you leave any lights on in your room before going to bed?"

"No."

"But you saw that his ski-mask was black, his eyes were dark, his undershirt was white, and you said earlier he smiled when he learned you were a virgin."

"Yes."

"Did you have a T.V. on, or were the shades up letting an outdoor light source in, or was there a light on in the hall that would have aided in your seeing those things?"

Jenna rolls her head from side to side. Her eyes travel from left to right as though searching for a light source, "I left the hall light on before going to bed, sort of as a nightlight. That must be it."

"The light came from the hall. You think the assailant left the bedroom door open while he was raping you?"

"I don't know." Jenna squirms in her seat, turns pensive, starts to say something and stops. Twice.

"Ms. Farnsworth, is there something you want to add?"

"Ask."

The detectives nod.

"It would make more sense that a rapist would have shut the door, right?"

"Why is that, Ms. Farnsworth?" Cambridge presses.

"Because the light in the hall gave me a chance to see him. And with the door open, he could have been interrupted by someone coming home. Unless. Unless he knew no one would be coming home," she shakes her head, gets up from the table, and paces a bit. "No. It wasn't Keith. It can't be Keith. Can it?"

"Ms. Farnsworth," Detective Chase begins, "do you have some place to stay until we have a chance to establish Mr. Moreno's whereabouts at the time of the attack?" *And to keep REDO from getting his hands on you*, he silently thinks.

"My grandparents place at Oneida Lake."

Interview fallout.

Jenna and Joey take the detectives' advice and head to Oren.

"I hope Keith is still at the University."

"Is he going back to your grandparents' place?"

"No." Jenna sort of blanks when Joey pulls to the curb.

"You ready? We should get in and get out."

Jenna opens the car door and leads Joey around back without word. The obedient roommate starts to remove her boots at the back door to protect the hardwood floors—the pissed woman thinks better of it and trudges through the entranceway and down the hall. She pushes open her bedroom door and gasps at the sight of her room. "What a fucking mess!"

"We'll be out of here in a few minutes," Joey consoles.

"Not talking about the room, Joey. My fucking life, it's a fucking mess!"

Jenna drags suitcases from under her bed, the ones she'd just finished emptying days ago, and slams them hard onto the stripped bare mattress. She grabs clothes and undergarments from bureau drawers that are covered in fingerprint dust, storms across the hall and sweeps personal items from a closet shelf into a carryall, goes to the den for her backpack and computer, slides it into a special slot, goes back to her room and shoves textbooks and notebooks in the main section, then puts various and sundry power cords in before zipping it shut. She hands Joey a suitcase, takes one for herself, and closes the bedroom door behind them. She storms down the hall with Joey tight on her heels, removes the housekey Keith gave her from her keyring, puts it on a shelf by the front door, and slams it shut behind her. She groans loudly when she sees her Subaru covered in a foot of snow.

"Forget it," Joey says, "Marilyn and I will come back later, dig it out, and bring it to Oneida."

Jenna tears and chokes her thanks.

Little more than a half hour later, Joey drops Jenna at the top of a driveway that leads to a sage green lakefront bungalow.

"I'd invite you in, Joey, but I'm hoping to sneak in and avoid any fanfare."

"No problem. As for the Subaru, Marilyn and I will drop it off sometime tonight. We'll leave the keys under the driver's side mat and leave the door unlocked."

"Thank you. I'll call you tomorrow to set up an appointment. There's something that's bothering me, and I'd like to discuss it with you." Jenna makes her way to the back porch and is caught completely off guard when she sees Mac sitting at the kitchen table with her grandparents. She suddenly wishes she'd made other plans for the night—*like jumping off a bridge.*

Mac leaps to his feet, opens the back door, and helps schlep her things to the small bedroom. She's just about to thank him for his help when he leans in. She leans away, awkwardly avoiding his intended hug.

He drops his arms and loses his smile.

"Mac. I think I'm a bit shocked. I didn't expect to see you."

His smile returns.

He's got a great smile, straight and even, and it makes tiny smile lines appear at the edges of his eyes.

She smiles into his name, "Mac."

"What?"

"You're getting laugh lines, and your hair, it's..."

"Darker," he says.

"Yeah. And buzz cut."

"Army hair," he says with a swipe of his hand across his head. "Maybe I'll let it grow out a bit now that I'm back."

"There's something else," Jenna tilts her head from side to side as she studies him.

Mac grins wide, "What?"

"I don't know. Something else is different," she says with wonder.

"God, Jenna, almost everything about me is different. I'm older, taller..."

"Yes," Jenna acknowledges, as her heart begins banging against her chest in response to Mac's close proximity in the tiny room.

An uneasy silence roots itself before Mac stomps it down. "Jenna, I'm so sorry about

Teddy and Maxine. I wasn't able to get time off to attend the services and..."

The awkward silence quickly morphs into an ugly cry.

"Shit. I shouldn't have said anything."

"Mac. I think you should..."

"Go. I should go," he groans his frustration, turns and leaves her bedroom and the bungalow.

SPD

Detective Chase reviews the notes Cambridge made during his interviews with Keith Moreno, Edith Cunningham, Zach Taylor, and Helena Verde before the latter shows for her interview.

"When we're done with the administrative assistant, I need you to talk to the snowplow driver to nail down a time for his work on Oren. And call Sargent Calhoun at SU, see if there are security cameras inside the computer labs at Hadley, the auditorium at Turner, and the parking lots at both places."

Chase nods and flips through a few more pages of notes. "Moreno's got a problem with his timeline. There's too much time unaccounted for."

Cambridge nods, "I think he told Helena Verde that he's in a jam, and she's trying to help establish an alibi."

"Being called in for an interview at the station might impress upon Ms. Verde that she'll be in her own jam if she lies for him."

Cambridge tilts his head toward the conference room window, "She's here."

The 'she' in mention enters the interview room, takes a seat and takes control, "I've decided to come clean. I talked with my lawyer, who is also my sister, and she advised me to tell you what I know."

Cambridge smiles wide at his partner, "Well that's a first, a lawyer telling a client to work with the police."

Helena notices the video equipment for the first time, "Are you recording this?"

"Not yet."

"I do not consent to being recorded. I want to say my piece and get the hell out of here."

The camera stays off.

Helena Verde says her piece. "Keith Moreno and I are having an affair."

Reveille and silhouettes.

Jenna stayed in her room after Mac left. She spent some time settling her things, a little bit of time pacing the small quarters, and way too much time deliberating details. She replayed the rape over and over in her head, pulling every damned thread trying to find out why he did what he did—and why she responded the way she did—whether she did. When she'd wound herself tight in a shitload of twisted threads, she moved on to the finer points, the ones she shared with the detectives. She wondered now if she'd left anything out of her statement, if she failed to emphasize the important things, if she even remembered the important things. After her grandparents retired for the evening, she snuck into the kitchen, grabbed an apple and a yogurt from the fridge, and a sleeve of square, salty crackers and a jar of peanut butter from the cupboard.

Morning light finds an antique alarm clock on a bedside table, its tick-tocks become way to loud for her to ignore. She focuses on the skinny gold hands, "Seven-twelve." She resigns herself to another day, pushes aside the covers, wraps herself in her ankle-length robe, pulls on a pair of rag socks and follows the smells of heaven. The young woman stands at the entrance of the kitchen watching the elderlies shuffle about. She takes in the sameness of the room she's loved since she was a kid. "This kitchen hasn't changed in decades," she says upon entering, "I'm so glad."

"The wallpaper's a bit faded, but I love my chickens," Grams smiles.

Jenna smiles wide at the array of plump white hens with orange feet and beaks and bright red combs that fill the yellow background, "I love them too, and the wire basket filled with the wooden eggs we painted, and the big rooster clock. Does it still cock-a-doodle-doo on the hour?" Jenna shakes her head, "No, I haven't heard it."

Grams clucks a chuckle, "No, dear, that cock hasn't doodled in quite some time."

The elderlies laugh.

"Did you notice the shelf Gramps put up? That's new since the last time you were here."

"Hard to miss with all those egg-shaped framed pictures of me."

While the old people share a laugh and a squeeze of their hands, Jenna reflects. "Everything's the same. Nothing's the same." A thought pushes through. "Hey, Gramps, I heard you, Keith, and Mac talking when I first arrived. I didn't mean to, but my window was cracked a bit and you three were on the wrap porch."

Gramps nods.

"You had a tone with Keith when you asked if he and Mary are still together. It was sort of harsh, almost like you were warning him not to hurt Mary."

"That's right."

"Why would you feel the need to do that? You don't even know Keith."

Grams jumps in, "We know of him. And we don't like what we know."

"What do you know?"

Grams places bacon, eggs, and toast in front of Jenna, "You eat, I'll talk."

"You two don't need me for this conversation." Gramps says, "I'll take Mac the leftover meatloaf plate you prepared him, Gracie. Shouldn't be gone too long."

"It's early, Emmett."

"Reveille, Gracie. You can take a man out of the military, but he won't sleep past dawn." On his way out the door, he places a kiss on the head of the only two girls who captured his heart the minute he laid eyes on them.

"He loves you so, Jenna," Grams sighs the words, then pats her granddaughter's hand. "I should have told you this before you moved in with **that** man. Maybe you wouldn't have—"

"Told me what?" Jenna cuts the sentence short.

"Ever since Mary moved this way, she's made it a habit to visit. She comes by at least once a month and stops in on every holiday. There was a time a year or so ago that Gramps and I were both down with the flu, and she came and stayed with us for three days. She's such a wonderful girl, Jenna."

"Mary's the best."

"Last fall, probably late October or early November, Gramps and I returned from a stroll along the water to find Mary sitting on the front stoop with her head pressed to her knees; she was caught in a real crying spell. We couldn't understand much of what she was saying except whatever set her off had to do with Keith."

Jenna stops eating to listen.

"When Mary pulled herself together enough, she explained that she returned home unexpectedly and found Keith and another woman in an intimate state. She said they had quite a row, I'm not sure what all was said, but the thing that stuck in Mary's craw is he blamed her for his actions. He said he felt slighted that she'd applied for and accepted the study program in Paris without discussing it with him first. He said that was the reason he did .... well, you know what he did."

"You don't believe him?"

"Jenna, the only person responsible for Keith being in bed with that woman is Keith. He said he was angry that Mary did this and Mary did that, and I'm sure he was angry, but taking another woman to bed had nothing to do with Paris or with Mary. He got caught with his pants down, and he blamed someone else for his actions."

Grams lets Jenna stew on that a bit before continuing, "I'm going to tell you the same thing I told Mary. There's a reason she didn't discuss Paris with Keith, and she should think about that. As for him, he might have had a reasonable complaint, but he had no right to sleep with another woman. And…"

"And what?" Jenna leans in.

"And then I told her that Keith's dalliance with that woman wasn't the first time it happened."

"Grams! You didn't!"

"I most certainly did. You and Mary are brilliant scholars, Jenna, but you are naive when it comes to scoundrels. Keith and Mary had a disagreement on an issue and less than a day later he pulled another woman into his bed? The man is handsome and charming and could have most any woman, but the one who landed in his bed that day had already been there before."

Jenna hasn't a notion why she starts laughing, but she starts laughing, and for quite some time she can't stop.

20 Shore Road

Mac quickly gathers his brushes and covers his paintings. It's the same thing whenever Gramps stops by. Fortunately, the elderly man comes to the back door of the McLaughlin bungalow and stays in the kitchen, out of sight from Mac's work. He's at the door before Gramps' third knock.

"Morning, Emmett."

"Didn't wake you, did I?"

The former enlisted man smiles wide, "Sir, no sir."

"Didn't think so. At ease. The missus asked me to deliver this." He hands off the remainder of last night's dinner, "Eat that, and you'll thank me for this intrusion."

"Thank Gracie for me."

"Will do."

As soon as Gramps leaves, Mac puts the covered plate in the fridge and heads back to the living room. He slides open the curtains at the bay window and pulls a sheet from his latest work. He assesses the easel-propped painting from different angles, and quickly eyes his other works. "Landscapes of the lake I love." He runs his finger along the outline of the silhouetted figure painted into a natural feature—a tree, an overhead cloud formation, a water shadow. The woman with long hair graces each of his canvases and haunts his dreams.

That could be awhile.

Caitlyn English is back in bed after a wonderful round of shower sex with her husband. Blissfully caught in a postcoital haze and wrapped in Egyptian cotton and fluffy down, she smiles wide at memories of their easy morning…

"Meet me in the shower," she pulled herself from his arms, sashayed naked through their bedroom, pausing at the en suite entrance, "I felt your wood pressed against my ass, so I know you're ready. What's the hold up?"

"Nice and toasty here, Caitlyn."

"It'll be nice and steamy there, Matt."

"Holler when you're ready for the wood, Ms. English."

Husband and wife were more than ready when he joined her. He stepped into the shower, ran his fingers up her thigh and didn't stop there. He slid two inside and did a little digit dancing.

She pushed at his wrist, "Stop. Matt. I'm almost…"

The ringing cell pulled them short.

He groaned.

She whimpered.

He thought about ignoring it. He didn't— he's a cop. And when he ended his call, he ended their longing with an orgasm for her and one for himself.

The totally satisfied woman left her husband to himself to finish the intended purpose of a morning shower, raced from the en suite and flopped onto the mattress.

"What are you doing?"

"I want to watch you dress."

"Did you bang your head or something?"

Caitlyn laughed big, "Those are the **exact** words people said when they learned I'd married you."

"That makes sense. You wanting to watch me dress does not."

"Well, that's what I'm going to do, and I'm going to narrate."

"Mark these words, Caitlyn English. Turn around is fair play."

She ignored him. "The dark haired, brown eyed, totally ripped husband of Caitlyn English dries patches of wetness from his arms, legs, broad shoulders, muscular chest and back. Muscles flex with every movement. The man sworn to serve and protect begins donning his idea of a work uniform: boxer briefs, T-shirt, socks, button-down shirt of white, pullover sweater of loden green, pair of perfectly faded jeans, navy tweed sport coat, boots, gun belt, and detective's shield." **She sighed then crawled into bed and pulled the covers high.**

"Why is your ass back in bed, Counselor?"

"I'm taking the day off."

The detective did something not generally done by him, he laughed—big. "You? **You** are taking a day off? Took me a damned week to convince you to take a few days off so we could get hitched."

"I believe you are presenting a revisionist history, Matt. It took you a damned week to convince me to **marry** you. My delay in answering had nothing to do with taking time off from work."

He laughed again.

She laughed with him, "As for this day off, I thought I'd rest up before the arrest and prosecution of REDO."

"Unless we get a break, a big break, those events could take a while, Counselor."

"But you think the Jenna Farnsworth rape is his?"

"Yes."

"And Jenna's roommate, any chance he's REDO?"

"Longshot, but his alibi sucks, and he's hiding something."

Caitlyn unwrapped herself layer by layer and crawled the length of the bed. "Could I entice you into staying for a longshot before you go?"

Cambridge eyed his naked woman, thought back to the fists of blonde hair he held as her denim-blue eyes lost focus and her orgasm tightened around him. He marveled at her modest curves, got hard at the sight of the intricately tattooed scales of justice on her hip, a celebratory act so unlike her, she said, and the simple gold of her wedding band. He growled deep. "Can't. But now that I know you're truant, I might sneak back and give you a longshot."

"Looking forward to it, Detective Cambridge," she hollered after him, "and call from the driveway so you don't scare the crap out of me when you come in."

"Or you could keep your classical crap low enough so you can hear me come in."

The detective isn't off the driveway when the ADA gets round two from her paralegal.

"You? **You** are taking a day off?"

"Yes," she laughs.

"Are you in need of medical assistance, ADA English?"

"No medical attention is needed, Michelle. My caseload is light, so I thought I'd pull a few threads on the Demi Warren case, see if anything leads us to Grant Timberlake. And I thought I'd surprise Cambridge with a homecooked meal."

"Okay, that's it, I'm sending the EMTs."

SPD

"What's with all the files, Old Man?"

"REDO's victims. Taking another look."

"Anything pop?"

"Just started. By the way, I talked to Steny Thomas. He said he started plowing Oren around midnight, probably got to the bend at ten past, then back to the bend by quarter past. He said the Fletchers' cars were on the driveway, both covered in snow, and there were tire tracks near them. Two cars were parked at Keith's, but no Jeep."

Cambridge jots down the information. "Anything else?"

"I talked to Calhoun at Styles. As for Hadley Hall, he said there are cameras inside the computer labs and along the hallways outside the labs. There are 'point of entrance' cameras on the administrative floor, as well as on the academic classroom floors, which are located one up and one down from the labs. At Turner, there are cameras inside the auditorium and along some hallways, but none backstage. As for the parking lots, there are multiple cameras, but they were black that night."

"Why?"

"Calhoun is checking if the power outage was related to the snowstorm, but you're wondering if the computer whiz PhD candidate knocked them out somehow."

"Apparently, so are you, Detective Chase."

Syracuse Rape Crisis Center
Joey Mayer finds Jenna Farnsworth sitting in the waiting area when she arrives.

"I hope you don't mind. I didn't make an appointment."

"Not at all, come on," Joey tilts her head, "follow me."

Jenna waits while Joey turns on lights, boots her computer system, and grabs two cups of coffee. The counselor takes a seat near the client in a small sitting area inside the office. She waits until Jenna is ready to begin. It's a very long wait.

"I'm sorry for wasting your time, Joey." Jenna gets up from her chair. The sudden movement causes her to bend with an "Ow."

"Your back is still hurting?"

"From time to time." She turns to leave.

"This wasn't wasted time, Jenna. Sometimes it helps to be in a safe place where you can organize your thoughts. You dictate the course of action and the timeline. When you're here, don't consider anything or anyone else. Okay?"

Jenna smiles, then almost immediately she hangs her head and begins sobbing, then shaking. "I .... I....... I think I climaxed."

Joey makes it to Jenna's side before the women slump to the floor. They are breathing heavy when Joey asks, "Are you alright? Do you want me to help get you into a chair?"

The emotionally wrought woman puts her hands over her face and shakes her head, slowly, then harshly. "And I can't get the chant out of my head."

Joey waits.

"No. No. No. It's in my head all the time. It's on a constant loop. No matter what I'm doing, or who I'm talking with, the words are there. No. No. No. .... No. No. No. I said those words when he was on top of me. I said it when he pushed in and .... when he tried to bring me to orgasm. How could I? Did I? It's disgusting. What is wrong with me?"

Joey offers Jenna her hand, palm up. Jenna takes hold.

"We'll work through this, Jenna, without assigning negatives. It's only been a few days. Right now, you are hyper focused on the sex part, in time you'll expand your vision. There was a lot going on in that room. You know all the big stuff, but your mind is in protective mode, right now. It isn't flooding you with all of the memories. Little by little things will be revealed, and then you can pull at some or all of the threads." The counselor gently squeezes her client's hand. "Do you feel like doing a little work?"

Jenna snort-laughs. "Joey, this has been the most work I've ever done."

Joey laughs and amends her question, "Do you feel like doing a little more work?"

"Okay."

"Okay. Can you tell me the first thought you had when you woke with him on top of you?"

"That I couldn't breathe. That I wanted to live."

"And you did."

Jenna has a good cry, pulls the final few racking sobs while she processes Joey's words. "I don't know whether I had an orgasm, but I do know I'm not ready to figure it out, Joey." She lives with the welcome silence, then offers a timid smile. "There's something I do know, something I already figured out, though."

"Okay."

"I'm not cowering in a corner. I might do that someday, but right now, I am not crippled with fear. I'm pissed. And in a bizarre twist of things, I feel a sense of pride. I know how weird that sounds, but I'm proud because I survived a rape. The actual event. I can work through the things that happened and the fallout from them. In time. But right now, what I cling to is this: I've been through the thing women fear most. It's done. It's behind me."

Joey is racked with guilt. *Nothing is behind you, Jenna. REDO will be back again— someday.*

REDO

The serial rapist is at the Syracuse DMV on a seek-and-he-will-find mission. He moves off a well-worn bench when a lovely young woman enters and takes a full scan of her surroundings. He casually makes his way across the crowded room. *Go to New Licenses,* he wills her.

She goes to New Licenses, hands the clerk her paperwork, and waits while it gets a quick review and a rubber stamp. The lovely young woman breezes through the mandatory eye exam, smiles pretty for the camera, takes her new license from the clerk, laughs at the goofy smile captured for posterity, and follows directions to the New Registrations window.

"She's new to town," he smiles as he heads outside. REDO waits in his idling ride until the light-skinned Black woman with warm honey eyes, friendly smile, and SU sweatshirt pops the trunk on her Volkswagen Passat, grabs a screwdriver and gets to work. She struggles with the dirty snow crusted Maine license plates for several minutes, then startles at a voice from behind.

"Do you need a hand with those?"

She stands upright and smiles, "How could you tell?"

They laugh.

REDO lowers his window and listens to their conversation.

She hands the screwdriver to the young hipster wearing a wool slouch hat, SU sweatshirt, and jeans. "Have at it. Fair warning, I think I might have bent the screw. Thank you, by the way."

"I haven't done anything yet," he smiles.

"You offered to help. I'm Bianca."

"Todd."

Ten minutes after accepting help, the lovely Bianca drives away having told hipster dude she is a transfer student at Styles, and she just finished moving into Meadowbrook. She smiles widely when he assures she chose a nice, safe area to live.

"Time for a drive through Meadowbrook," the serial smiles.

It's a boy.

Caitlyn spends the day surrounded by stuff. When she's in the kitchen, a room she is barely familiar with, she's at the counter surrounded by chopped vegetables and cookbooks. When she's in the master bedroom, her makeshift home office, she's on the floor surrounded by case files and legal pads. After countless trips between the two rooms, and with that night's dinner well underway, she settles herself for a review of a cold case file. It's her umpteenth probe over several years, but she's still looking for a thread to pull, one that makes any sense. She reads her summary of the case.

"Grant Alan Timberlake, aka Wood Timberlake, was twenty-five at the time of Demi Warren's murder. The victim was found partially nude and strangled near Sweetheart Lane, a frequently used cut-through to Onondaga Lake and a popular place for couples to walk, picnic, and watch the stars. There was no evidence of rape though her panties were removed and taken from the scene—both scenes. Evidence suggests the body was moved several hundred yards from the kill spot to the discovery spot. Friends told investigators Demi wasn't dating anyone, but two young women thought Timberlake was interested in the victim, though no one ever saw them together." She finishes her summary, only to ask the questions she's been asking for years. "Why was Demi Warren on Sweetheart Lane? Was there something going on between Warren and Timberlake, or was she involved with someone else? And more importantly, why was her body moved from Point A to Point B, but left in the same area? If you're going to move a dead body, then why not move the dead body?" She is interrupted by the stove's timer.

Cambridge parks next to his wife's Benz. He doesn't bother locking his Land Rover, "A quick dinner, and then back at it." He changes his mind when he enters their home. "Caitlyn! What is that smell?"

"I'd prefer you classify it as an aroma, Mr. Cambridge, and it's braised beef in red wine."

"Did you order in?"

"Nope. Thought I'd poison you myself this evening."

Cambridge enters the kitchen, steps around the apron-adorned woman when she moves in for a kiss, and pulls off the lid of a pot that has never been used before. "**You** made this?"

"You sound surprised. As a matter of record, Matt, you sound a bit too surprised. I can read a recipe, you know."

"No evidence to support that, Counselor," he reaches in and pulls a piece of beef.

"Matthew Cambridge. I think I would enjoy serving the meal that took me six hours to prepare. Go pour the wine. It's from Long Point Winery."

He groans when he sees the beautifully set table, linen, china, crystal, flowers, candles. "I only stopped by for a longshot, Caitlyn."

"No dinner. No drink. No conversation. **No** longshot."

After an amazing meal, The Counselor is served her very own, very powerful climax, brought about by the expert moves of **That** Cop. The couple spends a few minutes with their own thoughts before Cambridge moves his arm out from under his wife's head. "I hate to do this, Caitlyn, but I need to get back to the station."

"Why?"

"REDO is bugging the shit out of me. Chase was working the victims' files earlier, and I realized I haven't looked at them in a long time. REDO is in my head, every rape, every victim statement is burned into my memory, but something's missing. I need to find a thread to pull, so I'm going back to square one .... maybe find something useful before REDO pays Jenna Farnsworth another visit."

"You'll find it, Detective."

"Hasn't happened yet, Counselor."

Beard Park Condo

Joey has been quiet all night. Marilyn knows her wife is preoccupied with REDO and struggling with the decision to not tell Jenna that she's still in danger. Marilyn thinks about broaching the subject—thinks better of it. She leaves Joey with her thoughts and goes to the spare room. She stands in front of a closet door needing to open it, unsure if she should. She has little choice. She slides open the bifold, sighs at the sight of a wall-mounted pistol vault, and thinks back to the day they decided to take shooting lessons and buy a gun...

"The Speedvault gun safe provides easy weapon access," the salesman said before talking them through the design features. "Just mount the vault under a desk, or on the side of a nightstand, or on a closet wall, slide the gun in and close it up. If an emergency situation arises, key a security code on the digital-keypad, which activates a drop-down drawer that holds your gun. The keypad is silent and has a light feature if needed."

"It looks like an old-fashioned cowboy holster."

"Exactly. It's designed for a quick draw."

Marilyn reaches to a shelf above the Speedvault and grabs hold of The Box. She sits on the floor, opens the dust covered receptacle, and begins organizing pieces of her past. She removes journals that hold details of his crimes and her painful reflections. She flips through a handful of SRCC pamphlets she received at UU during her SART exam. She smiles at a banded stack of appointment cards from her sessions with Joey, "I never would have met you, if..." She sets them aside and digs through the rest of the contents until she finds the picture. She hasn't had more than a second with it, when she freezes at the sound of Joey's voice.

"Whose baby is that?"

Marilyn panics at her wife's question, and pulls the picture to her chest.

"Whose baby is ……. OH. MY. GOD."

Marilyn hangs her head.

Joey bolts from the room banging heavily against the doorframe on her way out.

Marilyn scrambles from the floor and grabs hold of Joey's hand before she makes it through the front door.

"Don't go! Please. Don't go."

Joey stops, remains at the door for several minutes, then closes it. She leans back. "Where is…"

"He. I had REDO's son."

Joey's mind starts a tortured trip down memory lane. "After the second rape?"

Marilyn nods.

"But you took Plan B. I was there. I watched you take the pill."

"Plan B doesn't work if you're already ovulating," Marilyn reminds.

Joey begins connecting dots. "That's why you left Syracuse."

"Yes."

"You said it was because of us, our relationship," Joey stumbles over the painful words.

"Yes."

Joey runs her hands through her short, black, curly hair as her green eyes fill. She shakes her head back and forth—slowly—quickly—slowly. When the movement ends, she lowers her head and stares at the floor. "You left me."

"I couldn't tell you, Joey. I tried, but I couldn't. That's why I left."

"Why didn't you…"

"Abort?"

Joey nods.

"I made an appointment, but a torturous loop started in my head. My thoughts and feelings were all over the place. The thought that held still for any length of time was this: I am a lesbian. I was raped, not once, but twice. After the first rape, I took Plan B and it worked. After the second rape, I took Plan B and it didn't work. I got pregnant with a child who **never** should have been. On one of two occasions—the only two occasions when sperm entered my body—a life was created." Marilyn walks to Joey and takes hold of her hands. "I was really fucked up back then. I was so emotionally battered that I couldn't find a path to ending the pregnancy."

"You should have told me."

"Jesus, Joey. There are no should haves here. All the shit that happened, happened to **me**. Every damned thing, every damned choice, every ounce of control over my body and my mind had been taken from me by REDO, a rapist, the father of my child. I wouldn't have made it through the rapes without you, Joey, but the decision to have or to not have a baby already inside me had to be my decision and mine alone."

"Where is he?"

"With Evelyn and Chet in Buffalo."

"Your sister and brother-in-law are raising him?"

Marilyn nods. "Since his birth."

"What's his name?"

"Joseph McGinn."

"Joey," Joey whispers.

Alibis are everything.

Keith Moreno is on the second floor of his house. For hours he's been working through a belly full of pissed energy. He's been measuring this, sawing that, fitting tongues into groves, shooting nails into planks, and sanding rough edges—and he's been practicing his alibi.

"I went to SU after dinner, worked at the computer lab, then went to Turner auditorium to watch a friend practice." He shakes his head. "Not good enough. Cambridge is gonna want a precise timeline." He thinks it through. "Okay. I went to SU around five, went to Turner around seven, and left campus around eleven-thirty. That timeline would put me home by eleven-forty at the latest. I didn't get home until twelve-thirty. I don't think I told Cambridge what time I got home, only what time I left campus. Shit. I don't remember, but I did tell him I stopped at Steny Thomas' place to get air in my tire. Cambridge will check about the tire. Steny was out plowing, so he can't say one way or the other if I stopped for air—but there might be cameras at his station. At the very least, the detective will ask Steny what time he plowed Oren. Cambridge asked me if the road had been plowed when I got home. It had, but there was some snow filling back in. Hard to tell what time Steny came through with the plow. The time I can't account for is between eleven-thirty and twelve-thirty.

Best thing for me is if Jenna said she was raped before eleven-thirty because Helena said she told Cambridge I was with her until eleven-thirty. That gives me an alibi for the early part of the night, and if there are cameras at Steny's, it might lower the heat all around."

The frustrated carpenter tosses the measuring tape into his toolbox, unplugs his circular saw, affixes a nail gun lock, and slams the cover. "I need to get my shit together. Food and sleep. I need both." He grabs a deli sandwich and a beer from a cooler and takes space on the floor. "Jenna left my house. Of course she left. She thinks I raped her. It won't be long before people at SU hear about this. Being investigated for rape doesn't look good for a fucking PhD candidate." He tosses an empty across the room, doesn't bother shielding himself from bits of glass that fly back toward him. He spends the next few hours eating, drinking, brooding, wiping blood from a facial scratch, and thinking about Jenna.

SPD

The detective has his feet up, open files are spread across his desk, one teeters on his lap. "Mendez, you looked good for that rape. The evidence looked solid, an eye witness put you outside Joanie Newton's place, and the woman you said could provide an alibi was a no show, until a year later, when you were behind bars. Well you're not behind bars now—you're back on the streets and you have been since the

REDO shit show started." The detective thinks for a few minutes, closes the file, knowing what he knew the minute he picked it up, "You aren't REDO."

It's well past midnight when the detective grabs a stack of victim files, sets them into chronological order, and gets to work, "Start at the beginning. Marilyn McGinn. REDO's first victim—so far as anyone knows."

The Statements

Marilyn McGinn
Victim Statement
Syracuse, New York

I relocated to Syracuse for paramedic training at Upstate Medical University. I did the Buffalo to Syracuse drive in record time, moved into my garden apartment, emptied boxes, set electronics, ran to the DMV, the insurance company, the college bookstore, the grocery store, cooked dinner, read for a bit, then crashed into the sleep of the dead. I woke to a terrifying scream—it came from me. A man on top of me was the reason for my scream. I tried to get out from under him. I tried to call for help. But he imprisoned me beneath him and muffled my screams with his hand. I couldn't move my body, but I thrashed my head back and forth and managed to get my face out from under his hand. I dragged a breath before his hand returned to my face. He pressed himself tighter against me and warned me not to move and not to scream. I nodded. He released his hand, but kept it hovering just above my mouth, ready to silence me, suffocate me, if I disobeyed. I pulled a desperate breath, my chest was rising and pressing against his. I felt him harden along my abdomen. I closed my eyes, he whispered for me to open them. The energy changed. He got seductive.

The masked man locked onto my eyes and ran his fingers the length of my hair. It was unnerving, intense, so I closed my eyes. I opened them when his hand raised quickly. I thought he was going to hit me, but he didn't. He traced the outline of my lips with his thumb, moved it down to trace along the clef of my chin. His touch was gentle, his dark eyes warm. **I don't want to hurt you. I only want to rape you.** He said those words with some weird inflection, as though the rape wouldn't cause pain. Then he asked me my name. I could barely speak, but managed to croak, Marilyn. **Beautiful name for a beautiful woman,** he said as he touched my face again. Then he said, **Marilyn, this can be a rape or a murder. You can get over one of those two events. I suggest you not fight this.** He pushed himself up and straddled my waist. A knife appeared out of nowhere, it was in his left hand. I closed my eyes and when I opened them again, I saw he'd freed his penis from his jeans. He took hold of my cotton tee, and sliced through it. He moaned when he saw that he cut too deep and drew blood. I could tell he was smiling beneath the wool mask. He warned me with his eyes, as he cut away the sides of my boxer shorts. I told him I was a lesbian and that I never. **Your lucky night,** he laughed as he pushed in, and in, and in. He whispered, **Marilyn,** when he released. He stayed deep inside of me for a minute, then moved off in one swift motion, walked to the head of the bed, leaned close, kissed me as though we were lovers, then pressed his lips to my cheek and whispered, **Maybe we'll meet again, someday, Marilyn.**

I checked the slice on my breast as soon as the rapist exited through the garden slider. I pressed zero on the landline phone I had installed earlier that day and asked the operator to connect me to the Syracuse Rape Crisis Center. I told the counselor who answered that I was raped at 44 Central Street, garden apartment, that I am an EMT and did not want ambulance service. I wanted someone to drive me to UU. Fifteen minutes later, I opened my door to a woman named Joey Mayer.

Signed under penalty of perjury: *Marilyn McGinn*
Witnessed: Detective Raymond Chase
and Detective Matthew Cambridge

Marilyn McGinn
Victim Statement
Syracuse, New York

I opened my front door and stepped inside my apartment. The door was kicked closed behind me. He said, **We meet again, Marilyn.**

Suzi Kekoa

The rape victim did not report her sexual assault at the time it took place. She carried the experience back to Honolulu, a mere twelve hours after arriving in Ithaca. She ignored the pleas of her cousin, Trini, to tell her why she had changed her mind about studying at Carver College and living with her in New York.

Suzi silently endured Trini's guilt trip...

"I rented a two-bedroom apartment for the two of us, Suzi. Why are you afraid to do things on your own? You're such a Momma's girl and will never find happiness under your mother's thumb. You should stay here and live your life!"

Suzi offered no defense, no explanation, no request that the barrage of insults and put-downs stop. She simply waited it out. When the cab came to take her to the airport, she addressed her cousin from the doorway...

"I'm sorry, Trini. Please send my belongings back to me, I left $100 on the bed. Goodbye."

Six months later Suzi Kekoa called the Ithaca Rape Crisis Center long-distance from Honolulu. She told a counselor her story and asked if it were too late to report the rape and could she report it at the police unit in Honolulu.

"I don't want to be involved, I just want the police in New York to know."

Suzi Kekoa
Victim Statement
Honolulu, Hawaii

After a 13-hour flight from Honolulu to Ithaca, I was sweaty, smelly, and in a foul mood. I took a taxi from the airport, found the key to the apartment right where Trini said it would be hidden, opened the door, put the key back so Trini could use it when she returned from her overnight shift at the hospital, and closed the door. I grabbed a water from the refrigerator, went into the bathroom to freshen up, and went to the pink bedroom, the one Trini designated as my room. I kicked off my shoes and undressed to my bra and underwear, then crawled onto the stripped bare mattress. I covered myself with a throw laying at the bottom of the bed. I woke to a hand covering my face and a man pressed on top of me. The first thought I had was, *Momma told me not to come.*

I didn't thrash about like I imagined I would have under the circumstances. I remained perfectly still. I am a small woman, 5' nothing, and 100 pounds if I had a big lunch. I knew I was not going to get away, so I resigned myself. I think he realized this and whispered, **Smart girl.** He asked me if I was going to scream. I shook my head and he removed his hand from my mouth. He became calm or something. This caused me to become very afraid. I started breathing quickly, too quickly. My chest was rising and falling rapidly. He put his hand onto my neck and said, **You need to relax. I don't want you to pass out.** I pulled a deep breath and went limp beneath him. I felt him harden when he started exploring my face with his thumb. He traced every inch, kept saying I was the most beautiful one. He told me to look into his eyes. I did. They were the only things I could see because of his mask. Then he said, **I don't want to hurt you. I only want to rape you.** I started breathing hard. He brushed my hair away and asked me my name. I lied to him. I said, Trini. That's my cousin's name, the woman I went to New York to live with. At the time, I didn't know why I lied. After thinking about it for the past six months, the only thing I could come up with was I didn't want to hear him say my name. If that was what he was going to do, I didn't want him to say my name.

As soon as he heard me say Trini, he said, **Beautiful name for a beautiful woman. Trini, this can be a rape or a murder. You can get over one of those two events. I suggest you not fight this.** He pushed himself up, straddled my waist, and pulled the fly of his jeans down. That's when I noticed the wedding ring, but it wasn't a ring, it was a knife. It had a hole in the center of it and he had his finger in the hole. I asked my cousin, Bomi, about it. He said it sounded like a Spatha knife, something climbers use. Whatever it's called, he used it to cut my bra and my panties, then he cut my breast. It wasn't a deep cut, but it was a long one. He got really hard when he saw my blood. I focused on the injury while he raped me, on whether I would have a scar. The worst part of that night was when he climaxed and called out my cousin's name. I almost lost it. When he pulled himself free, he walked to the head of the bed and caressed my face, kissed my lips, and whispered, **Maybe we'll meet again, someday, Trini.** I waited until I heard him leave, then ran to the back door and put a chair against it. Then I locked myself in the bathroom. I showered as fast as I could and sat against the locked door. At 7 AM I came out, removed the chair, and waited for my cousin to come home. As soon as I could, I left New York and returned to Hawaii.

Signed under penalty of perjury: *Suzi Kekoa*
Witnessed: Detective Akoni Mahelona

Connie Braxton
Victim Statement
Aurora, New York

I just moved into a new apartment off-campus and was really excited about a teaching job I got at Aurora Elementary. I'd been in the area for four years as an undergraduate at Wynona College and decided to stay put for a while. The previous week, I flew to Jersey to pack up things from my parents' home and to get the Jeep I'd never brought to campus. I spent that day unpacking and doing a thousand errands and teacher-related things that needed to be done before the first day of school. One of the reasons I rented the renovated barn apartment was because my landlord and his wife lived at the main house a stone's throw away. They were out of town that first weekend, and I was on edge the whole time. I thought about spending the night with my former roommate, but talked myself out of it.

I was asleep when everything started. A man in a ski-mask landed sort of on top of me and covered my mouth with his hand. I bit him and managed to roll away. I was out from under his upper body and his hand had come loose, so I screamed. It was the kind of scream I'd only ever heard in a horror film. He got hold of me and shoved me beneath him. He covered my mouth and nose and growled against my face,

Don't move. Don't fucking move. Don't fucking scream. I nodded and he pulled his hand away. **What's your name?** I told him Connie and he said, **You're a feisty one, Connie. I don't like your type, I much prefer the Trini's of the world.** I didn't know what he was talking about, but I knew I'd better chill. He brushed my hair away from my face, then grabbed a bunch and pulled really hard. He leaned low and said, **I have a sudden urge to hurt you before I rape the fuck out of you.** I teared up and went still beneath him. I was trembling and barely breathing. He said, **That's more like it.** He pushed himself up and straddled my waist. He was breathing hard, not from exertion, but from rage. He yanked his penis through the fly of his jeans, fisted my nightshirt and cut through it with a gold-tipped knife that appeared from nowhere. Then he sliced my breast. He got really, really hard, and inched his penis toward my mouth. I thought he was going to rape me orally, but he lowered himself on top of me and pushed into my vagina. When he climaxed he said he wished I were Trini. He pulled himself free and raged toward me. He spun the knife he was holding around and around. I thought we was going to cut me. He bent low and said, **The next time, it's going to be much worse, Connie.**

Signed under penalty of perjury: *Connie Braxton*
Witnessed: Detective Grant Simms
and Detective Brandan Kelly

Connie Braxton
Victim Statement
Aurora, New York

I opened my front door and when it closed behind me he said, **We meet again, Connie.**

The second statement was given and signed at Aurora Medical Center three days after the rape and savage beating of Connie Braxton.

Trini Kekoa
Victim Statement
Ithaca, New York

I stepped into the apartment and when the door closed a man grabbed me from behind, lifted me easily off the floor, and said, **We meet again, Trini.** He held me tight against him with one arm, and covered my mouth with his other hand. He carried me to the far bedroom, threw me onto the bed, and growled, **Take off your clothes.** When I started to strip, he said, **I've missed you, Trini.** When I had only my bra and underwear still on he laughed and said, **A bare mattress again.** I had no idea what he was talking about and started thinking he was insane. I began panicking inside, my breathing increased and I started shaking. He smiled and said, **You know you'll live through this.** I took that to mean he wasn't going to kill me if I behaved. He told me to lay down and said, **I don't want to hurt you. I only want to rape you.** He straddled my waist, pulled a knife from somewhere, and cut the bra strap between my breasts. He moaned and said, **This time I want you to unzip my jeans and take my dick out.** I started to move and he said, **Where's the scar?** I looked stupefied because I was stupefied. He pushed my shoulders to the bed and examined my left breast, he kept saying, **Where's the cut? Where's the fucking cut, Trini?** That's when we both knew the truth. I didn't have a scar on my breast because he hadn't cut my breast—because he hadn't raped me before. He became furious. He put a hand around my throat and the knife next to my cheek. He snarled, **Where is she? Who is she?** He loosened his grip so I could answer, and I coughed that her name is Suzi, that she is my cousin, and she was back in Honolulu. He was overcome with rage. He screamed at me, said if he couldn't have his second chance with that Trini, he'd have a whole new experience with this Trini. He moved up onto my chest and orally raped me. When he was finished he tucked himself away, leaned real close and said, **Maybe we'll meet again, someday, Trini.** As soon as I heard the door click shut, I called the SART nurse at Ithaca General to come get me. She took me to the Emergency department where I work every day, admitted me, and then called the police department.

Signed under penalty of perjury: *Trini Kekoa*
Witnessed: Detective Caleb Sanchez
and Detective Katherine Melber

The Investigation

A slip of the tongue.
A slip on the ice.

Detective Chase answers the phone just as a too-hot sip of coffee burns its way down his throat. "Chase," he coughs.

"Ray, it's Brandan Kelly."

"What can I do for you, Detective?"

"REDO visited Aurora last night."

"Goddammit it," Chase barks. "Your victim make a prelim statement?"

"Yeah, she told SART at Cayuga Regional that her rapist said he didn't want to hurt her, he only wanted to rape her, that she had a pretty name, and that maybe they'd meet again someday. The usual crap, until the end. This time he whispered the name Jenna when he ejaculated."

Chase sits straight in his chair, "Jenna? Is that your vic's name?"

"Nope. Her name's Monica. Monica Farrell. Your recent rape victim is Jenna, right?"

"Right. Looks like REDO had a slip of the tongue. Hey, Brandan, Detective Cambridge just sauntered in. I'll get him up to speed and one of us will get back to you."

Matt fills the doorway between their offices, "What's up?"

"REDO was in Aurora last night."

"That was Detective Kelly on the phone?"

"Yeah."

"Kinda quick for an FYI call."

"There was no problem putting the pieces together on this rape, Matt. The vic's name is Monica Farrell."

Cambridge shrugs his shoulders, "Is that supposed to mean something to us?"

"Nope. But the fact that REDO whispered the name *Jenna* when he filled her means our rapist just fucked up. There's a thread to pull."

"Fuckin A there is."

Oren

Keith Moreno is woken by robust banging on his front and back doors. He answers Door Number 1, immediately wishing he had opted for whatever's behind Door Number 2. "What the fuck, Cambridge?"

"What's with the scratch on your face? Call your lawyer, tell him to meet you at the station. You're coming with us."

Attorney Jack Rafferty moves through the squad room as though he's been there hundreds of times. That's because the defense attorney has been there hundreds of times. That's also why no one bothers to stop Jack Rafferty. "Where's Cambridge?" he hollers on his way through the huddle of cops. An automatic raising of arms and pointing of fingers show the way, followed by more than a few finger salutes when he's out of view. "Cambridge!" the attorney hollers from the end of a corridor housing a dozen interview and conference rooms.

Cambridge evil-eyes Keith Moreno, "Your lawyer is—"

"Jack Rafferty," the bellicose attorney finishes the detective's sentence from the doorway. "What the hell was so urgent that you needed to drag his ass, and my ass, out of bed before the damned sun took its morning piss?"

"Need to talk to Mr. Moreno about a rape."

"The rape took place days ago, Cambridge? Mr. Moreno gave you a preliminary statement, without legal representation, so that'll be tossed. And my client has agreed to sit down for a formal interview. What more do you want?"

"An alibi. For last night's rape."

"I was home."

"Alone?"

"Yes, Detective. My roommate moved out, probably at your suggestion."

Cambridge nods, "Mr. Moreno, any chance you'd like to do one of your cut to the chase alibis for last night, and is there any chance you haven't destroyed evidence?"

The lawyer turns to leave, "Unless you have specific questions, Detective?"

Cambridge remains quiet.

"Come on, Keith."

The suspect takes a step toward the door, shakes his head, then goes rogue. "How about I give you an alibi that begins about the time I learned my roommate abandoned my home because you two convinced her I raped her. I placed a called to this shyster so I could have the pleasure of paying him 500 bucks an hour to deal with you two assholes, went to the second floor of my place, laid, banged, and screwed a bunch of boards—not broads—and tied one the fuck on." He starts to move out of the room.

Cambridge smirks, "Starting to like these cut to the chase dumps you do. Before you leave, any chance you know Monica Farrell?"

Keith Moreno stops dead in his tracks and turns fifty shades of **what the fuck red.**

His lawyer grabs hold of Keith's arm and shakes his head, "Don't say another word." He addresses Cambridge, "Expect a call from your brass, Detective."

"Better up Mr. Moreno's retainer, Jack."

When the men are out of earshot, Cambridge scoffs, "Seems Keith Moreno knows Monica Farrell? That's an unexpected twist."

The Lake

Jenna is up and out of the bungalow a few minutes after the sun has claimed the morning sky. She's a good mile down the shore before she realizes she left without her gloves. She puts her hands in front of her mouth and exhales warm air onto her frozen digits then shoves her hands deep into her pockets. She finds no relief, so she goes to Plan B. She takes off her slouch, pulls her fur lined hood onto her head, and wraps both hands into her toasty warm hat. "Perfect," she exclaims, and it is perfect until she slips on a patch of ice and can't release her hands from her hat quick enough to break her fall. Her hip, then her elbow, then her shoulder take the impact. She is gasping for air when she manages to right herself to a sitting position. An ache quickly settles on her left side from top to bottom, and her ass quickly becomes part of the frozen firma.

"Jenna!"

She startles at the call, then relaxes when Mac rounds a corner. "Never been so happy to see you, Mac."

He looks at the felled woman, legs straight forward, an ungloved hand holding her shoulder, a too big hood partially obstructing her face, "I believe you. What happened?"

"Seriously, Mac?"

"Okay, you fell. Why haven't you gotten up?"

"I twisted my ankle and cracked the hell out of my shoulder, elbow and hip. And I'm quite sure my posterior is on its way to being permanently affixed to this icy spot."

Mac squats in front of her. "I'm going to pull you up onto my shoulder."

"You are doing no such thing."

"Can you walk?"

"Aided, perhaps."

"For a mile?"

"Doubtful."

"Lean toward me, Jenna."

She leans.

He hoists. He positions her hips in front of his shoulder, her torso over it, wraps his arm across the back of her thighs, and readies to move out, "Hold onto the back of my jacket and **Don't**. **Move.**"

She panics, begins flailing, and brings them both down.

"What the hell, Jenna?" He scrambles to his feet and looks at the emotional wreck in the making. "What's wrong? Are you hurt worse than you thought?"

Jenna Farnsworth is cowering in a metaphorical corner. Mac's words, "Don't. Move." brought it all back. She unravels.

He stands helplessly by. His questions go unanswered as the woman on the ground falls to pieces. He squats in front of her, "I don't know what's going on, Jenna, but you're hurt and hypothermia is the next thing on our list of problems. I'm lifting you, and we're moving out. This time, stay still." Mac easily handles the mile trek, takes her to a spare bedroom at his place, sets her onto a club chair, wraps her in several blankets and waits. On his fifth well-spaced, "Jenna," she breaks from the daze she'd slipped into. He kneels in front of her, looks into her eyes, and takes hold of her wrist, "Pupils dilated, pulse rapid."

She begins trembling and moves quickly to a full-on body shaking, "Cccold." The word takes her back to when Keith tried to help her.

"We need to get you out of your wet clothes."

"No. No. No."

"Can I help you?"

"No. No. No."

"I'll go get Grams and Gramps."

"No. No. No."

"Jenna, tell me how I can help."

"Pocket."

Mac removes the blankets she's wrapped in, puts his hand into her jacket pocket and pulls a business card. "Joey Mayer, Syracuse Rape Crisis Center."

Jenna's eyes fill at the words.

Mac pulls his cell from his jacket and begins punching in the number. He notices another number written on the back of the card, hits End, and punches in that one instead.

"Joey Mayer."

"Ms. Mayer, my name is Robert McLaughlin. I am a friend of Jenna Farnsworth. She's in really bad shape."

"Where is she?"

"20 Shore Road, out in Cleveland."

"Before or after her grandparents' place?"

"Before. The beige bungalow. How long before you get here?"

"Forty-five minutes."

Begs the question: Why?

Caitlyn English heard her man get home well after midnight the night before and start his Land Rover very early this morning. She wished he'd found his way to their bed, but when he's drilling down on a case, he usually bunks in the spare room. "I wonder if it would have been okay to join him there? Ah, the uncertainties of being a newlywed," she smiles. She pulls her sinfully fluffy comforter high and nestles deep into her California king. "Maybe another try at sleep." She closes her eyes and immediately starts thinking about REDO's victims. "I guess that's a 'no' on the sleep."

She inches up in bed as the contents of victim files shuffle like a demonic deck of cards. "Marilyn McGinn, two rapes. Suzi Kekoa one rape. Connie Braxton, two rapes. Trini Kekoa, one rape. Jenna Farnsworth, one rape, so far." The ADA thinks a bit more, "I need to take a fresh look at REDO start to finish." She bolts from bed, takes a quick shower, calls her paralegal, then waits for the files to be delivered from her office. While she waits, she enjoys the beautiful strains of Wagner's *Forest Murmurs* blaring from her sound system.

Oren

Edith Cunningham no longer watches T.V. She gets her excitement from her perch at the window. That's where she's been throughout most of the time since she heard Her Scream. Her perching has paid off nicely. She saw the new girl and another woman take suitcases from Keith's house, and two women take the new girl's car away, and Keith working until dark on the second floor. She was still upstairs this morning when two angry door bangers disrupted her sleep. "Can't imagine what the rush was all about. Can't imagine why Keith is being bothered and taken away like some criminal." She ponders a bit, "I wonder what happened at 10 Oren? Why did that new girl scream?" Her thinking is interrupted by a fancy black boxy car that pulls to the curb across the street and up a ways. She recognizes Keith as the passenger and can tell he's listening intently to the driver. Edith takes a seat on the rocker, "This shouldn't take more than a minute, my bladder will hold."

Jack Rafferty puts his Genesis SUV into park, "Who is Monica Farrell?"

"A girl I dated in high school."

"She lives in Syracuse?"

"Used to. She's been living in Aurora. She studied history and art at Wynona College. I ran into her over the holidays, and she said the College asked her to stay on and do research on some donated books and paintings."

"You ran into her in Syracuse?"

"Yes."

"And she told you where she lives?"

"Yes."

"And she was raped last night?"

"I guess."

"And you have a scratch across your cheek?"

Keith runs a finger across his cut, then shakes his head.

"Let me sum this up for you Keith. You are under suspicion for the rape of your roommate, Jenna Farnsworth. She left your home because she is unsure if you could be her rapist. Meanwhile, your high school sweetheart, the girl you spent time with over the holidays, was raped last night. You were brought to SPD this morning and without being directly asked, you went rogue and confirmed for Cambridge and Chase that you know the latest victim. And it's not even nine in the morning."

Keith gets out of the car.

The attorney shouts to him, "Don't talk to anyone about this. Especially not Cambridge or Chase." He bangs a U-turn and drives past Edith's place.

Keith checks to make sure his alibi is sitting at her window watching the comings and goings. He waves at the little old woman. "Thanks, Edith."

The Lake

Joey and Marilyn knock on the back door of 20 Shore Road a half hour after receiving Mac's call. He ushers them through the kitchen to a spare bedroom where they find Jenna sitting on a club chair, rocking back and forth, her teeth banging from the intensity of a full-body shake.

The paramedic goes to the patient.

The counselor takes Mac outside the room. "What happened?"

"She passed my place just after sunrise for an early morning walk. After a bit, I headed out to see if we could talk. We had an awkward first meeting, and it's been bothering me. Anyway, I found Jenna on the ground holding onto her left shoulder. She said she slipped on ice. I suggested I carry her over my shoulder. She balked at first but agreed when she said her ass was freezing to the ground."

Mac stops and begins shaking his head, drops it a bit. "I picked her up, got her hip situated properly on my shoulder and said, 'Don't. Move.' She **freaked** out, started thrashing wildly. Her movements pulled the two of us to the ground. Then she went into some sort of emotional break. I was worried about her mental state, but hypothermia was at the top of my concerns. I just picked her up, did the whole shoulder-carry-thing again, and brought her here. She was shaking uncontrollably, so I covered her with blankets and told her she needed to get changed out of her wet clothes. She started saying, 'No. No. No,' over and over, then said the word 'pocket'. I found your business card and called you. That's when I understood why she's been so distant." He walks away in an effort to hide his emotions.

Joey leaves Mac to himself and heads to the bedroom. Relief hits when she finds Jenna sitting on the edge of the bed, Marilyn struggling mightily to pull frozen stiff jeans from her legs. Jenna tears at the sight of yellow-purple bruises on her shins, "His boots did that."

The women help Jenna into an old-lady nightgown they find in a dresser drawer. Marilyn constructs a sling from a scarf hanging in the closet and immobilizes Jenna's left arm. They help her into bed, pull her very long hair into a very high ponytail, tuck her in with an array of pillows cushioned under her swollen elbow to help support her aching shoulder and another under her knees to help with lower back pain and to keep pressure off her twisted ankle.

Marilyn rummages through her medical bag and hands Jenna a pill and a bottle of water, "A muscle relaxant." Jenna swallows it. Marilyn hands her two more pills, "OTC pain relievers."

Jenna takes them. "I can't stay here," she whispers to the women.

"Because you don't feel safe here?" Joey asks.

"Because it's an imposition."

"Only if he says it is. I'll be right back."

Joey finds Mac standing at a bay window in the living room. He swings around and scans his surroundings as though looking for an enemy.

Joey jumps back.

His stance relaxes, "Sorry, a remaining reflex from life in the trenches."

"I'm sorry. I didn't mean to disturb you." Joey halts, then points to the easels. "Are these paintings yours?"

Mac covers his most recent work with a sheet. "My secret passion. I'm not very good, I'm afraid."

"I'd disagree, but I can tell this isn't something you want to discuss. The reason I'm here, Mr. McLaughlin—"

"Mac, please."

"Mac. We've settled Jenna in the spare bedroom. Marilyn, is a paramedic and thinks Jenna's injuries don't require a hospital trip, but she is in a considerable amount of pain and her ankle isn't weight bearing."

"Jenna is welcome to stay here, if she feels safe, considering."

Joey smiles. "We asked, and she does. If you don't mind my asking, Mac, were you an Army medic?"

"Ancillary responsibility, Ms. Mayer."

"Joey."

He smiles.

"And your primary responsibility?"

"I could tell, you but I'd have to—"

"Kill me," Joey finishes his sentence with a laugh.

Mac heads to the Farnsworth's to fill them in on what's happened, leaving Jenna in the capable hands of the paramedic and the counselor. The elderly couple walk the line between upset over the events and comfort that Jenna will be cared for by her childhood friend. When he returns it's with two pieces of leftover lasagna, a kettle of homemade chicken soup that he's been told to simmer for an hour before serving, and two pieces of Angel Food cake drizzled with Jenna's favorite chocolate ganache. He leads with the take-home menu when he knocks on the spare room door and is rewarded with a smile from Jenna—the smile he'd seen a million times as a kid, the smile he dreamed about when he was away.

On The Road Again
The detectives split up after the Keith Moreno non-interview. Chase plans to spend time with the REDO files while he waits to hear back from Detective Kelly in Aurora about their newest rape victim. Cambridge plans to hit the road for a little case processing.

He leaves a voicemail for his wife, "Caitlyn. I'm on the road. REDO paid a visit to Aurora last night. I need to process the shit out of this. Be back at some point. Don't wait up." He hops onto I-690W and lets his mind have at it. "Okay. Let's look at this again. First thing: REDO is escalating. Two rapes in a handful of days in two different locations. That's where the investigative focus will be. The main question right now—why is the rapist ratcheting things up? Second thing: REDO is leaving a few threads to pull. Up until now, the rapes have been nearly mistake-free, though not completely. First mistake was confusing Suzi and Trini Kekoa. Easy error to make. Similar looking women living at the same location. Still, the circumstances of those two rapes are worth another look to see if there's a thread, something other than mistaken identify. Second mistake was calling one rape victim by another's name. Easy error to make. Very tight timeframe between the two sexual assaults. Still, it's not like REDO to be sloppy. Begs the investigative question: Why?" The detective turns off his mind and his radio on, then heads to where he needs to be, "Aurora. That's where the heat's gonna be."

Location. Location. Location.

Caitlyn English is on the floor of her bedroom surrounded by REDO victim files. She is so into her work that she doesn't hear her cell ring, sighs when she hears the ping signaling a voicemail, and whispers, "Dammit," when she learns REDO attacked another woman. The ADA may be a newlywed, but she has worked with Detective Matthew Cambridge long enough to know he's on a road trip and that it will take him to Aurora, the scene of the most recent rape. The Counselor has been on the waiting end of **That** Cop's processing technique many times...

"Sorry I'm late, I was in Aurora meeting with Detective Kelly on the Connie Braxton rape."

"He's branching out. Syracuse, Ithaca, Aurora."

"He's setting up shop in the Finger Lakes college communities. Won't be long before the press starts stringing this shit together. That's when the shit will hit," he realized where he was and with whom he was speaking, "sorry for the language, Ms. English."

She laughed, "Detective Cambridge, I'm quite used to your salty language, in fact, I quite expected a Fuckin A by now."

He parked a hip onto her desk, "That must have hurt."

"What must have hurt?"

"Cuss words coming out of that Grace Kelly mouth of yours had to have caused some discomfort."

"Yes, well, Detective, it's not my favored part of communication, but it serves a purpose."

Cambridge smiled, "That's more like it. Refined and elegantly stated." **He handed off a case file on Braxton.** "SPD is unofficially making me point person, a liaison if you will, with the other PDs. Detective Chase and I will be building REDO victim files at the station, regardless of assault location, and handing off what we get to the Onondaga DA's office. I'll get the Suzi Kekoa file from Ithaca in the next few days."

"Good. This is a very good idea. DA Weston will find this quite useful and having this handled in his jurisdiction will be a feather in his cap."

"DA Weston is a—"

"Careful, Detective."

He smiled.

"You should do that more often."

"Do what?"

"Smile. You have a bit of a reputation of being a…" she hesitated, searched for the correct word.

"Continue, Ms. English."

"A bastard."

"Understatement of the year, Ms. English. Most people refer to me as a goddamn, son-of-a-bitching, asshole."

"Yes, that sounds about right, Detective."

Caitlyn laughs at the memory and slaps a label onto the event, "The beginning of our dance." The Counselor listens to That Cop's

voicemail a second time, then cheers her man on, "Push in, Matt. Get what we need to put REDO away." The ADA gets back to the task at hand. She grabs a victim file, a blank legal pad, and starts in.

Timeline

Marilyn McGinn arrived in Syracuse in August,
 the day of her rape.
Suzi Kekoa arrived in Ithaca in September,
 the day of her rape.
Connie Braxton lived in Aurora for four years
 before her rape.
Trini Kekoa lived in Ithaca for four years
 before her rape.
Jenna Farnsworth arrived in Syracuse in January,
 days before her rape.
New victim?

She assesses the list. Talks herself through it while making notes.

"Marilyn McGinn and Suzi Kekoa arrived in different months, but both arrived for the fall semester for graduate studies at two different college campuses. One drove from Buffalo to Syracuse. One flew from Honolulu to Ithaca. Both moved into off-campus apartments. Both were raped on the day they arrived." She ponders a bit, then continues.

"Connie Braxton and Trini Kekoa came to New York for undergraduate studies four years before their rapes. One studied in Aurora. One studied in Ithaca. One became a teacher and

143

stayed in NY. One became a nurse and stayed in NY. Both were raped when they moved from on-campus housing to off-campus apartments." She jots a few notes then continues.

"Jenna Farnsworth arrived for the spring semester of graduate studies. She drove from Philly to Syracuse and moved into an off-campus apartment. She was raped within a week of relocating. Plenty to work with." She draws a line across the page and titles the new section.

Victim Profiles

Age at time of attack:
Marilyn, 24. Suzi, 24. Connie, 25. Trini, 25. Jenna, 25. New victim?

College/University affiliation:
SUNY. Carver. Wynona. Carver. Styles. New victim?

"Okay. The victims are connected by age and pursuit of higher education, and ...." She leans against a wall, puts a legal pad onto her bent knees, and studies it. "Hmm. Let's look at that."

Living locations at the time of attack:
Marilyn moved into a garden terrace
      apartment.
Suzi moved into a second-floor apartment.
Connie moved into a renovated barn
      apartment.

Trini moved into a second-floor apartment.
New victim?

"Could this have something to do with real estate?"

Syracuse Rape Crisis Center
The director answers her private line, "Josephine Mayer."

"Hi Joey, it's Angie."

Joey knows in an instant why the director of Cayuga County Rape Crisis is calling. "REDO?" she asks anyway.

"REDO," Angie Kett confirms.

Affairs and alibis.

"I need to see you."

"Half hour."

Keith thinks about sneaking out the back door and cutting through the tree line that runs from the back of his property to a main road. He thinks better of that plan, walks out his front door, takes a right at the end of the sidewalk and moves away from Edith's prying eyes. He jogs about five minutes then gets into Helena's Mini Countryman. "What did you tell Cambridge?"

"Exactly what you told me to tell him."

"Then why is he still breathing down my back?"

"I told him you and I were together from seven-thirty until eleven-thirty at my place, and the reason you lied about working at Hadley Hall is because I have a soon-to-be ex-lover who would probably be my soon-to-be ex-employer, and your soon-to-be ex-faculty advisor if he found out about our relationship."

Keith calms a bit.

Helena continues. "I told the detective—"

"Detectives."

"No. They were both there when I arrived, but the nice one was called out of the room for a few minutes."

"That's weird. That happened with me, too. Must be an investigative routine of theirs, but since Cambridge is the one pushing hard on me, it's good he heard your entire alibi."

"He's an ass, and here's your alibi. You walked me to my car and cleaned it off before going into Turner Theater around seven. I told him that after spending a few minutes watching Zach, you and I went to my place and then I dropped you back at SU around eleven-thirty. Cambridge asked if I stayed to watch you clean off your Jeep. I told him no, but confirmed that your Jeep was covered and the parking lot was a mess. He asked if the lights were on at the SU parking lot and whether the streets had been plowed. I said I didn't remember anything about the lights, and some of the streets had been plowed, but not all."

Keith is quiet.

Helena is confused. "Why is Cambridge breathing down your back? He seemed to believe me, which means you have an alibi, and he needs to start looking elsewhere. And if he still has doubts, have him call Mary. She can confirm that we slept together in the past. In fact, your former girlfriend would love to tell him she found you up to your balls inside of me."

Keith is quiet.

Helena isn't stupid. "What aren't you telling me, Keith?"

"I need an alibi for last night."

Balls and bottles.

Cambridge makes a stop at a diner in Auburn, NY. He orders a Reuben, a half-sour pickle, a tall glass of ice and a can of root beer at the counter, then heads to a booth in the far corner. He opens a notepad and reviews, "One rape per year from 2014 to 2019 – six total. Two rapes in January 2020." Cambridge pushes his notes aside and works on his meal. Two words surface and bang over and over in his head, "Escalation and mistakes. This is the focus area. These are the threads to pull."

Aurora Police Department
"Matt, I'm glad you made the trip," Brandan says with outstretched hand. "I just got off a call with Cayuga County DA, Isla Conway. She said your DA is convening an Upstate NY task force to work REDO. Your name is being floated as head honcho."

Cambridge groans.

Brandan laughs, "You can deal with that honor on your time, but since you're here, you can sit in on Monica Farrell's statement. She's on her way in."

"I think I should stay in the background until the task force is official. Don't want to make things difficult for your ADA having an interloper in the interview room. I know our ADA would have my balls if I let you sit in."

"Your ADA is your wife, right?"

"Yeah."

"Hate to break it to you, Matt, but she already has your balls."

"Fuckin A she does."

Brandan laughs and directs. "Walk through the door at the back of interview room three. You'll be able to see through the two-way and hear through the system. Help yourself to coffee or whatever's in the fridge."

Cambridge takes a seat and watches REDO's newest victim, a slim, strawberry-blonde with dark sapphire-blue eyes and an edgy swagger enter the room. He foregoes taking notes in lieu of receiving the official transcript. "Straight off the top, there's an anomaly in the victim's statement." Cambridge dictates into his cell. "Monica Farrell has lived at Wynona College campus housing for four years. No mention of relocation during that period of time. That's new. Could be a thread." The detective waits until the victim leaves, then spends a few minutes with Brandan, "Anything click?"

"On-campus housing and a recent breakup with her boyfriend are anomalies. And the biggest thing is REDO calling her Jenna."

"'Threads," the visiting detective offers.

"We'll see."

"Okay, Brandan, I'm outta here." Cambridge calls his wife from the road, "Hey, Caitlyn."

"You sound tired, Matt."

"I am. Look, I'm going to be passing Long Point Winery, do you—"

"Yes. Yes. Yes. When you get there talk to Greg, he'll have a list of my favorite wines. Be nice. Long Point is my favorite winery, and the owners were lovely to let us get married there."

"Question."

"Okay."

"Are there a lot of wines on your Long Point list?"

"Yes."

"Feel like narrowing it to a red and a white?"

"Nope."

"Sounds like an expensive stop, Caitlyn."

"For richer, for poorer, Matt. By the way, I got a call from one of the ADAs in Cayuga County."

"Yeah," he groans.

"You know about the task force."

"Yeah," he groans.

"Are you going to accept the request to head it up?"

"Yeah," he groans.

When a mistake is not a mistake.

Detective Chase is taking a deep dive into SPD victim files. "If it's the last thing I do, I'm going to crack this case." He laughs and adds, "It's all but certain it'll be the last thing I do, so let's flip this sucker ass end to." He sets a sheet of paper to make notes and begins his review.

"One rape per year for six years, then two rapes in January 2020. He's off-pattern and escalating." Chase flips through the victim statements until he finds what he's looking for. "Trini Kekoa. REDO's last rape before his escalation in 2020. Trini was supposed to be a second rape, but REDO fucked up with the lookalike cousins. It threw him off his game, pissed him off. That's probably why he didn't cut Trini's breast and why he raped her orally." Chase bangs this point for several minutes then talks it through. "REDO showed up for a second rape and found himself caught up in a case of mistaken identity. Easy enough, the women look the same and the rapes happened at the same location, but..." Chase sips his coffee and thinks a bit. "We've been looking at Trini's rape as a mistake made by REDO. We need to stop looking at it in relation to Suzi's rape, and look at it as a standalone attack." The detective grabs a marker and puts a circle around Jenna Farnsworth's and Monica Farrell's names. "But using the wrong name when he ejaculated,

That. Was. A. Mistake." Chase grabs his coffee cup off his desk and heads to the break room. While he sets a pot, he heads down another path. "Something happened in REDO's life to set him off. Was it the Suzi/Trini debacle? Is his ego that fragile? Or did something else happen, if so, what?" When he gets back to his office, he puts down his mug of coffee, takes the list he made, and alters it to include rape locations.

Victim Timelines and Locations

Marilyn McGinn 2014
> (44 Central Street, Syracuse)

Suzi Kekoa 2015
> (6 Treble Way, Ithaca)

Connie Braxton 2016
> (2 Stone Lane, Aurora)

Connie Braxton 2017
> (11 Fern Street, Aurora)

Marilyn McGinn 2018
> (14 Turner-Styles Lane, Syracuse)

Trini Kekoa 2019
> (6 Treble Way, Ithaca)

Jenna Farnsworth 2020
> (10 Oren Street, Syracuse)

Monica Farrell 2020
> (Street unknown, Aurora)

"If you take Suzi and Trini Kekoa out of the equation, the victims who endured a second rape had moved after the first rape. REDO'S first go around with the women could have been random, but the second go around was planned. He tracked them down." Chase runs his hand along his scratchy, way-beyond-five-o'clock shadow. He's burning the candle at both ends and is feeling every bit the Old Man his partner calls him. "Asshole punk," he growls.

He takes a sip of caffeine and moves on. "After the initial rape, REDO had to do surveillance to track the victim from point A to point B, and then he'd have to do a little old-fashioned stalking of their new living location to see if they moved in with roommates, and to plan a good time for his return visit." He flips through the McGinn file looking for a note he made at the time of her second rape, abandons the task and relies on memory. "Marilyn McGinn moved in with Joey Mayer **before** the second rape. Jenna Farnsworth moved in with Keith Moreno **before** the first rape. These two victims had roommates. Kinda risky for our guy to enter a residence where someone might come home."

He takes his empty cup to the break room, washes it, dries it, and puts it in the cupboard. He's just about back to his desk when the penny drops. "If REDO is doing reconnaissance between Rape 1 and Rape 2, that would account for the spacing between repeat events. That type of recon takes time, patience, and resources. Add the sneak attack element, brute strength, ease with knives, and hand to hand combat, and you've got someone skilled in tactical training. Maybe that's why he isn't concerned with roommates, he probably knows he can handle a second person, especially a female. Maybe he's ex-military, or maybe he attacks only once a year because he's active military, and comes stateside or to upstate NY on leave." The detective thinks a bit more and concludes, "Military guy could be good for this."

The Lake
Mac knocks on Jenna's door and waits.

"Come in." She tries to push herself up against the headboard.

He doesn't fully enter the room. "Marilyn and Joey called to check in. They asked me to tell you they'd be back in the morning. And Grams called to check in."

Jenna smiles, "Something smells good."

"Grams' chicken soup. You must be hungry."

She nods.

"Do you think you can make it to the club chair? I have a T.V. tray I could set up."

She nods. "Would you help me to the bathroom first?"

"Sure," He helps move the mountain of pillows out from under her elbow and knees and pushes the covers aside.

She tries to wiggle her legs over the side of the bed, but pains when she puts weight onto any part of her left side.

"Jenna, would it be okay if I carried you?"

"Yes, please."

After a quick assessment, Mac lifts her into his arms, takes her to the bathroom, and waits until she hops and hobbles her way inside. When she has finished her business, she hops and hobbles her way to the door, manages to open it a crack, and calls Mac for another assist. He gets her into his arms, carries her back to the bedroom, and sets her in the club chair he already moved closer to the bed. He slides a T.V. tray in front of her and heads to the kitchen for her soup. "Your next round of pills are on the tray," he calls over his shoulder, then stops when she speaks his name.

"Mac. I really appreciate your help."

He smiles warmly, "I'd do anything for you, Jenna. You know that."

Even though they hadn't seen each other in years, Jenna does know that.

Silhouettes and suspicions.

Marilyn and Joey are at Mac's house early. The paramedic of the duo had concerns overnight about Jenna's injuries and wanted to reassess. "The ankle swelling has gone down a bit, but your elbow is still swollen and very tender, although the range of motion is okay, painful, but good." Marilyn takes a step back and surveys her patient, reaches into her medical bag and takes out an OTC bottle of pain relievers, "Here, take these."

"Mac already gave me my pills this morning."

Marilyn nods, "Have you been up yet?"

"No."

"Come on, let's get you into the shower."

Jenna moans at the thought, but moves to the side of the bed and inches her feet over just as Mac knocks on the doorjamb, "I went and got some of your things from Grams." He smiles at Jenna. "Do you need another lift?"

"Yes, please." She addresses Marilyn, "I think I could make it to the shower or endure the shower, but I don't think you'll get both from me. If you don't mind, I'd like Mac to schlep."

Marilyn steps out of the way, "Go for it."

With ease, he takes her to the bathroom door and leaves her in Marilyn's good hands. On his way back, he finds Joey in the living room, an apology on her lips as she turns away from his paintings, "I'm so sorry, Mac. I know better than to invade someone's personal space, but these are so beautiful. They call to me. Still, that is no excuse for my intrusion."

"Apology accepted. I'm one of those artists, and I use that word lightly, who paints strictly for their own pleasure. I'm untrained and uncomfortable with prying eyes."

Joey nods, "Again, I'm sorry I overstepped, but still sort of glad I did. They are breathtaking."

"Thank you."

An hour later, the paramedic and counselor leave. They get into Joey's Saab and set out for Buffalo. Marilyn takes hold of Joey's hand, "Don't be nervous. Meeting Joseph will be good for you, for us."

"I'm not nervous, Marilyn, I'm so excited I can hardly contain myself." Joey places a kiss to her wife's hand. "Let's grab some breakfast and when we get back on the road, I'll tell you a story about Mac."

Fayetteville
Caitlyn is waiting in the kitchen for Cambridge. The door to the guest bedroom is closed, so she knows he's home. She's had her morning coffee and read the paper front to back before she hears him stir. She leaps from her chair and goes airborne into his arms when he rounds the corner. The momentum pushes them back against a wall.

"I'm thinking assault charges, Caitlyn."

"Sorry, Matt, I'm just happy to see you. It's been ages."

"Days."

"Feels like ages."

He hooks his head to the left, "I come bearing gifts."

His wife squeals when she sees four, six bottle wood crates of wine sitting at the back door. Her hand flies to her heart, "Matt Cambridge! I'm speechless."

"That'll be a first, Counselor."

"Why the extravagance?"

"Insurance."

"Come again?"

"I'm bound to forget a birthday, an anniversary, Flag Dag, or some other shit I'm supposed to remember. You get one bottle for each of my screw ups. Then I'll get you four more crates."

Caitlyn goes airborne and nearly upends him.

"Definitely, assault charges."

"Sue me," she says with a kiss.

Buffalo-Bound

Marilyn spent their entire breakfast talking about her son, and how wonderful her sister and brother-in-law have been, and how eager she is to introduce Joey to her boy. When they're back on the road, it's Joey's turn to chatter on. She starts with the story about Mac's paintings.

"They're landscapes of Oneida Lake, really beautiful landscapes. They catch the mood of misty mornings and shadowy evenings. He is very talented and very guarded with his work."

Marilyn raises a quizzical brow, "Then how do you know about them?"

"I snuck into the living room to see them."

"Joey, that isn't like you. You're so conscious of personal space."

"I couldn't help myself. I saw them by accident yesterday, and I just had to see them again this morning. I'm telling you, Marilyn, they are enthralling, breathtaking; some of them have such a sense of longing. Almost heartbreakingly so. I told Mac what I thought, then I apologized for my intrusion."

"They're landscapes of the lake?"

"Yes, but some," Joey pauses, "maybe all," she pauses, "have the silhouette of a woman painted somewhere in the scenery." She pauses. She tenses. "The woman looks like—" Joey stops mid-sentence.

Marilyn notices the very strange look on Joey's face. She taps her wife on the knee, "Joey, where'd you go?"

"Go back. Go back. The silhouette is Jenna."

"What? We can't go back, Joey. We won't have a valid reason for showing up again, and my sister is expecting us." Marilyn thinks a minute. "Call Cambridge, tell him about Jenna's fall, and the paintings, and ask him to check on her."

Fayetteville

Cambridge stops at the front door to answer his phone, turns around and goes back inside the house. "This morning just hit the shits. What do you want, Joey?"

"I have an update and I need a favor. You get the update if you agree to the favor."

"How good is the update—how big is the favor?"

"Comparable."

"Shoot."

"Jenna Farnsworth had an accident yesterday, a slip on some ice, but she's banged up pretty badly. Marilyn evaluated her yesterday and again this morning. She's holed up in a bungalow at 20 Shore Road out in Cleveland."

"Her grandparents' place?"

"No. The beige bungalow before the sage green one. It belongs to her childhood friend, Robert McLaughlin, he goes by Mac. He's the one who found her after her fall. Anyway, Mac is a closeted artist. He's done a bunch of really beautiful landscapes of the lake. The thing is Cambridge, each painting has a silhouette of a woman. I think the woman is—"

"Jenna."

Art studios and dimpled darlings.

Cambridge knocks on the front door of the beige bungalow at 20 Shore Road. He's shoved his hands into the pockets of his jeans so his detective's shield is easily seen. From his vantage point on the front porch, he can see two easels set in the living room and a scowl on the man who moves through that space.

"Can I help you?"

"Mr. McLaughlin, I'm Detective Matt Cambridge. I understand Ms. Farnsworth is staying here."

"Yes. Is that a concern of the Syracuse Police Department?"

"No concern, but I have a few questions regarding—"

"Her rape?" Mac fills in the obvious blank with a tone that suggests the detective should have done something to prevent the crime.

Cambridge gives a slight nod.

"How did you know Jenna is here?" he asks, still blocking the front door.

"Joey Mayer. I talked with her this morning about another recent assault, and she mentioned Jenna's fall. I thought I'd check on her since I have a couple—"

"Questions," Mac finishes another sentence. "Wait here, I'll check with Jenna, make sure she's up to seeing you." Mac shuts the door in Cambridge's face.

"A bit territorial." The dogged detective moves closer to the bay window and focuses on the paintings leaning against the wall, "Impressive. Joey was right about this guy's talent. She's right about the silhouette being Jenna, too."

He turns his back and looks out at the lake when he sees Mac retracing his steps through the designated art studio.

"She doesn't seem happy about it, but she agreed to see you, Detective." Mac steps aside.

Cambridge steps inside and does a prolonged stomping of his boots as he takes in the artwork. "Those yours?"

"Yes."

"Is it a hobby, or do you sell them?"

"Hobby."

"Don't want to part with them?" the detective jabs.

Mac sneers, "Jenna is in the spare bedroom."

Jenna is in the paintings.

The injured woman is propped against an antique brass headboard, a pillow under her left knee and ankle and another tucked under her elbow. Her shoulder is immobilized by a sling brought in that morning by Marilyn.

"Detective, I'm warning you upfront, I'm in no mood for your surliness."

"I can see why. You banged yourself pretty good, Ms. Farnsworth. Are you sure you don't need to be checked out at the hospital?"

"She's fine," Mac says from the doorway.

"Are you a doctor, Mr. McLaughlin?"

"Army medic, but my assessment of Jenna was cursory, at best. Paramedic McGinn did an extensive evaluation. I trust her abilities."

Cambridge takes a seat next to Jenna's bed. "Mr. McLaughlin, you can shut the door on your way out." He stares the man down, and when the door shuts the detective moves his chair closer, "Ms. Farnsworth, are you comfortable in these accommodations?"

"Detective, you've made it so I left Keith's house, are you going to suggest I leave Mac's too?"

"No suggestion. Just a question."

Jenna nods and remains quiet.

"You fell."

"Yes."

"Was there a reason?"

"I slipped on ice."

"Did anything startle you, a noise, a presence, anything?"

Jenna tilts her head and furrows her brow, "Now that you mention it, I heard a noise right before I fell. Maybe the ice settling." Another tilt of her head, "Definitely the crack of ice."

"How long after your fall did Mr. McLaughlin find you?"

"Not long."

"Did you tell him you were going for a walk?"

"No, but I passed by his house."

"And he followed you?"

"I...I don't know. I never asked him why he was there. I was just so happy to see him."

"He brought you back here."

"Yes."

"Why didn't he bring you to your grandparents' home?"

"His house was closer to where I fell."

"Right." Cambridge lets his word hang a minute. "Ms. Farnsworth, have you ever seen Mr. McLaughlin's paintings?"

Jenna tilts her head, "Paintings?"

"When you're on your feet, you might want to check out the art studio in his living room. I think you'll find his pieces very interesting."

Buffalo

Joey stands off to the side while Marilyn and Evelyn embrace. Young Joseph happily babbles while squished between the sisters. His "Mma, Mma, Mma," chant is directed to Marilyn.

Evelyn leaves the dark haired, dark eyed, dimpled darling in Marilyn's arms and approaches Joey. "It's nice to see you, again." They share a warm, long hug, then Evelyn takes her sister-in-law's hands in hers, "I'm so glad you know about Joseph. It has been hell on Marilyn. She knows she should have told you, but honestly, Joey, when she found out about the pregnancy she became frozen by fear. Two rapes at that sadist's hands ruined a part of her. I hope your being here means you forgive her," Evelyn's words are punctuated by misty eyes.

Joey hugs Evelyn again, "I have forgiven her, and I understand." She walks hand in hand with the woman who has raised the son of a rapist as a favor to her sister.

Evelyn reaches her hands out, and Joseph McGinn fills them. She stares into the trusting eyes of the eight-month-old whose chubby hands are on either side of Evelyn's face. She addresses the boy, "Joseph McGinn, I want you to meet someone very special. Her name is Joey." She hands the little boy to her sister-in-law, kisses his head, and goes inside her house.

Joey turns astonished eyes to her wife, "Marilyn, does your sister think we're taking him?"

"Not today, but eventually. If you think that's something you're interested in."

Joey runs her hand through the soft, tufted hair of the squirming worm in her arms. "What about Evelyn, wouldn't that be hard on her?" Joey spins when she hears Evelyn's approach, making note of an overnight bag in her hands.

"It will be the most difficult thing I will ever do, Joey, but it still won't compare to the things my sister has endured."

"Where are you going?"

"Chet and I are taking the night away. You two can stay here with Joseph. Enjoy your time. I'll only be a phone call away if you need me." The emoting woman places a kiss to the head of the boy she's raised since birth and inches away.

Cancer, coeds and cowboys.

Ray Chase has a hell of a time getting out of bed. He's dog tired from burning the candle at both ends and damned depressed about the Stage 4 pancreatic cancer diagnosis he received the week before. He moves the covers back and his legs over the side of the mattress, then waits for the world to right itself, "I **have** to solve this case. It's the only thing on my bucket list—not because there aren't other things I want to do, or should do, but because there's not enough time for anything else."

Chase drags his ass into the station and taps on Diane's window as he passes by.

"Morning, Detective," she singsongs.

He functions on autopilot, eventually finding his seat with his ass. He wants to pick up where he left off the previous night, but he expects Cambridge will want them to press into Keith Moreno. "That's wasted time and I don't have time to waste." He delays the sip of coffee he desperately wants and answers an incoming call. "Chase."

"Morning, Ray. It's Brandan. Did I catch you at a bad time?"

"An un-caffeinated time. What's up, Brandan?"

"Did you and Matt get a chance to bang around the information he got from the Monica Farrell interview?"

What information, Chase wonders? "Not yet, why?"

"Heads up, then. There are some irregularities beyond REDO calling the victim by the wrong name."

"Like?"

"First, the living location is off. The victim has been at the same place for over four years—a cabin that's part of on-campus housing at Wynona College. Second, Monica Farrell was in a long-term relationship until just before the holidays. She said the guy roughed her up from time to time, nothing she objected to, but late last year he got abusive."

"Boyfriend's name?"

"Evan Sayles."

"Anything else?"

"The ejaculation thing, but I already told you about that. Hey Ray, are you and Cambridge working this case together?"

"Yeah. Just haven't crossed paths with him, yet. Can you give me the address of Monica Farrell's place?"

"CL-12, at the very edge of the Wynona College campus."

"CL-12?"

"Cayuga Lake, at the 12th mile. The lake is nearly 40 miles long and the addresses are designated by the nearest mile marker."

"Yeah. I think Seneca Lake's addresses are similar."

"And Hemlock's, too. Since you haven't talked to Cambridge, you probably don't know about the task force."

"Nope."

"Your DA is putting together an Upstate group to work REDO. Cambridge's name is being floated as head honcho."

"No shit? Good for him. Listen Brandan, I've got to pound the pavement on our latest case. Anything comes up, give me a call."

"Ditto."

When the call disconnects, Chase makes a decision, "Fuck Keith Moreno, I'm pressing into REDO."

SPD

Cambridge calls Chase when he gets to the station, "I've got some things to fill you in on. You coming in today?"

"Already been in and heard plenty from Brandan Kelly. I've got some things to handle, Matt. I'll check in with you later."

"Pull back on investigating Keith Moreno."

"Why?"

"I'll fill you in later, but there's an ex-military guy in the Jenna Farnsworth picture."

"Yeah?"

"Robert McLaughlin, goes by the name Mac. He lives next door to Jenna's grandparents on Oneida Lake. Our victim is holed up at his place after taking a fall the other day. McLaughlin **did not** want to let me into his place when I showed up to see her. Once I got inside,

I knew why. He's done a shitload of landscape paintings of Oneida Lake. Nice work, especially the silhouettes of Jenna he drops into each painting. She is in his head."

"Huh, ex-military. Any idea when he discharged out?"

"Not yet, but it's the first thing on my to-do list."

District Attorney's Office

Caitlyn is at her desk earlier than she's ever been. She isn't working through the Timberlake file as she should be, she's ruminating on REDO. "What makes you tick, what sets you off?" She's asked that question often enough that it is automatically followed by the next question, "One rape per year for six years, then two rapes in a matter of days. You're escalating. Why?" She shoots from her seat when a knock comes on her office door, and the crack of her name comes from just beyond.

"ADA English." In quick succession, the door opens, the man conquers the space, and she goes weak in the knees. It's the same thing every time—it's the same thing with every woman.

Weston James, graduate of Columbia Law, and youngest DA in the history of New York state by a mere four days to James Murphy III, is ALL MAN. The 6'3" Harrison Ford lookalike, circa *Indiana Jones and the Temple of Doom,* hails from Montana and goes by the nickname Cowboy. That reference is not a tip of a Stetson to his home state, but rather a wink of an eye for his supposed riding of more than his fair share of women. At least, that's the rumor.

"Counselor, you will be working with **that** cop on the new REDO task force. The Upstate DAs want an ADA on the committee to make sure there are no legal issues regarding jurisdiction and anything else that could get the case tossed once we make an arrest and get it to trial. No other ADA in a seven county area wants anything to do with Cambridge, even though being on this task force could be a crown jewel in their careers. Have to tell you, English, you marrying **that** cop is a head-scratcher."

"Permission to speak freely?"

Weston James nods.

"I'm with Matt for the same reason you want him on your team. No one thinks a case through like Matt Cambridge. It's thrilling."

"We'll see how thrilling it is when he's sitting in a position of power over you. Get results, and no mistakes on this, English."

The ADA waits until *he* is down the hall. She drops her ass onto her seat and begins ruminating a whole new subject, "Matt will be my boss? Not sure I like that idea."

Not. About. This.

Cambridge calls Joey Mayer, "Do you have time?"

"You at the station?"

"Yeah."

"On my way."

Cambridge and Mayer share opposite ends of a hallway. He can tell something is up simply by watching her walk toward him. He doesn't care what's up. He gets to the point of their meeting when they enter his office. "What's your take on McLaughlin?"

"There's a vibe. Could be something related to the military, or could be nothing more than he's trying to fit back in to civilian life, but something seems off."

"It's Jenna."

"He has a thing for her," Joey nods, "but he isn't REDO."

"Why not?"

"He's a recent discharge."

"So?" Cambridge stares, assesses. *She's usually way more reasoned in her thinking. She's unfocused. Something's up with her.* "Military guys get leave, you know."

Joey shrugs.

"Did McLaughlin say how Jenna got injured?"

Joey nods.

"No sign language, no miming, no charades, Joey. Start talking or get out."

"Sorry, Cambridge."

An apology? Something big is up with Joey Mayer.

"I got an early morning call from a guy identifying himself as Robert McLaughlin, a friend and neighbor of Jenna Farnsworth. He said she fell on a patch of ice, injured herself pretty good, and when he tried to help she freaked out."

Cambridge slams his hand on his desk, "Mayer. I need more than a chronological, here. Start again. Tell me what he **said**."

"Right. Sorry. His story was that Jenna passed by his house for an early morning walk. After a while he went out to see if he could meet up with her so they could have a talk. Apparently, their first meeting in a very long time was awkward, and he said it had been bothering him. When he found Jenna, she was sitting on the ground unable to get up. She told him she fell and hurt her shoulder, elbow, and hip, and had twisted her ankle. He convinced her to let him shoulder-carry her and when he was positioning her, he said, Don't. Move. and she freaked out. She took them both to the ground with her sudden thrashing, and she went into an 'emotional break'—his words. He said he feared hypothermia, so he got her onto his shoulder again and brought her to his place. He told her she needed to get out of her wet clothes, and her response was No. No. No. over and over. At some point, she said the word pocket so he checked her jacket, found my business card, and called me. Jenna was an emotional wreck when we got to her. Marilyn administered medical care while Mac and I talked in his living room. That's when I saw his paintings."

"What did you think of them?"

"I thought they were beautiful. When I saw them a second time, I noticed the silhouette. It didn't register until right before I called you that the shape of the woman, the long hair, and the…" she pauses looking for the right word.

Cambridge tilts his head, furrows his brow, clenches the muscles in his jaw. "What?"

"Don't shit on me, Cambridge, but there's a quality or an essence that makes me sure the silhouette is Jenna. They are so beautifully done that I'm sure he has a thing for her."

"I agree."

"For real? Or are you fucking with me?"

"Wouldn't fuck with you. Not today."

"Why not?"

"Something's up with you. Don't know what it is—don't want to know—unless it has something to do with REDO or one of my cases."

"REDO," she whispers.

Cambridge waits. And waits. And waits. "Not playing 20 Questions today, Joey."

She pulls a deep breath, "You do not say **one word** to Marilyn about this."

"I say what I want when I want."

"Not. About. This."

Cambridge nods.

"I need your word."

"You have it."

"Marilyn gave birth to REDO's son."

Matt Cambridge runs that bit of information and declares, "There's DNA—the golden thread to pull. Fuckin A!"

That's some twisted shit.

Ray Chase climbs the stairs at a brownstone in the Rosalind section of Syracuse. He came by the day before, but never managed to get out of his car. This time he's out, and this time he's knocked. He should have knocked on this door any number of times over the years. He didn't. He should have come by during the holiday season that just passed. He didn't. He should have come on the day he received his death sentence. He didn't. He knows he wouldn't be here today if he didn't need help. His gawk through the window is rewarded with the sight of his son walking toward the door. The father is hopeful when a hand pushes aside the lacy window cover—is saddened when the curtain drops back into place. Ray expected the rebuff; still it stings.

He speaks through the closed door, "Chris, I'm dying."

Christopher Chase falters. He returns and unlocks the door, "Come on in."

Ray steps inside the home he once shared with his former wife and son. He looks long at the grown man standing in front of him, the one with the same height and build as his own, but the lighter coloring and skeptical look of his mother. Out of the corner of his eye he catches movement. He knows it's Camille—the woman who asked him to leave their home decades ago—the woman who should have asked that favor of him years before that. He turns to the petite brunette with topaz eyes and spine of steel. "Cami, I've come to say goodbye."

"You did that twenty years, four months, two weeks, and two days ago, Ray."

Chris immediately owns the space between his parents, the space he filled as a young boy, "He says he's dying."

Camille's eyes wet. "Come on," she says on a turn, "I'll put on a pot."

Ray spends the brewing time walking the floors he paced day in and day out all those years ago. He knows every dip, every scuff, every groove, like muscle memory. "Place looks good, Cami."

"Thank Chris, he's the one who's been doing the upkeep."

Ray nods to his son, "You still living and working from upstairs?"

"Yeah."

"When we're done with the coffee and cancer talk, can I come up and talk to you about something?"

"Yeah."

The former Chase family sits at the kitchen table. It's the same table Ray and Camille sat at the morning she asked him to leave. The irony is not lost on the dying man. *I'll be leaving more than a house this time around.* "I was diagnosed with Stage 4 pancreatic cancer. It's spread all the fuck through me. The only treatments being discussed are of the palliative variety. My life expectancy is months, and they can be counted on one hand." He lets his former wife and son catch up before continuing. "You still carrying a mortgage on this place?" he addresses his son.

Chris scoffs, "Yeah."

"I have a life insurance policy for two-hundred-fifty-grand. I'm leaving it to you for the sole purpose of paying off the mortgage. Whatever is left, give it to your mother." Ray finishes his coffee in a gulp, gets up, hitches his head, "Chris, I need your help."

Raymond Chase leans over Camille Chase and presses a long kiss to the top of her head. "I love you, Cami. I should have done better by you. I won't be coming around again," he kisses her one last time, "Goodbye."

Camille takes hold of the hand that rests on her shoulder, drops it only when Ray walks too far away.

The detective begins his spiel before Chris has a chance to talk about cancer and mortgages. "I need your help with a case."

Chris laughs, "Your damned cases. The only things you ever thought about. Even now, it's the only thing you're thinking about."

"The case I'm working is the biggest case I've ever worked. It's a serial rape case. The rapist is a sadistic piece of shit that's hit several Upstate NY counties."

"I've heard about rapes over the years, but none that were linked to a serial rapist."

"We've been keeping it on the downlow. He's hitting college communities, which is problematic for admissions and..." The detective checks himself one last time before bringing his son into this mess.

"And what?"

"His tag is REDO. He has a penchant for paying a second visit to his rape victims."

"What. The. Fuck." Chris shakes his head, "That's some twisted shit."

Ray nods. "Chris, I **need** to crack this case before I die. That means we don't have much time."

"We?"

"I need your computer skills on this one."

"You want me to work with you on a serial rapist case?"

"Yeah. You in?"

"All-in, Old Man."

Ray shakes his head at the reference. He hands Chris a slip of paper, "Research this guy. I'll be in touch in a couple days."

Off the grid.

Matt Cambridge has gone deep into the investigation of REDO. He's hell bent on working the DNA angle by himself. "No way I'm letting Ray in on this. If he finds out from Joey, then he can have a run at it. Until then, this baby is all mine."

Ray Chase has gone deep into the investigation of REDO. He's hell bent on working a DNA angle by himself. "No way I'm letting Matt in on this. If he figures it out for himself, then he can have a run at it. Until then, this baby is all mine."

The detectives surface two days later.

Once in a Blue Moon.

Caitlyn English opens her front door. "Well this is a surprise, Ray, come on in."

He follows her to the kitchen and takes the stool she points to, "Matt isn't here, and he won't be until late, but you probably already know that."

Ray shakes his head, "I wasn't at the station today. I had a personal matter to attend. That's why I'm here, Caitlyn."

"Before we talk, do you want me to put on a pot of coffee, or would you like a cold beverage?"

"You got a beer?"

Caitlyn nods, pops the top on two, hands one off, and takes a sip. Then she waits. In her line of work, waiting for people to organize their thoughts and start talking is the norm.

Ray takes a long pull. "I've got a personal favor to ask."

She nods.

"I'd prefer it stay between the two of us. If Matt knows, he'll be obligated to tell the brass at the station, and I'm not ready for that."

Caitlyn leans against the island at which Ray sits. "If this is a lawyer/client issue, Ray, I won't be discussing it with anyone."

Ray smiles, "I need you to draw up a will. I know it's not your thing, but it is a simple distribution of assets."

Caitlyn nods, knowing there is more to come, fearing what it is.

"I have a handful of months to live, Caitlyn, so I need the paperwork fast."

She reaches across the island and puts her hand on top of Ray's, "Whatever you need. Let me get a pad and pen." When she returns, he is standing at the back door deep in thought. She coughs to get his attention. He points to the wine crates at his feet.

"Long Point Winery, that's the one near Aurora, right?"

Caitlyn beams. "Yes, it's my favorite winery. That's where Matt and I got married. He brought those bottles back after his trip there the other day."

"I didn't know people got married at wineries."

Caitlyn laughs, "That's what Matt said when I suggested we have our ceremony there. Long Point doesn't generally host weddings, but I've come to know the owners over the years, so they granted my request. After a beautiful, albeit cold Thanksgiving Eve wedding, we stayed at a nearby place on Cayuga Lake. It was idyllic." She suddenly remembers why Ray Chase is standing in her kitchen. "So, to answer your question, you can get married at a winery." She waves the legal pad, "Do you want to sit at the table?"

"Rather stand at the island."

"Okay."

The detective goes off subject for a minute. "REDO is wreaking havoc and ruining lives throughout Upstate NY, Caitlyn. I'm glad there's a task force being put together. I heard Matt's heading it."

Caitlyn nods, "And apparently he's going to be my new boss. DA James assigned me to the task force. I haven't told Matt, and to be perfectly honest I'm not sure how that's going to fly."

Ray laughs, "It'll be fine. Some say you've tamed that beast."

Caitlyn raises her beer, "Well, from your lips to God's ear."

Ray scoffs, "God and I aren't on speaking terms right now, Caitlyn."

"I suppose not."

The dying man and amused woman laugh themselves into quite a fit.

The lawyer gets what she needs to draft Ray's will, then walks her guest to the door. She hugs him before he can object, and watches until he's gone from sight. She wipes the tear or two that have started their journey down her cheek, cleans the kitchen through a good long sob, and takes the legal pad with her client's personal information and last wishes to her bedroom. She works on it for an hour or more, tucks the pad under her pillow and answers the very first beckon of sleep. Painful considerations of Ray's situation torture her slumber, then give way to sweet memories of her romantic wedding with Matt...

"Beautiful," he whispered when she stepped from the building where she'd dressed for the ceremony.

She walked alone to the lovely makeshift altar assembled and decorated by the husband and wife owners of the winery. Lace draped, wooden wine racks were placed lengthwise creating an aisle that led to two upturned wine barrels displaying baskets of lush Autumnal Mums and lit pillar candles set inside tall hurricane glass vases. Beyond the beautiful display was a magnificent view of Cayuga Lake surrounded by the blaze of New England fall.

The bride was stunning. Her long-sleeve, cashmere white waist-length jacket was tailored and refined. Her full-length, multi-layered, organza skirt was fun and sexy. It's movement on the windy hillside was carefree, like the bride, herself.

"Beautiful," he said a second or third time. He took hold of her hand when she reached him, "Are you sure about this?"

She beamed brightly, "I'm thirty-four Matt, and if memory serves me, you're the only one who's asked."

"Dumb fucking luck on my part," he kissed her cheek.

The owners of the winery officiated and witnessed the marriage of Caitlyn English and Matthew Cambridge.

~

That dream gave way to the unsettled reactions of those who learned The Counselor married **That** Cop.

"You what?" the astonished paralegal snapped, forgetting for a moment to whom she was speaking.

"I got married over the holiday weekend," Caitlyn raised her left hand, the one that sported a brand-new, gold wedding band, and wiggled her fingers.

"Who did you marry? Have you been seeing someone? How did I not know? Who did you marry?"

"Matt Cambridge."

Michelle cracked up laughing, "Yeah, right." She swallowed the rest of her guffaws hard and apologized swiftly, "I'm sorry, Ms. English, I thought you were kidding. I should go .... finish the .... case."

Caitlyn plopped her ass onto her chair, "That went well."

~

And when her boss learned of her marriage, it felt as though she jeopardized her job, somehow.

"Ms. English, did I hear correctly?"

She waited for more, answered his sort-of-asked question, "Yes sir, I married over the weekend."

"*Him?*" the word drenched in disapproval.

She thought about defending her actions, only to realize there wasn't an adequate defense—of her secret relationship—or her impromptu vows.

The married woman wakes in a cold sweat, raises her hand first to her pounding heart, then to her cheek to wipe away tears that fall. "I didn't do right by myself, or Matt. I should have—we should have—been open and upfront about our relationship. I should have—we should have—faced the disapproving lot together, before our nuptials. If we had, maybe others would see the side of Matthew Cambridge that I see."

A six pack, Caitlyn?

Groggy, and with a bit of a hangover, she slaps at the alarm. Once again, the newlywed finds herself alone in bed. This time she doesn't linger in the California king, she hurries to the bathroom, then down the hall ready to breach the sanctity of Matt's shelter for a little snuggle. She releases a groan when she finds he's not there. She places a call to the wayward one.

"Where are you, Matt?"

"On my way back from Geneva."

"REDO hit Walters College?"

"Yeah. I was pulling onto our driveway last night when I got a call from Geneva PD saying they had a rape victim uttering, I don't want to hurt you. I only want to rape you. They were directed to me by their ADA."

"Because you're the head of the task force."

"Yeah."

"About that. You're going to be answering to my boss. I'd appreciate it if you'd play nice."

"Your boss is an asshole."

"Funny, that's what he says about you."

"General consensus, wifey."

Caitlyn laughs, "I've been missing you."

"Can you skip work?"

The lawyer remembers the will she needs to draw up for Ray, "Wish I could. Maybe you can cut out early?"

"If Ray decides to pull his weight."

Caitlyn ignores the comment but can't ignore the pain that comes from it.

60 Preston Parkway

Ray opens his front door to find his son's Tacoma parked at the curb. He heads to it and bangs the roof. Chris jumps a mile then lowers the window.

"Hell of a way to wake up, Old Man."

"What are you doing out here?"

"Freezing my balls off."

Ray turns around and heads back to his place, "Come on."

His son grabs a backpack from the passenger floor, slams the truck's door, and sprints up the stairs. Once inside, he takes a look around, "Nice place."

"I rent, so don't get any ideas."

Chris smiles, although it's a forced one. "I researched the hell out of Staff Sergeant Robert McLaughlin. He left the Army a couple months ago after eight years in. He spent the last four years at Fort Benning in Georgia as part of the 75th ranger regiment. He's a trained medic and was part of a quick strike force."

Ray smiles.

"You're smiling too wide for the rest of the information, Detective Chase. Getting military records on a special forces member will take some time. I don't have anything specific on when he went on leave from that end, but I'm starting to pull personal financials to see if he was in Syracuse, Aurora, or Ithaca during the time of the rapes."

Ray nods, "Don't do anything that will get you screwed, Chris. I won't be around to help you out of a jam, but if some shit happens, go to Caitlyn English, Onondaga County ADA. Do not talk to **anyone** but Caitlyn English. Do you understand?"

Chris nods. "Is she a friend of yours?"

"If you stretch the word friend. She's married to Matt Cambridge."

"I heard he's an asshole."

"Understatement. Getting away from that son-of-a-bitch is worth dying."

Chris laughs. "How'd the asshole nab the counselor?"

"Damned if I know." Ray thinks back to the day he heard the news about The Counselor and **That** Cop...

Diane Earls flew from her seat when she saw Ray Chase walk past her office. She grabbed hold of his sleeve and pulled the mammoth man her way.

"Do you want to see me, Ms. Earls?" he laughed.

"Get in here. Shut the door."

"What's going on, Diane?"

"Matthew Cambridge got married."

"Wasn't born yesterday, Diane."

"Hand to God."

The detective read her face, "Who the hell would marry him?"

"Caitlyn English."

The detective took a seat, "What the hell is wrong with that woman?"

"Well, they spend an awful lot of time together working case files, and he's really good looking, and she's too beautiful for her own good."

"Too beautiful?"

"Women that gorgeous, and that successful, intimidate men. They tend to not get asked out much."

"That so?"

"It takes a man with a strong ego to even think about asking a Grace Kelly clone out on a date." **She scoffed.** "We both know there's nothing wrong with Cambridge's ego, but…"

"But, he's a mean son-of-a-bitch. Pardon my language, Diane."

"No worries, Detective Chase, I was going to say he's an asshole."

Chris waited in silence for a few, then pushed in, "Any ideas?"

"On what?"

"On how Cambridge got English to marry him."

"No fucking clue."

Fayetteville

Cambridge drags his ass to the kitchen after several hours sleep in the spare room. He presses the single brew function on the coffee pot, runs the tap in the sink and cups a mouthful of cold water. The bit that isn't scooped for a sip is sent splashing against beer bottle empties that have been rinsed and are drying on a wooden rack. "A six pack, Caitlyn?" He ponders a minute, eyes the wine crates still at the back door, "A bottle of wine, maybe—but a six pack of beer? Not by yourself. Who were you drinking with?"

Mistakes and marching orders.

Detective Chase is in the break room pouring a cup of coffee when his partner comes barging in. Chase hands off the filled mug, "Looks like you need this more than me."

Cambridge takes it and walks away.

Chase forgoes a mug and follows the surly one, "Something set you off this morning?"

"Too much driving, too little sleeping."

"Were you on the road last night?"

"Geneva."

"Walters College?"

"Yeah."

"REDO?"

"Yeah."

"To quote you, Matt, 'Fuckin A.'"

"I got a call late last night from Geneva PD asking me to stop by since I'm the patsy who agreed to head up the task force." He takes a handful of sips then plunks the cup onto his desk, splashing some over the sides. The shake of liquid off his hand reminds him of the empties in the sink at home. A nudge of suspicion pushes up from somewhere, he pushes it aside. "REDO visited Mandy Kelleher, a twenty-three-year old junior at Walters. The coed rents a two-bedroom terrace apartment in a small off-campus building on the shore of Seneca Lake. Her sister-roommate and nearly everyone else in the building was away on an annual senior class trip. REDO got in, said his thing, did his thing, and left with his warning that he'd be seeing Mandy again."

Ray takes a seat that isn't offered, "This is his third rape in three weeks. He's escalating, and we need to figure out why, drill into his mistake."

"Mistakes."

"I'm no longer looking at the Kekoa rapes as a mistake."

"Why the fuck not?"

"REDO raped Marilyn McGinn and Connie Braxton twice. He raped Suzi Kekoa and returned for the repeat event. The fact that he ended up with a doppelganger for his second go around isn't on him. REDO didn't fuck up, the circumstances fucked him up."

Cambridge leans forward, "I'll bite. So that leaves us with only one mistake: calling Monica, Jenna."

Ray nods. "Look, REDO's going off the deep end could be about the Kekoas, could be about something else. Let's look for something else. The bastard is raping with more frequency, his territory is expanding, he made a verbal mistake, and he's changing up victim selection. That's what we need to look at."

"Changing up victim selection? What are you on to?"

"His first victims lived alone, that's not the case with his most recent victims. Two of his last three had roommates, Farnsworth and Kelleher. Now for the side notes: Farrell had a roommate until just before her rape, and McGinn lived alone for the first rape, but she moved in with Joey Mayer two days before the second rape, so technically Marilyn had a roommate on her redo."

"Right," he pauses, "that notation isn't in my files."

"It's in mine. You need to keep your files in better order. You keep too much in your head."

"Head comes with me—what's in my head comes with me, Old Man."

"Yeah, but records are important. I've seen your files. They're on the thin side. I've got some big-ass files full of stuff."

"Shit, Ray. We're running a case using two sets of files. I should have your notes. Shit, I should have your files."

"You can have 'em when I'm dead."

"You keep besting me on this investigation, the dead part will be sooner rather than later, Old Man."

Ray laughs. "I'll get you copies." *As part of my estate, asshole.*

"I'll read them."

"You should. There are threads we should be pulling."

"Like?"

"For years, REDO was a fall semester rapist. For years, he chose victims who didn't have roommates. For years, he chose victims who'd just moved into new apartments. At first look, those constants suggest REDO lived by some sort of orderliness, but there might be an alternate explanation."

"Like?"

"Looking solely at his first six rapes, maybe they took place in early fall because they were part of a fucked up anniversary thing, or maybe college coeds filling campuses unleashed something in him, or maybe he's from out of town and swings into Upstate NY once a year for a little R&R—rape and repeat."

"And now?"

"He's off kilter. His frequency is up and his territory is expanding. Something set him off."

"Seems obvious. There were six rapes over the course of six years. The last rape of that first batch was Trini Kekoa. She was a mistake—at least in his mind. Maybe that mistake pissed him off and the uptick in rapes is the result."

"Okay, but that rape happened at the end of August. REDO didn't start acting out until the New Year. Why the delay?"

"Jesus, Old Man, I don't know. It could be anything. Maybe he took a sabbatical, maybe he broke his leg, maybe there's a victim or two out there who hasn't come in?"

"**That** angle is something the task force should flush out. Are there other victims? If we find out that's the case, we'll get new threads to pull. One way to shake out other victims is if the task force holds a news conference. There's going to be a public announcement made about REDO, right?"

"Don't know. The DAs are in charge and will be making that call. You're on the task force, you know."

"Didn't know. Who else is on it?"

Matt shrugs. "Onondaga District Attorney James wants to see me this afternoon. He'll probably give me names and marching orders."

Elbows, ankles, and orange slices.

Jenna is ambulatory, mostly moving from her bedroom to the kitchen and to the bathroom on her own. She spends long hours sitting in the club chair reading the SU textbooks Mac brought from her grandparents' place. She is beyond well-rested from full nights of peaceful sleep in an incredibly comfortable bed. She decided she'd spend two more nights at Mac's place, and in celebration of her impending move back to Grams and Gramps, she and Mac have invited them for dinner.

"Still haven't figured out what you're cooking, Mac, but it smells awesome," she says on her way to the bathroom.

"I need to get something from Eileen's. I'm trusting you to stay out of the kitchen, Ms. Farnsworth."

"You have my word, Mr. McLaughlin." As soon as Jenna heard the screen door slam, she rushed into the bathroom and back out. "You should have made me swear not to enter the living room, Mac." At first, she's surprised by the makeshift art studio, then she is captivated by the beauty, the serenity, the mastery of Mac's paintings. "Amazing," she declares with a quick comparison look at Oneida Lake beyond the studio. "He captured it perfectly on canvas." It's on her second look that she sees the silhouetted woman. The image is nestled into the landscape, nearly indistinguishable. "Is that?" She moves from one painting to the next, studies each from different angles. "Is that? Is that me?" She is pulled from her thoughts by the slamming of a car door. She hurries from the front room, accidently banging her injured elbow on a doorframe and twisting her ankle a bit as she moves back toward the bathroom. She is safely there when Mac enters the house. He calls out from the kitchen, "Jenna!"

The very unsettled woman fights tears that spring and pants through the pulsating pain in her arm and leg. "In the bathroom, Mac."

"Okay," He calls out from the living room. "She was in here."

Jenna spends quite a bit of time behind the bathroom door cupping her elbow and rocking back and forth with the pain. Her head is reeling. "I wish I had my cell phone. I'd call .... who? Who would I call?" She sits on the closed toilet, cradles her elbow and prays that the whirling mess inside her head stops. "I need help. But from who? Grams and Gramps—two elderlies? Joey and Marilyn— my rape people? Keith or Mac—my possible rapists?" She thinks back to the first time she saw Mac at her grandparents' house. "It was so awkward and uncomfortable—because I'd been raped? Or because he raped me? I pulled away from him. I'd never done that before. It'd been years since we were together, and he's so different: older, taller, and his blonde hair is dark now, and..." She startles at the knock on the door.

"Jenna, are you alright? Do you need help?"

197

She opens the door, "My elbow and ankle are hurting again. I was just resting a bit before my return trip."

"Would you like a lift?"

She does not want a lift, but accepts his offer. *I can't let him know I don't trust him. Can't let him know I can't walk, let alone run if I need to—do I need to?*

District Attorney's Office

Caitlyn is waiting in the lobby of her office building. "We need to talk," she says as she grabs her husband's arm. "Get in the elevator."

"Is this about last night?"

Her face reddens, "What about last night?"

"The empty beer bottles. A six pack, Caitlyn?"

She nudges his shoulder, "I didn't drink them by myself, Matt. Michelle came by with some files. We started talking and started drinking." Caitlyn laughs. "What did you think?"

"Same thing I'm thinking now. There's more to this story."

"There is. That's why I met you downstairs. Weston James is going to give you the list of names for the task force."

"Yeah."

"I'm on the list."

"Fuckin A."

When they arrive at the upper floor, Detective Cambridge is directed to a conference room where Weston James is waiting. ADA English rushes to her office suite, grabs hold of her paralegal's arm and pulls her inside her office.

"Michelle. Sit. Listen. I had a meeting last night at my house that Cambridge cannot know about. During that meeting, a six pack of beer was consumed. Cambridge is curious about the empties. I told him you stopped over with some files, and we started talking and drinking."

Michelle nods, "What did we discuss?"

"The fact that I was named as a member of the task force, and I wasn't sure how Matt would take the news."

"Got it." When she gets to the door she asks, "What kind of beer did we drink?"

"Genius! Blue Moon."

"With or without the slice of orange."

"Without. Jesus, you're good at this."

"And you suck at this, Counselor."

Michelle leaves the office door open so Caitlyn can see how good her paralegal really is. Michelle makes a phone call, says a few words, then disconnects. An hour later Michelle's office line rings. She ignores it and steps to her boss' door, "The detective just left the DA's conference room." The paralegal is back at her desk holding a bottle of OTC pills and sipping from a bottle of water when the detective walks into her area.

"Tough night?" he asks.

"Tougher on me than the Woman of Steel in there."

Cambridge peeks at his woman, "Beer doesn't bother her, but wine, that's a different story."

"Good to know," Michelle opens her drawer and drops the OTCs in.

"What did you think of the beer?"

"Would have been better if my boss offered an orange slice."

Cambridge nods and moves past. *Good try, Michelle.* He shuts the office door behind him.

Caitlyn comes from around her desk, "Do I still have a job?"

"Two, apparently."

"Is this going to be a problem between us, Matt?"

"Nope."

A bite of dessert.

Grams and Gramps slept in after their big night out at the next door bungalow. The elderly woman shuffles to her bedroom the minute Gramps leaves for Eileen's on an unnecessary errand. Gracie Farnsworth lifts the heavy black receiver from its cradle and dials an international number. It is answered on the second ring.

"Bonjour."

"Mary, you sound so Parisian. I hope I didn't wake you."

"Grams! Oh, Grams! I'm so happy to hear from you."

"Maybe you won't be. Mary, dear, I have a story to tell you, but I need an honest answer from you, first."

"Of course."

"Could Keith be a rapist?"

Fayetteville

Cambridge arrives home to find his wife sitting at the island in the kitchen, surrounded by REDO case files. A kettle with what appears to be homemade chicken soup is simmering away on the stove.

"Soup? You made soup?"

"Again, I can follow a recipe. As a matter of fact, I followed two." The proud wife straightens on her tall stool and points to the oven, "Open it."

He does. He smiles. "Bread?" He pulls a whiff, "I haven't smelled homemade bread since my mother died. She baked it every Sunday."

"Will there be a comparison coming?"

The husband closes the oven, moves to the island, and wraps his arms around his wife's waist from behind, "Not stupid enough for that trap." His hands get very busy.

She slaps them away, "Are you *copping* a feel, Detective?" She laughs freely.

He groans loudly, "Never heard that before," he kisses her head then walks away. "Let me know when dinner is ready, I'm starved."

The domestic diva serves dinner in the dining room. The horny husband wants dessert in the bedroom. He starts by copping that feel along the way. They're holding hands when they enter their room. He spins her toward him and leans her against the closed door. "I've missed you."

"I've—"

"No talking, Caitlyn." He runs his fingers through her hair, along the shell of her ear, to a pearl earring. "Beautiful."

She pulls a deep pant when he presses against her, when his lips find hers, and his tongue playfully explores.

He lifts her sweater over her head, watches the rise and fall of her breasts before cupping, kissing, sucking through the beige silk. He reaches around and unzips her skirt, helps it on its journey over her hips, then inches her thigh-high hose down each leg, touching this, stroking that along the way. He leans in for another kiss, pressing himself against her.

"Matt," she pants.

"Can't talk right now, Caitlyn." He kneels in front of her, "Spread 'em."

Her legs tremble at his touch, his lick, his suck.

He brings her to a powerful orgasm in seconds.

Her legs weaken.

He continues his mouthing, bringing her to an almost painful second release.

"Matt, I'm ... I'm." Her legs buckle.

He grabs hold before she hits the floor and carries her to their bed. He enters her, and within seconds he fills her. When his wife surrenders to the slumber of the sexually satisfied, the husband goes searching.

He still has a Blue Moon nudge.

Do you think it's Mac?

Matt spends some morning time with Caitlyn who is working from home again, "Does this mean there's another culinary event in my future?"

"Lasagna."

"In that case, I'll be home by six."

He showered and dressed, this time sans her narration, and when he is ready to leave he joins her on the bed. The detective starts flipping through the files she's scattered about, "Every place I go, someone is looking for REDO."

"I think we're going to crack this. We're close."

"We? Don't want you stealing my thunder on this one, Counselor."

"Then you'd better get cracking, Detective."

His goodbye kiss is tender, his parting words, whispered. "Looking forward to dinner—and dessert."

The Lake

Cambridge stews about his wife on the drive to Oneida. "Been spending a lot of time away from the office, Caitlyn. Why is that?" He shuts off the radio and works the question. "There's no way she's cheating, it's not who she is, but maybe she's working from home because she's uncomfortable at work. Her fucking boss has always had a thing for her, but I don't think he ever acted on it. Weston James isn't one to cross the line of impropriety. If he didn't make a move in the past, it's unlikely he'd make a move now that she's married. But she said he thinks I'm an asshole, so the topic of our marriage came up." He bangs that through his head a couple times then moves on. "Now for the beers, there's a story there. Someone came by. My gut says it wasn't Michelle. It wasn't Weston James, either. There's no way the DA and his ADA would sit around drinking beers in our house. Someone helped her drink those beers, though."

By the time the detective arrives at his destination, he's pretty combustible. He knocks a little too hard on the back door of the bungalow owned by Robert McLaughlin. A black Humvee that was parked on the driveway during his first visit is gone. "He could be out." He knocks again. "She could be asleep."

The 'she' in question moves a curtain aside, rolls her eyes, and opens the door. "Detective."

"May I come in, Ms. Farnsworth?"

"To tell me what? That Gramps is a suspect now." She feels the world tilt on its axis and rights herself by placing a steadying hand on the doorjamb.

"Ms. Farnsworth, you should sit down before you—"

"I'm fine," she interrupts. "As I was saying, aside from you and Detective Chase, Gramps is the only other man I know in Upstate NY who you haven't accused." She blanches, falters, and nearly faints. Cambridge catches her and moves her into her bedroom and onto her bed.

"Ms. Farnsworth, what the hell happened out there?"

"He said ……. he said," she begins crying. "He said maybe we already know one another." She grabs the detective's sport coat, "I saw the paintings. They're of me. Do you think it's Mac?"

At that moment, the victim and the detective realize they are no longer alone.

"Do you think it's Mac, **what**?"

Cambridge stands and moves between the two. "Mr. McLaughlin, Ms. Farnsworth and I are working. Please shut the door on your way out."

Mac looks past Cambridge, "Jenna, do you think I raped you?"

Cambridge rescues her from having to answer that question. "Mr. McLaughlin, when was the last time you were in Aurora or Geneva? Maybe you made a trip to either or both of those communities within the last few days?"

"I've been here with Jenna."

"Not an answer to my question, Mr. McLaughlin."

Beard Park Cemetery

Ray Chase is sitting on a stone bench at the top of a tiny hill beneath a towering barren elm. He's bent at the waist, his forearms resting on his thighs, and his head hung as low as possible. From time to time he wipes away a tear or two, blaming each on the bitter cold wind that whips by. "Twenty-two feet," he whispers. He knew which direction to head when he arrived at the cemetery, but didn't know for sure where his plot was located, where he'd spend his eternal rest, so…

"Excuse me," he interrupted the young woman with pink-tipped hair at a small office at the entrance to the cemetery.

"Can I help you?"

"I'd like to look at my burial plot, but I can't remember exactly where it's located."

"Name?"

"Raymond Chase."

"Raymond and Camille Chase?"

"Yes."

"Here you go," she handed him a slip of paper, "your plots are located in section E. The cemetery grid is alphabetical, so follow along, and when you get to E, head west and travel to Eternity Hill. Your plot is at the top, under the big elm. The beginning marker of your space is twenty-two feet from the stone bench, heading in a westerly direction."

"Twenty-two feet from the stone bench." He's said the words several times, but has yet to count them out. "I wonder if Cami still plans on ……. doubtful," he shakes his head. "I didn't treat her right in life, no reason she'd want to spend eternity with me." A few tears slide, these hold regret—he doesn't try to pretend otherwise.

Ray sits straight and looks past his final resting place. He scans for the headstone of his former partner, scoffs when he finds it. "My number's almost up, Brian. I wonder what direction you headed, and whether I'll be following your lead?" Raymond Chase gets off his duff, walks twenty-two feet from the stone bench and freezes in place.

Not because of the cold—
but because he knows.

--- *Pulling Threads* ---

Ray finds his son in the kitchen when he gets home. "I see you let yourself in."

"That's why you gave me a set of keys, right?"

"Yeah. How long have you been here?"

"Hours. Mom wasn't sure about your diet, or if you'd feel like eating, but she sent the bisque and baguettes you used to like."

Ray makes his way to the stove, "I thought that's what I smelled. Tell Camille it was great."

"You haven't had any."

"Don't need to have any to know it's great."

Chris smiles and nods.

Ray helps himself to some heaven, "Do you want any?"

"Had some."

"From mine?"

Chris laughs, "No, at home."

"Move your files and tell me what brought you here. I'll eat while you talk."

"I'm still researching McLaughlin and Moreno, but I was wondering, are they your only suspects?"

"Nope."

"Should I be researching someone else?"

Ray nods, "Keep digging on those two, and add Evan Sayles. He's the abusive boyfriend of one our victims. My gut is saying that none of these guys is REDO, but my gut's filled with cancer, so who the fuck knows." He stops for a few bites before continuing, "Chris, look for exculpatory evidence. McLaughlin was active duty for eight years. He took leave and went somewhere during that time, find out where. If he didn't come to the Lakes region, move on. As for Moreno, he can get himself out from under suspicion of rape by giving a DNA sample, see if there's a reason why he won't. Sayles had a physical thing with our newest victim for years, see if you can figure out what caused him to cross the line from smacking to battering. I'll give you a couple names tomorrow. They're former suspects, guys who deserve another look. But I think I know who REDO is."

"Then why have me do this work?"

"You need to weed those men out. I need to start pulling threads." Ray mulls some while he finishes dinner, "I'm gonna work upstairs and then hit the hay. If you leave, lock up on your way out. If you stay, don't wake me."

Ray makes a call before getting into the case files, "Cami, thank you for the bisque and baguette. You still have it."

"Thanks, Ray," she says on a choke of tears and the disconnect of the phone.

Ray shakes the image of the only woman he ever loved out of his head—it is a very long shake. He sits at his desk, puts his feet up, and leans back.

Two hours of contemplation later—he puts pen to paper and writes the name of his suspect.

MATTHEW CAMBRIDGE

The Suspect

Now what?

The detective's hands shake vigorously when he finishes writing the name of his suspect—the name of his partner. Part of the shake comes from a surge of adrenaline, most comes from anger. "What the fuck took you so long to figure this shit out? You've had suspicions about Matt Cambridge over the years, that he planted evidence, or left shit out, or put shit in to victim and perp statements. Why the delay?" The debating detective no sooner said those words when he starts talking himself out of this bold step, and then right back in again. "You don't like Cambridge .... Speak the fucking truth, you hate him .... He's a cop for fuck's sake .... You know that means shit ....Yeah, but suspicions don't mean anything. You. Need. Evidence."

Ray pushes back from his desk and begins pacing. "You never went there with Cambridge, never allowed yourself to go looking for evidence because of Brian Stewart." The man of blue hangs his head low and accepts the hard truth. "I lost every-fucking-thing when I accused Brian of being dirty. I lost friends on the force, lost years trying to gain a foothold at the station, lost my marriage, and lost my kid." Reality hits him harder than the truth of his past. "Jesus, Ray. You're about to lose your fucking life. You're teetering on the edge of death.

You're going to **have** to go there. You're going to chase the thoughts that have haunted you at night. You're going to ask the questions that have festered in your gut and tore your heart to shit. You are going to find out if Matt Cambridge is REDO."

The ill man is winded when he falls back onto his chair, but he is not done with his beratement, "If you'd done this shit sooner, you would have saved those poor women from the ruins of REDO and maybe from the gut-rot that's killing you." On a new sheet of paper the detective writes three words.

WHERE WAS HE?

Ray adds victim names and their rape dates to the list, logs onto his SPD system, goes to personnel records, and starts looking for threads to pull and perhaps to bind.

Marilyn McGinn   8/29/2014
        personal day
Suzi Kekoa   9/2/2015
        personal day
Connie Braxton   8/28/2016
        vacation week
Connie Braxton   8/26/2017
        vacation week
Marilyn McGinn   8/3/2018
        sick day
Trini Kekoa   8/29/2019
        personal day

Jenna Farnsworth	1/8/2020
on-call	
Monica Farrell	1/14/2020
day shift	
Mandy Kelleher	1/20/2020
day shift	

He adds a circle around Monica's and Mandy's names, "Matt was at the station on those days, but ......" Ray tries to remember exactly when their paths crossed. "I'll work on that, but I'm clear on one thing, he wasn't home during Mandy's rape because I was at his house with Caitlyn. He was in Geneva. It'd be interesting to know when he arrived in that little Upstate village."

Ray conducts another round of debates, then asks himself a question on the way to bed, "Would Matt Cambridge investigate **this** guy? Fuckin A he would."

Stay safe, Caitlyn.

Chris was up most of the night cyber searching and head scratching. He is in the kitchen making scrambled eggs and toast when Ray comes down.

"Coffee ready?"

"Yeah. Grab a cup, and I'll plate you some of this."

"Not sure I can eat it."

"Then smell it."

The father laughs. "You stayed."

"Seems."

"Not complaining, but don't you have a life, maybe a girl, or a job?"

"I'm gay, and I own my own business."

"Gay, huh? That might have pissed me off some, but I've got bigger fish to fry now." Ray takes a sip, "You know, broads can be a handful, maybe you're onto something."

"Not how being gay works."

"Don't want to know how it works, Chris."

The son laughs. "So last night you said to concentrate on things that disqualify a suspect. What do I do about ambiguous things?"

"Like?" Ray says around a mouthful of toast.

"I found a couple threads to pull on Staff Sergeant McLaughlin."

Ray smiles big, "Threads?"

"Yeah. When in Rome."

"What're the threads?"

"His financials turned up normal and consistent ATM usage in and around Fort Benning, but there's random usage during the time period of two of the early rapes."

"Go on."

"August 30 to September 15, 2015 and August 22 to 28, 2017."

"Suzi Kekoa and Connie Braxton."

"What?"

"Never mind. Where was the random ATM usage during those times?"

"Philadelphia, Pennsylvania."

Ray gets up to pour himself a cup of coffee, leans against the counter and raises his cup, "Jenna Farnsworth is from the Philly area. Maybe he was in town visiting."

"Who's Jenna Farnsworth?"

"Looks like you need to know some stuff about the victims. It will help you link the shit you're finding." He puts his cup in the sink, "The thing is, I won't be around to kill you if you say anything about this to anyone."

"No problem, Old Man. My lips are sealed."

"Still having a problem with your gay thing, Chris. Let's not talk about your lips, okay?" Ray says on his way upstairs.

"Asshole," Chris yells after him.

"For fuck's sake. Do. Not. Say. Asshole. Ever. Again! Come on, I'll give you the list of victims."

SPD

Cambridge is alone in the office and will be all day since Chase called in sick again. He stacks SPD REDO case files on one side of his desk, opens an expandable legal file he brought from his storage unit and sets it on the other side. "Good thing I kept the original victim statements and interview sheets," he flips through a handful of papers, "and these notes from Ray, they'll give me some stuff to analyze, but not nearly enough if Ray's been keeping a second set of records on every rape for all these years." He takes three clipped packets from his expandable file, "Marilyn, Suzi, Connie. I wonder what these three will reveal? I was still new to the division and the investigations were Ray's dog and pony show. He called the shots, and I handled the files. Turns out I didn't handle them good enough. I **need** Ray's files. That's where the threads are going to be. The Old Man has been reviewing shit for weeks, maybe longer. Fuck only knows what threads he's found—and pulled. And I won't know until I get my hands on his files."

The detective gets up from his desk, pulls the slatted blinds on the window facing the hallway, locks his office door, and does the same in Ray's office. "I can review the files later, I should check his computer now, while he's out. Computer password. Fucking IT changes them every three months. Chase wouldn't remember his. He'd write it down. Where would he put it?"

He searches under the desk blotter and inside its four corners, runs his hands under the skinny center desk drawer and checks inside, moves the In-Box and Out-Box aside. "Nothing." He empties a coffee cup filled with pens and markers, reads its inscription, **World's Best Detective**. "You better hope not, Old Man." He returns everything he's touched and continues his search. "Desk drawers unlocked. Nothing's gonna be there." After a cursory look, he moves on. "L-desk and slide out keyboard. Password. Password. Password. Where?" He runs his hands under every section of wood and metal feeling for something taped beneath. He lifts the mouse pad—nothing. Lifts the keyboard—nothing. He moves to the credenza, "Center door locked." He is about to pick it when there's a knock on his office door. He moves through Ray's office, closes the adjoining door and yanks his wide, "What!?"

Diane jumps back from the verbal assault, "Is your phone broken, Detective?"

Cambridge scowls, "What?"

"ADA English is on Line 1. She's been holding for ten minutes. And here's your mail."

"Any mail for Detective Chase? We're waiting on a few things."

"At my desk if you want to thumb through," the admin says before leaving.

Cambridge grabs the receiver, "What's up, Caitlyn?"

"Could ask you the same thing, Matt. I've been holding long enough to have had a pedicure."

"Yeah. Sorry. Ray's out, so it's gonna be a balls to the wall kind of day."

"You forgot your cell at home."

He slaps at his pockets, "Any chance you could."

"On my way."

"Not sure where I'll be when you get here. Leave it with Diane up front. I'll grab it from her later. Thanks, Caitlyn." As he hangs up he hears his cell ring in the background. "Shit." *Mental note: check to see who called because she's gonna read the name.*

Caitlyn reads the name on Matt's cell, "Detective Kelly, Aurora PD. A member of the REDO task force." The woman saddens, "Syracuse, the place I live, and Aurora the place where I married, have been marred by REDO. Little by little he's encroaching on the whole of Upstate NY. I can't wait to nail this sadistic rapist's balls to the wall." She laughs at the words tumbling from her once refined lips. "You're wearing off on me, Matthew Cambridge." She is no sooner back to her car from dropping off Matt's phone when she receives a call from Ray Chase. "Good morning, Ray," she says lightly.

"I'm not at the station."

"I know. I just dropped off Matt's cell with Diane Earls."

"Is Matt on to us?"

"No, but he's been very curious about the consumed six pack of Blue Moon."

"You need to hide evidence, Caitlyn."

"Yes, well, I'll do better next time," she laughs. "Is there something I can do for you, Ray?"

"Nope. Just checking in. Thank you for the prelim documents. I put a few notations and sent them back to your office."

"I'm out today, Ray, but I'll work on them first thing tomorrow."

"Stay safe, Caitlyn," he says as he hangs up.

Caitlyn watches her cell fade, feels her smile fade with it, "He's such a nice man."

Crimson, blue, and brown, too.

Jenna is exhausted. She slept the night through, but it was a disrupted slumber. Questions about Mac rolled and crashed through her subconscious like waves pounding the shore during an emotional tsunami. She's awake now, but the tormenting thoughts are at it again. "Why is he painting silhouettes of me? Is he painting silhouettes of me? Could the woman at the lake be someone else? Why did I fall on my walk? Because there was a sound. Was there a sound? Was it made by Mac? Why was he out there? Why is he so different?"

Jenna's eyes close and she drifts off, her hands slowly unclenching a Granny-quilt tucked under her chin. She surrenders to a dream that quickly turns to a nightmare…

"May I look?"
"Not yet."
"When?"
"Soon, Darling."
She was perched on a stool in a painter's studio, canvases lined the walls, some rested on easels beneath showcase lighting. She was silhouetted in every work, the constant in an ever-changing landscape. The moods were controlled masterfully, the budding greens of spring, the sparkling blues of summer, the boastful orange, red, and yellow of fall, and the unforgiving gray of winter.

The artist rested his palette onto a splattered stand. He stretched his back and arms, then offered his hand to his model, his muse. She moved lithely to him, suddenly aware of his faceless form. She halted at the sight, then succumbed to the pull of his work. She took hold of his hand and smiled with expectation. A chill ran through her; a scream died before it could announce her horror. She turned condemning eyes to the man, "The silhouette. It's hideous, hateful. Crimson paint is dripping from the woman's breast. From my breast."

"Not paint, Jenna, blood."

"The mask. Take off your mask."

"There is no need. You know who I am, Jenna. Look into my eyes."

"One is blue. One is brown. It's you!"

Mac pushes open her door at the sound of her scream, "Jenna! What's wrong? What's the—"

"Get out!"

"Jenna. Please."

"Get Out! Get Out!"

He turns to leave.

"Wait! Give me your cell phone."

"I'll get it." He returns and starts to enter the room.

"Just leave it on the floor. Close the door behind you." Jenna listens to his retreating steps, then waits until there is enough distance between them. She hobbles to the door, flips the flimsy lock, grabs the phone, and calls Gramps.

"Come get me. Now. Please." The distraught woman is desperately pulling a pair of rag socks onto her feet, one of which is still swollen and sore when there's a knock on the bedroom door, "Gramps?"

"Yes."

She welcomes him in. "I need you to get me out of here. Can you support me?"

Gramps nods, helps her to the kitchen, and addresses Mac, "Can she use your mother's crutch?"

He nods. "It's in the closet by the back door."

"Come on, Jenna." Gramps encourages. "I'll be back for her things, Mac."

"Wait." She pats Gramps' arm before hobbling from him. She gets into Mac's space, "Your eyes. The first day I saw you, I asked what was different about you. I couldn't put my finger on it, but I knew there was something. You said you were taller and had darker hair, but you never mentioned your contact lenses. Why? Why?"

"Jenna, I wear brown contact lenses because my eyes bother the fuck out of me. Hell, you had a problem with them when we were kids. I don't understand what the big deal is about wearing brown contact lenses."

"My rapist has brown eyes. The man who paints silhouettes of me and supposedly found me at the shoreline **wears** brown eyes."

"Jenna. I had no…"

"Don't, Mac." she turns, loses balance, then pulls her arm from him when he helps right her. "Don't, Mac. Don't ever touch me!" She hobble-storms out the door.

Gramps squares his shoulders and straightens his spine, "Mac don't come around. I spent time in the Army. I know how to shoot, and I'll be armed."

"Emmett, I didn't."

"Don't think you did, Mac, but Jenna does."

Binders full of women.

Caitlyn struggles to put Ray out of her mind; actually, it's his parting comment she struggles to tuck away. "Stay safe, Caitlyn." Several times over the past few hours, she finds those words rolling free as though they're errant pinballs with nothing to bump against. As she is wont to do, she's been sitting on the floor of the master bedroom working REDO. Expandable legal files, different colored binders, and a ream's worth of printed emails and faxes are spread all around her. And still, her mind keeps going back to that comment. "Stay safe, Caitlyn."

"How odd. Stay safe. From what? Life's unexpected curve balls, like pancreatic cancer?" She tries hard to shake the comment, but it ends up circling around again, "Stay safe. From whom? REDO? I don't fit into his demographic." She stays with it, pushes for a thread to pull, something that might explain his comment. She gets nowhere. "Poor man, he's carrying the burden of this unsolved case to his grave and leaving the women of Upstate NY vulnerable to a serial rapist." A chant of sorts whispers from her lips, "We Need To Solve This Before ... We Need To Solve This Before ... We Need To Solve This Before ..."

"Before what?" Cambridge says from the doorway.

She screams at the unexpected intrusion. "Jesus, Matt. You scared the hell and the piss out of me!"

"You were deep in conversation with yourself, Caitlyn. You didn't hear me, and you didn't hear the timer on the oven."

Caitlyn pushes off the carpet and rushes past.

"I shut it off, and I took it out," he calls after her.

"Thanks!" she hollers back.

The detective's eyes are drawn to three stacks of colorful binders. He takes an orange one from the first stack and silently reads the label on the inside cover.

Monica Farrell
Date of Rape: January 14, 2020
Location of Rape: CL-12
Aurora, NY, Cayuga County
Detective of Record: Brandan Kelly

He flips through. "Not much, although there are several emails and faxes from the Cayuga County DA's office tucked inside the back pocket. She's just starting to assemble this." He eyes the label again, "There's enough stuff right here to go on if she starts connecting dots." He takes the next binder, a lime green one, and silently reads the label on the inside cover.

Connie Braxton
Date of Rape: August 28, 2016
Location of Rape: 2 Stone Lane
Aurora, NY, Cayuga County
Detectives of Record: Simms and Kelly

He flips through the plastic-sleeves. "Same stuff SPD files have. That's because she gets what I want to give her." Toward the back he finds two sections labeled Evidence and Questions. "Empty sleeves." He fingers through a pile of papers on the floor, "These are in chronological order. She removed them from the binder." He reads a few handwritten notes before putting them back in a pile, skips the second lime green binder, "Braxton's second rape," he surmises. He moves to the next stack of binders and takes the black one, "This belongs to the first victim," he scoffs, "not by a longshot," he laughs.

Marilyn McGinn
Date of Rape: August 29, 2014
Location of Rape: 44 Central Street
Syracuse, NY, Onondaga County
Detectives of Record: Chase and Cambridge

He takes the second black notebook from the stack. "Marilyn's REDO." He doesn't open it; he doesn't need to. He plays the rape scene through his head, holding still the memory of his climax—the one that created his son. He quickly rearranges the stacks when Caitlyn calls from the kitchen.

"Dinner is ready, Matt."

"Smells great," he hollers. "**You** are becoming a problem, Caitlyn." He quietly closes the bedroom door.

The Lake

Emmett and Grace Farnsworth spend a few minutes with Marilyn and Joey who drove to the bungalow at Jenna's request. As soon as the elderlies leave, the visiting women sit at the kitchen table with the young woman who is barely holding it together.

"Mac has a blue eye and a brown eye, except he doesn't because he has brown eyes. My rapist has brown eyes. They may or may not be real eyes. Mac paints landscapes with silhouettes of me in them. Mac found me sprawled on the ice. He may or may not be the source of the sound that caused me to fall. Mac hoisted me over his shoulder and said, Don't. Move. They were the same words with the same inflection as my rapist. Mac took me to his house instead of my house. He rummaged through my pocket for a business card and didn't react when he saw the words Syracuse Rape Crisis Center. He didn't ask if .... Wouldn't he have asked if…?"

Jenna draws a breath and continues her roll, "On the other hand, he said he wears contacts because he hates his eyes—they are kind of freaky. The sound could have been from the ice moving and settling. I've heard that sound lots of times. When I was on his shoulder, he needed me to stay still, so he told me not to move. I was in an emotional state when he looked at the business card, maybe he did react, maybe he didn't make the connection between me and the word rape." She stops and thinks for a minute and continues, "Besides, *he's Mac*. I've known him forever. And he's taken such good care of me, cooking for me, schlepping me to the bathroom, and giving me my medication."

Marilyn jumps all over **that** comment, "What medication?"

"The pills you left me, you know the OTCs for pain and the muscle relaxants." Before her final word is out of her mouth she realizes Marilyn hadn't left any pills for her. She goes from stunned to panicked in a matter of seconds, "Oh my God. Oh My God! He's been drugging me? And doing what? Oh my God. Oh My God."

Marilyn moves in front of her patient, "Jenna, look at me. Jenna, you need to calm down. Breathe in through your nose and exhale slowly from your mouth. Again. That's good." She speaks over her shoulder to Joey, "Call Cambridge."

Jenna shakes her head as the words *No. No. No.* assault her from within.

Fayetteville
The call comes in as he's helping clear the dinner table. He rolls his eyes and groans. Loudly.

"Joey Mayer?" His wife asks.

"Honing your detective skills, I see." He shakes his head and exhales before answering the call, "Better be good, Mayer."

"Can you come out to Oneida Lake? Grams and Gramps Farnsworth just left for BINGO at the Rec Center, so it's a good time for you to talk to Jenna."

"Been out that way a lot lately. What's going on this time?"

"Jenna thinks McLaughlin has been drugging her."

"Be there in forty."

The Lake

Jenna has moved to the living room and is quietly looking at the shadowed lake when Cambridge joins her more than an hour later. "Ms. Farnworth, you're looking better."

She snarls, "I look like shit, I feel like a used piece of meat, and I wonder…"

The detective waits. "You wonder what?"

"My rapist said it could be a rape or a murder, and that I could get over one of those events. I wonder if I can get over this new betrayal."

Cambridge eyes Joey, "I'm going to give you a few minutes with Ms. Farnsworth." He tilts his head toward Marilyn. She follows him to the kitchen.

"Is there any coffee?"

Marilyn sets about making a pot. Cambridge watches her. *She's strong and tough, but soft and sensuous.* He remembers being in her, the feel of her silk. He gets hard, then is pulled back to reality.

"**Cambridge**, how do you take your coffee? Where the hell were you?"

"Sorry. We had two more rapes, one in Aurora and one in Geneva."

"You're working them? Kinda out of your territory, isn't it?"

"Upstate DAs put me in charge of a task force."

"No shit."

"Shit you not."

Joey, who'd come into the kitchen for some coffee hears the tail end of the conversation. "Glad you're heading it up, Cambridge. This bastard needs to be stopped."

The detective scoffs. "Maybe he can't be stopped."

Joey pulls her slack-jaw together and suggests, "You might not want to use that as your opener with the task force."

Ratatouille and goodbye kisses.

Ray and Chris have been working the REDO files all day. The son left his father for an hour or so and is back with travel dishes full of food.

"Your mother cooks when she's upset."

"Well, she's upset, Old Man."

"I can't think about Camille."

"I know."

For many minutes, the men quietly share generous helpings of ratatouille and chunks of crusty French bread. "Maybe it's not guilt rotting my insides, maybe it's because I stopped eating Camille's food," Ray says, forgetting his son is there.

"What do you have to be guilty about?" Chris confuses.

"You for starters. Maybe if I'd been around, you'd be straight."

"Not how gay works, Old Man."

"Still don't want to know how it works, Chris."

They share a laugh—a good laugh.

"Come on, let's get back to work. Clean the kitchen then drill down on the suspect list I gave you. Start with Grant Timberlake, but it's not gonna be him."

"Why not?"

"Mr. Timberlake is being looked at for Demi Warren's murder—"

"The coed found near Sweetheart Lane?"

"Yeah. Ms. Warren was strangled, stripped of her underwear either ante- or post-mortem, and her body was moved from one location to another. Timberlake might be good for Warren, but he isn't our serial rapist. REDO rapes his victims inside their homes, and they're alive when he kisses them goodbye. Check Timberlake though, then move on to Aldo Mendez. We had him for a rape a few years ago, but the conviction was tossed. We run Mendez through the mill whenever there's a new rape, but come up empty. Your turn to take a whack at him. You know enough about the victims and the circumstances of the crimes to leave the men in as suspects or take them out. Your work on McLaughlin and Sayles looks good, but dig deeper on Keith Moreno. I'm going upstairs to work."

Ray drops his physically drained ass onto his chair, grabs a piece of paper, and labels it. Then he pulls the victim statement files, reads through them, and underlines certain sections.

CHOOSING HIS VICTIM

Marilyn McGinn: <u>moved into my garden apartment, emptied boxes, set electronics, ran to the DMV, the insurance company, the college bookstore, the grocery store, cooked dinner,</u>

read for a bit, then crashed into the sleep of the dead.

He reads Suzi Kekoa's victim statement, the one made in Honolulu, and stops half-way through. "What the fuck? Why didn't this penny drop before?" He makes a note at the top of the paper. *REDO **did not** do reconnaissance on Suzi Kekoa. She arrived from Honolulu the night she was raped. The reconnaissance REDO did was on Trini Kekoa. **She** was the woman who was supposed to be raped in 2015.

Connie Braxton: I flew to Jersey to pack up things from my parents' home and to get the Jeep I'd never brought to campus. I spent that day unpacking, and doing a thousand errands and teacher-related things that needed to be done before the first day of school.

He puts the statements aside and makes a quick note: *Trini Kekoa: When did she move into the apartment in Ithaca? Where did she live before the move? Did she make any trips to the DMV?

He voices a thought as he makes a call, "DMV. One of the first three victims mentioned a trip to the DMV. One victim brought a Jeep from home and might have gone to the DMV." He stops talking when his call is answered.

"Detective Kelly."

"Brandan, it's Ray Chase."

"You calling about the info I sent on the Monica Farrell rape?"

"Yes and no. I took a sick day, so I didn't see the file. I'm probably going to be out again tomorrow. Can you fax whatever you have to my house? I'd ask Matt, but he's out straight with the investigation, the task force, and covering my ass."

"What's your number?....... Okay, it'll be on its way in five."

"Thanks, Brandan." Ray has his feet on his desk and has nodded off when the grind of his fax brings him back around. He waits until it stops whirring, drops his feet to the floor, and grabs the pages. "Let's see if there was any reason for you to be at the DMV, Monica." He flips. He reads. He comes up empty. He checks his watch, and though it's late he calls Detective Caleb Sanchez at Ithaca PD.

"Sanchez."

"Detective, it's Ray Chase in—"

"Syracuse," Sanchez interrupts.

"Didn't think you'd remember me."

"Saw your name on the task force list. What can I do for you?"

"Any chance you remember whether Trini Kekoa got a new car, or had a reason to visit the DMV before her rape."

"Wouldn't have remembered anything along this line, but I buried myself in the Kekoa files over the past few days. Cambridge wants copies of everything for the task force, so I did a little clean-up before **That** Cop reviews our work. Anyway, I don't know if she did any DMV visits before her rape in 2019, but she did some before her cousin's rape in 2015. Remember that huge pile up on I-81 that summer?"

"The truck/boat/car shit fest?"

"That's the one. Trini's Lexus was totaled in the wreck. She had to have made a trip or two to the DMV to register her new ride late that summer. Don't know for sure why the sexual assault file had accident shit in it, but it might have been there because Trini moved into the apartment on Treble Way a short time before her cousin was raped there. You thinking there's a tie to the DMV?"

"Longshot, but that's all I've got."

"You working with Cambridge on this angle?"

"Nope."

"He's an asshole."

"Yup."

"You didn't hear that from me," Caleb laughs.

"How could I have heard anything from you? We never spoke. Thanks a lot, Detective."

There's a new thread to pull.

Ray makes a few more notes: *If REDO is identifying victims through the DMV, then the reconnaissance he did in 2015 was on Trini. He definitely went to Treble Way to rape Trini. Suzi was in the wrong place at the wrong time.* He sits with that information for a few then opines. "Raping the wrong woman would piss off Matt Cambridge. That may be why he orally raped

Trini, but it's not why he's escalating." Ray thinks back to his recent conversation with Caitlyn…

"Long Point Winery, that's the one near Aurora, right?"

Caitlyn beamed. "Yes, it's my favorite winery. That's where Matt and I got married. He brought those bottles back after his trip there the other day."

"I didn't know people got married at wineries."

Caitlyn laughed, "That's what Matt said when I suggested we have our ceremony there ……. After a beautiful, albeit cold Thanksgiving Eve wedding, we stayed at a nearby place on Cayuga Lake. It was idyllic."

Ray drags his ass to bed without enough energy to change out of his clothes. It's only 8 PM.

Footstools, ski-masks, and flat tires.

The women at 22 Shore Road wait for Cambridge to return from Mac's place. The wait becomes too long for Marilyn and Joey, "I'm really sorry, Jenna, but my overnight shift starts at eleven. I need to get back to Syracuse."

"Don't worry. Grams and Gramps will be back soon. In fact, they're usually back by now. Maybe they're giving us a little extra time. I'll lock up and be fine. Besides, Cambridge will probably stop back when he's done with Mac."

Within minutes of being alone, Jenna gets a call from Joey. "The detective's Land Rover is still at Mac's. He's not in it, so that must mean he's inside the bungalow. Depending on how long the talk goes, he might just give you a call on his way back to Syracuse. Be safe."

Jenna hangs up feeling anything but safe. She putters around the kitchen and walks the bungalow, checking locks on windows and doors, and shutting shades and blinds as she goes. She thinks about distracting herself with some T.V., but opts for a quiet book instead. She has just settled onto the couch in the living room when she senses something amiss.

Mac is freezing his ass off. He's been outside his bungalow since shortly after Cambridge headed toward Jenna's. The former elite forces member knew he'd be paid a visit by the detective, so he dressed in layers, grabbed his tactical rucksack, and set out. He hopped into his Humvee, drove it to a secluded pull-off up the road and backtracked on foot. He headed to a trench that runs along a retaining wall at his property line, pulled a pair of night vision binoculars from his gear, and waited. His instinct and his wait pay off.

Detective Cambridge pulls his Land Rover onto the empty driveway at 20 Shore Road. He goes to the back door and knocks, waits, then knocks again. He makes his way to the front door and repeats the process, this time adding a shout out, "Mr. McLaughlin. Open the door." Within minutes, the detective heads to the back porch, unscrews the lightbulb above the door, bends down, and picks the lock. Then he steps inside.

"What the fuck?" Mac trains his night visions on the big bay window, watches the detective move throughout his house, eventually leave through the back door, twist the bulb back in place, and head toward his Rover. "What the fuck?" Cambridge removes his sport jacket, puts on Mac's Army-issue camouflage parka, gets in the vehicle, and waits. When he sees a set of headlights move toward him from the direction of the Farnsworth's place, the disguised detective ducks down. "What the fuck? That son-of-a-bitch," Mac snarls when Cambridge gets out of his vehicle and enters the wooded tract of land between 20 and 22 Shore Road. As soon as

Cambridge moves deep into the thick, Mac tracks his subject.

Jenna stays frozen on the couch waiting for the eerie feeling to pass. It. Does. Not. Pass. Every nerve ending tingles. Every muscle tightens. Whatever spooked her is confirmed by the sound of footfalls. Instinct tells her it's not Grams and Gramps returning home. She is in danger, and she needs to take action. She moves as quietly and as nimbly as her injuries allow. She leaves the lighted living room and moves to the darkened kitchen. She stands in the center of the room unsure what to do, where to go, "My bedroom? Their bedroom? Should I try the loft? What? Where?" **Pick a place!** the voice in her head screams. She is hobbling toward her room when she sees a space between the refrigerator and the cupboards. Tucked into that space is a small footstool. Jenna squeezes in, sits upon the stool, and makes two calls. The first is to Detective Cambridge. It goes unanswered. The second is to the Cleveland police department.

Cambridge puts on a black ski-mask, and removes the outdoor lightbulb pitching the porch into total darkness. He is crouched low, working the door lock, when he feels the vibration of his cell phone in his pocket. He takes it and silently reads the display: **Jenna Farnsworth.** "Could be checking about McLaughlin. Could have heard a noise. If she's scared, she'll call CPD." He screws the lightbulb back in and is on his way back to his car when the distant wail of sirens breaks the serenity of the tiny lake community. He moves quickly through the tree line, gets into his Land Rover and waits for the responding officer to drive past. He hops out, changes jackets, then drives to Jenna's. He casually shows his detective's badge to the officer standing at the back door, "What's the problem, Officer?"

"We received a call from a woman, who identified herself as Jenna Farnsworth, saying she heard noises outside her place."

"I'm working with Ms. Farnsworth on a case, step aside."

Jenna hears the conversation and calls out, "Detective, I'm glad you're here."

"That's a first."

"There were noises outside. I called you thinking you might still be in the area. When you didn't answer, I called Cleveland."

"I've been waiting for McLaughlin."

"All this time?"

"His Humvee was at his place when I first arrived, it was gone when I went back to talk to him. I figured since I was out here, I'd wait for him to return home."

The CPD officer interrupts, "Did you see or hear anything, Detective?"

He shakes his head, "I was back a ways."

The officer nods, "Noise travels pretty good at the lake."

"Still didn't hear anything, Officer."

"Yes, sir."

"Why don't you take a look around outside. I'll stay with Ms. Farnsworth until her grandparents return."

It's nearly two hours before Grams and Gramps pull onto the driveway. The young CPD officer escorts them to the door, then heads out.

"Jenna. Oh, Jenna, what's happened?" Grams calls out.

"Just a little scare, ma'am. I'm Detective Cambridge from Syracuse PD. Ms. Farnsworth became spooked earlier and called your local police department. I was at the McLaughlin place and came back here to check on her, but now that you're here, I'll be heading out."

The last thing the detective hears Jenna ask, "Why are you so late getting home?"

And her grandfather's answer, "We had to stop for air. One of our tires was flat."

Quiche and takeout.

Camille Chase is at the front door when she hears his voice from behind, "You coming or going, Cami?"

"I was supposed to be gone by now."

"Okay, the answer to my question is going. Something smells good, so I'm thinking you stopped by to cook?"

"Chris let me in to make breakfast. He went to mail an envelope you gave him and then to his place to shower and change. I hope you don't mind." Her topaz sparklers say she doesn't care one way or the other.

"Don't mind. What am I smelling?"

"The spinach and cheese quiche you like. It's all set to cut. I should go."

"You should stay," Ray closes the space between them and closes the door behind her. "We could talk."

"We **should** talk, Raymond Paul Chase," she says while stiffening her spine.

He laughs, "Pushy broad."

"Don't you know it, Raymond?"

He lets her putter around the kitchen a bit, then takes hold of her hand. "Sorry that it took a death sentence for me to…"

She squeezes his hand, "Ray, you're sorry, and I'm sorry. There isn't time to deal with all of that, but there is time for you to tell me what's eating at you."

Ray scoffs, "You should have been a detective, Cami."

She laughs, "You're the detective. I'm an intuitive woman."

"Chris is helping me work a case, he's handling a small part, but an important part."

"And you're working the bigger part, the more important part?"

Ray nods.

"And you're working in secret?"

Ray nods.

"You did this once before, and it almost killed you."

"I know."

"Are you investigating your partner?"

Ray nods.

"Oh, Raymond, is this really how you want to spend your time?"

Ray's eyes mist. "Cami. Where I spend eternity depends on my solving this case."

"What the hell does **that** mean?" Chris demands from the doorway.

Ray gets up from the table, "You shouldn't have heard that."

"Yeah, well I did. You need to tell me what's going on. Last night you said you felt guilty about something, and today you say your eternity depends on your solving this case. Spill it, Old Man, or I'm out of here!"

"Chris!" Camille shouts as she gets up and stands next to Ray.

"Cami. Don't. He's right. Chris, the suspects you're investigating may be rapists, but they aren't our serial rapist. I know—I think I have always known—who the serial rapist known as REDO is. That's all I can tell you, right now."

Chris processes that information and nods.

Ray continues. "You need to pull those guys apart. Clear them fair and square, and when you do, I'll bring you into **my** investigation. Don't cut corners. Don't make mistakes. When the shit hits the fan, I want everyone who reviews your work to confirm its thoroughness and fairness, that way the authorities can turn their focus on the suspect I give them."

Chris turns and walks away.

"Where are you going?" Ray and Camille ask.

"To work. I suggest you do the same, Old Man."

Fayetteville
Caitlyn bumps into her husband on her way out of the master bedroom. "Just getting home?"

"Nope. It was a late one so I crashed in the spare room. I'm heading for a shower, care to join?"

"Wish I could, but I've got a long day ahead. There's a meeting on Grant Timberlake. We're taking another look at him for the Demi Warren killing." She gives her head a little shake, "Sorry, Matt, I can't talk about the case with you."

"Because I studied psychology under Dr. Timberlake."

"Yes."

"For what it's worth, I haven't had any interactions with my former professor for years, and I don't know his son."

"Sorry, but I'm working with Detective Chase on this one. Hopefully, I'll be able to work the REDO case a bit, too. I want to be as prepared as I can be for the task force meeting next week. I hear the guy in charge is a real son-of-a-bitch," she says with a huge kiss. "I'll get takeout on my way home, any preference?"

"Nope. See you tonight." He waits until he hears her Benz purr away, then goes to the master bedroom for a little file review. He starts with the expandable legal files stacked against the wall, "Plenty of stuff to keep me busy."

Planting evidence and DNA testing.

Mac learned pretty quickly what Cambridge was doing during his breaking and entering; he was planting evidence in the former ranger's duffle. The soldier dragged the bulky bag from a closet in the spare room and put it onto the bed Jenna recently vacated, then he paced the small room debating what his move should be and whether he even had a move. "Jenna left that bed and fled my home after Cambridge suggested I was her rapist. Now, he's planted evidence in my duffle, and lurked around her house in my camouflage jacket so she'd think it was me if she looked outside. I have been masterfully setup as the patsy who will go down for the rape of Jenna Farnsworth, especially if there isn't any DNA from the crime scene or Cambridge fucks with it somehow." In the wee hours of morning, Mac parked his ass on the floor, closed his eyes to quell the pounding in his head, and fell asleep. He's plugging in morning coffee when there's a pounding on his back door.

"Mac, we need to talk!"

"Gramps? Hang on."

Emmett Farnsworth isn't through the door when he starts in, "Son. Were you the one terrorizing Jenna last night?"

"No."

"Do you know anything about what happened last night?"

Mac pauses. *I can't tell him. He won't believe me. Nobody will believe me.* "No."

"You weren't lurking in the woods?"

"No."

"You were here, at the bungalow?"

"Yes."

"Did you talk with Detective Cambridge? He said he was waiting for you."

"No."

Gramps tries to square Mac's answers with what he's heard from Jenna. "Don't come around my place. That is not a request, Mac, it's a warning." Gramps turns to leave and almost trips. "What's in the ruck, Staff Sergeant McLaughlin?"

Mac does not answer the question.

SPD

Diane Earls places a call to Detective Chase even though he's called in sick, "Detective, I'm sorry to bother you at home. I know you called in sick, and if you really are sick then please say so, but if you are well enough to come in, I think you should."

"What bee settled in your bonnet, Diane?"

"The brass is in, and they're looking to talk to someone about REDO."

"Where's Cambridge?"

"MIA."

"Be there in ten." He hangs up, gets up, then wishes he hadn't. He waits for a swirl to pass before moving on. "MIA. Jesus, Matt, that better not mean you're out raping."

Diane is MIA from her office when Ray arrives. He leaves a voicemail, "When you have a minute, my office."

The Maggie Gyllenhaal lookalike, steps into the detective's office just as he's removing his Fedora and overcoat. "Need something, Detective?"

"An explanation as to why my blinds are closed."

The admin looks around the room, "Not sure, but they were shut yesterday when I delivered mail to Detective Cambridge. His were too, maybe the cleaning crew closed them."

"Was there any?"

"Any what?"

"Mail."

Diane extends her hand and gives him several envelopes. "There were other pieces, but Detective Cambridge said you two were waiting on something, so he took what he needed."

"Remember what he took?"

"Something from some DNA phenotyping lab." She turns to leave, turns back. "The brass ducked out. Maybe you should go home, Detective. You don't look too good. This place will spread whatever you've got faster than a speeding bullet," she laughs.

"Don't worry, Diane, I'm not contagious."

Ray waits until she closes his door and is down the hall before he sends his trash can sailing. The tin receptacle dents on all sides as it bangs across the room and empties onto the floor. "Fuck. Cambridge has the results. He knows I sent his sample and my sample for DNA testing." The detective busies himself with trash retrieval as he works the problem. "Okay. If Cambridge doesn't suspect I'm on to him, he might think I wanted to test the phenotyping process for accuracy. If he's on to me, I'll be meeting my maker, sooner than expected."

Fayetteville
Cambridge finished rummaging through Caitlyn's files before noon. He removed a few post-it-notes written in the counselor's script and several pieces of paper from the older files that didn't make sense back then, but will come into focus now "**If** she has enough time to connect the dots." Before he starts his next task, he makes a call.

"Ms. Farnsworth, this is Detective Cambridge. Just checking in after last night's excitement."

"It was probably nothing more than my being alone for the first time since the attack. My Gramps went to Mac's this morning and asked him if he was snooping around the bungalow. He denied it and told Gramps that he was at home last night, but you said his truck was gone."

"It was. McLaughlin is lying."

"I guess so."

Matt hangs up in a raging mood. He storms through the house, "If McLaughlin **was** home last night, then he was outside his house. If Mr. Army Man had me in his sights, then he saw me break into his place, take his parka, skulk through the tree line, and try to break into the Farnsworth's place. Well, that fucking plan might have blown up in my face. I wanted to scare Jenna into thinking it was Mac trying to break in, but if he saw me then he knows—way too much. **Fuckin A!** There's incoming from all sides. I need to neutralize one of my threats— Caitlyn. Ray. Mac. Which one is the biggest threat?"

He spends a few minutes fuming then another few minutes reading the DNA phenotyping results on Raymond Chase and Matthew Cambridge. "Have to tell you, Old Man, I'm pretty pissed you ran this test. Question now is whether you were checking DNA phenotyping for its accuracy OR you were testing me." A memory pops, actually two...

"How long were you inside Turner Theater?"
Keith shrugged.
"Venture a guess, Mr. Moreno."
"Ten, maybe fifteen minutes."

~

"Go ahead, Ms. Verde, fill in Moreno's timeline."
"Keith walked me to my car a little before seven, cleaned it off, then went to Turner to watch Zach Taylor. By seven-fifteen or so, we were heading to my place."

Cambridge paces while the pennies drop. "The interviews were interrupted by a knock on the glass. Chase left the room and was back in a few minutes. Two interviews interrupted by Tam Hagino, a CSI tech. What the fuck was so important that she had to interrupt an interview? Two interviews." Cambridge slides his badge onto his hip, his service revolver into his shoulder holster, a second handgun into the back of his jeans, pulls on his trademark sport coat, and threatens the space around him, "The Old Man knows. Ray Chase just became my Number One target."

Cambridge examines the upside of that decision. "One sure way to slow the investigation of me is to get rid of Ray. One way to slow the investigation of REDO is to take out one of the lead detectives. Looks like I'll be killing two birds with one kill shot."

A suspect's kitchen.
An old lady's bedroom.

Ray got back-to-back-to-back calls that morning, all of them interesting, all of them worth his being in the office, even though he felt like shit. He's kicked back now with a mug of coffee, running the calls...

"Ray, it's Caleb Sanchez. I got a call from Trini Kekoa this morning."

"No shit."

"She's an Emergency Room nurse at Ithaca General. She said the SART nurse practitioner told her about the task force. Trini said she wanted to add something on behalf of her cousin. Apparently, they'd been estranged for years, but have been in touch with one another recently. Anyway, there's a place in the Suzi Kekoa statement when she said she started breathing too quickly and the rapist put his hand onto her neck and told her she needed to relax."

"I remember that, Caleb."

"Trini said Suzi thinks the rapist was checking her pulse and might have medical training."

"Anything else?"

"Yeah. I wasn't sure the other day when we talked, but I'm on the task force."

"Is that a good thing?"

"We'll see, Ray."

The detective no sooner hung up when he received a call from Paris, from a woman identifying herself as Mary Raines...

"What can I do for you Ms. Raines?"

"I received a call from Grace Farnsworth, Jenna's grandmother, asking me if I thought Keith Moreno could be a rapist. For what it's worth, and it's probably not worth much coming from his former girlfriend, but he's absolutely not capable of rape. He's a cheater, and he shades the truth, but I know he is not the type of man who would violate a woman."

"How's that, Ms. Raines?"

"Keith told me he and his high school girlfriend ended things because she liked it rough, and he couldn't go there."

"And this girlfriend's name?"

"Monica Farrell. Okay, I've said my piece. Is there anything else you need from me, Detective?"

"Your phone number in Paris."

The third phone call was from Diane Earls, and it set him free...

"Detective Cambridge is on his way in."

"Good. If you need me, I've got a stop to make, then I'll be at home."

Oren Street
Ray grabs the statement Keith Moreno made at SPD from the passenger seat, and before he even knocks, Moreno pulls open the door.

"Where's the asshole?"

Ray laughs. "Not sure. Can I come in?"

"Not unless my lawyer's here."

"How about we both record this conversation?"

Keith gets his cell and presses record. "I'm recording this conversation, Detective Chase. Again, I won't answer questions without my lawyer."

"I won't ask any questions. I just want you to read something."

"Come on in," Keith says with more curiosity than annoyance in his voice.

Ray follows him to the kitchen, "Nice place. You did the work?"

Keith raises a brow, "That's a question and I'm not answering it."

"Right. Sorry." Ray hands him the statement, "Was anything left out of that statement?"

Keith reads, raises his head in thought, reads it again. "Yes."

"Do you want to tell me?"

"It doesn't mention my stopping at Steny Thomas' place to get air in my tire."

"I don't remember you mentioning that."

"You left the interview room to talk to someone in the hall. I told your asshole partner. I think I asked him to check with Steny to see if he has security cameras at the station. Did that asshole leave it out on purpose? You'll check with Steny, right?"

Ray nods. "Nice work on your place, Mr. Moreno." When he rounds his car to get in, he sees someone standing at the window in the house across the street. He drives slowly, sees it's an old lady and pulls to the curb.

Edith Cunningham meets Ray at the front door. She pulls it open before he even knocks, "Don't go setting me right about opening the door without asking who is calling, the other detective already did that."

Ray smiles, "Don't suppose you have a few minutes, Mrs. Cunningham?"

"Have we met? And call me Edith."

"No. I read your name in a report Detective Cambridge wrote up. I'm Detective Ray Chase."

Edith steps aside, "Come on in, Detective. You can put your hat and coat on the sofa. I was just readying myself a cup of tea. Care to join me?"

"Please."

"Let's move to the kitchen. Haven't seen a Fedora much these years."

"I take some ribbing over it, Mrs. Cunningham."

She laughs a sweet old woman's laugh, "I expect you do. Have a seat."

Ray takes the chair that doesn't seem to get much use. When Edith sets the cups, saucers, and teapot onto the table, Ray stands and pulls her seat for her. She smiles at the courtesy.

"So, Ray," she pauses, "I hope you don't mind the informality."

He shakes his head.

"First thing, I like that you drive a car and not one of those boxy things Keith and that other detective drive."

"The boxy things are very popular now."

"I dare say so. Keith drives one, and there was one parked at the Fletcher's place across the street on the night the new girl screamed."

Ray takes a quick look at the interview sheet Cambridge wrote up on his conversation with the elderly woman. *No mention of a car, boxy or otherwise.* "Would you mind telling me about the vehicle at the Fletcher's?"

"Like I told your partner, you best let me talk without interruptions."

Ray nods and sips.

"A scream woke me from sleep, and when I looked out the window there was a boxy car at the Fletcher's place. The snow was blowing at a good clip, but I could tell it was a dark boxy car." She sips, "There's something else about that." Another sip, "Oh yes, the street hadn't been plowed, yet."

"Were there cars at the Moreno place, at the time of the scream?"

"Just the girls' cars, and they were buried deep in snow. Did I mention that the boxy car at the Fletcher's place didn't have a bit of snow on it?"

"No, ma'am. Do you happen to know when Keith got home?"

"No, but I heard Steny's plow come through after I was back in bed. I had some trouble falling back to sleep." She lifts her teacup for a sip, "Did I mention the light was out at Keith's back door? He's usually very good about leaving it on. I told the other detective that the new girl probably forgot to put it on."

Ray checks Matt's interview sheet. *No mention of a back porch light being on or off.*

"Edith, would you mind if I take a look out your bedroom window?"

The woman thrills, "Mind? I haven't had a man in my bedroom for two decades, come on, Ray."

The detective stands at the window overlooking Oren Street. He ponders a bit then assesses. "Blue Victorian next to Moreno's. Driveway is on the left. There's tree cover between the Fletcher's house and the Moreno house. He gets out of the boxy thing—gets into the tree line—gets to the back door—kills the light—gets in—gets out."

"Are you speaking to me, Ray?"

"Talking to myself, I'm afraid," Ray smiles.

"Don't worry, Ray, I do it all the time."

Ray escorts Edith downstairs, grabs his hat and coat from the sofa as she grabs a seat on her rocker. He waves as he gets into his ride, spins his non-boxy thing around, and heads back to 10 Oren. The detective knocks on Keith's door again, waves his phone in his direction and presses record, "Mr. Moreno, what entrance did you use on January 8th?"

"The back door."

"Do you have an outdoor light source at the back door?"

"Yes."

259

"Was it on or off when you left?"

"On."

"And when you returned, on or off?"

"On."

"Are you certain?"

"Yes. The back of the house is really dark because of the tree line. I put it on when I left and it was still on when I got back. That's how I could tell the inside door was open."

Ray is no sooner in his car when he receives a call from Cambridge.

"We keep missing each other, Old Man."

"Count your blessings."

"What?"

"I've got some sort of intestinal thing. Not sure if it's contagious."

"Diane said you were in this morning."

"Yeah. She called me at home, said the brass was in and wanted to talk to one of us. Diane said she couldn't reach you, so I went in."

"What did the brass want?"

"Don't know. They didn't talk to me, they probably wanted to talk to you, so heads up."

"You coming in over the weekend?"

"Nope." Ray ends the call and begins tumbling the last part of the conversation. *Matt Cambridge has **never** asked me about my weekend plans. He's on to me.* Ray grabs his ringing cell from the passenger seat, sees the call is from Cambridge. He lets it go to voicemail then listens to it.

"**Ray, I need a copy of your files on REDO before the task force meeting. Make sure you bring them on Monday.**"

60 Preston Parkway

Ray pulls to the curb in front of his place. He's too tired to get out and climb the half-dozen steps to his front door. He decides to sit awhile. He grabs his cell and places a call. "Brandan, it's Ray Chase. A couple questions for you about Monica Farrell, and one about Evan Sayles."

"Shoot."

"First, does Monica own a car?"

"Nope."

"Second, are you looking at Sayles as being REDO?"

"Nope. Sayles likes to get rough with his women, but it's a mutual thing. Don't understand it, but there you have it."

"But he got rougher than usual with your vic? Any idea why?"

"Monica said Sayles came home one afternoon and found her talking to some guy outside her cabin. She told Sayles the dude was on a ramble and stopped to say hello. When it happened a second time, she said Sayles accused her of cheating. That's when he started smacking her hard."

"Did she have a name for the rambling man?"

"Nope."

"His name is Matt Cambridge," Ray says after he hangs up.

Poofy buns and outdoor naps.

Caitlyn drags her weary ass home well past eight without having stopped for takeout. That forgotten errand smacks her upside the head when she steps through the front door and breaths in. "What is that smell, Matthew?"

"I'd prefer you classify it as an aroma," he mocks her previous braised beef comment.

She enters the kitchen and moves past him toward the stove, removes the cover from a baking dish and inquires, "You cook?"

"I've cooked once or twice in my thirty-eight years."

Caitlyn breathes in, "What is this?"

"My version of chicken pot pie."

"Are those poofy buns on top?"

"Yes, poofy buns," he laughs.

"Is it ready? Can we eat? I'm starved."

"Go sit. I'll serve."

Caitlyn squeals when she sees the table adorned with flowers and candles and her favorite white chilling in an ice bucket. She is smelling the flowers when he speaks from behind.

"Not sitting, Caitlyn."

She smiles and takes her seat. "Is there an occasion I've forgotten?"

"Nope. I figured I'd surprise you."

"Matthew Cambridge, everything about you is a surprise."

"You ain't seen nothing yet, Ms. English."

"I was supposed to get takeout." She eyes her plated chicken pot pie with poofy buns and declares, "This is so much better."

"Maybe," her husband smiles.

60 Preston Parkway

The blare of a horn wakes Ray from an unintended nap. He is slumped over the steering wheel of his car, stiff from the cold, and in desperate need of a piss. He tries to right himself, but can't. He struggles to get his phone from the passenger seat, presses the number three and is instantly connected to Chris' cell phone.

"Dad?"

Ray smiles at the reference.

"Dad?"

"I need help. I'm outside," he struggles.

Chris is at his father's car in seconds, leans him away from the steering wheel, goes around and climbs into the passenger seat, turns on the car, blasts the heat and waits. "What the fuck?"

"I couldn't get out. Must have passed out."

"How long have you been out here?"

"Since two."

"It's almost nine. Do you think I can get you into the house?"

Chase nods.

"The steps. Are you sure?"

"I'll do it."

The men barely make it through the front door when Ray's legs give out and he collapses. He warns his son, "Do. Not. Call. An. Ambulance. Call Cami."

By the time Ray's ex-wife arrives, Chris has managed to get his father sitting upright against one of the walls just inside the front door. Though covered by a mound of blankets, he's in a full-body shake.

"What happened?"

"He passed out in his car and was nearly frozen solid when I found him. He insisted I help him get inside."

The worried woman presses her hand to the slumped man's forehead. He struggles to raise his hand, eventually finds hers, takes it from his head and presses it to his lips. "Cami."

Her sparklers fill with tears, "Ray." At his mother's direction the son rushes to the kitchen, "Chris, put on a kettle of water, dissolve a chicken bouillon, pour a glass of orange juice, and bring them to me." She spoon feeds her former husband, relaxes some when color returns to his ashen face and his shaking begins to slow.

"I need to piss, Cami."

With less struggle than before, Chris gets his father up and to the bathroom.

Upon their return, Cami points to the living room couch that she's set with pillows and blankets, "Get some rest, Ray. Then I'll tell you how things will be from now on."

Ray's lip curls. He plops his ass onto the couch, "That's my Cami."

Peek-a-boo and pizza.

Caitlyn crawls from bed in search of her husband. She checks the clock, "Four-forty?" She grabs her robe and pitter-patters through the house. She is just about to call his cell when she finds the note he left. **Needed to hit the road. I'll call.** The abandoned wife heads back to the master, flips on the lights, grabs a throw from the foot of the bed, takes a seat on the floor, and begins her search for REDO. "Who are you? Where are you right now?"

60 Preston Parkway
Early morning sun shines bright against the living room window. Ray groans at the glare, gets himself to a sitting position, and waits for the world to right itself. He makes his way to the bathroom and then to the kitchen without any assistance. He startles his ex-wife and son when he enters.

Camille bounces off her seat, "Here, sit. I'll get you something."

Ray does as he's told. "Sorry for the inconvenience last night. I need to slow it down a bit."

"You will. We'll make sure of it," Camille bosses.

Ray nods and eagerly accepts the mug of coffee she offers.

"This is how things are going to be, Raymond. Chris and his friend, Jonah, are setting a bed in the spare room down here for you. Your desk and chair, and anything else you need from your upstairs office will be moved into the corner of the living room. Chris will be bunking on the couch, and I'll be moving into your upstairs bedroom." Camille's sparklers defy rebuff. "Any comments, Ray?"

"Nope. A question though."

Camille nods.

"What kind of friend is Jonah?"

"Boyfriend. Any comments, Old Man?"

"Nope."

"Any questions?"

"Good God, no."

BUFFALO

Matt Cambridge arrives in The Nickel City shortly before 7 AM having already stopped for breakfast. He pulls his Land Rover to a stop on Maplewood Lane, not far from Chet and Evelyn Dolan's place. He reads the information he found online about Marilyn's sister and brother-in-law. "Chet Dolan, 35, Buffalo lifer, BS in electrical engineering from Buffalo University, makes $100 grand a year. Evelyn Dolan, 35, Buffalo lifer, BS in landscape design from Buffalo U," he pauses and looks up the street, "Nice yardwork at their place. Evelyn probably putts around outside while she stays home with my boy."

The investigator puts his research aside and starts the Rover when he sees the happy little family heading to their car an hour later. He waits until they pass then bangs a U-turn and follows them away from the tree-lined, immaculately cared for neighborhood. The Dolan's park their SUV at a grocery store and head in, Cambridge follows suit. He grabs a cart and goes shopping, arriving at checkout right behind the happy family.

Chet does the conveyor-shuffle, while Evelyn occupies a very inquisitive Joseph strapped into a kangaroo carrier. When she and her ride along reach for a magazine at the checkout counter, the man in line behind them says, "Peek-a-boo."

Joseph's face lights up.

"Peek-a-boo," Cambridge says over and over.

The boy open-mouth, drool-laughs.

"He likes you."

"He's a cute kid. He looks a lot like my son," Cambridge smiles.

"Really? How old is your boy?"

"Eight-months. This guy looks a little younger, though I can't tell for sure because of the carrier."

"Nope. Joseph is eight-months."

"Joseph. That's a great name." He turns his attention away from the woman and addresses the boy, "It's nice to meet you Joseph. I'm Matt."

"Nice to meet you, Matt." With that, the Dolans are on their way with a final wave from Joseph's bio-dad.

Cambridge lets the family get home before he pulls out of the grocery store parking lot. He's back on Maplewood Lane in no time, and is just about to settle in for the long haul when he sees a bronze Nissan Rogue heading his way. He grabs a ball cap from the passenger seat, pulls it on and sinks low, "Marilyn." He waits. He watches.

Marilyn pulls onto the driveway behind the Dolan's SUV. She greets her sister, then takes Joseph into her arms.

Cambridge remembers when he took Marilyn. Remembers the release that created his boy. He hardens.

Fayetteville

A bitter cold assaults Caitlyn as she makes her way to her Mercedes SUV. She hurriedly opens the door and pulls it closed with a solid thwomp. The engine purrs to life with the touch of a finger, the one she runs along an envelope she tossed onto the passenger seat. Sorrow fills her. She bats away a tear, turns on the headlights and is half-way down the driveway when Matt pulls next to her. "Shit," she whispers. She waits for him to get out of his car before lowering her window. "I have an errand to run. Shouldn't be more than an hour."

"You want company?"

She smiles. "Can't. It's a lawyer/client thing. Do you want to meet at Michael's for dinner?"

"Sure. I'll follow you out, then head to the station. I'll meet you at the restaurant in an hour."

"Perfect," she beams as she puts her SUV in reverse.

Matt gets back into his Rover and follows from a distance.

60 Preston Parkway

Ray greets Caitlyn at the door and ushers her in. The reconfiguration of his home is complete and his company is in the kitchen. He takes Caitlyn's coat, hangs it on a hook, and leads her inside. Ray walks to Camille's side, "Caitlyn English, this is my ex-wife, Camille Beausoleil Chase." The women greet one another with knowing smiles.

Ray pushes on, "And this is my son, Chris, and his friend, his boyfriend, Jonah."

Chris laughs, "That couldn't have been easy."

"Easier than the cancer, kid."

Caitlyn walks to the men and shakes their hands. She turns to Ray, "Am I to talk freely?"

"Yes."

"Very well. I have the revised Last Will and Testament, and I did a trust as well. Is it your intention to sign off on them today?"

"Yes."

"Camille and Chris are beneficiaries, so I'll need Jonah to witness them. Is that acceptable?"

"It is."

"Okay. Why don't we sit while you read them."

Camille, Chris, and Jonah leave the lawyer and the client alone.

A dark boxy vehicle inches down Preston Parkway for the fifth time. "What the fuck?" was asked when Cambridge saw his wife enter his partner's place. Those words have been repeated with each ensuing circle around the block. "What the fuck?" Nervous energy pulses and a burn settles in his gut. "Are they working together? Does she know? Is he telling her?" The detective keeps a close eye on the time. Fifty-five minutes pass before the front door opens. He seethes when his wife enters his partner's arms. "What the fuck?" He starts his car when she enters hers.

He waits for her to leave.

She doesn't leave.

He places a call. "Hey, Caitlyn. Where are you?"

There's a sniffle and a pull of a breath, "On my way."

"Are you crying?"

"No. No. I think I'm getting a cold. Would you mind if we do Michael's some other time?"

"Nope. How about I grab a pizza and meet you at home."

"Thanks, Matt."

They disconnect. She sits another five minutes thinking about Ray's parting words. "Stay safe." She starts her Benz, the welcoming purr wraps warm thoughts of Ray. "Stay safe. It must be something he says when people leave. It's sweet."

Cambridge hangs back until long after Caitlyn leaves, "Let's see if anyone else comes out."

One down, two to go.

Chris shuts the front door after Jonah leaves and heads to the kitchen to help his mother cleanup. "Where's Dad?"

"Resting. He said to forget the angle you've been working. The two of you are going all-in. I think he senses time is running out."

Chris opens his arms to his mother. "Do you wish he didn't tell us?"

Camille gently pushes from her son's embrace, "Not even a little bit. I **need** this time with him."

"Me too."

Fayetteville
Caitlyn is sitting on the floor of the living room, a red and white checked tablecloth spread out in front of the fireplace and throw pillows pressed along the front of the couch. She directs her husband to her with a shout out, "Bring the pizzas in here, we're having a picnic."

"What is it with you and the floor?"

She smiles. It fades.

Matt puts the pizza on the cloth and tosses his sport coat onto a chair. He plants his ass on the floor next to his wife and stretches his arm across the back of her shoulders. Caitlyn buries her face into his shoulder and falls apart.

"Caitlyn."

She sobs.

"Is something wrong?"

She sobs.

"I'm a detective, and I'm detecting you might be upset."

She starts laughing, then crying, then combines the two in a rather ugly display. "Matt, I'm sorry. The errand I did earlier. A client of mine is dying, and I delivered his final paperwork."

"This person is more than a client?"

"Yes."

"I'm sorry, Caitlyn. How long before…"

"Not long," she says on a new set of tears.

Matt hugs his wife close. *One down, two to go,* he smiles.

60 Preston Parkway

Ray sits at his desk and Chris sits on the couch with two laptops open in front of him. "What's first, Old Man?"

"Research Matthew James Cambridge. I want to know every-fucking-thing about the son-of-a-bitch. Where he was when he took his first piss—where he was when he took his last piss—and where he was for every piss in between. Get as much as you can before we talk. I have some work to do."

Chris pushes off the couch and begins pacing. He easily clocks a quarter mile before stopping, and staring, and stammering. "Matt Cambridge? Your partner? Matt Cambridge? The husband of Caitlyn English? You think Matt Cambridge is REDO, a serial rapist?"

"I know it."

"Holy shit!" He paces a bit, then addresses his father, "No interruptions. I have major work to do."

Ray smiles. "Chris. In case I forget to tell you, I'm glad we had this time together, and I'm proud of you."

Chris doesn't comment because he can't.

"Son. Before you start, why don't you sit and listen for a few. I'll read the victim statements, maybe something will jump out."

"I'm going to key in stuff, and I'm making a recording, okay?"

"Yes."

"Okay, shoot."

Ray begins reading. "Marilyn McGinn, August 29, 2014 ...."

Chris stopped keying as soon as Ray started reading. He's been as still as a statue, absorbing every disturbing word, his mind cataloguing like a computer.

Ray tosses the pages onto his desk. "I'm gonna hold off on Monica Farrell's statement, and I don't have Mandy Kelleher's yet. Anything interesting jump out?"

"First off, I'm removing Trini Kekoa from this review. There are too many variables. She wasn't a repeat rape, and in the rapist's mind, she wasn't really a new rape either."

"Okay."

"As for the others, Marilyn, Suzi, Connie, and Jenna, they all mentioned: mask, knife, jeans, and a cut breast. They recounted near-identical sequences of events and sentences spoken. There were little nuances like minty breath and chapped lips, and there are a few notable variables as well. Suzi was the only one who said he touched her neck when she became upset. She said the knife he used had a hole in the center of it, and he had his finger through the hole. Connie Braxton said the rapist used a gold-tipped knife. Jenna said he wore an undershirt. The other women didn't mention what he wore on top. He had to have worn something, right?"

Ray nods. "And whatever he wore would have his victim's blood on it. I need to dig deep into these files and check the information on the new victims." His plan is cut short.

"Right now," Camille says from the kitchen, "you need to take a break."

Ray yawns his agreement.

Fayetteville

Cambridge clears away the pizza box and the red and white checked cloth from the floor. He places an array of throw pillows in front of the fireplace and grabs a cashmere blanket from the couch, "You need some unwinding."

"Here? On the floor?"

"When in Rome, Caitlyn."

The husband unwinds the hell out of his wife, on the floor, in front of the fire. When she turns the corner to slumber, he eases himself up and gets to work. He grabs his sport coat, heads to the spare bedroom for his work bag, and

Sheryll O'Brien

heads outside to slap a GPS tracker onto his wife's Benz.

Wedding rings and suspicious minds.

Ray gets out of bed and moves to the living room, waking Chris in the process. He rummages through a cardboard box, then another, grabs the Jenna Farnsworth file, and flips through it.

"What are you doing? It's two in the morning. What are you looking for?"

"The transcript from the UU SART examination on Jenna Farnsworth. I don't think I made a copy for my home files—"

"Wait, Dad. Let me record this."

"Okay."

"Let's start again. What are you looking for?"

"The transcript from the UU SART examination on Jenna Farnsworth. I don't think I made a copy for my home files."

"But you saw one at work?"

"Yes."

"There's something in it."

"Yes, I think." He runs his hand across his head, then shakes it. "I'm tired, Chris. My brain's fried, but I think Jenna mentioned a wedding ring during her interview, but it's not on the victim statement I read you earlier. Right?"

"Right."

"I'm getting mixed up with all of the victim's details."

"Can you get a copy of the SART sheet or get the information from someone without having to go to the station?"

Ray stops looking through the files. "Yes." He checks the clock and makes the very inappropriate late call.

Beard Park Condo

Joey Mayer answers on the second ring. "Detective Chase, I don't think I've ever received a call from you, certainly not at this hour."

"And you didn't receive this one, either."

Joey feels the weight of that statement especially since it's coming from Chase in the middle of the night. "What's going on, Detective?"

"First, we **did not** talk. Second, I'm working an angle on my own time. I do not want interference from **anyone**. Third, even though we did not talk, you can and should discuss this call with Marilyn, although stress to her the importance of not repeating any of this. Fourth, is the reason for this intrusion. I need to know if you accept my previous terms."

"Whatever it takes to get REDO, Detective."

"Good. I can't get my hands on the SART recording or transcript made during the exams of Jenna Farnsworth. I want you to think it through, then rattle off things you remember from her description of the rapist."

Joey jumps right in, "Mask, jeans, undershirt, knife, dark eyes, minty breath, wedding ring."

Ray's hands tremble. "Wedding ring," he repeats, "You're sure?"

"Yes."

"Okay. This next part, you might not know the answers, but I'm hoping you can flush them out for me. Ms. Farnsworth was new to Syracuse and had to have run mundane errands associated with relocation. Can you find out where she went?"

"I'm meeting with her tomorrow." She checks the clock, "Actually, I'm meeting with her later today at her grandparents' place on Oneida Lake. Is that soon enough?"

"Yes. I don't expect anything to happen between now and then."

Marilyn snuggles close to Joey, "What was that about?"

"I'll tell you, but you can't repeat a word of this."

Marilyn unsnuggles. "I won't say anything to anyone."

"Ray Chase is working the REDO case on his own time. He doesn't want **anyone** knowing or interfering with his work. I think we should assume that includes Matt Cambridge, although Chase didn't say so explicitly. He asked me to repeat identifiers Jenna used during her exams."

"I heard."

"Then he asked me to check with Jenna about errands she did when she arrived in Syracuse."

"This is odd, Joey."

"I know." She quiets. She bounces the conversation around in her head, then does a compare and contrast of all of the victim statements. As SRCC counselor, she was in the room when Marilyn did her first and second SART exams and when Jenna did hers, and she's read reports from other crisis centers on REDO victims. The information starts a swirl in her head. One by one, the threads start twisting together and wrapping around Ray's words.

Don't talk about this. **Mask.** *Working an angle.* **Jeans.** *My own time.* **Undershirt.** *Don't want interference from anyone.* **Knife.** *We did not talk.* **Dark eyes.** *Tell Marilyn.* **Minty breath.** *Talk to Jenna.* **Wedding ring. Wedding ring.** *Wedding...*

Joey bolts from bed.

"What's wrong!? What is it!?"

"Ray Chase thinks the newly married Matt Cambridge is REDO!" A terrifying memory bangs...

"You do not say **one word** to Marilyn about this."

"I say what I want when I want."

"Not. About. This."

Cambridge nodded.

"I need your word."

"You have it."

"Marilyn gave birth to REDO's son."

"There's DNA—the golden thread to pull. **Fuckin A!**"

Fayetteville

Cambridge wakes with a start and finds an empty place on the floor where his wife once lay. "Caitlyn!" he shouts. Awareness edges in as he moves through the rooms. He pulls a deep breath, "What is that aroma?"

His wife laughs, "Cinnamon buns. They're from some sort of popping can. Michelle told me about them, and they look delicious. They're almost ready for the icing."

"Ice them. I'll be back in two for two."

The husband and wife sip coffee, eat cinnamon buns, and lick melty icing from their fingers. Their time is playful and easy. *She doesn't know*, Matt smiles inside. "Do you have plans today?"

Caitlyn lip-smacks some icing from her fingers, "I think I might polish off these scrumptious little yummies while I catch up on some REDO work."

"It's Sunday."

"It's REDO."

"If you're gonna eat these in the bedroom, don't get any icing on the carpet."

"Not to worry. If I drop some, I'll lick it off," she teases.

"Maybe I'll stick around to watch."

"Are you heading out?"

"I'm way behind at the station. I'll be there most of the day. Do you feel like cooking?"

"It'll have to be something like omelets. I haven't shopped."

"I did. Check the fridge drawers."

Caitlyn pushes from the table and runs to the mammoth stainless side by side. "Oh. My. God. I didn't see all this when I grabbed the popping can this morning. When did you shop? What do I do with...?"

"Stew beef and veggies," he says as he makes his way out of the kitchen.

"But how do I?"

"I believe you said you can read a recipe, wifey."

"Read this, hubby," she says with a snip, then laughs at his laugh. A memory of that laugh pushes in...

"I'm done," Caitlyn dropped her pen onto her pad, pushed away from the conference table at which she'd been sitting for hours.

The detective checked his watch, "Eleven-thirty. Sorry for keeping you so late Ms. English."

"Not a problem, Detective. We made some very good headway, so the time was well spent." She started picking up and packing up, stopped at the knock on the door, straightened her skirt, and ran a hand through her hair when *he* entered the room.

"ADA English, Detective Cambridge. Looks like you're about finished for the evening."

"Yes, sir. Just packing up before heading out."

"If you have a moment, English, my office."

She shoved the remaining files and paperwork into her briefcase, smiled at the detective, and followed her boss. When she and he arrived at her car more than an hour later, the detective was waiting.

"Did you forget something, Detective Cambridge?"

"Just making sure Ms. English made it to her car safely, DA James. Have a good evening you two."

The ADA smiled when she saw the detective behind her at the red light...continued smiling when he followed her home.

Matt opened her door and offered her his hand.

"Did you forget something, Detective Cambridge?" She mimicked her boss.

"Just making sure you made it home safely, Ms. English."

"I doubt much could happen with you—"

"Stalking you?" he laughed big.

"I was going to say following me," she laughed.

Beard Park Condo

The women left their bed in the wee hours. They have been on the couch since then talking in fragmented sentences brought on by the shock of Joey's theory about Matt Cambridge. They are exhausted from lack of sleep and have headaches from their early morning mentalcartwheeling. "Hope this helps," Joey yawns, as she hands Marilyn an enormous bowl of coffee.

"Are we still thinking Matt Cambridge is REDO?" Marilyn yawns into the bowl.

"I haven't changed my mind on that, although my mind's not functioning."

Marilyn gets up and goes to the spare room, "Meet me in the kitchen." She grabs The Box from the closet shelf, shuffles down the hall, and puts it on a counter. She removes this and that, rummages through the remaining contents, and removes a stack of pictures of her son. The two women take seats at the table and pass them back and forth. They say nothing. One begins to cry, followed soon by the other.

Fayetteville

Caitlyn finds a recipe for crockpot stew online, then finds a crockpot on a shelf under the counter. "Huh. Where'd you come from?" She pulls the instruction booklet from inside the never-been-used-cookery, reads the step by steps, loads it up with ingredients, and plugs the sucker in. "That's it?" she ponders as she sets the kitchen timer for six hours. "I think I **like** the crockpot!"

While dinner is being made in the kitchen, the ADA takes to the floor in her bedroom. She divides the colorful binders into three stacks, "There's a Syracuse stack, an Aurora stack, an Ithaca stack, and now there is a lone notebook for Geneva. Another community. Location. Location. Location. Stay with that angle. But which location? There has to be a thread running through these communities, or one that binds them. Why can't I find it?" Hours of review pass. She's analyzed REDO's actions, compared and contrasted victim timelines and statements, took copious notes, created numerous charts, drew a map of Upstate NY, and in the end she divided the binders back into their original stacks having accomplished little for her day's effort. "Syracuse and Aurora have the highest number of rapes. Maybe he lives in one place and visits the other."

"You're talking to yourself again."

She yelps like a frightened puppy, "Will you **please** announce yourself from the door!?"

"I just did."

"The other door, Matthew."

"What other door?"

"The one you enter from outside."

He laughs, "Sorry. By the way, something smells amazing."

She rights herself from the floor and pushes past him. "I'll call you when the table is set."

He grabs an orange binder and flips through the pages. "You've been busy, Caitlyn." Tucked into the back pocket of the binder is a hand drawn map of the Finger Lakes region with Syracuse, Aurora, Ithaca, and Geneva spaced appropriately, and travel routes and travel times between locations written beneath them, "Too fucking busy."

They know.

Ray moves aside the curtain and looks out the front window. He lets the cover fall back into place with annoyance. "It's Cambridge. Chris, take your mother to the spare room and be quiet." Ray puts on his coat and hat before opening the door, "What are you doing here?"

"Came to see how you're doing. You've been out of the station a lot lately. You heading out?"

"No. Don't want to catch a chill."

"I could come in," Matt suggests.

"Not a good time. What do you want, Matt?"

"Just checking in, Old Man," he says on a turn. Cambridge opens the door of his Rover and before sliding in he offers the real reason for his visit.

"You look like **death** warmed over, Ray."

He knows I'm dying.

"And you're a piece of shit, Matt."

He knows I'm REDO.

Fayetteville

Caitlyn is finishing dinner dishes when Matt returns from his errand. "That was quick."

"So was your cleanup. How about we go fuck a bit?"

Caitlyn smacks him with a dishtowel, "Matthew James Cambridge, don't be so crass," she laughs.

"Don't be so uppity with me, Counselor. You know you love a bad boy. I'll give you to the count of ten, then I'm coming for what's mine."

Caitlyn squeals and scampers away. She starts for the master, opts for the spare room, the one Matt crashes in. She slides between two pieces of furniture and hunkers low. Her heart begins pounding as he searches for her.

"You'd better come out, Caitlyn. The longer it takes for me to find you, the worse it's going to be," he singsongs.

She silences a giggle.

"Your fate is in my hands, wifey."

Her heart thumps wildly as playful thoughts of her man finding, conquering, and sexually pleasing her, excite. Then she hears something in his voice.

"Remember, you **caused** this."

The trembling woman senses her husband is near. She looks up and finds him towering over her, tears sting her eyes. "That wasn't fun, Matt. You sounded so..." She begins sobbing.

Cambridge reaches down and helps her out of her place. "I'm sorry. I didn't mean to scare you." He takes her to sit at the edge of the bed. Holds her until she stops trembling. "That wasn't fun for you?"

"No."

"Don't worry, Caitlyn, I won't chase you for fun, ever again."

Caitlyn relaxes into his embrace, begins bouncing a bit at the edge of the mattress. "Why don't we spend the night here? It's a comfortable-cozy little den," she whispers against his chest.

"Den of iniquity," he laughs. He lifts her and tosses her onto his bed. Imagines that her playful squeal is her rape scream.

The entwined couple is pulled from sleep by the ring of Caitlyn's cell. She looks at the display.

He looks at the clock. "It's three-thirty, Caitlyn."

"Hello ……. Yes, this is Ms. English." She inches her way up as she listens intently. "I'll be right there."

"Right where?"

"My client is passing," she says on a choke.

He holds his smile until she rushes away.

The passing of Raymond Chase.

Camille stays with Ray while Chris talks to his father's doctor in the living room. "It's happening so fast," the son chokes.

"Ray's cancer was invasive. There wasn't much we could do beyond palliative measures. Your father wanted no part of any care we could provide. He said he didn't want to wither away."

"But he said he had a handful of months."

"On the high end with rest and care. I suspect Raymond has pushed himself to the limits, making every second count." The doctor touches the son's shoulder. "Do you want any medical staff to come in?"

"To do what?"

"Be with your father, and they could assist you and your mother."

Chris looks to his partner for help.

Jonah shakes his head. "Camille won't want anyone."

"He's right. Just tell me what to do when it happens."

"Call me. I'll notify the proper authorities. If there is anyone who needs to be here you should call them."

"I already did."

Chris ushers the doctor out and the arriving Caitlyn in. "My father asked to see you. Come on."

Camille smiles when Caitlyn enters the room, "He's very desperate to talk to you, Ms. English."

The lawyer, the friend, sits next to the dying man and takes his hand, "Ray, it's Caitlyn."

He opens his eyes and tries a smile. He mouths a few words.

She leans close, puts her ear to his lips and waits.

"MATT CAMBRIDGE IS REDO."

Her eyes fly wide with shock—
his fix and dilate.

Before the body's cold.

Chris helps move Caitlyn away from the deathbed and out of the room. He sets her on the living room couch with Jonah and heads back to his mother. He finds her lying beside the only man she ever loved—the man who was gone for decades—the man who came back for a handful of days before leaving again.

"Mom. Can I do anything for you?"

"You can give me some time alone with Ray."

The young man leaves his mother to her grief, takes a moment for himself, then continues his father's work. When he enters the living room, he finds Onondaga County ADA English slumped over her knees in a full-on state of panic, his boyfriend rubbing soft circles on her back.

"I'll get some .... What should I get?" Chris asks numbly.

"Tissues. Get tissues," Jonah suggests. "And water?" he shrugs.

Chris returns from his hunting and gathering, "Ms. English, can you drink some of this? Should I call—"

She raises her head and stammers the words, "Don't call **him**!"

"No, of course not," Chris ensures. "Do you need medical assistance?"

"No." She begins trembling, "You shouldn't be assisting me, Chris. Your father." She breaks down in tears. "You should be with Ray."

"My mother wants some alone time." He considers his next words... "ADA English. I know what my father said to you. I know his words are true, or at least as true as his investigation into Matt Cambridge suggests at this point."

"Investigation?" She follows the point of Chris' hand to a desk completely covered with paperwork and cardboard boxes stacked nearby on the floor. She is pulled to them by some unseen force. She sits in Ray's chair, sure she still feels his heat. Tears sting again. She wipes them away and begins reading. With each paper she puts aside, the tremble in her hand becomes greater and greater. When she can handle no more, she swivels the chair and addresses Chris. "We need help with this. Why was your father conducting this investigation in secret?"

Camille Chase answers from the doorway, "Because of Brian Stewart."

"Who is Brian Stewart?"

"Was, Ms. English. Brian Stewart was Ray's partner when he first joined the force. They were beat cops when Ray accused Brian of being dirty. My husband took a huge risk coming forward with his accusations, both personally and professionally. Brian was part of a long line of Stewart cops, and Ray felt the immediate weight of his charge of impropriety. The blue line stood in solidarity with Brian. No one wanted to partner with Ray, and for his own safety, the brass kept him off the streets. Going into the station every day took every ounce of strength that man had. And as bad as all of that was, everyone thought Ray was wrong—I thought Ray was wrong. By the time the full story came to light, Ray and I were over, and Brian was dead, by his own hand. Raymond Chase was vindicated, but it took years for him to piece his life together and to get a foothold at work. I'm sure your husband benefited from Ray's inability to see what was in front of him, or his fear of acting on it."

"I never heard any of this."

"It was long before your time, Ms. English. And the SPD has a way of keeping dirty secrets secret."

Caitlyn stands, puts on her coat, gathers her things, and heads for the door. "I am very sorry for the passing of Detective Ray Chase. I know what I have to do, and I hope you will allow me some time to do it. If it is your hope that Ray solves the REDO case, please do not notify any authorities about his death." Caitlyn looks at her watch, "I'll be in contact with you within four hours. If I miss that mark you may proceed as you wish."

Camille walks to Caitlyn and embraces her. "Do what you must, and please stay safe."

The counselor's eyes sting, "Ray said those words to me. Quite often, actually."

"That's because he wants" Camille pauses and fixes, "that's because he wanted you to stay safe, Caitlyn."

REDO

Please listen, there's more!

Caitlyn makes a phone call from her Benz. The call may very well get her fired.

District Attorney Weston James barks into the phone, "ADA English, there'd better be a good reason for this pre-sunrise call."

"I know who REDO is, and I'm in trouble, sir. Will you meet me at the office? Please?"

"Forty-five minutes."

"I'll be there in an hour. I'm sorry for my delay, sir, but I want your car in the underground garage and away from prying eyes before I pull in."

"English, do you need protection?"

"Not yet."

She disconnects from the call, sits in her car, sure that when she takes it back onto the road she will be followed by Detective Cambridge. "My car has GPS tracking on it, I just know it," she aches with the knowledge.

Fayetteville
Matt Cambridge waits in his Rover for his wife's SUV to move from in front of Ray's house. When she begins to roll, he watches the tracker. "You're not heading home, Caitlyn. You're heading downtown. To your office?" He bangs that around a bit, "Maybe you're filing some sort of death papers? Let's hope," he smiles. He puts

his thoughts and questions aside when his cell rings, "Caitlyn, where are you?"

"I'm heading to the office. I need to produce another document before," she chokes. "It might be awhile. I'm sorry."

"No problem."

The detective drives downtown and pulls his Rover to a stop across the street from the DA building just as his wife pulls her Benz into the underground parking garage. He waits a half hour before leaving. "Looks like you're alone—for now. When you leave your office, wifey, you'll have company."

Cambridge starts his Rover and heads to Ray's street.

District Attorney's Office

Caitlyn goes directly to the inner sanctum and shuts the door behind her. "I would appreciate it if we could put formalities aside, sir."

"Proceed."

"Detective Ray Chase passed away an hour ago from complications of a recently diagnosed illness. There are four people who know of his passing: his ex-wife, his son, his son's partner, and yours truly. A handful of days ago, Ray told me about his illness and asked me to handle his final papers. At the end of each meeting he cautioned me to stay safe. Curious, but nothing more. Two days ago, I delivered his final papers to his home which had been turned into some sort of work center. There were several laptops, files strewn about, and several cardboard boxes used for file storage. At three-thirty this morning, I was called to the home of Detective Raymond Chase. I was escorted into his bedroom and ushered to his deathbed where he whispered his final words into my ear." Caitlyn begins trembling and slumps into a seat that has not been offered. "Detective Chase identified the serial rapist known as REDO as my husband, Matthew Cambridge."

The DA leans against his desk, "ADA English—"

"Please let me finish. Once I gathered myself from the shock of those words, I had a discussion with Chris Chase, Ray's son. He said he knew what his father whispered to me and that the investigation Ray was doing would support his claim. Then Chris directed me to Ray's workstation. I spent many minutes reviewing months' if not years' worth of investigative information. There are copies of SPD files, documentation from Aurora and Ithaca PDs, and handwritten notes about the recent Geneva rape. Ray had records of recent phone conversations with members of APD and IPD, and had connected data he received from both. I saw charts, and pages and pages of notes, and questions, and outlines. There is a page that has the words, DNA phenotyping on it. After sitting with that a bit, I think Ray wanted to use this type of profiling to get the ethnicity and physical composite of the rapist. I'm not sure how long Ray suspected Matt, but he might have been planning to use phenotyping to weed through other suspects before accusing his partner."

The DA ponders, "Getting DNA from the forensic department on known rape victims to run phenotyping would be near impossible, and if he did it without going through proper legal channels his results would have been fruit of the poisonous tree. Any defense attorney would succeed in getting the results tossed. But .... if he ran a sample on someone who wasn't a suspect who later became a suspect—"

"Sorry for the interruption, but I have a thought. Ray knew his time was running out, maybe his intentions had nothing to do with the court system. Maybe he just needed to know."

"Possible, but it's still an incomplete process without DNA from our crime scenes to tie things together."

"We may never know his intent, but this is what I do know. The work Ray did is remarkable. He developed compare and contrast grids for the victims, and..." The counselor blanches.

The DA notices. "English, what just happened?"

"His work product is very much like my work product. Sir, I've been working the REDO case from home recently. When I sat with my files yesterday, I realized there were things missing, post-it notes I'd made, and a few documents and faxes. At the time, I thought I might have misplaced things on the shuffle between my house and the office, but..." The counselor has a flashback to earlier that evening. She begins trembling and pulling rapid breaths. "And tonight … tonight … my husband, the man who might be a sadistic serial rapist stalked me through our home. I thought we were playing Hide 'n' Seek and that it was fun and games, until it became anything but fun—it became downright terrifying."

DA James picks up his phone.

"No! Don't! You can't have him arrested!"

"ADA English. I can, and I will!"

"Not yet. Please listen, there's more!"

You have a plan?

The DA hands his employee a finger of whiskey. "Proceed."

"Do you know anything about a situation with the Syracuse PD involving Ray Chase and Brian Stewart."

"The situation, as you refer to it, was before my time, but I am aware of the particulars."

"I only learned about this a few minutes ago and the information came from a biased source, Camille Chase, the ex-wife of Ray Chase. Her story is that Ray accused his partner of being a dirty cop. At first, it appeared Ray was wrong, but the full story eventually came to light after Brian Stewart's suicide. Ray was vindicated, but by then, the situation had taken a toll on the man's personal life, and the detective's professional life."

The DA nods.

"The implication made by Camille was that Ray couldn't accuse another partner without rock-solid proof. If we charge in too soon, it will be the Onondaga DA against the Syracuse PD. Cooperation will cease, and any evidence Ray's accumulated will have a taint."

The DA returns the receiver to the cradle and moves behind his massive desk. "You have a plan?"

"I do. The first part is distasteful, but necessary. I suggest we transport Detective Chase by ambulance to UU, admit him as a living patient. Of course, his body would be transported to the morgue."

"Why on God's green earth would we do that?"

"If Cambridge thinks Chase is still alive, but hospitalized, he'll think the Chase family will be by Ray's bedside, leaving the Chase home empty. He'll make a move to get into Chase's house and snoop around. Ray's been working from home, Matt knows that. If he thinks Ray was onto him, he's going to want Ray's files. If we get those files moved here and let Cambridge go in, maybe we could get him on camera and start building our case. Once we have the files, we could put together a task force to work the information, maybe put our investigators on the case." Her momentum stops, "Would you permit me a moment? I'd like to get something from my office."

The DA nods.

A minute later, Caitlyn returns. Her hands are latex-gloved and she's holding a navy blue journal in one hand and an overstuffed yellow envelope in the other. "This is what I went for," she waves the journal. "This is what I found in my In-Box," she waves the envelope. "It's from Ray Chase."

The DA gets up and leads Caitlyn into his adjoining conference room. She dumps the contents onto the table. He grabs a pair of gloves from a credenza. They start unfolding this and reading that. "Get some legal pads and pens, ADA."

"Before we do that, sir, we need to decide how to handle Ray Chase. I told his family I would be in touch with them within four hours, and if they didn't hear from me in that amount of time they could do whatever they felt appropriate."

"Call them. Tell them an ambulance will be transporting Detective Chase to UU where he will be admitted. Tell them not to talk to anyone about Ray. Get supplies, put on some coffee, I need to make a call."

Before the DA shuts the door, the ADA hears him say, "Sorry for the early hour, Franklin, but I need a rather big favor."

"Franklin Moss, Syracuse Medical Examiner." Caitlyn smiles. It fades when she thinks about the deceased Raymond Chase.

The DA returns with a nod, then he and she begin working the documents scattered on the conference room table. At the bottom of the pile, Caitlyn finds several small envelopes. "There are seven in all." She reads the names written on the front of each: "Marilyn McGinn. Joey Mayer. Detective Brandan Kelly. Detective Caleb Sanchez. Chris Chase. Caitlyn English. Ray Chase." Her brow raises at Ray's envelope, but her attention goes to the one addressed to her. "The words confidential and urgent are underlined." She opens it and begins reading aloud.

Caitlyn.

There is no doubt in my mind that Matthew James Cambridge is REDO. I told Chris to make sure you get the files from my house when I die or if I become incapacitated. Matt knows I am on to him, and he will make a move to get my stuff.

He recently learned that I've been keeping a second set of records. I inadvertently mentioned something about one of the cases and Matt was all over me. He knew the tidbit I shared wasn't in the SPD files—he knew that because Matt picks and chooses what gets entered into SPD files. My first suspicion of this deceitful practice dates back to the Mendez fiasco. Ever since, I have been keeping my own records. As for my suspicions that Matthew Cambridge is the serial rapist known as REDO, I'm not really sure when I first suspected, but I am sorry to say that I didn't do enough to get him off the streets. I will take the pain and suffering of REDO's victims to my grave.

The first order of business, Caitlyn, is getting my stuff before Matt does. He told me to bring my files to the station so he could review them before the task force meeting. If I am no longer around, he will use his authority to get my files.

The small envelopes included with this letter have the names of people who can help you get this case solved. Inside mine, there are things about REDO, and something for Camille. Please make sure she gets it – you'll know when the time is right to give it to her. The other envelopes are for people who have information, or skills, or insights that will prove very useful. I think Marilyn McGinn has the most conclusive proof connecting Matt to these crimes. Tread softly with her. I hope your higher ups will let you form your own task force and include the recipients of these envelopes. This rapist, your husband, needs to be taken down.

Caitlyn, you are in danger. You know too much, and you are too close to Matt. I don't know how to get you out of this situation. Hopefully DA James will help. Once you and the DA decide how to proceed internally, I think it is wise for him to contact his counterparts, especially those working on the task force. Keeping Cambridge busy in that capacity will keep him from racking up any more victims, minimize his time with you, and give you time enough to put together a case against him.

Thank you for your help handling my final wishes. I offer one of my own to you: Stay Safe, Caitlyn.

Ray

The DA moves to a wall of windows. He stands for many minutes before speaking, "You are in danger, ADA English. Knowing that, I cannot proceed in the way that best suits this investigation."

"Excuse me for saying so, sir, but you don't have any choice."

"Awfully close to insubordination, English."

"Yes, sir."

Connecting dots—or not.

Cambridge does his third drive-by, then pulls to the curb across from Ray Chase's place. Most of the house is dark, yet there is a lone light shining from somewhere in the back. "Kitchen?" He is just about to leave when the house is flooded with light and commotion. In the distance he hears the wail of a siren that moves closer and closer. The Chase front door opens as the ambulance comes to a stop, blocking the street—blocking his exit. Two EMTs and a paramedic race inside. "Marilyn McGinn." He grabs a baseball cap from his front seat, puts it on, and sinks low. Several minutes pass before the medical team gets a gurney into the house and several more before they move the loaded gurney down the stairs. Cambridge's attention leaves the medical commotion and focuses on the people standing in the doorway. "Camille and Chris Chase."

When Ray is loaded in the back of the ambulance, Marilyn joins him. The mother and son duo shut the house door behind them, get into a Tacoma, and drive away. Cambridge waits until Ray's neighbors go back behind closed doors before getting out of his car. He eyes a narrow path between 60 and 62 Preston and has started in that direction when he sees a man move past the living room window.

"Fuckin A. Who's that?"

Jonah puts his cell phone onto the coffee table in the living room and pulls the front curtains closed. As he does, he takes a casual look outside. He picks up the cell and answers Chris' question. "Yes, the Land Rover is still across the street, and the detective is getting back into it."

"Back into it?"

"Yeah, he must have been near the house when I went to the window."

"Lock up, Jonah. I'm calling Ms. English. Find a way to watch Cambridge, and if he gets out of his Land Rover, call the cops."

DA's Office

Caitlyn reads the display screen, "It's Chris Chase." The DA nods. She answers. "Caitlyn English. You're on speaker with the District Attorney, Chris."

"Ms. English, my father is being transported to UU. My mother and I are following the ambulance. On our way out, we saw Cambridge on our street. After we left, he made a move toward the house, then stopped when he saw Jonah inside. Do you have a plan to keep him out of the house while we're gone?"

The DA nods.

"Cambridge will leave Preston Parkway as soon as I call him. I'll be telling him I'm dropping off paperwork at my client's house. He won't want to be seen loitering outside a dying man's home, certainly not by his wife. Tell Jonah to expect me and to let me in immediately."

"Will do. Watch yourself, Ms. English."

She disconnects and presses number 5 on her cell. She puts the call on speaker. It's answered on the fourth ring, "Matt. Did I wake you?"

"It's alright. Where are you?"

"I'm leaving the office and heading back to my client's house. I should be home after that. Maybe an hour more."

"Call me when you're heading home. I'll keep an eye out."

Weston James stands to his full height over Caitlyn English. "I'm on record, here. I do not like this. First thing tomorrow, we get you some protection."

60 Preston Parkway

Matt moves his Rover several spaces back from the Chase house. Within minutes his wife pulls to the curb, climbs the stairs, talks to some dude at the door and steps inside. No more than two minutes later she is back in her car and heading to UU hospital. "Better rush that paperwork to your client, Caitlyn. Things don't look too good for the dying detective."

UU

Medical Examiner, Franklin Moss, has corralled his morgue transport team and paramedic, Marilyn McGinn, in a conference room in the bowels of UU. "Not one word of this to **anyone**. Not one word amongst yourselves. This is a classified and sensitive matter. I am going to list the people who know about this situation: the Syracuse Medical Examiner, the Syracuse District Attorney, one of his ADAs, the wife and son of the deceased, and you three. If word gets out about any of this, the authorities will know who to investigate and prosecute. Ms. McGinn, I trust my employees implicitly. The person who chose you for this operation has the same faith in you."

She nods.

He addresses his employees, "Get out of those EMT uniforms and incinerate them. Then get back to work." The men leave, and the ME addresses the remaining medical conspirator, "Ms. McGinn, you may be tempted to connect dots. **Do not.** That is all."

Marilyn McGinn steps off an elevator on the main level of UU and right into the floor space of ADA Caitlyn English. The women share a look and walk past.

"I suppose **that's** a dot I'm not supposed to connect," Marilyn scoffs. And when she steps out of the ambulance bay and sees Matt Cambridge's Land Rover parked at the far end of the lot she whispers, "And **that's** another dot I'm not supposed to connect."

Finding comfort where you can.

Matt's Rover is on the driveway when Caitlyn gets home. Heat emanating off the engine chills her to the bone as she moves toward the house. "How am I going to pull this off? How am I supposed to play the happy, contented wife when I'm—"

"Talking to yourself, again. Not a good sign."

She startles at his voice and stops at the kitchen. "You're still up," she smiles through a yawn as she enters.

"I said I'd wait up," he reminds from a kitchen stool.

She moves to him, wedges herself between his legs and kisses him. "I'm glad you did. It's been a long, depressing night."

"Your client. Did he or she pass?"

"Not as of twenty minutes ago. But I'm afraid it won't be long now." She pulls from his arms and moves to the refrigerator. "I lied to you, Matt." She reaches in, takes a carton of orange juice and pours two glasses. "The night I consumed the six pack of Blue Moon," she takes a sip, "my guest that evening wasn't Michelle, it was Ray Chase." She waits for a response, continues when she receives none. "He showed up asking for my help in preparing his final documents."

He pauses. "So it's not the flu?"

"No, it's pancreatic cancer. I was called to his house tonight. When I arrived, he was in very bad shape. He asked me to change something in his paperwork, that's why I went to the office. When I brought the papers back to his place, I learned he'd been transported to UU. I went over there, but he was out of it. I'm not sure if he'll be able to sign the paperwork."

Matt gets off his stool and pulls Caitlyn into his arms. "Is that all you want to tell me?"

"No. I want you to know I'm sorry I lied."

"Don't sweat it. We all lie."

She buries her head into his shoulder and shivers.

"Let's get you to bed. You're practically dead on your feet."

Oh, God. I have to sleep with a serial rapist.

UU

Camille and Chris Chase meet with the ME and Ray's oncologist, Dr. David Philips, who was brought into the plan.

"Per Franklin's request, I have admitted your husband to room 818E on the oncology floor. If anyone calls the hospital to inquire about Raymond, the operator will see that he is a patient and that he is not allowed visitors. The medical staff on the 8th floor will be informed that 818E is a VIP transfer with his own nursing staff, but admitted through me—a somewhat infrequent occurrence at UU, but it shouldn't raise suspicions, given I'm head of oncology.

Franklin and I think this ruse will give the DA three days to handle his investigation."

"And Ray?" Camille asks.

"Your husband is being tended to in the morgue, Mrs. Chase."

"Thank you. I'd like to go home now." Chris helps his mother with her coat and takes her to his father's home.

Fayetteville

Matt grabs his cell off the nightstand barely an hour after his eyes shut, "Cambridge ....Yes, sir. I just learned about Ray's illness. I'm on my way."

Caitlyn snuggles beneath the covers until she hears the close of the front door. She jumps from bed, scurries down the hall, wedges herself into a corner by the front door and peers through the etched glass to make sure he leaves. She sighs mightily when she sees his Rover drive away.

She hurries back to her bedroom in time to shout, "Hello!" into her ringing cell.

"English."

"Yes, sir."

"Your husband just left. Is that correct."

"Yes. Did you assign protection, sir?"

"Yes. Peripheral surveillance. What is your ETA to the office?"

"Within the hour."

"My office when you get here."

"Yes, sir."

60 Preston Parkway

Camille climbs the stairs to Ray's room, goes to his closet, takes one of his shirts from a laundry hamper, puts it to her face and breathes in. She. Just. Breathes. In. When she's had her fill, she removes her clothes, puts the shirt on and climbs into his bed, where she cries herself to sleep.

I never liked him.

Matt is where he's wanted to be for days—camped out in his partner's office getting things in order, his things, REDO's things. The conversation he had with his CO bangs through his head as he pulls Ray's office apart...

"No pullback from the investigation, Cambridge. You like working on your own, so have at it. Chase's replacement will be assigned after he's passed. Get to work."

The duplicitous detective is so deep into his task and his headspace that he doesn't see Diane in the doorway.

"Good Lord, what are you doing to Ray's office?"

Matt bangs his shin as he stands and takes a look around, "I was looking for something."

"Looks like you were trying to exorcise some sort of demon."

"Nervous energy."

Diane pulls a shaky breath, releases it slowly and adjusts her tone. "Of course. I'm sorry, Detective, he's been your partner for years. Is there anything you need? Do you want me to put this place back in order?"

"Any chance you have his computer password?"

"No, but maybe I'll come across it when I rearrange," she smiles.

"You don't like chaos and mess," he says flatly.

Her body answers before her mouth does, "Good Lord, no. Just standing in this swirl of debris is wreaking havoc on my system."

Matt smiles and walks to his office, "Have at it." He gets lost in silent debate about a little B&E at the Chase house or a knock on the door asking for the files. He's still working his way through the back and forth when the phone rings, "Cambridge," he barks.

"Detective, this is District Attorney James."

"Sir."

"I heard about Detective Chase. Very sad situation. The reason for my call, Detective, in light of the situation with your partner, do you see any reason why you won't be in attendance at the first task force meeting?"

"No reason."

"Good. I'll need you to take the reins for Onondaga County. A pressing matter at the DA's office will keep me and ADA English from attending. An unfortunate circumstance that cannot be helped. Since the venue for the gathering is in Cayuga County, District Attorney Isla Conway will be co-chair with you. Her contact information is in the paperwork my office sent over. She's expecting your call."

"Yes, sir." Matt disconnects with a "Fuckin A!" He's reminded that he's not alone when Diane clears her throat.

DA Office
Weston James steps from behind his desk and addresses his ADA, "English, this office is going to finish the work Detective Chase began. When we have enough evidence we are going to call for the arrest of Matthew Cambridge on behalf of the people of the great state of New York. Let's get to work."

The two head to the DA's private conference room. He tosses a legal pad onto the table and talks while he makes himself a coffee, "First, we need to get Ray's files out of his house. I'm working on a plan. Second, you need to contact the people whose names appear on the small envelopes Ray sent you. Make sure every one of them is in attendance at our secret task force meeting on Wednesday. I don't suspect you'll have any problem getting them here. A request from the DA's office carries a certain amount of sway," he smiles. "As for Detectives Kelly and Sanchez, the District Attorneys in Cayuga and Ithaca will make sure they are in attendance at our meeting. Stress confidentiality to the others. Is there anyone on staff here that you trust with your life, English, because I'm sorry to say you are in the crosshairs of Matt Cambridge?"

The woman who is most aware of her peril ignores the last part of the DA's sentence and answers the first part. "Michelle Young."

"Bring her on board. We're going to need administrative assistance. Talk to her here, this room is gravitas central. Scares the shit out of most people," he smiles.

She nods.

"Wasn't including you in that blanket statement, English. It's fully evident that nothing scares you, although certain things should."

Caitlyn waits until the DA closes his office door and closes his room-dividing shades before buzzing Michelle, "Would you please bring the Timberlake file to the DA's conference room? And get phone coverage, you'll be here awhile." Caitlyn has the door open for Michelle, "Come on in, close the door, and take a seat." The ADA has been standing at the wall of windows preparing her words. She takes a seat across the table from Michelle. "There is a situation that I need to inform you of and include you in. No words from you until I have finished."

Michelle nods.

"There is a secret task force being assembled to work REDO. You are being brought on board because you work with me and more to the point because I trust you. I am involved with this case on a professional level and now on a personal level." A look of utter despair crosses her assistant's face. Caitlyn responds accordingly. "Michelle, I am not a REDO victim, and if we all play our cards correctly, I won't become one." She moves to the seat next to her paralegal and swivels toward her. She takes Michelle's hands in hers and pulls a cleansing breath, "My husband,

Detective Matthew Cambridge, is the rapist known as REDO."

Michelle gasps then reacts as she is wont to do, "I never liked him."
Caitlyn laughs big.

Wrong fucking dead detective.

Cambridge decides the only way to get Ray's files is to go get Ray's files. "Hey, Diane. I'll be back in an hour."

60 Preston Parkway
Chris disconnects from a call with District Attorney James and takes control of the room, "The DA thinks Cambridge is on his way for Dad's files. Jonah, go to the mudroom, get the rolling recycling bins emptied and out onto the back patio and start carting the boxed files outside. Mom, get your coat on and stand at the front door. When you see Detective Cambridge pull up give me a shout then answer the door as though you are heading to the hospital. Stall him, and if he insists on coming in, I'll take it from there. GO. GO."

Jonah is rolling the last of three bins through a gate at the back of the property when Cambridge pulls to the curb out front. Jonah shuts the gate and hides on the other side of the receptacles and waits.

Camille Chase gives her heads up to Chris and steps outside. She is locking the front door when she senses someone at her back. She turns and puts her hand to her chest when she comes face to face with the rapist.

"I didn't mean to startle you, Mrs. Chase. I'm Matt Cambridge, Ray's partner."

Camille does a scorching once over, "I know who you are Detective. I can't imagine why you are here, but whatever your reason, I don't have time to deal with you. I'm on my way to the hospital to be with Ray. If you will excuse me." She makes a move toward the stairs.

He blocks her. "I understand you're in a hurry, Mrs. Chase, but Ray is in possession of some files that are needed by the SPD. Perhaps I could..."

"Why don't you give me your card, and I'll call you with a time."

The Detective hands it off and lets her proceed ahead of him down the stairs.

"She's gonna be a problem," he spews when he is behind closed Rover doors. "Fuckin problems are popping up everywhere. Problems can be solved, some by cancer, some by bullets," he reminds himself.

Beard Park Condo
Preoccupied by her role in 'The Detective Is Dead, But Don't Connect The Dots' escapade, Marilyn McGinn answers a call from a blocked number. "Hello."

"Is this Marilyn McGinn?"

"Yes."

"Ms. McGinn, this is ADA Caitlyn English."

"What can I do for you Ms. English?" Marilyn eyes her partner whose jaw drops.

"The District Attorney requests your presence at the DA building Wednesday morning at nine. He has an urgent matter to discuss with you. Your attendance requires utmost confidentiality. Do you have any questions, Ms. McGinn?"

"I do not, Ms. English."

"Wednesday at nine," Caitlyn reiterates. "If for any reason you are unable to attend, and there should be **no** reason, Ms. McGinn, please call this number, 315-555-9725."

Before Marilyn has the chance to discuss the call, one comes in for Joey. "Hello."

"Is this Joey Mayer?" Caitlyn asks.

"Yes."

"Ms. Mayer, this is ADA English ...."

The women take seats in the living room and confirm the calls were identical in nature. Marilyn goes silent and begins connecting the dots she was warned not to connect. She gets up and begins pacing, "Joey, I have a story to tell. The thing is, I've been warned not to tell anyone. But since you and I have been summoned to the inner sanctum of DA Weston James, I **cannot** keep this from you."

Joey nods, r.e.a.l.l.y. s.l.o.w.l.y.

"After your very early call from Ray Chase, you said you thought Matt Cambridge is the serial rapist known as REDO. I wasn't quite sure what to think. After the events of last night, I **know** Matt Cambridge is REDO."

Joey leans in—all the fucking way in.

"I got the weirdest call of my professional life last night from Franklin Moss, the Medical Examiner. He asked me to report to the morgue.

When I got there, there were two EMTs waiting in his office, except they weren't EMTs, they were part of the ME transport team. The three of us were told, by Moss, that we were commissioned for an operation ordered by the DA. We were told to report by ambulance to a home where we would find a deceased male. We were told to transport the deceased male to UU and to make it look like he was a live transport. In my role as a paramedic, I participated in a sham emergency call, prepared a dead man for transport to UU for admittance to the hospital as a VIP, accompanied two fake EMTs to the morgue, waited while they did their thing with the dead man, then went with them to the ME's office."

Marilyn shakes her head a bit at the absurdity of what she is saying, but she continues along. "The ME told the fake EMTs and me that we are involved in a classified and sensitive matter. That the only people who know about the matter are the ME, DA, an ADA, the wife and son of the deceased, and the three people who transported the dead guy. He let us know that life would be very difficult for us if word got out. He told his employees to change out of the EMT uniforms and incinerate them, then he told me to resist the urge to connect the dots. I no sooner left his office when I ran into ADA Caitlyn English, who is most definitely a dot in this situation. And when I went outside I saw The Big Dot: Matt Cambridge was sitting in his Rover staring at the ambulance bay."

"Holy fuck, Marilyn. This is so cloak and dagger. I can't imagine what you've been thinking."

"I've been thinking that not only is my son's father REDO, a serial rapist, the rapist is also the detective who worked my rape case. And he has been in my company any number of times. Mostly I've been thinking that I fucking hate Matt Cambridge, and I want him to pay, BIG!" The rage-shaking woman puts up her hand to stop her partner from giving her the hug she needs, but does not want.

Joey stares at the floor for several minutes, clearly deep in thought. "Hey, Marilyn."

"Yeah."

"You never said who the dead guy is."

Marilyn shakes her head, scoffs and shakes some more, "Ray Chase. The deceased man is Detective Ray Chase."

"Wrong fucking dead detective."

Another mountain of a man.

Chris moves across the second floor alternating between watching Cambridge at the front curb and his partner freezing his ass off at the back gate. On one of his trips to spy out the back, he sees a van pull to the curb and the driver approach Jonah. The man from the van hands Jonah a phone, then presents him with a paper that requires a signature. The driver and his assistant roll the three bins to the van, put them inside, and drive away. Jonah jogs back to the house and sneaks in. He and Chris remain hidden on separate floors until Cambridge pulls away from the curb.

DA Office
Caitlyn is on the floor of the conference room with Ray Chase's files and notes crescent mooning the floorspace around her. She is dictating her thoughts into a handheld recorder while Michelle is marking whiteboards, one of which contains information on the first rapes, the other, information on redo rapes.

Caitlyn begins processing Ray's thoughts as though he is still part of the team. "Detective Chase thinks there are two distinct tactics being used to find the women. He was pushing the idea that REDO initially chose his victims at the DMV. Why don't we run this, Michelle."

"Okay. The women were new to the area, so they would need utilities turned on, groceries brought in, a bank account opened, a new driver's license, and maybe a vehicle registration and license plates."

"Right. So if the woman went to the DMV and got a new license **and** a vehicle registration and license plates, it'd be a safe bet that she was new to the area. All REDO had to do was hang out at the DMV then follow his victim home. Within a couple of hours of watching, he'd know if she lived alone, and then he'd make his move." She startles at her boss' entrance and his words.

"Are you alright, English?"

She sits upright, grabs a new file and answers without making eye contact, "Yes, sir."

"You're on the floor."

"Yes, sir."

He moves further into the conference room and examines the whiteboards, reads DMV, and nods. "Interesting. Detective Chase could be onto something."

Caitlyn smiles at the DA's present tense consideration of Raymond Chase.

The DA addresses Michelle, "Ms. Young, would you please order lunch for the three of us?" When Michelle is gone from the room, the DA offers his hand to his ADA, "Join me in the office, please."

Caitlyn remains silent as he looks out corner to corner windows. "Cambridge will be busy tonight trying to get his hands on Chase's files. When he is unsuccessful, he is going to be very upset. He will be bringing his frustration and anger home. I don't want you alone with him, Caitlyn. Take a seat."

Caitlyn? That's a first. "May I stand, sir. I've pretzeled myself on the floor a bit too long and seem to have put a crick in my back."

He preoccupies himself with some paperwork, still he manages to watch as she leans against the wall near the door, stretches her legs out in front, rolls her shoulders forward, and hangs her head low. He hips a corner of his desk and gets lost in the beauty of Caitlyn English ……. *I should stop thinking about her,* he silently admonishes. He clears his throat, "You shouldn't be alone with Cambridge this evening. As I see it, we need to keep you away from him tonight, tomorrow, and tomorrow night. He'll be heading to Cayuga County for the task force meeting on Wednesday morning. Do you think he'll spend Tuesday night there?"

"I doubt it. Door to door, Aurora is less than an hour from Syracuse."

The DA thinks a minute, "What if Conway tells Cambridge she wants him to handle part of the press conference scheduled for Wednesday afternoon, and she'd like a sit down dinner on Tuesday to prepare?"

"That could work, but the request needs to come from DA Conway."

60 Preston Parkway
Chris answers a dinnertime knock at the front door and immediately begins playing **good cop**

with the **bad cop**. "Detective Cambridge, my mother said you'd be coming by. I'm Ray's son, Chris." The men shake hands. "Come on in. I've boxed up whatever I could find that's SPD related. The box is on my father's desk," Chris points, "You can take a look through or take it with you."

Matt nods, "How is Ray doing?"

"He's holding on," Chris offers a smile and the shake of his head. "I hope this won't take too long, we're anxious to get back to the hospital."

Cambridge follows the man into the living room. He is tempted to rifle through the box; he doesn't. "Is this it?"

"It's all I could find."

"What about his laptop?"

"That's his personal laptop, Detective," a woman says from the kitchen.

"It might have SPD stuff on it."

Camille strolls into the living room, "And it might have copies of the love letters he sent me. The computer stays."

"You heard the lady. I think your business here is done." Chris points to the door, follows the detective to it, closes and locks it behind him. He places a call, "Ms. English, the detective just left with the files you wanted him to have, and I let him know the house would be empty tonight. He made it very clear that he wants the laptop."

Cambridge is slow moving away from the door at 60 Preston. He knows the box he's carrying contains diddly-squat, "Ray's files have been picked over, but by who? If it's the son, then he knows far too much about REDO. If Ray packed up a special box for me then the stuff I want is still in that house. Guess it's back to Plan A. Time for a little B&E, but first—"

Caitlyn answers a call within ten minutes of Cambridge's departure from Ray's house. "Hey," she says with a happy lilt in her voice.

"Hey."

"You sound tired."

"You don't. How come?"

"I caffeinated myself rightly. The caffeine crash is just around the corner. I think I might be able to make it through dinner at Michael's. You game?"

"If you can make it within the next half hour, I'm in. I have to work tonight, so I could use some food."

"And."

"And, what?"

"And you could use my wonderful company," she laughs.

"See you at the restaurant."

Caitlyn English has a quick fall-apart in the conference room, scans her surroundings, and is relieved no one else is nearby. Minutes before her departure, DA James enters the room with a mountain of a man, who on first look could be a young Ray Chase. She gasps at the resemblance, then circles her attention back to her boss.

"ADA English, this is Stanner. He is your security detail. Would you please give him your phone?"

She does as she is told, watches the man take her phone apart, stick something inside and reassemble the pieces.

"That is an audio device, Ms. English." He hands her a fountain pen, "That is a GPS tracker, and we have put a secondary tracker on your SUV. You are aware that your husband has been tracking you?"

"I suspected it last night."

"This is the plan for this evening. You will go to dinner with Cambridge. You will go home and do whatever you normally do. When you are tired, go to bed. Don't throw him any signs that you are in distress about being with him. Meanwhile, we will be tracking him. We anticipate he'll be doing some B&E at the Chase house. We are going to let him eat some time inside before calling 9-1-1 about a disturbance at 60 Preston Parkway. The more time he spends on his B&E, the less time he'll be at home with you. Understood?"

"Yes."

"Make sure your cell phone is near you at all times. I will conduct my intervention based on what I hear from you. I can only hear you if you have your phone nearby. Understood?"

"Yes."

"Approximately one half hour after Cambridge gets home, you will receive a call from Chris Chase saying his father is in his last rally and requests you be there for the signing of his last papers. That's our plan to get you out of the house and away from your husband. It's a simple plan, Ms. English." He waits for a response. Receives none. He can sense she's getting too far into her head, or zoning too far out of it. He tests her. "The best plans usually are. Isn't that right, Ms. English?"

"I'm sorry, what was that last part?"

"The best plans are usually simple. Isn't that right?"

"Yes."

"If Cambridge tries to stop you from leaving your home, it will be entered by force. Do you agree to all of these terms?"

"Yes." Her mind drifts again or she might have slipped into an exhaustion coma.

The DA pushes in. "ADA English ……. Ms. English ……. Caitlyn."

"I'm sorry, did you say something?"

The DA steps near, "If you want to end this operation? Just say the word."

"Absolutely not."

What the fuck is that?

Caitlyn enters Michael's, wraps her arms around her man and holds on tight.

"What's that for?"

"I've been missing you—missing us. That's all. How long of a wait?"

"Maybe five minutes."

"Good. I'm starved."

"You look tired," he brushes an errant strand of hair from her face, twirling the ends around his finger. He continues his exploration with the run of his thumb along her cheek to her chin, "Beautiful."

The REDO seduction, the thought loops through her head as a fear-shiver dances along her spine and raises goosebumps. She tries to cover her creeped-the-fuck-out-feeling with a yawn, "As soon as dinner is over, I'm hitting the sheets."

"Good."

The hostess seats them and sends over a carafe of Long Point wine. "Why Matthew Cambridge, I do believe you're becoming a romantic."

"Or I wanted some wine."

Caitlyn laughs mightily.

They enjoy their drink and some silence, place their orders, and just mellow out in the dimly lit eatery. "I could surely curl up on this booth and sleep the night away."

Matt puts his arm across the back of the booth, "Nestle in, Mrs. Cambridge."

As she nestles, she tamps her desire to smack the fuck out of him and scream, "*get away from me you sadistic son-of-a-bitch.*" When she sees the waitress heading their way, she pushes free, "Scoot, scoot. Make room for our food."

Somewhere Close By
The mountainous bodyguard and the larger-than-life district attorney listen to every word said between Mr. and Mrs. Cambridge from the comforts of a Cadillac XT6. Stanner is concentrating on the rapist; Weston James is concentrating on the woman. As soon as the degenerate escorts the debutante to her Benz and drives away, the District Attorney gets out of the Caddie. "I want updates every hour."

"Yes, sir."

"Nothing happens to her, Stanner."

"Yes, sir."

The Lake
Joey Mayer gets w.a.y. i.n.s.i.d.e her head on the trip to Oneida. She talks herself into believing Matt Cambridge is REDO and talks herself right back out again. "Ray Chase never said anything about Cambridge during that phone call. He didn't name him when he said he didn't want me discussing his investigation with anyone, and even if he were keeping the investigation from his partner, there could be

any number of reasons why he'd do that, professional competition for starters. And Chase didn't connect Jenna's 'wedding band wearing rapist' to Cambridge, I did that. And Caitlyn English didn't say Cambridge **wasn't** part of the secret task force, so he very well may be. That'd be a fucking kick in the pants to walk in and see him sitting there. And as far as Baby Joseph is concerned, he looks like Cambridge, but he probably looks like a million other guys, some who probably aren't even rapists," she laughs. The woman who is losing both sides of her argument pulls onto the driveway at 22 Shore Road having absolutely no recollection of how she got there. Not surprisingly, her preoccupation continues when she's inside the bungalow.

Jenna taps Joey's leg with her foot, "Are you alright?"

The counselor zooms back in, "I'm sorry, Jenna, did I miss something?"

"I think you've missed most everything," she smiles. "Right then, I said something's been bothering me about the other night."

"Okay."

"After you and Marilyn left, you called to say Cambridge's Land Rover was at Mac's. While I was waiting for him to return, I sensed something amiss, like something dangerous was lurking, then I heard footfalls outside the bungalow. I hid in the kitchen and called Cambridge thinking he was up the road at Mac's. When he didn't answer, I called

Cleveland PD. A few minutes after CPD arrived, Cambridge came back. He stayed until Grams and Gramps returned. He told us he was at Mac's place and came back to check on things when he saw the patrol car."

Joey sort of blank-eyes Jenna, "Can you tell me what bothers you about all that?"

"If Cambridge was waiting for Mac, why didn't you see him when you drove past his Land Rover, and why didn't he answer my call? If he was busy interviewing Mac and chose to ignore my call, that's understandable, but if he was just hanging out, why didn't he answer my call?"

"Maybe he was on another call," Joey offers.

"Or maybe he wasn't at Mac's."

Mac was at the kitchen sink washing paint brushes when he saw Joey Mayer's car head toward Jenna's place; he is standing at the top of his driveway when it returns an hour later. He rushes to the center of the road when she nears.

Joey slows.

"We need to talk," he shouts.

"Interesting way to initiate a conversation."

"I did not rape Jenna. But I think I know who did."

"You should go to the police. Tell them."

"The rapist is a cop."

Joey pulls onto Mac's driveway and follows him into his house. "You have five minutes to state your case. If you make one

337

move toward me, I will kick your balls so far north you'll need a dentist to extract them."

Mac winces, "Understood. The other night I saw Matt Cambridge drive down to Jenna's."

"Marilyn and I called him when we found out you were drugging her."

"Drugging Jenna? I wasn't drugging her."

"You gave her muscle relaxants."

"Yeah. The same ones Marilyn gave her."

"You gave medication to a woman without her knowledge."

"I. Did. Not. I told Jenna I had the same kind of muscle relaxants Marilyn gave her and asked if she wanted to continue taking them. She said she did."

"When did this conversation take place?"

"That first night. She must not remember, but I **absolutely** asked her if she wanted a second dose. She **absolutely** accepted. She said the relaxants and the OTCs were helping with her aches from her fall and with spasms she was experiencing from a previous back injury."

"Go on with your story."

"I didn't want a visit from the detective, so after he drove to Jenna's, I ditched my car up the road and hid outside." Mac makes a move to get up. Joey bolts up. He points to a backpack on the floor. "I just want to get that ruck." She looks. She nods. He puts his tactical gear onto the table; he can almost read Joey's negative thoughts. "It looks bad, but let me explain. I used my night vision binoculars to spy on Detective Cambridge."

"Or Jenna."

"Please don't interrupt. I only have four minutes left. After spending some time at the Farnsworth's, Cambridge drove to my place, got out of his vehicle, knocked on the back door of my bungalow, knocked on the front door, and called out to me. He returned to the back door, unscrewed the porch light, picked the lock, and went inside."

Joey leans in.

"I watched him move throughout my house. At the time, I didn't know what he was doing, but I clocked him. He was inside for three minutes. On his way back out, he twisted the bulb back in, went to his Rover, put on a camouflage parka he stole from my closet, and sat until he saw your headlights coming toward him. He ducked down so you wouldn't see him when you drove past."

Joey raises her hand, "Wait, I need to think." Jenna's words begin a tumble through her head, "If Cambridge was waiting for Mac, why didn't you see him when you drove past his Land Rover, and why didn't he answer my call?" Joey nods, "Continue."

"The minute your car was out of sight, Cambridge got out, walked into the wooded tract between the two bungalows, went to the Farnsworth's back porch, put on a black ski-mask, untwisted the lightbulb, and began picking the lock. Then he pulled a cell phone from his pocket, read the display, stood back up, twisted the lightbulb back in and moved back through the trees. He hid in his Rover until the Cleveland police drove by, then he drove down to the Farnsworth's."

"Let me repeat this the way your arresting officer will. You avoided a conversation with a detective by ditching your car and hiding outside with a pair of night vision binoculars. You watched a man break into your house to do who-knows-what without challenging him, then watched this man sneak through a tree line to a house where a recently raped woman was staying, again without challenging him. You watched this man put on a black ski-mask and try to gain entry to that house, again without challenging him."

"It sounds bad. That's why I lied to Emmett Farnsworth when he asked me if I was outside my bungalow that night. That's why I haven't gone to the police, even after I found ...."

"What? Even after you found what, Mac?"

Wait here. He returns with an Army duffle and slams it onto the table. He unzips it, removes a set of dog tags, several perfectly pressed articles of clothing, several Army insignia envelopes, and points at the remaining contents.

Joey stands. Joey peers inside. Joey stammers, "What the fuck is that?"

"It is a man's T-shirt stained with what looks like blood. Wrapped inside the shirt is what feels like a knife, which I will assume has blood on it, and something that feels like a ring, which I haven't a clue about. I do not know if the rapist cuts his victims, but if he does then I'd bet anything the blood on that T-shirt belongs to Jenna Farnsworth."

"We need help with this," Joey says as her ass finds her seat again.

"We?"

Joey nods, "Go put that back. I need to make a call."

This can't be good.

Cambridge is rolling the dice. The few times he's seen people go in and out of Ray's place no one has stopped to activate or deactivate the alarm system that's just inside the front door. He runs a thought, "Maybe they don't know the codes. Ray's been on his own ever since I've known him, and he never once mentioned his ex or his kid, so maybe they're back on the scene because he's dying."

The would-be-thief drives past 60 Preston then parks his Rover several streets away, cuts across a few properties, opens the gate at the back of Ray's yard and steps through. He leaves the gate open for a hasty retreat, then moves with purpose to the darkened shadows by the house. "Showtime." Without pause, he chooses the door at the mudroom as his point of entry, "Always the least secure area." He tries the knob, smiles wide, and steps inside. He tries the next door, "Locked." He easily picks it, opens the door, and waits for the wail of an alarm. Cambridge smiles wide as he enters the home of Ray Chase. He goes to the only place of interest: Ray's desk. He unplugs Ray's HP laptop, puts it on the floor, eases a backpack from his shoulders, unzips the center compartment, slides an HP from inside, sets it on the desk and plugs it in. He rummages through a box of files, grabs several, slides them and Ray's laptop into the backpack—just as the first strobe of blue light moves toward the house. He grabs his gear and gets the hell out of 60 Preston Parkway, smiling wide as he drives from the scene of his most recent crime.

Fayetteville

Caitlyn reads the display screen and answers a call. "This can't be good." She pulls a breath, "English."

"This is Joey Mayer. Can you talk?"

"Yes. Is there a problem?"

"A development, a rather big development. Is it possible for me to bring someone with me?"

"**To the secret meeting?**" Caitlyn whisper-shrieks.

"Yes. This person doesn't know anything about the meeting, but he knows a very important thing about REDO, and he has evidence—planted evidence to make this person look guilty. I was suspicious of the man and believed I was unswayable in changing my opinion. I have fully changed my opinion."

Caitlyn's free hand begins to shake and sweat, "I'll call you back."

For the second time in two days, ADA Caitlyn English places an afterhours call to her boss. This call is received in a very different manner than the first, "English, is there a problem?"

"I received a call from Joey Mayer. She wants to bring someone to the meeting."

343

"Did you explain the secrecy of this meeting?"

"I did."

"And that the DA created the invitation list?"

"I did."

"And yet this invitee wants to bring a plus one?"

"She said she spoke with a man who knows a very important thing about REDO and has evidence."

"What's your take?"

"She wouldn't have called me unless she believed she's on to something."

"Tell her to have him come in at noon. That will give our group some time to work the case."

"Thank you, sir."

"Before you hang up, English, how was dinner?"

"Uneventful, sir."

Caitlyn startles when Matt speaks from behind her, "Who are you talking to?"

She disconnects her call. "Please stop sneaking up on me. I don't like it."

"I thought you might be asleep," he explains. "What's got you wound up?"

"That was the DA. This damned case I've been pulled onto, it's a stressor."

"The case that's keeping you from the meeting?"

She blanches, "What meeting!?"

"The REDO task force meeting in Aurora."

"See! I've already forgotten about that, and **that's** where I should be. I work in the sexual crimes unit, not the homicide unit."

"Why the change?" he starts undressing.

"The second-chair is going out on maternity leave, and I'm being briefed as her fill-in. The trial won't start until she's back, but there will be filings for this and pre-trial motions for that, and they want someone up to speed in the event she doesn't return."

"Which case?"

"What?"

"What case did the DA assign you?"

Caitlyn pauses. "Must we continue this conversation? I'm exhausted."

He heads to the shower. "She's lying."

She crawls into bed. "He knows I'm lying."

The passing of Raymond Chase. Again.

Chris Chase places a well after-midnight call to Caitlyn English, she bolts upright and yells, "Hello!"

Matt bolts upright at the shout.

"No. No. Chris. I'm awake." She listens. "Lucid?" She listens. "Yes, of course, a deathbed rally, I've heard of this." She listens. "I'll be right there." She jumps from bed, "Ray's sort of awake and wants to sign the papers." She quickly strips off a pair of sleeping shorts, tugs on a pair of leggings, pulls a purple and white SU sweatshirt over her spaghetti-strap camisole, pushes her feet into a pair of sneakers, and affixes a headband in place. She rushes to the bathroom for a brush of her teeth and a minty-fresh gargle only to return to ....

Matt is out of bed and dressing. "I'll come with you."

"You will do no such thing. I don't know how long I'll be, and I do not think the Chase family wants interlopers during their final moments with Ray."

"I'll drive and stay outside."

"Again, you will do no such thing." She pushes past him, grabs her cell from the nightstand and her briefcase from next to her bureau, "Be back when I get back, I guess."

With the click of the front door, the suspicious spouse finishes dressing and leaves the Fayetteville house of lies.

Stanner watched Caitlyn's Benz head out. Within minutes he watches the serial head out. He hangs back until Cambridge is parked at UU before heading in that direction. He alerts the DA of the detective's whereabouts. "He followed her."

Weston James knew **That** Cop would follow The Counselor, and he's taken steps to make sure the deathbed ruse goes off without a hitch.

Caitlyn is met at the entrance and escorted to the empty VIP hospital room by a tall, distinguished Black man who identifies himself as Dr. Philips. He escorts her to Ray Chase's room. She startles when she sees the DA waiting inside for her.

"Your husband followed you, he's parked outside."

Caitlyn 360s, "This isn't going to work. This **isn't** going to work. He's too smart. He knows I'm lying," she begins to hyperventilate.

"English, sit down and calm down."

She does one of those two things.

"Cooper," he says.

"Cooper? What the hell is Cooper?" She sees the look on the DA's face and tries to amend, "I'm sorry for the tone, sir."

"The homicide case to which you've been assigned." He shakes his head, "Not giving you the name of a case was an error on my part."

Caitlyn blinks astonished eyes and goes a bit slack-jawed, and when she unslacks that jaw she 360s, "Oh. My. God. Oh. My. God. You were listening .... to my bedroom conversation. Oh. My. God." The hyperventilating returns full force.

The DA takes a step toward her.

She shakes her head vigorously, "Please, sir, no."

"I wasn't listening. Stanner heard the exchange and gave me a heads up."

She connects the dots. Her breathing returns to normal—for a very short period of time.

Weston James answers a call, relays the information, "Cambridge is in the hospital."

The detective hopes to charm and disarm. He heads to Information and to the young woman who is eyeing him hard.

"May I help you," she asks with a little pant in her voice.

"I hope so." He moves his sport coat aside to reveal his detective's shield. "My partner is in pretty bad shape upstairs. I've forgotten his room number."

"The patient's name?"

"Raymond Chase."

The lovely young woman with dark hair and eyes that show sorrowful knowledge says, "Your partner is in room 818E. Follow the yellow lines on the floor to Ambulatory-E elevator. Detective, you know your partner is not receiving visitors?"

Matt nods and sprints away.

Dr. Philips is standing at the nurses' station when Cambridge arrives. He is busying himself with his tablet and stops his pretend work when the detective tells the duty nurse, "I'm here to see Ray Chase."

The nurse runs the name through her head, comes up empty, so she keystrokes her computer only to be halted by Dr. Philips.

"I'm Mr. Chase's physician, may I help you?" he addresses Cambridge.

The detective reads the lettering on the doctor's lab coat, "Dr. Philips, I'm Matt Cambridge, Ray's partner."

The men shake hands, "It's nice of you to come, Detective. If you would like to wait for the family at the visitors' waiting area, it's at the end of this corridor."

"Actually, I was hoping to see Ray."

The doctor opens his tablet, finds Ray's chart and swipes through a few screens, "I'm sorry, Detective, but you aren't on the family's list of approved visitors. I'm sure they will appreciate your coming by." The doctor ends his conversation with the detective by answering his ringing cell, "Dr. Philips." He listens. He answers. "Yes, that's correct."

Matt makes his way to the visitors' waiting area under the watchful eye of Dr. Philips.

DA James disconnects from his call with the doctor. "Cambridge is on the 8th floor."

Caitlyn's phone rings. "It's Matt."

The DA nods.

Caitlyn connects, "Matt, is everything okay?"

"Yeah. Why?"

"I'm busy."

"I'm at UU."

"Where? Why?"

"Come to the 8th floor visitors' waiting area."

She storms from the room, rounds the corner at the nurses' station, sees Matt at the far end of the hall, and marches toward him. **"What. Are. You. Doing?"** she whisper-yells and raises her hand when he starts to say something. **"Matt, you need to leave. I am sorry if your feelings are hurt, but you and Ray were never close, and his family knows that. I am trying to do my job and you are interfering. I shouldn't be out here discussing this with you, I should be inside that hospital room helping a man sign the last thing he will ever sign."** She stops her whispered rage, looks beyond her husband at Chris Chase who is waving his hand, beckoning her from the far end of the corridor. **"I need to go, and you need to leave."**

She jogs down the hall, nearly bumping into Ray's oncologist as they round the corner out of sight.

Cambridge storms from UU, throws himself into his Rover and peels out of the parking lot. Stanner sits tight, keeps his eyes on the GPS tracker, and reports in. "He's heading home. I'll let you know if that changes."

Caitlyn storms into room 818, paces furiously from one end to the other and does one more 360. "I can't do this. I'm wining, dining, and sleeping with a rapist. What am I thinking? What am I doing? He's going to kill me. I can't do this. We need to arrest him. Why aren't we arresting him?"

The DA stops her on one of her trips past. "English. Stop!"

She stops.

"Ray Chase may have built a case against Cambridge, but it is far from being a solid one. It is no secret that the detectives disliked one another. Part of their animosity stems from professional competition. The senior-most detective was overshadowed by his underling, the cock-of-the-walk Detective Cambridge. That fact throws suspicion onto this unsanctioned investigation. Add to that, although you don't need to, Detective Ray Chase could be accused of gunning for another partner. Cops do not like cops who cross the blue line of loyalty. Straight out of the gate, the entire SPD will be pissed that one of their own is going after one of their own."

Caitlyn interrupts, "Yes, but most, if not all of SPD can't stand Matt."

"That won't matter. They will side with Cambridge, especially when they learn Chase is dead. Speaking of that, Ray Chase dies tonight."

Escalation.

Cambridge is in the kitchen when Caitlyn gets home a few hours before dawn. He is in a foul mood having spent the remainder of the night trying to break the security code for Ray's laptop with no success. He calls out to his wife, "Caitlyn!"

She enters the kitchen, offers a glare, but says nothing.

"I don't appreciate the way you spoke to me," he says as he moves toward her.

She stands her ground, "I don't really care." She turns to leave. He grabs her upper arm. She tries to shake him off. He holds on tight. "Let go of me!" He squeezes tighter, "Matt. Stop! You are acting like a fool. Your partner is dead, and you are in the grips of some hissy fit. Let go of my arm!"

"Ray is dead?"

She storms away.

He smiles, big.

Stanner is out of his Caddie and moving toward the house as soon as voices raise; he pauses when the ramping tensions slow. He places a call, "The detective got physical. It could have escalated further, but he had a change of mood at the death announcement. Still, she's in danger, West." Caitlyn's bodyguard stays near the house listening and reporting. "Ms. English told Cambridge to sleep in the guest room. I'll call you in an hour."

Stanner moves to the shadows, leans tight against an exposed fireplace wall to pull the last of its heat. He speaks caution to the woman who cannot hear him, "Lock your bedroom door, Ms. English. If he tries to get in, I'll need the extra time to get to you."

Caitlyn startles awake.

Matt is towering over her.

"Are you trying to kill me? I nearly had a stroke."

"I'm heading out. I came in to discuss a few things."

She inches her way to a sitting position, presses her back against the headboard and finger combs her hair away from her face. "Discuss what?"

"Last night."

She stays silent.

"We've never been that way."

She stays silent.

He hitches his head, "Sorry about your arm."

She examines it, notices perfectly defined fingerprint bruises. She stays silent.

He walks away.

As soon as she hears the front door close, she scurries to it and peers out the etched window. She relaxes back against the foyer wall when she sees him drive away.

Stanner gives Caitlyn a few minutes before calling. "Ms. English, things escalated pretty quickly last night. I know you are under stress and taking incoming from all directions, but I don't think it's wise to poke the bear right now, particularly this bear."

"You're right, of course."

"He hurt you."

"I'm fine."

"He hurt you."

"I'm going to shower and go to the office. Thank you for checking in."

"I'll be within earshot if you need me."

Caitlyn drags herself to the shower. On the way, she rubs her bruised arm and tries to ignore her breaking resolve.

Weston James takes the call from Stanner.

"He left marks on Ms. English. If she's in his company again, she'll end up dead."

24 Hours.

Caitlyn takes a call on her way downtown, "Chris, how are you and Camille doing?"

"Better now that we can live with our grief. The reason I'm calling is to let you know Cambridge took the decoy laptop you gave us and a few files last night. He left his decoy in its place just as you predicted. Mom tossed a sheet over it as a reminder that none of us are to touch it."

"Good. Do you think you'll be able to attend the task force meeting at the DA's office tomorrow? I don't want any of this interfering with your plans for Ray."

"I'll be there. I need to speak on my father's behalf."

DA Office
Michelle knocks before entering Caitlyn's office. "The DA wants to see you. He asked that you bring whatever you have prepared for the meeting tomorrow. Do you have anything prepared?"

"No."

"Can I help with anything?"

"You can clear your evening. I'm going to need you to work late, very late."

"Done."

Caitlyn arrives at the inner sanctum empty-handed. The DA points to a seat, "I heard you were roughed up last night. We are going to rethink this situation."

She is silent.

"English. No arrest is worth you being in harm's way."

"We need 24 hours. If I stay at work until late tonight and he stays in Aurora overnight, I won't be in his company for the remainder of today. He'll be at his task force meeting tomorrow while I'm at ours. Maybe we'll have enough to put an end to all this after that."

"And if he only pretends to stay in Aurora overnight? He's erratic, which means we should expect the unexpected."

"If he heads back tonight, Stanner should know, right? Because of the GPS he attached to Matt's Rover, right? And he'll be watching my home, right?"

"Yes."

"Then we work off this plan; I'll go home when I'm done here. If Matt comes back to Syracuse, I'll leave with Stanner."

"I don't like it, Ms. English."

"I don't like any of this, sir, but we're so close now. About the work product you asked to see."

He raises his hand, "Let's meet after the rest of the office heads out for the night. You and Michelle should work in my conference room out of sight of questioning eyes." He takes a file from the corner of his desk, "And you should familiarize yourself with NY v Cooper in the event the homicide case comes up in conversation again. That's all, English."

The ADA steps into the adjoining conference room, studies the file, then places a call. In minutes her paralegal joins her. "Michelle, grab a pad and pen. We need to organize for tomorrow's meeting. This isn't an ordinary task force. We can't bandy about this idea or that idea, we need to hit hard with the attendees, come to a consensus, and take action."

SPD

Cambridge calls his wife's cell from the SPD parking lot. The call goes to voicemail. He calls her office; that too goes to voicemail. He drives to the DA building, "A little surprise visit never hurt anyone."

Stanner makes a call from the parking lot across the street, "Ms. English, Detective Cambridge is on his way into the DA office building."

Caitlyn grabs Michelle's arm and the NY v Cooper file. They make a mad sprint to her office. "Sit. Type whatever I say."

Michelle sits and types.

Caitlyn stands between her office and Michelle's workspace. "See if I can meet with Maggie before she goes out on maternity leave. I have some questions about her notes."

"Specifics?"

"Timeline. Our suspect left the bar and was gone for an hour. He said he came back for last call. We need to talk to the bouncer again, find out whether it's his practice to let people into the bar when he should have been getting patrons out?" Caitlyn notices Matt standing just outside Michelle's workstation. She turns and moves into her office. She addresses her assistant, "Michelle, why don't you walk that down to Maggie's paralegal and see if you can get an answer." She waits until she and Matt are alone, "Why are you here?"

"I called your cell and your office line."

"Not an answer, Matt."

"We need to talk."

"Yes, but I'm swamped, and I'm looking at a very late night."

"I wanted to talk before the task force meeting."

"How's tomorrow morning over coffee?" *She knows he won't be at home for morning coffee.*

"I'm heading out this afternoon and staying the night in Aurora."

"Why?" *She knows why.*

"DA Conway is having a press conference tomorrow afternoon and she wants me alongside. She wants to prep me tonight."

"Press conference? To announce what? The task force? The public doesn't even know there's a serial rapist."

"They will tomorrow." He walks further into her office. Caitlyn doesn't move, not even when he is inches from her. "I need to spend some time with you before I head out. My headspace is all about you, about us. I need to get it into the case."

"Even if I wanted to be with you, and at the moment I do not, I just don't have the time."

"Caitlyn, I'm sorry about last night. I never should have—"

"Excuse me," the interruption by the DA puts a halt to the husband's apology.

He turns in greeting, "DA James."

"Detective. I'm sorry to interrupt. Ms. English, there's a meeting being put on the schedule regarding the questions you raised on NY v Cooper. That was a good catch, we're calling the bouncer in for another round of questions. When you are done here, bring your notes. I want to discuss this issue before the meeting." The DA turns to Cambridge, "Good luck tomorrow, Detective."

Matt seethes on the inside. "Thanks." He turns to his wife who has moved to her seat, "I guess lunch is a no go?"

She scoffs, "Lunch, dinner, and every piss I need to take is a no go. Maybe our not being able to talk is a good thing. Maybe we both need a cooling-off period. Why don't we plan on talking over dinner tomorrow night. It'll have to be takeout. How's seven sound?"

He nods. He thinks about approaching for a kiss, thinks better of it when Michelle returns.

"Excuse the interruption, but there's a meeting at..."

"I already heard," Caitlyn says as her rapist husband turns and leaves.

Matt loiters the sidewalk a bit pretending to ignore the black Caddie SUV across the street. *Nice ride. It was at the hospital last night, near the station earlier today, and now it's outside the DA building. Someone's going to a lot of trouble to keep eyes on me.*

Threading it together.

Cambridge pulls to the far corner of the parking lot at the diner he frequents on his rape and redo trips. Before going inside, he checks the undercarriage of his Rover and finds what he knew he'd find. He leaves the tracker in place. "Who put you there?" His first guess is Ray Chase. "But that fucker's dead, and I've still got a tail. Could be the dude in the Caddie hasn't heard about Ray yet." He heads inside the candy-cane painted diner and orders his usual at the counter, "A Reuben, half-sour pickle, tall glass of ice and a can of root beer," then he makes his way to a booth in the far corner and ruminates while he waits. "Who wants eyes on me? The most obvious culprit is Ray Chase. The Old Man's been on to me for a while, though he couldn't act because he turned his first partner in for being dirty. That played to my benefit—but he knew. Maybe he hired someone to follow me around, to try to catch me in the act."

"I'm sorry it took so long," a waitress in a red and white striped uniform says when she tables his order.

He ignores her, takes a bite and gets back to the questions at hand. "What tipped Ray off?" He chews a bit, replays every part of every REDO rape story: the surveillance, the attack, the words, the actions. "Ray was onto me before the 2020 rapes started, so whatever sent him my way happened between 2014-2019." He pushes his meal aside, feels a rise in agitation, "I've done this mental exercise a million fucking times. I need to look at this from a different angle." He taps, taps, taps his fork, thinks back…

"Head comes with me—what's in my head comes with me, Old Man."

"Yeah, but records are important. I've seen your files, they're on the thin side. I've got some big-ass files full of stuff."

"Shit, Ray. We're running a case using two sets of files. I should have your notes. Shit, I should have your files."

"You can have 'em when I'm dead."

The detective leans back against the vinyl booth, stares out the grimy roadside window, and zones out for several minutes. "The files. Ray's been keeping his own set of files because he knew I was fucking with evidence, altering victim and perp statements." He takes a bite, a sip, and a minute to run stuff. "He probably thought I was fucking with shit so I'd move up the ranks at SPD. At first, anyway, but something happened to make him start thinking I was good for rape. What? When?" A memory from the day Aldo Mendez was sent up bangs the fuck out of his head…

Detective Ray Chase raised his glass, "Let's celebrate another arrest by the Hot Shot detective ……. You know, wherever I go I'm asked what the secret is to Matt's success. People in and out of law enforcement want to know why it is he always gets his man? This is what I say ……. Matt Cambridge catches the rapist because he thinks like a rapist."

Cambridge throws his fork. It hits the wall and bounces across the table. He storms from the diner and squeals from the parking lot, his eyes searching for the Caddie all the way to Aurora. "No tail." He mulls it through. "If the tail is Ray's, then maybe it pulled back because Ray's dead. Nope. Doesn't feel right. Maybe the Caddie stayed in Syracuse because there's no reason to tail a man if you already know where he's heading. Now, who knows where I'm heading. Caitlyn English. Son-of-a-bitch." Some shit starts banging—hard…

"It's three-thirty, Caitlyn."
"My client is passing."

"Caitlyn, where are you?"
"I'm heading to the office. I need to produce another document. It might be awhile. I'm sorry."

"Matt. Did I wake you?"
"It's alright. Where are you?"
"I'm leaving the office and heading back to my client's house. I should be home after that. Maybe an hour more."

"You're still up?"
"I said I'd wait up."
"I'm glad you did. It's been a long, depressing night."

"Your client. Did he or she pass?"

"Not as of twenty minutes ago. But I'm afraid it won't be long now."

"Who are you talking to?"

"That was the DA. This damned case I've been pulled onto, it's a stressor."

"Which case?"

"What?"

"What case did the DA assign you?"

"Ray is awake and wants to sign the papers."

"I'll come with you."

"You will do no such thing. I don't know how long I'll be, and I do not think the Chase family wants interlopers during their final moments with Ray."

"I'll drive and stay outside."

"Again, you will do no such thing."

"I don't appreciate the way you spoke to me."

"I don't really care. Let go of me! Matt. Stop! You are acting like a fool. Your partner is dead and you are in the grips of some hissy fit. Let go of my arm!"

"Ray is dead?"

"Why are you here?"

"I need to spend some time with you before I head out. My headspace is all about you, about us. I need to get it into the case."

"Even if I wanted to be with you, and at the moment I do not, I just don't have the time."

"Excuse me."

"DA James."

"Detective. Good luck, tomorrow."

"My wifey sure had lots of reasons not to be in my company or in my bed, lately. And she had a lot of interaction with, and redirection from, her boss. They know. The fucking dude in the fucking Caddie is surveilling me because of Caitlyn, and there's no fucking way she hired the muscle. This has DA James' hands all over it." Cambridge slams the steering wheel, "Fuck. Fuck. Fuck. Weston James wanted me away from Caitlyn, that's why I'm in Aurora a day early. Well, I'm here. Let's see what happens next."

We're damned fools.

District Attorney Weston James' call is put through to SPD Chief of Police, David Barelli.

"I hope this is a social call, West, because I'm up to my balls today."

"Afraid not David, and your balls are about to get crushed. I need you to come to my office."

"When?"

"As soon as you hang up."

The Chief hangs up.

Caitlyn had just gotten used to being in the inner sanctum without having her stomach twisted in knots. That comfort level hits the shits when she walks in and finds Matt Cambridge's boss standing flank to her boss in front of corner to corner windows. Both men are stiff kneed, their arms are folded across their chests, and their scowls speak before their mouths do. She feels the blood drain from her face and the tingle of sweat run her fingers.

"Have a seat, ADA English."

A seat? I was planning to crash to the floor, but okay. She plops down, rather ungracefully.

"Chief Barelli has been briefed on Matt Cambridge. He has his concerns about the way we are handling things."

"Ms. English, is it true that Matt Cambridge caused you bodily harm during a recent argument?"

"Yes."

"Is that a usual occurrence?"

"It is not."

"Has he caused physical injury to you in the past?"

"No."

"Ever?"

"No."

"The rapist is escalating—your husband is acting out. There's a stressor in Matt's life, Ms. English. The first part of that pressure point was Detective Chase. Matt probably figured Ray was onto him, but through a tragic turn of events, that stressor died, no pun intended. Matt figured he was in the clear, until the second pressure point became apparent. Matt probably knows that your absence from his life in recent days isn't about deathbeds and final papers. If he doesn't know for sure that the DA and the ADA are investigating him, he will. I think we should assume he knows. That means Cambridge is formulating a plan, and you are at the center of that plan, Ms. English. If we don't bring Matthew Cambridge in, he will do more than squeeze your arm the next time he is with you."

She nods.

He continues. "I understand your desire to honor Ray's wishes, but I'm going on record that we should bring REDO in now."

"Due respect, Chief, we need evidence, real evidence, in 24 hours we will have that evidence."

"Why can't we get the evidence now?"

"The person in possession of it says it was planted in an attempt to frame him. It's a huge risk for him to come in and give us something that could incriminate him. If we change things up now, he may back out."

"Do you know who this man is?"

"I do not."

"And the intermediary?"

"Yes, but I am unwilling to identify that person."

Chief Barelli walks swiftly past the woman who is in peril. He opens the door to leave, turns and drops his final salvo. "West, you should heed this warning, Matthew Cambridge is brilliant and cunning, and more to the point, he is a mean son-of-a-bitch. Your best shot at getting him is to plan a sneak attack, otherwise you might find he's outmaneuvered you." He gives a long look at Caitlyn, "And when he takes to his final battlefield, Ms. English, you will be the first casualty."

"Not if you help us," she pleads.

He closes the door, "We're damned fools. Every one of us."

Aurora Police Department

Cambridge stops by APD to kill some time before his meeting with DA Conway. Detective Kelly is in a conference room working through some files. "Everywhere I go, someone is working REDO," Cambridge says from the doorway.

Brandan smiles, "Wait until you're announced as the go-to guy for every police department with an unsolved rape and every news outlet looking for a comment. You should take a seat and rest up." Detective Kelly pulls his files toward him, folds them, and stacks them. "You ready for tomorrow?"

"Yeah. You?"

"Won't be at the first meeting."

Cambridge scoffs, "DA James, ADA English, Detective Kelly, all no shows at the first task force meeting. Not getting off to a good start."

"Don't know about Onondaga, but Aurora will be well represented. Captain Simms is sitting in for me. He and I handled the Connie Braxton rapes, so he's up to speed. You want to meet him before tomorrow?"

Cambridge shakes his head, "I already know him."

"Right. You've been working REDO for years."

Cambridge checks his watch, "Don't want to keep DA Conway waiting."

"Smart man. Good luck tomorrow."

Cambridge admits the walls are closing in, and momentarily thinks about leaving, but... "I've already put myself in Aurora. If I'm a no show at tonight's meeting, I'll have every law enforcement agency on my ass, and I'm not prepared for a run. I need to get back to Syracuse to get my shit. So I'm stuck—for now." He parks his Rover in the hotel parking garage, grabs his gear, checks in, requests his things be brought to his room, and goes to the restaurant/bar. Twenty minutes later, **she** walks in.

Isla Conway is a tall, tanned, toned clone of Cameron Diaz. So far, she's done nothing more than enter the room, and every eye in the joint is on her, especially those of the two men flanking her.

Cambridge stands from his seat and waits her arrival. The men disappear into the background. Sort of.

"Detective Cambridge," she extends her hand, "It's a pleasure meeting you. Your reputation precedes you."

"I bet," he smiles wide.

"I appreciate your making time for this meeting. I don't ever go onto a dais without knowing who is up there with me and what they are likely to say."

Matt moves to pull her chair for her.

"Thank you," she eyes his drink and smiles wide "Amaretto?"

He raises his glass in salute and motions for the cocktail waitress, "Two, please."

The DA smiles, "We do have work to do, Detective."

"Do we?" He throws a wide smile her way.

The DA smiles in return. *Oh. My. God. A serial rapist is flirting with me. Weston James is going to owe me for a century.*

Fayetteville
Stanner calls Caitlyn as soon as she arrives home. "Cambridge is still in Aurora. Leave your phone on, and please do not take any sleeping aids."

The exhausted woman would laugh herself silly at that notion if she weren't beyond exhausted, "I'll be asleep in five minutes. Feel free to time me, but please refrain from recording should I begin to snore." She manages to change out of her clothes and into a pair of leggings and a camisole before passing out. She ignores Matt's 2 AM text and immediately calls Stanner, "Are you sure he's still in Aurora?"

"Yes, Ms. English."

The task force gets to work.

Michelle Young waits at reception for the task force members. They have been announced by lobby security, and they exit the elevator en masse. "Follow me," she says sans introductions. She leads Marilyn McGinn, Joey Mayer, and Detectives Brandan Kelly and Caleb Sanchez to the inner sanctum conference room. Onondaga County District Attorney, Weston James, commands the room, "Thank you for coming. Quick introductions. ADA Caitlyn English is to my left, and the woman who just skipped out is Michelle Young, a paralegal on my staff." Going clockwise, Marilyn McGinn, a paramedic with UU hospital; Joey Mayer, the director of Syracuse Rape Crisis Center; Detective Brandan Kelly with the Aurora PD; and Detective Caleb Sanchez with the Ithaca PD. Please take a seat on that side of the table."

Everyone, excluding the DA and the ADA sit. The DA continues, "Three additional people will be joining this meeting. One of those two individuals says he has evidence that relates to the topic at hand. The second person is a computer analyst, and the third person is the reason we are having this meeting—he will be in attendance in spirit only. Detective Raymond Chase began a clandestine investigation prior to his death and named a suspect in the REDO case. For reasons that will be explained later, he did not act on his very well-founded suspicions, rather he left that shared responsibility to the members of this task force. You were named to this committee by Ray Chase. ADA English will present his work. We ask that you share your knowledge so we can fill some holes in the detective's case and get a sadistic rapist out of our communities." The DA nods to his ADA.

Caitlyn walks on shaky legs to an easel on which sits a covered whiteboard. She lifts the cover back and lets the participants read Ray Chase's final words.

MATT CAMBRIDGE IS REDO

SILENCE FILLS THE ROOM

Caitlyn breaks the silence. "Those were the final words spoken by Raymond Chase."

Michelle knocks at the conference room door. She enters with another member.

The DA makes the introduction, "This is Chris Chase, Ray's son. He worked with his father during the last stages of this investigation and is here to share his insights and to render his services. You've brought your laptop as requested?"

Chris pats his messenger bag, "Two actually," he smiles.

"Please give your messenger bag to Ms. Young." He does. The paralegal hands him a laptop, the DA informs.

"Before you begin working with us, Mr. Chase, you need to become a member of my staff. Your employment will be effective immediately and will last through the period of this investigation. The laptop you've been given is property of the District Attorney's office and will allow access to certain databases that are outside your purview."

Chris chuckles.

The DA smiles, "Let me rephrase, the computer you've been given will allow **legal** access to certain databases that are outside your purview."

The attendees laugh.

"While in this building, Mr. Chase, you will be required to use the laptop assigned to the District Attorney's Office of Onondaga County. Your work product will remain the property of Onondaga County. Whatever work you do on this investigation will be protected by the legal scope of confidentiality. You will not be required to answer questions in a court of law regarding the work you do today as it falls under protections of work product of this office. What you do on your own time is of your own concern. Do you agree to this proposal?"

"Yes."

"Very good."

Michelle hands Chris a contract, asks him to read it and sign it. She hands it to Marilyn and Joey, "Please sign as witnesses to the District Attorney's explanation, and Mr. Chase's consent."

Once that is finished, the DA introduces Chris to the other members and gets down to business. "ADA English, the floor is yours."

"I received an envelope from Ray Chase. The contents inside were pieces from an investigation he conducted on his own time and separate from his work at the Syracuse Police Department. Also included were seven envelopes, hand-addressed by Raymond Chase, to the following individuals: Marilyn McGinn, Joey Mayer, Detective Kelly, Detective Sanchez, Chris Chase, Caitlyn English, and Ray Chase. Inside my envelope was a letter from Ray," she nods to Michelle who hands a copy to each member. "Please take a moment to read the letter."

Caitlyn.

There is no doubt in my mind that Matthew James Cambridge is REDO. I told Chris to make sure you get the files from my house when I die or if I become incapacitated. Matt knows I am on to him, and he will make a move to get my stuff.

He recently learned that I've been keeping a second set of records. I inadvertently mentioned something about one of the cases and Matt was all over me. He knew the tidbit I shared wasn't in the SPD files; he knew that because Matt picks and chooses what gets entered into SPD files. My first suspicion of this deceitful practice dates back to the Mendez fiasco. Ever since, I have been keeping my own records. As for my suspicions that Matthew Cambridge is the serial rapist known as REDO, I'm not really sure when I first suspected, but I am sorry to say that I didn't do enough to get him off the streets. I will take the pain and suffering of REDO's victims to my grave.

The first order of business, Caitlyn, is getting my stuff before Matt does. He told me to bring my files to the station so he could review them before the task force meeting. If I am no longer around, he will use his authority to get my files.

The small envelopes included with this letter have the names of people who can help you get this case solved. Inside mine, there are things about REDO, and something for Camille. Please make sure she gets it – you'll know when the time is right to give it to her. The other envelopes are for people who have information, or skills, or insights that will prove very useful. I think Marilyn McGinn has the most conclusive proof connecting Matt to these crimes. Tread softly with her.

Marilyn and Joey gasp. All eyes turn in their direction, their eyes lock onto one another. Joey reaches for Marilyn's hand. She gives her head a gentle shake. "Sorry for the disruption, Ms. English."

"Marilyn, do you—"

"No."

Caitlyn nods.

The participants go back to their reading.

I hope your higher ups will let you form your own task force and include the recipients of these envelopes. This rapist, your husband, needs to be taken down.

Caitlyn, you are in danger. You know too much, and you are too close to Matt. I don't know how to get you out of this situation—hopefully DA James will help. Once you and the DA decide how to proceed internally, I think it is wise for him to contact his counterparts, especially those working on the task force. Keeping Cambridge busy in that capacity will keep him from racking up any more victims, minimize his time with you, and give you time enough to put together a case against him.

Thank you for your help handling my final wishes. I offer one of my own to you: Stay Safe, Caitlyn.

Ray

When all are finished reading, Michelle collects and shreds their copies. When the grinding is done, Caitlyn begins again. "Along with my letter, I opened the envelope with Ray's name on it. I will be sharing the contents of that later. The ones with your names will be handed out before we disband today. We have a lot of ground to cover, so let me explain how this is going to work. I am going to present Ray's case, there are parts that follow a chronological order, and other parts that include random thoughts, suggestions, and questions. I need your input. I expect on any given subject, there will be more than one of you who have information to add. In front of each of you there is a color card. Please hold up your card if you want to jump into the conversation, Michelle will be keeping a running log of who participates. Additionally, today's proceedings are being video recorded." Michelle hands authorizations of approval to each participant. "Please read and sign," Caitlyn directs. Michelle gathers the forms.

The task force gets to work.

Filling holes.

All eyes are on the wife of Matthew James Cambridge.

"**Where was he?** That was a question Detective Chase asked—he found the answers. On August 29, 2014, when Marilyn McGinn was being raped, HE had a personal day. On September 2, 2015, when Suzi Kekoa was being raped, HE had a personal day. On August 28, 2016, when Connie Braxton was being raped, HE was on vacation. On August 26, 2017, when Connie Braxton was being raped for the second time, HE was on vacation. On August 3, 2018, when Marilyn McGinn was being raped for the second time, HE had a sick day. On August 29, 2019, when Trini Kekoa was being raped, HE had a personal day. On January 8, 2020, when Jenna Farnsworth was being raped, HE was on-call. On January 14, 2020, when Monica Farrell was being raped, HE was on day shift. On January 20, 2020, when Mandy Kelleher was being raped, HE was on day shift."

Joey Mayer raises her card.

Brandan Kelly raises his card.

Caitlyn English raises her card and nods to Joey.

"For those of you who don't know, Marilyn McGinn and I are married. Prior to our marriage, we moved into an apartment building at the corner of Turner and Styles. Move in day was August 1st—move out day was August 5th. On August 3rd Marilyn and I planned a day of unpacking and settling in. Those plans were changed by Detective Cambridge. He might have called in sick to SPD that day, but he also called me and asked that I meet him at SRCC about a case. I waited three hours. He never showed. During my absence from the condo, Marilyn was being raped." She nods to Detective Kelly, "Your turn."

"Cambridge made a trip to APD on January 15, 2020. He arrived moments before Monica Farrell was scheduled to come in for her interview. I asked Matt to sit in on that interview. He gave me some bullshit about jurisdiction. Actually, he said his wife, the ADA in Onondaga, would have his balls if he let a visiting cop sit in on an SPD interview."

All eyes turn Caitlyn's way. "That depends on the circumstances of course, but there were no jurisdictional boundaries for Matt Cambridge. SPD loans him out to Finger Lake communities with regularity. He has limited-scope access to several police department databases, and he'd been tapped to head the REDO task force which would have put him in any interview room in any police department in Upstate New York. There's more to his refusal. We'll circle back." She turns her attention to Michelle, "Please make a notation that we should readdress this issue. Matt's real refusal might come into focus the farther we get into this. Okay, the reason I raised my card—Matt was on day-shift September 14, 2020, but he left our home after dinner and didn't return until well after midnight. That period of time easily gets him to and from Aurora. As for the rape of Mandy Kelleher, her investigative file is on the thin side, and we don't have input from Geneva PD, however, as for Matt's whereabouts on September 20, 2020, he was on day shift, but he was gone all evening. I called him when I woke the morning of September 21st. He said he was on his way back from Geneva, and that he'd been notified by Geneva PD about a rape at Walters College." She holds up a blue leatherbound book, "This is my personal journal. I document events, special dinners, important dates, that sort of thing. It will help establish Matt's timeline on several dates. It most assuredly documents a sizeable purchase from Long Point Winery in Aurora made on September 15, 2020, sometime after he met with Detective Kelly."

"Before you continue, Ms. English," the DA hands Chris Chase a slip of paper. "That is an access code for the Syracuse Police Department personnel database. Chief Barelli has authorized you to go in and get records for Matthew Cambridge for the dates on that slip of paper. Do not review or manipulate any other records."

Caitlyn starts the next topic of discussion. **"Missing information from official files.** Ray made a notation, actually he made several notations about pieces of information missing from SPD files, or things not included on victim or suspect interviews. We are going to take a look at Ray's notations on this, but if Marilyn agrees to a personal testing?"

"I'm in."

"I'm going to read certain sections of your victim statement. Raise your card if there's something to discuss. You arrived in Syracuse from Buffalo, moved your belongings into your garden apartment, ran to the DMV, the insurance company, the college bookstore, and the grocery store. You returned to 44 Central Street, cooked dinner, read for a bit, and retired for the evening. You woke with a masked man on top of you. You mentioned two articles of clothing, a facial mask and a pair of jeans."

Marilyn's card goes up. "He wore a white T-shirt, and a pair of boots, like shitkickers."

"Did you mention those articles at the time of your interview, or are you remembering them now?"

"Both, Ms. English."

"Thank you. Getting back to the statement. You said that after an initial struggle, the rapist became seductive. When he was ready, he straddled you, showed he had a knife, and freed his penis from his jeans. When he cut your top, he sliced your breast, drawing blood."

Marilyn's card goes up. "That was an accident."

Caitlyn silently reviews the statement. "There's no mention of that here."

"I didn't know it at the time. When REDO came back for his second rape, he ran his finger across my scar and said he didn't mean to cut me, but that it made the experience memorable. That notation should be in my second victim statement."

Caitlyn and the rest of the DA staff review their copies. Each shakes their head in the negative. "Michelle, make a notation to circle back." She pulls a breath and continues. "The rape was vaginal. The rapist left a goodbye kiss and the suggestion that the two of you might meet again."

Marilyn nods.

Chris Chase's card goes up.

"Yes, Chris."

"My father was pushing hard about the discrepancies between his files and the SPD files. When he pulled me into the Cambridge investigation, he played catch up by doing a brief rundown on some stuff. I recorded our conversation, and…"

The DA pushes in, "Was the recording made with Raymond Chase's consent?"

"Yes. It's stated on the recording."

The DA and the ADA share a consenting nod. "Proceed, Chris."

Chris finds the recording on his cell…

"Son. Before you start, why don't you sit and listen for a few. I'll read the victim statements, maybe something will jump out."

"I'm going to key in stuff, and I'm making a recording, okay?"

"Yes."

"Okay, shoot."

Chris stops the recording. "The next few minutes are a complete reading of each victim statement. For time purposes, I'm going to skip through and pick up where we begin talking."

"Proceed."

"I'm gonna hold off on Monica Farrell's statement, and I don't have Mandy Kelleher's yet. Anything interesting jump out, Chris?"

"First off, I'm removing Trini Kekoa from this review. There are too many variables—she wasn't a repeat rape, and in the rapist's mind, she wasn't really a new rape either."

"Okay."

"As for the others, Marilyn, Suzi, Connie, and Jenna, they all mentioned: mask, knife, jeans, and a cut breast. They recounted near-identical sequences of events and sentences spoken. There were little nuances like minty breath and chapped lips, and there are a few notable variables as well. Suzi was the only one who said he touched her neck when she became upset. She said the knife he used had a hole in the center of it, and he had his finger through the hole. Connie Braxton said the rapist used a gold-tipped knife. Jenna said he wore an undershirt. The other women didn't mention what he wore on top. He had to have worn something, right?"

"And **whatever** he wore would have his victim's blood on it. I need to dig deep into these files and check the information on the new victims."

Joey raises her card.

Chris raises his card.

Joey starts. "I received a phone call in the middle of the night from Detective Chase—"

"I'm sorry to interrupt, Joey, but my father called you while in my presence, and I taped his end of the conversation, with his permission."

"Play the recording, Chris."

"Wait, Dad. Let me record this."

"Okay."

"Let's start again. What are you looking for?"

"The transcript from the UU SART examination on Jenna Farnsworth. I don't think I made a copy for my home files."

"But you saw one at work?"

"Yes."

"There's something in it."

"Yes, I think. I'm tired, Chris. My brain's fried, but I think Jenna mentioned a wedding ring during her interview, but it's not on the victim statement I read you earlier. Right?"

"Right."

"I'm getting mixed up with all of the victim's details."

"Can you get a copy of the SART sheet or get the information from someone without having to go to the station?"

"Yes."

The DA interrupts, "Chris, stop the recording. Ms. Mayer is this the conversation you were beginning to tell us about?"

"Yes."

"Please tell us what was discussed."

"Detective Chase called around two in the morning. He stressed that he and I were **not** having the conversation we were about to have, and that aside from Marilyn, I was to tell no one about it. He said he couldn't get his hands on the SART recording or transcript made during the exams of Jenna Farnsworth. He asked me to rattle off things I remembered from her description of the rapist. I told him Jenna mentioned mask, jeans, undershirt, knife, dark eyes, minty breath, and a wedding ring. He repeated the words 'wedding ring' and asked me if I was sure. I said I was. Then he asked me if I would ask Jenna what she did, what errands she ran, when she first arrived in Syracuse. I told Marilyn what the detective said, and after running the conversation over and over and over again, I floated the theory that Detective Chase thought the newly married Matt Cambridge is REDO."

Caitlyn is rendered temporarily mute, she self-consciously checks her watch while she reorganizes her thoughts. "Okay, someone will be joining us in an hour. His input relates to the Jenna Farnsworth case. I'd like to push through some discrepancies Ray found on that investigation before our guest arrives."

She gets nods from all around.

Caleb Sanchez's card goes up. "I'm not familiar with the assault on Ms. Farnsworth. Do you have time to give some details?"

"Of course. Jenna Farnsworth is the first REDO victim of 2020. Her investigation is in the preliminary stage, but there is plenty for an initial review. Ms. Farnsworth relocated from Philly to Syracuse at the beginning of January. She moved into a sublet a few days before her rape at 10 Oren Street. On the night of January 8, 2020, she shared dinner with her male roommate, Keith Moreno. He left the premises at 5 PM, and she retired for the evening sometime after 9 PM. She woke in the midst of a scream with a man on top of her. The rapist stayed on script verbally and through his actions. He seduced the victim, straddled her, exposed himself, pulled a knife from his ankle area and sliced her breast. She said he took pleasure knowing she was a virgin. He vaginally raped her, left a goodbye kiss, and the intimation that they might know one another."

"To sow suspicion," Chris mumbles.

All eyes turn his way.

"Sorry."

"No. No. It's a point to consider given that Matt Cambridge might have been doctoring statements to frame Keith Moreno, the only man she knew in Syracuse. In the days preceding his death, Ray Chase did a follow-up interview with Mr. Moreno, and Edith Cunningham, an elderly woman who lives across the street from 10

Oren. I'm going to read the discrepancies Detective Chase found."

Chris' card is raised. "I have my father's cell. He recorded his conversation with Mr. Moreno."

"Did he get Mr. Moreno's consent to the recording?"

"A few seconds into the conversation."

"Proceed."

"Where's the asshole?"

"Not sure. Can I come in?"

"Not unless my lawyer's here."

"How about we both record this conversation."

"I'm recording this, Detective Chase. Again, I won't answer questions without my lawyer."

"I won't ask any questions. I just want you to read something."

"Come on in."

"Nice place. You did the work?"

"That's a question, and I'm not answering it."

"Right. Sorry. Was anything left out of that statement?"

"Yes."

"Do you want to tell me?"

"It doesn't mention my stopping at Steny Thomas' place to get air in my tire."

"I don't remember you mentioning that."

"You left the interview room to talk to someone in the hall. I told your asshole partner. I think I asked him to check with Steny to see if he has security cameras at the station. Did that asshole leave it out on purpose? You'll check with Steny, right?"

"Nice work on your place, Mr. Moreno."

Chris shuts off Ray's cell.

Joey Mayer's card goes up. "Ms. English, I want to address the flat tire issue when the next participant arrives."

"Michelle, please make a note to remind me. Okay, moving on to the interview Ray did with Mrs. Cunningham. I'll handle this unless Chris has a surprise recording for us."

"Sorry."

"Okay. These are the discrepancies or omissions Ray noted. 1) Mrs. Cunningham said that shortly after she heard a woman scream, she looked outside and saw a dark colored 'boxy car' without a bit of snow on it parked at the Fletcher's house. Ray highlighted the following words: **There is no mention of a car at the Fletcher's house in Cambridge's report**. 2) Mrs. Cunningham said the back porch light at Mr. Moreno's house was off when she looked out the window. She said she told the other detective that Keith is very good about putting it on, but assumed the new girl forgot. Ray highlighted the following words: **There is no mention of a back porch light being on or off in Cambridge's report**."

Joey Mayer's card goes up. "Ms. English, I want to address the back door light issue when the next participant arrives."

"Another reminder, Michelle. Okay. Ray made the following notes. **Blue Victorian. Driveway is on the left. There's tree cover between the Fletcher's house and the Moreno house. He gets**

out of the boxy thing—gets into the tree line—gets to the back door—kills the light—gets in—gets out."

Joey Mayer's card goes up. "Ms. English, I want to address the tree cover between the houses when the next participant arrives."

Michelle preempts, "Got it ADA English."

Chris' card goes up. "There's an additional piece to my father's conversation with Keith Moreno. It relates to this topic."

"Proceed, Chris."

"Mr. Moreno, what entrance did you use on January 8th?"

"The back door."

"Do you have an outdoor light source at the back door?"

"Yes."

"Was it on or off when you left?"

"On."

"And when you returned, on or off?"

"On."

"Are you certain?"

"Yes. The back of the house is really dark because of the tree line. I put it on when I left, and it was still on when I got back. That's how I could tell the inside door was open."

"Thank you Chris. Most of you know that Matt Cambridge drives a black Land Rover. I suspect he parked his vehicle at the Fletcher's house the night of Jenna Farnsworth's rape, and that's why he left that bit of information out of Mrs. Cunningham's report." The ADA checks her watch, "Okay, I think we have enough time to squeeze the next topic in. Ray titled the next page **What happened in REDO's life between September and January?"**

The DA answers the question.
"He married you, Caitlyn."

Z ... Y ... X ... W ... V

Michelle ushers everyone out of the conference room leaving the DA and the ADA alone.

The man helps the stunned woman to a chair and kneels in front of her. He ignores propriety and takes her hands in his, "I'm sorry I blurted that out. The thought came, and I wanted it on the record." He takes a handkerchief from his breast pocket and hands it to her.

"I'm his trigger? For the last three rapes?" She bends at the waist, puts her head into her hands, and her hands onto her knees.

"English." The DA places his hand onto the back of her head and gently strokes, "English, you do not share **any** responsibility for the actions of that degenerate." His spoken words cause the opposite desired effect.

Racking sobs muffle up from the breaking woman.

Weston James runs his hands down her arms, wraps them around her wrists and pulls her upright. She presses into his open embrace and welcomes his comfort—until she doesn't.

She pushes free and stammers her objection, "You're my boss. This is inappropriate. I need to..." she squares her shoulders, dries her tears on his hankie, and marches out of the room.

Robert 'Mac' McLaughlin carries his Army issue duffle bag to his Humvee, puts it on the floor of the passenger seat, starts the engine, shifts into gear, and heads to downtown Syracuse. "Review your plan. Execute each step. Keep your head clear." That's the beginning of a chant that will stay with him until he reaches his destination. It's the one he used on every ranger mission he conducted. "Review your plan. Execute each step. Keep your head clear." As the miles pass, he moves beyond the mantra and settles into the business at hand. "Your future is on the line. Jenna's safety is on the line. **Get your head in the game!**" By the time he enters the DA building, he has his shit together. He stops at lobby security, "District Attorney James is expecting me."

"Name?"

"Robert McLaughlin."

"Put the duffle on the counter. We need to inspect it before you go upstairs."

"I am refusing that request. You need to call DA James or ADA English. If you open that duffle you will have compromised evidence in a case I'm working on with them. Call them."

Within seconds, Mac is approached by the head of security. "I'll escort you upstairs, Mr. McLaughlin."

Michelle greets the duffle-toting man at reception. "We are in the DA's conference room, please follow me. My name is Michelle Young, Mr. McLaughlin."

"Call me Mac."

The attendees file back into the room and take their seats. The DA nods to Michelle who introduces the new arrival. She hands him a release form and makes a move toward the duffle. He stops her hand and holds onto it. "I am not relinquishing that duffle or its contents to you, or anyone in this room until I've had my say and procured assurances."

Michelle eyes the DA who nods.

Caitlyn returns in time to catch the tail end of the conversation. She approaches the new attendee and extends her hand, "Mr. McLaughlin, I'm ADA Caitlyn English."

"Ms. English, are you aware that your husband is a very dangerous man?"

She breathes deeply and exhales slowly, "I am. I hope you are willing to do your part to put him behind bars for the rest of his miserable life."

Mac smiles. "I am."

"Good. Let's get down to business. Michelle, please give Mac a color card. Simple rules about the card, if someone is speaking and you have something to say raise your card. Okay, a few more things before we break for lunch. After that, it'll be the Joey Mayer and Robert McLaughlin show."

Everyone nods.

"We have completed this morning's chart work. I wish I could catch you up, Mac, but we need to push through. In a nutshell we are finishing an investigation started by Detective

Raymond Chase. He identified Matthew Cambridge as the serial rapist known as REDO." Caitlyn assesses the non-response from Mac. "You don't seem surprised."

"I am not."

"Okay, let me push through the following topics. They are miscellaneous, almost throw outs by Ray. They were sealed inside the envelope with his name on it. I'll offer my insight when I have it, but I really hope this team has information to share. Let's begin with a note from Ray saying he talked to a woman named Mary Raines in Paris."

Mac's card is raised.

Joey's card is raised.

Marilyn's card is raised.

Mac takes this one. "Mary Raines is the childhood friend of Jenna Farnsworth and former girlfriend of Keith Moreno. Mary is doing a study abroad in Paris, and it's her room at Oren Street that Jenna is subletting."

Joey and Marilyn lower their cards.

Caitlyn nods. "Okay, next to Mary's name Ray noted. **Keith is not a rapist,** and next to that he noted, **former boyfriend of Monica Farrell.**"

All eyes are on Brandan Kelly, "First I'm hearing of this, but Monica said she was originally from Syracuse. She said she ran into a former boyfriend over the holidays, but as far as boyfriends who hit her, she only mentioned Evan Sayles."

DA James pushes in, "Farrell is the interview Matt Cambridge watched through the two-way?"

"Yes."

"Detective Kelly, in retrospect, would you say Matt Cambridge was purposeful in his avoidance of Ms. Farrell?"

"Yes."

"Michelle, please make a notation that our investigators should press into the connection between Monica Farrell and Keith Moreno. We need to make sure there's nothing between these two. Please continue ADA English."

"The next topic for discussion is DNA Phenotyping. How many of you have heard of this in general terms?"

Three color cards are raised.

"And in relation to this case?"

Three color cards are lowered.

"For those of you unfamiliar with DNA phenotyping, it is a controversial analysis procedure, favored by some in law enforcement and opposed by most of the general public. The process accurately identifies genetic ancestry using DNA: eye color, hair color, skin color, and face shape of individuals from any ethnic background, including those with mixed ancestry, are part of the end result of the testing procedure. We're going to conduct a demonstration that will illustrate the process and explain why its use is controversial. Everyone stand up. If I identify a characteristic that does not apply to you, please sit down. Okay, the police answer a 9-1-1 call and find a dead body on a lonely stretch of highway. During a cursory review of the crime scene, a detective notices a hair on the lapel of the murder victim's jacket. The hair is run through DNA phenotyping. Without canvassing the area for witnesses, or conducting a single interview, the police learn their suspect is of African descent."

"Of course he is," Chris jokes.

"I didn't mention gender, Mr. Chase. Okay, anyone who is not of African descent, please be seated."

Three people remain standing: Chris Chase, Joey Mayer, and Caleb Sanchez.

"Our suspect is male." Joey takes a seat. "Our suspect is also of French ancestry." Chris and Caleb remain standing. "Our suspect has brown hair." The men remain standing. "And blue eyes." Chris takes a seat. "Mr. Sanchez, you are under arrest for the murder of our fictitious victim. You have the right to remain silent." The room enjoys the levity. "Detective Sanchez, would you please explain your ancestry?"

"My maternal family came from Africa as slaves, settled in the French Quarter of New Orleans, and my paternal family is Mexican descent."

"Thank you, please be seated. Thanks for playing everyone. Now imagine how shallow the pool of suspects would be if law enforcement knew they were looking for a man of African and French descent with brown hair and blue eyes.

Now imagine the public outcry if the police began rounding up men who fit that description. Now imagine if someone wanted to frame a man of African and French descent with brown hair and blue eyes."

The DA offers his thoughts. "The ADA and I think Detective Chase considered running his partner's DNA after Ray was delivered a death sentence. He knew his time was running out, and we think he needed to know for sure if Cambridge was REDO before he died. Getting Cambridge's profile through DNA phenotyping would have been useless without running it against DNA from our crime scenes, and there's nothing to indicate Ray did that, but he was definitely after something."

Marilyn McGinn pushes from the table and shouts, "DNA Phenotyping! OH. MY. GOD. Joseph!" She turns to DA James. "My son needs protection, now. Right now!"

"Who is your son?"

She falls back onto her seat. "I am the mother of REDO's son."

The DA reacts. **"Everyone except Marilyn McGinn, Joey Mayer, and Caitlyn English, leave this room."**

Mac moves past the DA, "I'm a medic and Ms. McGinn needs medical attention."

The DA nods.

Mac kneels in front of Marilyn and puts his fingers to her pulse point. He speaks softly, "Marilyn, concentrate on my voice. Breathe in ......

Breath out .... Can you recite the alphabet backwards?"

She shakes her head.

"Try. Concentrate on the letters not on anything else."

"Z ... Y ... X ... W ... V." Her breathing slows. Her pulse slows.

"Good, keep going."

She begins shaking her head, "No. No. No. Evelyn." She searches for her wife. "Joey! Do something!"

"What is it, Marilyn. Look at me, babe. Breathe with me. Whatever it is, we'll work it."

Marilyn fights for composure. "Evelyn said some guy started playing peek-a-boo with Joseph while they were in line at a grocery store. The guy said his name was Matt and he had a son who looked just like Joseph."

Joey bolts up and addresses the DA. "Evelyn Dolan is Marilyn's sister. She and her husband Chet have been raising Joseph since birth. They live at 77 Maplewood Lane in Buffalo. Can you send the police to do a wellness check?"

The DA is in motion before Joey stops speaking. "Marilyn, it's best that you call your sister while I'll call the authorities. Come with me."

When they leave the room, Caitlyn English slumps back against a wall, slides its length, and drops to the floor. She shakes her head at Mac when he approaches, "Please leave."

The DA finds her on the floor many minutes later, "Are in you need of an assist up?"

"No."

He joins her, "The Dolans of Buffalo are safe and are being placed into protective custody."

She sniffles.

He hands her a crisp, new handkerchief, "This is becoming routine, ADA English." He waits several minutes before speaking. "Are you resting or thinking?"

She scoffs, "Are you serious?" As soon as the words find air, she remembers to whom she is speaking. She begins to apologize—stops when he puts up his hand.

"You have permission to speak freely for the duration, English."

SO. SHE. DOES. "In a matter of days, I learned that my husband is a serial rapist who finds sadistic pleasure in raping his victims, not once, but twice, that he is the father of a son born to one of his victims, and his future atrocities will most likely begin with my rape, followed by my murder. My thoughts on all that? I'm disgusted, ashamed, horrified, desperate, and scared shitless, sir." She pulls a breath, "Moreover, I am driven to nail his balls to the wall. Not sure if those were the thoughts you expected, but there you have it. If you will excuse me, I am starved." She pushes from the floor, turns on her heels and heads to the lunchroom.

Syracuse state-of-mind.

Members of the REDO task force—the one in Cayuga County—are on a lunch break. Matt Cambridge is seated next to Isla Conway, though his thoughts are 34.67 miles away.

Onondaga County DA Weston, no show. Onondaga County ADA English, no show. Cayuga County Detective Kelly, no show. Tompkins County Detective Sanchez, no show. Looks like there might be another REDO task force in Syracuse. I need to get on the road.

DA Isla Conway repeats herself, "Isn't that right, Detective Cambridge?"

"Ma'am?"

"I was saying that the momentum of the task force suggests REDO's days are numbered," she smiles wide.

"We'll see," he smiles wider.

Planted evidence and retribution.

"Before we get to Robert McLaughlin, I'm going to open the floor for comments and additions."

Brandan Kelly's card is raised. "I want to circle the drain for a minute." He addresses Marilyn. "May I ask you a few questions?"
"Yes."
"Matt Cambridge sat in on your post-SART exam interviews at UU?"
"Yes."
"And he conducted your police interviews at SPD?"
"Yes."
"And he prepared your victim statements for signature?"
"Yes."
"Marilyn, I read Ms. Farnsworth's statement a few minutes ago. You were the paramedic on scene after her rape, and Matt Cambridge was the detective on scene."
"Yes."
"And Detective Cambridge was present for Ms. Farnsworth's post-SART interview at the hospital?"
"Yes."
"Matt Cambridge doesn't shy away from being in the same room with his victims after he raped them. One could argue that being with

them after the fact was part of his thing. Except when it came to Monica Farrell. Put a pin in that for a minute. A few days ago, I got a call from Ray. He asked if I was looking at Evan Sayles as being REDO. I told him that Sayles is an ass and he likes to get rough with his women, but it's a mutual thing. Ray pressed in, he wanted to know what made Sayles turn the corner from smacking Monica to beating her. I told him Sayles got pissed when he found Monica chatting up a man outside their cabin. She told Sayles the guy was out on a ramble and just happened by and that she didn't even know the guy's name."

"His name is Matthew Cambridge," Caitlyn whispers, then repeats, "His name is Matthew Cambridge."

"That's what I'm thinking, Ms. English. And that's why Cambridge didn't want to be in the same room with Monica Farrell. If he is Rambling Man, then she would have connected the detective from Syracuse to the guy from Cayuga Lake."

Caitlyn starts pacing. Her breathing becomes quick and her hands take on a life of their own. "Cayuga Lake. Long Point Winery. Aurora." She paces a bit more, "Cayuga Lake. Long Point Winery. Aurora."

She stops when the DA addresses her. "English. Explain what's going on."

"The night Ray Chase came to my house to ask me to draw up his final papers, he remarked on the wine crates in my kitchen. I told him Matt and I got married at Long Point Winery, and he stopped on his way home from Aurora to buy some wine. Ray said he didn't know people had weddings at wineries and asked if they have overnight accommodations. I said some do, but not Long Point. Then I told him Matt and I spent our wedding night at a little cabin on Cayuga Lake." The energy in the conference room intensifies.

"Cayuga Lake," Chris mumbles, his fingers start flying across his keyboard. Michelle leans over and watches. She knows what he's looking for.

Caitlyn knows too, "Chris keep looking. I need to keep pushing." She pulls a note from Ray's files, "Cut breast. Bloody T-shirts."

Everyone raises their color card.

Mac stands up, "I'll take this one." He lifts his duffle from the floor and bangs it onto the table. "Inside this bag is evidence Matt Cambridge planted in my house to frame me for the rape of Jenna Farnsworth. Underneath my neatly folded Army gear is a bloody T-shirt. I believe there is a knife tucked into the shirt, as well as a round object."

The room stills.

"A few nights ago, Matt Cambridge parked his Land Rover at my bungalow. He knocked on both the front and back doors, and when I didn't answer, he unscrewed the lightbulb at my back door, picked the lock, and went inside, where he remained for three minutes. When he left, he screwed the lightbulb back in, went to his Land

Rover, put on a camouflage parka that belongs to me, and waited for Joey Mayer and Marilyn McGinn to leave their meeting with Jenna Farnsworth. After they drove past, Matt Cambridge exited his vehicle, moved into the tree line between my house and the Farnsworth's house, put on a black ski-mask, went onto the back porch, removed the outside light and began picking the lock. He stopped to remove his cell phone from his pocket, tightened the bulb back into place, and hightailed it back to his vehicle arriving moments before a Cleveland police car arrived. Apparently, Jenna placed an emergency call to them when she heard a noise."

The DA addresses Joey Mayer, "Can you attest to any of this?"

"Yes. Marilyn and I were with Jenna that night. We had to leave her alone because Marilyn was on 11-7 duty. Emmett and Grace Farnsworth were very late getting home from BINGO because they needed to stop to get air for their flat tire."

"He flattened their tire, just like he flattened Keith Moreno's tire. He planned on raping Jenna again that night." Caitlyn stammers.

"No," the DA, the ranger, and the two detectives say in unison. Three men remain silent—one explains.

"Cambridge dressed like me so that when he scared the shit out of Jenna, she'd think it was me. After all, who else would be wearing my Army-issue camouflage parka? Not only would she have been convinced I was her rapist, but she probably would have moved out of her grandparents' bungalow to get away from me and gone back to Keith Moreno's. Cambridge was setting the stage for his return to 10 Oren Street for his REDO performance."

The DA raises his hand. The room silences. He makes back-to-back calls, "DA James for Judge Landers ……. Henry, we need a search warrant for the home of Matthew Cambridge and Caitlyn English. We are looking for evidence pertaining to the serial rapist known as REDO. My office will fax over probable cause documents and a list of items for search and seizure. I need to cut this short, Henry. He places his second call to Chief Barelli. "David, a request for a search warrant for the Cambridge and English house in Fayetteville is in the works. Please make a call to DA Conway to inform her. Hopefully, she can have REDO arrested at the task force meeting, or better yet at the news conference."

Chris addresses the DA as soon as he ends his call, "Sir, you might want to get a search warrant for a cabin at mile marker CL-14 in Aurora. It is owned by a trust listed as MJC: 18-5-4-15. The alpha and numeric for that listing is Matthew James Cambridge: REDO."

The DA directs Detectives Kelly and Sanchez, "Get to Aurora. I'm contacting DA Conway to make the arrest of Matthew Cambridge and the issuance of a search warrant for the cabin located at CL-14. I expect you'll find a cache of bloody T-shirts and maybe a set of cutlery. Keep in touch with this office, Detectives."

After the men leave, the DA addresses Marilyn McGinn, "Would you consent to a DNA test on your son?"

"Yes."

"English, draw up the paperwork. I need to make a call."

Isla Conway's cell vibrates. She ignores it. She'd answer the call, but she is too busy watching various and sundry law enforcement professionals scramble in their effort to locate Matthew Cambridge. Her heart picks up speed and her hands tingle with sweat when the assembled media realizes there's a story unfolding around them.

"DA Conway. The announcement. Is this about a string of rapes in Upstate NY?"

"Ms. Conway, DA Conway. The public has a right to know if there's a rapist targeting college coeds."

Isla steps away from the microphones and answers the incoming call. She fumes at DA James. "He's gone!"

Wifey, I'm coming to get you.

        Matt Cambridge boosted a ride nearly thirty minutes before the press conference was set to begin. He knows he should be heading away from Syracuse, away from trouble, but his need for survival isn't as powerful as his need for retribution, and his need to hear —

Her Scream

Caitlyn English

A mere touch away.

The DA accompanies the ADA to her home to get a few things. He'll learn in short order what a few things means to Caitlyn English.

Stanner parks the Caddie on the street leaving enough driveway space for the expected arrivals. He stands guard at the front door until the Chief of Police and other SPD brass enter the lovely brick home to conduct a search and seizure. Within minutes, the street fills with patrol cars. Stanner moves to the perimeter as cops take sentry all around.

"Good show, boys. Now go get the fucker."

When the dignitaries exit the home of Caitlyn English, each is carrying a suitcase, or duffle bag, or messenger bag, or backpack—all of which hold the belongings of Caitlyn English. She is carrying her files on REDO. Stanner takes the baggage, packs his ride, then takes his place in the shit show of flashing lights.

Cambridge is no longer up close and personal for the comings and goings at his home in Fayetteville, but he's still watching. He laughs big at the ignorant muscle in the Caddie. "Rule #1, never leave your ride unaccompanied and out of sight, you might end up being the victim of a slap-and-tack. Now, let's see where you're heading because wherever you go, my bitch goes." Forty-five minutes later the Caddie stops in Marietta, NY. "DA James lives in Marietta. Looks like DA James took my wife home. Quite the consolation prize for the Cowboy. Maybe she'll let you take her for a ride. Enjoy yourself Weston because the next time I see you, it will be through a scope. And you, Mrs. Cambridge, the next time we're together, you'll be at the wrong end of a blade." He checks his surroundings, ditches the stolen car, and makes his way through the streets of Syracuse. "Right now, I need to go low, but I won't stay down for long."

Caitlyn is quiet.

The DA uses that time to prepare for his conversation with Isla Conway, and mentally formulate the statement the two will give the press. "That'll be a shit show."

"I'm sorry, did you say something?"

He laughs. "Not used to having company on my ride home. I tend to talk things through in the car."

"I'm a shower-talker, myself, but the car works." The next several minutes are quiet.

"Penny for your thoughts, English."

"Hardly worth a penny, sir." She sits straight in her seat when they turn off a very dark, very forested two-lane road onto a well-packed dirt and gravel road that travels through thick woods and over a split log bridge that spans a wide babbling brook. The two-vehicle caravan moves slowly, their way lighted only by headlights. The scant illumination makes the transition from dirt and darkness to a beautiful tree lined path with antique wrought-iron lampposts quite remarkable. And when they arrive at the home of Weston James, it deserves comment, if one were able to speak.

"Cowboy," she whispers.

He laughs, "I'm from Montana. This home is a replica of my granddaddy's place. Come on, I'll show you around, **after** we eat, I'm starved." Weston sets Caitlyn's briefcase inside the front door, takes her coat and hangs it on a black iron arched hook. "Stanner and I trade off on the cooking. I'm afraid to say, it's my turn. Why don't you look around while I change unless you'd also like to."

She shakes her head. He nods then bounds up the double-wide staircase. Caitlyn walks and talks the space. "Massive center foyer, wide open rooms, vaulted ceilings, all wood construction. Masculine designed—woman adorned. Slate gray leather sofas, softened by dove gray and plum pillows. Built-in bookcases flank a beautiful stone fireplace with the last throes of dying embers. Built-in gun cases of glass and black iron and an array of cowboy inspired paintings and sculptures. Cowboy." She leans toward a particularly impressive painting to read the artist's name, and startles when the homeowner speaks from behind.

"Frederick Remington is a personal favorite."

"Mmm. His work is so lifelike. My eye goes to the horse rather than the rider, or even the landscape. I expect the horse to turn toward me and snort."

"Remington was born in New York, but the heart of his work is all Montana. Do you ride?"

"Mmm. English is my preference, but I ride Western too." She blushes at the play on words, *English riding Weston.* She turns from the paintings and startles again when she sees the MAN crouched low, attending the fire. He's wearing a flannel shirt, pair of well-worn jeans, and buckskinned slippers. She rethinks changing out of her work clothes, "I think I'd like to freshen up."

"Stanner brought your bags upstairs. Turn left at the top, last room on the right."

When she returns to the first floor, her face has been scrubbed free of the little makeup she usually wears, and her hair has been pulled high into a ponytail. She's replaced her business attire with a form-fitting, pale pink turtleneck, a pair of button-front, bootcut jeans, and ankle-high Mukluk booties. She thinks she hears a moan when she enters the kitchen. "The guest room is lovely, and though I could only see lights in the distance, the view off the bedroom deck is breathtaking. Can I help with anything?" He points to a high stool at a granite island. She takes a seat, then points to eggplant stained cabinetry, "Those are beautiful."

His thanks is filled with pride.

"You built them?"

"Built, yes. Installed, no."

"I have to tell you ……." she stops unsure of what to call him.

He laughs, "While you're here, call me whatever is comfortable for you."

She nods, "I have to tell you ……." she rolls the options through her head and settles on what she's most comfortable with. "I have to tell you, sir," she smiles and continues, "I half expect that you are hiding a superhero persona somewhere. DA by day—gun-toting, horse-riding, hero by night."

"Let me return the compliment, ADA by day—steely-spined, razor-focused, heroine by night. I've yet to lay eyes on a woman so fierce."

"I don't feel fierce at the moment, but I am very grateful for the reprieve from needing a steely spine—even if for only one night. Being tucked away on a heavily forested cowboy fortress won't be enough to keep Cambridge from getting me, I'm afraid. I've brought danger to your doorstep, sir, and it needs to be a temporary situation."

"You will be staying here indefinitely."

She ignores the comment and rescues herself from further discussion by pointing to what appears to be a built-in pizza oven. She raises a quizzical brow.

He smiles and explains. "That is the only structural difference between my ranch and my family's ranch back home. Prior to my coming to New York for college, I'd never had a slice of pizza."

"Did you say you're from Montana or Mars?"

He laughs. He is finding her company enjoyable. "My family's ranch is as far from city life and city food as a place can be. We live off the land and our idea of living large is heading into White Sulphur Springs, in Meagher County, Montana, population some below a thousand. There are no pizza joints in the Springs. The first time I took a bite of a New York pizza pie, I was struck deep and hooked for life. I try to live off my land here, grow what I can and cook from scratch whenever I can, but a man's just got to have his pizza—this man, anyway. If you're here long enough, I'll make you a pie."

Chef DA has been gathering this and that from the huge side by side refrigerator and mammoth cupboards while he talks. Plastic bags of pre-chopped veggies line the counter, a cast iron skillet has been drizzled with olive oil and sprinkled with a variety of herbs and spices that sizzle when the cold peppers, broccoli florets, mushrooms and slices of red onion hit the pan. He lowers the heat to simmer after a minute or two, covers the pan and sets about pouring some wine. Clearly comfortable in his kitchen and in no need of help, Caitlyn offers to set the table. He smiles, "Plates and glasses are there. Silverware and napkins are there. And we'll eat in the kitchen, so the table is there."

Making quick work of her chore, she heads to French doors that lead to an expansive deck, "May I?"

He points to a Sherpa-lined, buckskin jacket, "Better put that on."

She is swallowed by the heavy jacket that smells of outdoor freshness and man—all man—that man. She is pulling her third deep breath of night air when he steps outside. He pulls a deep breath of his own as he hands her a glass of red.

"It's the stars."

"What?"

"The stars, they're the ones I'd be seeing if I were in Montana. They're why I found my way to staying here after law school."

Caitlyn gets lost in the beauty of the nighttime sky.

West gets lost in the beauty of the woman a mere touch away—the one who needs to stay a mere touch away.

I should have known.

Marilyn and Joey meet Mac at the Farnsworth bungalow. They are welcomed in. Sort of.

Joey takes control of the gathering. "Have you been listening to the news?"

She receives three headshakes.

"Good. We wanted to tell you what's going on." She steps in front of Jenna, "There's an arrest warrant out for Detective Matt Cambridge. He is the man who raped you. He is the serial rapist known as REDO."

"REDO?"

"His pattern is to rape his victims then return for a second rape."

Jenna doubles over and struggles to breathe. Marilyn helps her sit, and begins rubbing her back, "Concentrate on my touch, I'm with you, Jenna. Slow breaths, That's right."

After a minute or two, she rights herself. Tears fill her cobalt-blues when she looks at Mac. Fat droplets are quick to run the length of her face and slide silently onto her folded hands. "Mac," she whispers.

He kneels in front of the woman he loves, the one he's loved since her first summer visit. "Can you handle more information?"

She nods.

"The big picture is this. The detective committed the crime of rape on multiple occasions, manipulated or omitted evidence in official reports, threw suspicion toward suspects, then framed them. In your case, the first person Cambridge tried to frame was Keith Moreno. When it looked like he had an alibi, Cambridge came after me. The night you called the Cleveland police, the detective was outside your back door trying to break in." He gives her a minute before continuing. "After meeting with you three, he went to my place on the guise of wanting to ask me questions. What he really wanted was to break into my place and plant evidence: a bloody T-shirt with your blood on it and the knife he used during his attack. After he put that stuff into my duffle, he stole one of my jackets, snuck through the trees that buffer our properties, put on a ski-mask, unscrewed the lightbulb at the back door, and began picking the lock. He reversed course and made it back to his vehicle moments before CPD arrived. I know all of this, Jenna, because I was spying on him from the ditch along the retaining wall. I would not have let him enter your bungalow."

Jenna pulls a shaky breath and offers her part of the story. "I called his phone right before I called Cleveland police. That's probably why he reversed course." She turns to Joey, "Remember, I told you there was something wrong when Cambridge didn't answer my call even though he said he was at Mac's."

Joey nods.

"And Keith? Does he know?"

"If he's watching the news," Joey answers.

Jenna begins shaking again. "Cambridge is a serial rapist. The man who came to my aide. The man who interviewed me and listened to my story of pain and suffering was the man who inflicted that pain and suffering. The man who stole my virginity is the man who said he'd hunt the man who raped me. If I had a gun I would hunt him myself and blow his balls off!"

"Emmett has a gun," Grams says as she begins toward her bedroom.

Gramps slides his arm around his wife's shoulder, "Gracie, I think it's best we let the police handle this."

Jenna bends at the waist as though she's been sucker-punched. "Oh, Mac. I'm so sorry," her rage scatters and leaves her weak and trembling with guilt.

He approaches, "May I hold you, Jenna?"

She nods, and when he pulls her into his arms they tighten around. She sobs into his chest. "I should have known it wasn't you."

A place to hide.

Cambridge left his boosted ride miles from his place of shelter then made his way through evening shadow. He unlocked the main gate at a storage facility on the outskirts of Syracuse and entered a code at his personal unit, 18-5-4-15. He slipped inside and took a deep breath then coughed greatly. "Gas fumes." He rolled the door, slipped a piece of wood beneath it, and let the space air out. He grabbed a duffle from the corner, tossed it onto the bed of his stored F-150 and passed the fuck out.

Twisted son-of-a-bitch.

Weston James and Caitlyn English are cleaning the kitchen when his cell rings. He knows who's calling without looking at the display. "Excuse me, Ms. English."

Isla Conway doesn't bother with pleasantries. "We got the warrant an hour ago. Captain Simms, along with Detectives Kelly and Sanchez searched the cabin at CL-14. There are bloodstained T-shirts, ten of them, West. There are other victims." She pauses, chokes a bit. "There are several knives, and a handwritten journal that details his crimes. He's been at this a long time. There's a section in the journal that is beyond disturbing. It's titled, **Her Scream**. It goes into haunting detail about, **The sound that brands our souls for all eternity**. That's the subheading in the journal. This guy is a twisted son-of-a-bitch, and he's one of us, West."

"I agree with the first part of that sentence, but you're way off the mark on the rest. Are you processing this shit alright, Isla?"

She laughs, "You do know who I am, right?"

"Yeah, you're the Iron Hand."

"I'd love to get my Iron Hands around this fucker's throat. By the way, you owe me for the next hundred years for making me dine with a serial rapist, who I'm sure would have fucked me and sliced me if not for my detail. Speaking of which, Weston, you might want to up your security. You're secluded, but your property is penetrable."

"Working on it. I'll call you tomorrow. Good work, Isla."

Are they involved? Caitlyn wonders as she puts away the last of the dishes.

The man and woman make their way to a den off the kitchen located very near the DA's home office. After she takes a look around, they take seats on two overstuffed, upholstered club chairs. They swing their legs onto ottomans set in front of each and get lost in the flicker of a fire in a black iron corner fireplace. He reads a text, then turns on an oversized, wall-mounted T.V.

Breaking news: Outcry across Onondaga County is fast and furious. Citizens are clamoring to know why District Attorney, Weston James, and Chief of Police, David Barelli, withheld information about a serial rapist targeting college-aged women in the Finger Lakes region. Though not confirmed, our news team has linked sexual assaults near college campuses throughout Upstate New York beginning as early as 2014. Neither James nor Barelli have issued a statement or returned calls for comment.

"And so it begins. It'll get worse when they know the suspect is a detective at the SPD," he says with the press of a button on the remote.

"When they know how hard your office worked on this, they'll thank you."

"Thankless job, English."

She smiles, "You can call me, Caitlyn."

"You're still calling me, sir."

"Touché," she says with a smile. She sits in quiet reflection. "Here are my thoughts on the name calling. If I start calling you Weston, I will undoubtedly have a slip of tongue at the office. Calling you, sir, under these circumstances is a bit awkward, but I've nothing beyond those options, I'm afraid. Of course, I could call you Cowboy, though I've heard that's what your women call you."

"Rumors, Caitlyn."

"Uh, huh."

"Back home they call me West."

"It suits you although I still might slip up at the office."

"We'll jump off that bridge when we get to it."

"Speaking of bridges, the one on your property is a work of inspiration. It fits naturally into the surroundings, and it felt rock-solid when we crossed over the brook."

"The split logs came from the trees I had to cut during the clearing of the land. It's my pride and joy."

"You built it?"

"Stanner and I built it."

"He's more than your security detail."

"Best friend."

"His only friend," Stanner says from the doorway. "Sorry for the interruption, but I'd like to give Ms. English a tour of the security features inside the main house. You want in, West?"

"No. I've got work to do. Goodnight, Caitlyn."

The bodyguard and the boarder hear the beginning of the DA's phone call as they walk away, "David, tell me the SPD knows the whereabouts of Matthew Cambridge."

Caitlyn is alone in her room. She is sitting at the edge of her bed absorbing Stanner's words…

"Behind this dividing wall are two areas, an en suite bathroom and a dressing room. There are four wall-mounted monitors in the dressing area. If there is any concern about a breach, check the monitors before you make a move. They'll project what's going on at the front and back of the property, and on the first and second floors of the main structure. The monitors are to remain on at all times. West will be staying in the room across the hall. If anything happens while he's there, go to him, but that room has no access to the outside. A drop from the window on that side of the house is too steep for you. Your room has a short drop. If you need to get outside, that's your best option. Take a look."

She looked. She shivered at the memory of Matt stalking her through their home. She started to tear, but pushed them back and swallowed them hard.

"Do you know how to use a gun?"

"Sort of."

"There's no sort of when it comes to gun handling, Ms. English. We'll work on getting you a better answer tomorrow. And before you ask, you will not be going into the office, or anywhere else, for the foreseeable future."

She gets off the bed, goes to the dressing room, leans back against a wall and watches the monitors. Images flash from vantage point to vantage point. On the monitor labeled, Out #2, she sees Stanner checking a small building off the back deck. On the monitor labeled, In #1, she sees flash images of rooms on the first floor, one of those images is of West pacing the den, a highball glass in hand. *He looks good in flannel and jeans.* "Stop it! He's your boss. And you are married!" She chokes on her next words, "To a serial rapist." Caitlyn heads to the en suite, draws a bath in a jetted claw-foot brass tub, immerses herself deep in an aromatic froth of lavender and sage and surrenders herself, body, mind, and spirit. As her muscles relax, so too her ability to keep her emotions buckled up. When there's not a single tear left, she drags her weary self to bed.

The man of the house leaves his door wide. He's still enjoying the wafting lavender and sage of Caitlyn English long after her lights go out. It is quite some time before he settles.

Wakey. Wakey.

Morning sounds invade. The Wanted Man hops from the pickup bed, grabs the block of wood from under the door, and closes the rolltop. He has his back to the wall when the beep of his security pad puts him at the ready. He listens. "No cop sounds. It's Ricky. He heard the news report, and he's checking my unit. Mistake. A fatal mistake."

Ricky Brown, owner of, A Place to Store Your Shit, never felt a thing.

Cambridge watches the bludgeoned man thud to the floor. He kicks aside the guys feet, closes the door, taps on a few bubble shaped wall lights, moves a few storage containers from a back corner, and drags Mr. Brown to his not-so-final resting place. He grabs a tarp from a far corner, drops it onto the prone man, wrenches off the top a paint can, and takes his morning piss. "Fuckin starved." He rummages through a container for food and water, tosses his bounty onto the bed, then leans his ass onto the tailgate. When he's done eating, he jumps inside the truck and turns on the radio.

Statewide search underway for Matthew James Cambridge, former detective with the Syracuse Police Department. Cambridge is wanted for a string of rapes across Upstate New York. Onondaga and Cayuga County District Attorneys, Weston James and Isla

Conway, issued a joint statement identifying Cambridge as the serial rapist known amongst law enforcement communities as REDO.

Cambridge turns off the radio and gets out of his truck. He hops onto the truck bed, opens the duffle he used as a pillow, moves some clothes and cash aside, grabs a handgun and tucks it into the waistband of his jeans. "Marietta, New York. Pretty enough place for the bitch to die." He checks his watch, "Six-thirty. I need to pack my shit and get the fuck out of here." He's ready to roll ten minutes later. He addresses the recently departed as he slides into his ride, "Sorry about the blood stain at the rolltop. Keep my security deposit, and we'll call it even."

He may live to regret that.

Stanner takes Caitlyn to a firing range not too far from *Remington*, the name of the DA's homestead. The usually buttoned-up barrister is dressed casually, and suitably for the unseasonably warm day: white turtleneck, pair of jeans, bright purple and white Styles sweatshirt, and her favorite pair of shitkickers. She dons a pair of shooting earmuffs and gets down to business. Stanner goes over the safety rules of weapon handling, then lets Caitlyn work a target, "I want to assess where you are," he hands her a Ruger LCR snub nose .38 revolver.

The Grace Kelly clone smiles demurely then sights and fires six rounds. The stunned Stanner pushes a button and watches the paper target move toward them. "Sort of?" he repeats her words from the night before.

She smiles, "Cambridge taught me."

"If he crosses your path, Ms. English, he may live to regret that decision."

"Or not."

"Didn't hear that, Ms. English."

"Hear what, Stanner?"

When they return to *Remington*, Caitlyn's bodyguard takes her on a tour of the grounds. "That clearing back there, just beyond the five stall stable, is the location for a paddock that will be built in the spring. The pool over there has a nearby bathhouse. The b-ball half-court over there has an athletic shed and quarter mile track around it. There are two root cellars off the deck, there and there. If you go inside, use the lights, it's a long drop. All of the structures I named have keypad entry, as does the main house. The code is 2114. Always check the upper righthand corner of the keypad before punching in the code; it shows the last time the unit was deactivated for entry. You may decide going into the facility is the more dangerous option. Let's head to the house, follow the rules I just set and gain access."

Caitlyn bounds the deck stairs, goes to the back door, checks the time in the righthand corner: 11:30a. "Someone deactivated security at eleven-thirty this morning."

"Yes. What's your plan, Ms. English? Are you going to enter the house?"

"West might have entered the premises."

"Cambridge might have entered the premises. I repeat, are you going to enter the house?"

"With you, yes. On my own, no. But what should I do?"

"Follow me." Stanner leads her off the deck and around the far right corner of the house, "This keypad reads 07:00a. This door leads to the basement. The basement is used by West for his woodworking and by delivery services. I have cancelled all deliveries for the foreseeable future, and West will not be woodworking, so no one will be entering the basement via this door, except us. I will be resetting this entrance with the readout 07:00a. If you are unsure about the safety of the main house, come here, and if the readout is 07:00a key in the security code, enter, and wait. This is the safest area of the entire spread."

Stanner has Caitlyn work the keypad and open the door. "If you are being pursued, Ms. English, step through the door and push it closed behind you. Do not let it simply shut. Do not give your pursuer an easy in." He leads her through the basement and on their way through, he instructs her, "Do you have your cell phone with you?"

"No."

"Starting now, you will have your cell phone with you at all times. It will be on silent/vibrate at all times. No need to let Cambridge know where you are hiding when he calls your phone trying to find you—and he will try to find you."

She nods.

They move along an aisle set between several sawhorses with several pieces of woodworking projects mounted on them. "West's?"

"Most. There are plenty of tools down here that could be used as a weapon. Learn this space. If you are in danger, think outside the box. Remember this, if you can use things as weapons, your attacker can too. As soon as you're feeling ready, Ms. English, I'd like you to have your piece with you at all times."

She nods.

"This panel at the top of the stairs controls the electricity in the house. If you move this red switch to the opposing position the house will be plunged into darkness, and the police will be notified by silent alarm. Lights in the basement will be off for ten seconds before the generator kicks them on. If anyone breaches the house, you should try to get into this section and get to this panel to flip the emergency switch. If you do all that and stay in this area, you are safe. As for the door at the top of the stairs, it has a keypad. Read it."

Caitlyn reads the time in the corner, "11:30a."

"Are you going to enter the house?"

"Yes."

"Why is that?"

"I saw West inside when we left the deck to come down here."

Stanner laughs big.

Caitlyn presses 2114, pushes the door open, and enters a room she hasn't yet been in, "A second office."

"Yours for the time you are with us. Your files and laptops are here for your use. There's one last thing, Ms. English," Stanner reaches behind his back and takes the revolver she used at the firing range. "Are you licensed to carry concealed?"

"No."

"Don't take that gun off these premises. Is that clear?"

"Very."

The DA asks from the doorway, "Ms. English is well-enough trained?"

Stanner pulls from his pocket the folded body target he took from the firing range, slaps it against the DA's chest and says, "Yup."

U-turns.

"What's your plan for the Ruger?"

Caitlyn opens her desk drawer and puts it in, "I'm leaving it here until I'm a little more comfortable having it on me. I think that is the ultimate goal, right?"

He smiles.

God he has a great smile.

He takes a seat opposite her, "There have been no sightings of Cambridge. Do you have any ideas where he might be?"

She scoffs. "I think we've established that I didn't know much about the man I married. I'm not trying to make light of this, but I just don't know. I was awake well into the night thinking about the time he and I spent together, and there's nothing that stands out. He said he was an only child and his parents are deceased."

"That's true."

"He said he was from Maine."

"That's true."

"He graduated from the Styles."

"That's true."

"And never went back to Maine because his parents were both dead by the time he finished graduate work."

West shakes his head. "His parents were dead before he started his freshman year. He began setting roots in Syracuse the day he arrived in 2001. He bought CL-14 while he was still in college. I'm sure there's more that will come to light about Matthew Cambridge, but SPD isn't investigating what he did in the past, they're interested in where he is now."

An involuntary shiver runs her spine, does a U-turn and runs it again.

"So far, Caitlyn, the only thing SPD has to go on is the car he stole to get out of Aurora, it was found abandoned on the outskirts of Syracuse. Cambridge made his way back to the area for a reason, and we know what that reason is."

Another U-turning shiver runs its course.

"Cambridge either boosted another car, or he had one stashed somewhere. He had to have known he'd be found out eventually, so he probably made contingency plans, mode of transportation, stashed money, maybe even a false ID and passport."

Caitlyn gets up from the desk and stands in front of side by side windows overlooking the back part of the spread. "*Remington* is a very nice name for your place. I spent a few minutes on the deck off my room this morning. The view of Otisco Lake is spectacular."

"It is. You should stay off the deck," he says on his way out of her temporary office.

Easy Fucking Peasy.

Cambridge closed up shop at Ricky's place, left a sign saying the owner was on vacation, then hit the road. He does a circuitous route on and off an interstate and travels a two-lane highway for many minutes, declaring "No tail." He debates whether he should cut his losses and leave New York or cut the bitch and leave her for dead. "Coin toss. I'll take a ride through Marietta and see if I can get near the DA's place."

An hour later, he pulls onto a parking lot, grabs his go-to cell phone, the one he lifted from the street-walking whore known as, Sonia Perez. He laughs at that whole fucking charade. "Found the hooker right where Aldo said she'd be, working the corners in Brownsville. Took the bitch for a ride, lifted her phone when she was face-fucking down on my dick, then let every call to the bitch go unanswered—the calls from SPD and the calls from Aldo's defense attorney. Fucking whore. If she hadn't sauntered her ass into SPD to provide an alibi for Mendez, Detective Chase wouldn't have put two and two together, and he wouldn't have figured out I'd been doctoring files. Aldo Mendez was the case where I made **the** mistake. The one that sent Ray in my direction. That mistake is keeping me from doing and redoing what I do best," he slams his hand on the steering wheel.

Cambridge plugs GPS coordinates from the slap-and-track he put on the Caddie into Sonia's phone, and lets the sultry sounds of some computer babe set his course. "Okay, now for a little drive-by. Don't get cocky," he cautions himself. "Just a drive past the main turn-off to his place, then a wide circumference around the property. Fifty acres is going to give me plenty of options. There's no rush. Find the right entry point."

Whispers and whimpers.

The DA spends the remainder of the day behind closed doors. Caitlyn heads outside to burn off some nervous energy by jogging the track at the basketball court. Stanner joins her, "Everything all right, Ms. English?"

"Hunky dory," she jabs. She stops cold, "I'm sorry, Stanner. You didn't deserve my flippant response."

He smiles, "No apology needed. I'd say under the circumstances you're entitled to a flippant response, maybe more."

She starts running again.

He joins her.

"You can call me Caitlyn, if you want."

"No, Ms. English, you are my subject."

"Right now, I am your jogging partner."

"One who I will tackle the hell out of if need be. In the future, Ms. English, I'd like a heads up before you exit the main house."

She smiles wide. "I will comply with your request if you beat me back to the main house," she catches her flatfoot flatfooted, and takes the lead, but the 6'5" guy makes up the distance in three exceedingly l-o-n-g s-t-r-i-d-e-s.

"Better luck next time, Ms. English."

The two stiffen when the DA steps out onto the deck, "Caitlyn, a word please."

She follows him into the kitchen, "Could this wait until I get out of this sweaty gear?"

"I'm afraid not. There is some breaking news, and I want you to hear it from me. Five women have come forward saying they are victims of REDO, and another woman's family blames him for their daughter's rapes and subsequent suicide."

Caitlyn doesn't react—or move—or breathe.

West rubs his hands up and down her arms until she comes around.

She turns sad eyes to him. "Would you say I'm somewhat intelligent?"

He smiles, "I would."

"Then would you please enlighten me as to how I ended up married to a rapist, a twisted one who thrills at raping his victims a second time around?"

The DA leaves the comment unanswered and changes subjects. "What do you know about Matt's mother?"

"She used to bake bread on Sundays."

"That's it?"

"Yes. Why do you ask?"

"There's a picture emerging about Matt's past. He's originally from Farmington, Maine, the only child of Dade and Amy Cambridge. Detective Kelly began researching him as soon as he was done with the CL-14 search. The detective spoke with Captain Moses Plank in Farmington who said he and his officers did plenty of wellness checks on Matt's mother at the request of neighbors who feared for her safety. The officers would offer to take Amy to a shelter, but she'd insist there was no reason to, and since she never had a mark on her, their hands were tied. Plank said things would settle at the Cambridge place for weeks, or even months, before they'd get another call. Detective Kelly said there's a lot more to the story, but Captain Plank didn't want to discuss it over the phone. Brandan's heading to Farmington next week."

"Learned behavior, but he never hurt me." She reflexively rubs her bruised arm, hangs and shakes her head.

The DA remains silent.

"He had to have known I wouldn't fall into his mother's role, so what? He took himself a wife to what—lessen his rape urges?"

"I don't think his marrying you was about love, romance, or rape. Matthew Cambridge benefitted greatly by being part of the arresting and prosecuting duo known as The Counselor and **That** Cop. Evidence is mounting that supports Ray's supposition that Cambridge was doctoring files at SPD, which means he was doctoring files at our office. He was controlling his twisted life by controlling everything and everyone around him, including you."

"Keep your friends close, your enemies closer."

"Yes. Cambridge had no reason to question your loyalties to him. Sadly, Caitlyn, that circumstance has changed. He intends you great harm now."

"When he finds me, he's going to rape me and then he's going to kill me."

Weston and Stanner hear resignation in her voice.

The emotionally deflated woman leaves the kitchen without further comment. She showers, pushes her wet hair back with a soft headband, pulls on a spaghetti strap camisole, a pair of bikini-panties, and slips into bed. She tosses and turns fitfully, pushes her blankets free, kicks her sheets away, then defiantly cracks open the deck door for a little fresh air. She hops back into bed, covers herself, and falls into a deep sleep. In the stillness of night she wakes with a hand pressed tight against her mouth. Fear rises and pushes until she hears *his* voice.

"Security at the main entrance reported a black F-150 on the road. They think the driver is doing reconnaissance." West feels a breeze at his back, turns to find the deck door open, "Jesus, Caitlyn." He shuts the door, goes back to her bed and extends his hand, "Come on. You're bunking in my room until we get the all-clear."

She kicks back the covers and rushes from bed. Her near nakedness doesn't register with her. It most certainly registers with him.

"Wait here," he groans when they enter his room. He steps into his dressing area, returns with a long-sleeved Columbia University T-shirt and tosses it to her. "Remind me later to tell you how much I hated covering you."

She sports a small smile as she pulls the shirt over her head, emerges with a huge smile when the shirt is in place. "Remind me later to tell you how much I hated putting this on."

He groans. "This is not the time to have the conversation we need to have."

"We need to have a conversation?"

"Not now, Caitlyn," he groans. He walks into his dressing room again. When he returns, he tosses her a pair of sweatpants. "Put them on or get into bed."

She points to the California king, "That bed? Your bed?"

The pacing man puts up his hand and answers his cell. He listens. He answers. "I'll be down in a minute. Stay here Caitlyn. If you have concerns you can watch the monitors in the dressing room. Do not leave this room, and if you need protection there is a Ruger in the end table drawer. Please do not shoot me upon my return."

"There's no way I'm shooting you **before** we have our conversation."

He laughs. He leaves.

Stanner is leaning against his Caddie when West joins him. The pissed off security guard hands his boss a small black plastic item. "It's a GPS tracker. It must have been put on my Caddie when it was parked at the Fayetteville residence. That's the only time my ride's been out of my sight. Cambridge knows Caitlyn is here."

"I should get her out of New York, maybe take her to the ranch in Montana."

"West. You're crossing the line with Caitlyn. It's a line you said you'd never toe let alone cross. What's going on?"

"I should have found a way to be with her. I let my damn job, the fact that I'm her boss, keep me from developing a personal relationship with her, and look where it's gotten us. Cambridge is after her and he is going to keep after her until he rapes and kills her. There is no fucking way I'm letting him anywhere near that woman. If I have to take Caitlyn English to Montana or to Mars to keep her safe, that's what I will do."

Stanner nods, "Let's get it done."

Caitlyn is standing at the door that leads to a deck off the bedroom when West returns. She is wearing the very roomy T-shirt and enormously wide and long sweatpants he tossed her way. West laughs when he sees her.

"Is Cambridge anywhere near this house?"

"No. But he knows you're here."

She nods and reflects a moment. "So we are safe."

"I wouldn't attest to that in a court of law, but, yes."

"Good. I know you want to have a conversation with me, but..." She pulls his T-shirt up over her head and his sweatpants down her legs. "But I'd much rather spend what could be my last night on earth whispering sweet nothings to you."

West crosses the room, swings the wanting woman into his arms, takes her to his bed and turns her whispers into whimpers.

Trailers for sale or rent.

"Guards at the access road," he grouses. "They weren't there this morning. Maybe nighttime reinforcement? Doesn't matter, they saw the truck. Probably not unusual for a truck to be on this road, but if the security detail is new, then the DA is fortifying the homestead." He takes the long way around the property. "No way I'm hoofing it from out here. I need to go in near the guard shack. Time to make some plans."

Half hour later, he is parked on the wrong side of a locked chain barrier at a closed campground in Auburn, New York. Rutted tire tracks suggest someone has used the access road since the January 8th storm. "Good." Within minutes, he has the padlock in one hand and the steering wheel of his truck in the other. He drives just beyond the chain, gets out and replaces the lock, then goes in search of a place to stay. His trip through the grounds doesn't take long, "Tracks run the lower roads. Can't put new treads down, so I need to choose one of these trailers." He does another creep through, pulls his truck to the far side of a sixty foot, double-wide. Checks the unit for cameras and a wall-mounted security pad before picking the lock and slipping inside.

Higher stakes.

"Caitlyn."

"Mmmmm."

"We need to get up. We need to talk."

"I would very much prefer whispering and whimpering, thank you kindly."

He leans close, kisses her shoulder, wraps his arm around her waist and pulls her tight into his spoon. He moans deep and moves his hand to cup her breast. He groans. She moans. He groans again.

"Caitlyn, if I promise there will be some more whispering, whimpering, and an occasional yeehaw scream of release, would you consent to getting your ass out of my bed?"

She laughs and rolls, "The real you is nothing like the buttoned-up man of command that need only look at his subjects to render them speechless and trembling."

West swings his leg over her, rights himself above her, brushes her hair away from her face, looks deeply into her denim-blues and warns, "Set yourself, Caitlyn. I'm about to render you speechless and cause a bit of trembling."

Stanner waits for the DA and ADA to join him in the kitchen. When they walk in he knows—they all know—the stakes became higher overnight.

The security expert kicks things into high gear, "West, have you spoken with Caitlyn?"

She tilts her head and raises a brow at the mountain man, "Caitlyn? I thought you couldn't address your subject by her first name."

"I believe you are West's woman now. Correct me if need be."

"No correction, Stanner, please continue."

"West wants you out of New York and would like to settle you in Montana for a spell."

The men expect pushback. The men get none.

"Okay. When do we leave?" She turns to West, "Of course, I'll need to inform my boss, or my former boss should he refuse to grant me a leave of absence."

He smiles big and pulls her near, "Your leave request is granted."

"Good, now that that's taken care of," Stanner continues, "I've booked three first-class tickets on a redeye out of Syracuse at 1:30 AM. It will arrive in Butte, Montana, a long-ass time after that. West, if you plan on going to your office, you need to be back no later than 10 PM. I'll have the Caddie packed with everyone's gear, so plan on leaving the minute you get here."

West smiles. "Are we allowed to have coffee and something to eat now?"

Stanner nods and leaves.

Caitlyn stands on her tippy-toes, plants a kiss on West's cheek and teases, "I'm really enjoying this side of you." He wraps his arms around her waist, lifts her so they are face to face and growls, "I'm really enjoying everything about you, Caitlyn, most particularly your eyes when they hood and lose focus. I should have told you I wanted you. I should have asked for a chance to be with you. And I should have demanded that you leave Cambridge when I saw him worming his way into your life. I was a damned fool, and my inactions are plenty to blame for this fucking mess."

She wriggles in his arms, then slides the length of him. When she is on somewhat solid ground, she shares her wonder, "You? You wanted to be with me? In a personal relationship—with me?"

He nods. "Since the day you walked into my office for an interview. I actually thought about not hiring you so I could date you."

"Shut up!"

He laughs and pulls her near, "You never sensed my want, my longing?"

She playfully rubs her abdomen against him, "I'm sensing it now," she smiles. "But good God, NO, I never sensed it. I must say you are very good at this dual-life of yours—dastardly DA by day, sexy suitor by night."

West takes hold of her shoulders and leans her body away from him, "Are you in urgent need of coffee and breakfast?"

"No."

"Good." He takes her hand and leads her into his office, swipes off whatever is on his desk, lifts her, and seats her on the edge of an intricately carved block of wood, "Set yourself, Ms. English, because I am about to live out the fantasy I've had for the past six years, and I expect you'll be offering one of those yeehaw screams of release I warned you about."

Caitlyn leans forward, releases him from his jeans, giggles when he pulls her butt near off the desk, and moans when he enters her, "Oh, District Attorney James, I had no idea this was in your briefs."

He laughs, then pushes deep.
"Yeehaw!"

Mantras and final wishes.

Cambridge has a plan, and he begins executing it. "Duffle of money, behind passenger seat on the floor. Backpack of water and provisions, in the bed of the truck. Duffle with rolled sleeping bag, ski-mask, and gloves, in the pickup bed. Rifle with scope, in the bed. Handgun, back of jeans. Knife to cut the bitch to pieces, in the glovebox." He tosses a twenty onto the counter inside the trailer and hits the road. He turns his plan into a chant and lets it keep him company.

"Stash the truck two miles south of the entrance. Cover tire tracks at point of entry. Hike in on foot. Hunker low until nightfall. Take out the guards, then…" He takes a sip of coffee and a bite of breakfast sandwich he grabbed at a morning food franchise then repeats his mantra. "Stash the truck two miles south of the entrance. Cover tire tracks at point of entry. Hike in on foot. Hunker low until nightfall. Take out the guards, then…" He takes his last bite and sip.

Just before the sun claims the full of day, Cambridge backs his truck as deep into the woods as possible. He leaves the duffle of money with a handwritten note in the cab.

If my ass ends up dead, use this money to raise the cabin at Cayuga Lake, CL-14 owned

by me, Matthew James Cambridge on record as MJC: 18-5-4-15. Bury my ass. There will be no objections from my wife, Caitlyn English, because she will be dead. DO. NOT. BURY. HER. WITH. ME.
Signed: Matthew James Cambridge.

He goes to the bed and grabs the backpack, second duffle, and rifle with scope. He goes around to the passenger side of his truck, takes a sheathed blade and affixes it to his ankle. He smiles wide and relaxes into himself, then begins a whole new chant, "Go get the bitch and eliminate anyone who gets in your way."

Tying up loose ends.

District Attorney Weston James leaves *Remington* with orders from Stanner to return home on time. He stops at the guard shack, lowers his window, and exchanges a few words with the man on duty, "Stanner asked you to do a day shift?"

"Yes, sir. My partner is doing a walkabout, and there will be two other guards here tonight."

"Very well," he says with the raising of his window.

Caitlyn spends a good amount of time in her office getting her files in order. She isn't sure how the whole working from Montana will play out, but her boss said he'd make it work, so she puts that concern aside. She goes in search of Stanner, finds him in West's room packing. "I'm in need of a run, but don't want to put you out if you've a lot left to do."

"Go change. I need about ten minutes."

Caitlyn turns to leave, turns back when he begins speaking again.

"I've decided to give you until the count of ten before I join our race to the house, Caitlyn."

She smiles wide, "My odds of winning just increased exponentially."

"Doubt it," he laughs.

The DA calls a meeting with his senior staff and includes the ADA's assistant, Michelle Young. "You are all aware of the situation regarding ADA English. For safety reasons she has been in seclusion. We believe Matthew Cambridge knows where she is and made an attempt to gain access to her. Ms. English will be moved to another location. I have arranged security for her during this move, but I feel it is my responsibility to ensure she arrives safely at her destination. I will be out of the office for a week beginning tomorrow. The only person in this room with whom I will be in contact is Michelle Young, although she will not know my whereabouts. Work your cases, and communicate any concerns or issues that come up with Michelle. That is all. Ms. Young please remain seated." He waits until his staff files out then sits across from the paralegal. "Set up shop in ADA English's office. No one is allowed at your workspace or in her office. As for workload while ADA English is away, concentrate on the task force cleanup. You will be assigned no other cases. One last thing, SPD Chief of Police Barelli will accept your calls. Do not contact him unless you suspect someone is dead or close to being so. That is all."

Plans and threats.

Cambridge is ready. He has set camp very near a split log bridge that crosses a babbling brook. He estimates that he's three quarters of a mile from the now empty guard shack and a quarter of a mile from the main residence which he's scoped with his binoculars. When he saw the log cabin estate for the first time he scoffed at its owner, "Fuckin tool thinks he's living on a goddamn ranch. Bet Cowboy's taken a ride or two on my bitch. But don't worry Caitlyn, I'll make sure my final mount breaks the fuck out of you. Then I'll put you down, for humane reasons, of course."

Think. Move. Think.

The DA calls Stanner when he's nearing the guard shack as is standard operating procedure. He thinks about placing another call when he finds the shack empty, thinks otherwise when concern burns his gut. He takes the corner onto his property and presses his foot to the floor. As soon as he starts across the log bridge, he loses control of his Lincoln Aviator and goes airborne. The vehicle hits all sides, finally landing wheels down in the brook—though West is currently unable to attest to that point.

Cambridge pats his scoped rifle, "One down. One to go."

Stanner had the Caddie mostly packed when he got the call that the DA was nearing the guard shack at *Remington*. The man looked at his watch, "Well, I'll be damned. West's gonna be here on time." The bodyguard of Caitlyn English steps into the house and calls up to her from the staircase. "West is on his way. I'll need the rest of your things, Caitlyn." Silence. Stanner charges up the stairs when there is no response, relaxes when he hears classical music blaring and the blow dryer running from inside the en suite. He is just about to knock when he hears the sound of a crash outside. Stanner bolts from the main house and heads down the access road. He has just entered the tree line when he is felled by a bullet.

Caitlyn is dressed very casually for the fifteen-hour trip to Montana. She is lacing her sneakers when she hears the slam of the front door and the words that send terror through her.

"Caitlyn, I'm home!"

The panicking woman PANICS, quickly remembers Stanner's words, "Think. Move. Think." She gathers her wits, then moves quietly into the dressing room and watches video images of Matt Cambridge searching the rooms on the first floor. She wants to scream for help. *If he's inside this house, there is no help, Caitlyn. Think. Move. Think.* She does both. She turns the lock on the bedroom door, makes her way onto the deck, slides the curtains back in place and then pulls the door shut. She swings one leg over the railing then the other. She wedges the toe of her sneakers as close to the slats as she can, inches her hands down, lowers her limbs off the deck and drops to the ground—just as she hears the inside door of her bedroom being kicked opened.

Cambridge steps onto the balcony above her and yells down, "Remember when we played Hide 'n Seek and I said I wouldn't chase you for fun ever again? Consider this fair warning. This isn't going to be fun!"

Caitlyn pushes to her feet and bolts. Matt hurtles himself over the deck railing, way too hard, grunts in pain when he lands with a thud onto the cold, hard ground. He rights himself as she rounds the corner at the far end of the house. She keys 2114, gains access to the basement, slams her back tight against the door and presses hard when it catches his hand. She keeps pressure on until he shimmies his fingers free, then pushes harder, closing it tight.

His screamed threats are in concert with his forceful kicks. "I am gonna rape the fuck out of you. You'll be begging me to fuckin kill you. AND. I. WILL!"

Caitlyn stands frozen in fear as he fires his weapon at the keypad and lock. She snaps out of her headspace and rushes through the underground room. She flicks the red switch on the electrical pad at the top of the stairs signaling the need for Marietta police. She bangs 2117 into the keypad. ACCESS DENIED. She tries again, 2114. The lock clicks. She opens the door and sneaks into her office, gets to her desk, takes the Ruger into her hand, and slips back through the basement door. She is pulling it shut behind her when tension pulls from the other side and Cambridge fills the doorway. He raises his foot and kicks her down the flight of stairs.

"How fuckin perfect. You love sitting and sleeping on the floor, Caitlyn. Let's see how much you like being raped and killed on one."

West wakes at the sound of a shot. He's aware of the freezing water filling the space around his lower body. He swipes at a cut on his forehead, rinses his hand in the water and tries to push through the fog in his head, "Accident." The next thought slams him into action, "Caitlyn!" He struggles, twists, turns, pushes, and kicks his way out of the car, falls onto the bank of the brook, pulls a few painful breaths, rights himself and limps toward his house and his woman. Off in the distance he hears the faint wail of sirens. "Please be heading this way."

Her Scream

Cambridge scrambles down the stairs and backhands Caitlyn as she's halfway to a stand. She stumbles back, bangs into a wooden workstation, upending it and herself, both falling to the floor amidst the sounds of metal tools hitting concrete. Cambridge tucks his gun into the back waistband of his jeans. He flexes his hands as he takes the last few steps toward his ultimate victim. She scrambles up, missing a handhold of a screwdriver laying very near. He laughs. She scoots left, pushing a sawhorse between them, rights herself, and runs toward the back exit. He laughs again as he hurdles the fallen piece. The sound of his boots heavy on the floor bring it all back to him…

"Get in our room."

The boy shook his head, "Please, I don't want to."

"You'll lay under my bed and learn how you keep your woman in line."

The boy shook his head, "No, Daddy, please."

"Get your ass in that room, or it'll be you who bears the brunt of this evening."

The boy inched into the room, slid under the bed, and swallowed the tears that threatened. He held his breath when he saw his mother's feet turn the corner, watched in horror as his father's booted feet moved toward her, listened in anguish to Her Scream when she was thrown hard onto the mattress.

This husband stalks **this** wife through the dank, dark basement, quickly closing the space between them. He grabs her from behind, lifting her feet high off the ground. She flails in his hold, trying to make contact with her pumping feet. He growls into her ear, "Having fun, wifey?" Her Scream of terror strengthens the ramrod between his legs.

"This is gonna be good. For. Me." He throws her to the ground, her head thudding hard on the concrete floor. He pounces on top, straddles her waist, pins her arms beneath his knees, slaps her hard to bring her around, and grabs his knife. He cuts through her camisole, smiles wide when he takes his first cut of her nakedness, a slice across her left breast. He ignores her, "No. No. No." Concentrates on his erection pulsing hard against its dungaree binding, feels it strengthen at the sight of her blood. "Now, you're like all the rest." He grabs hold of her leggings and easily slices through. He yanks himself from his jeans, lays the length of her, thrusts several times, struggling against her moves for her entrance. He misses the mark. He pushes and rages. Misses again. **"Don't. Move."** He pulls a few slow breaths, trying to lower his rage. He needs to seduce to perform. He struggles between his desire to rape and his desire to murder—this woman. He whisper-rages against her ear, **"I want to rape you. I want to kill you."** He laughs manically.

Caitlyn's panic soars. She inches her hips away from his grunting plunges, barely avoiding entry. She pushes her hips hard against him, her body moves upward and leftward. He grabs her hips and pulls them toward him, cutting her thigh in the process. He locks her beneath his weight. "I will cut your fuckin throat if you move another muscle." She stills.

West exits the tree line and limps to his felled friend who took a bullet to his chest.

"Take my gun. Go," Stanner pants.

West grabs the weapon and moves clumsily toward the house, his breathing halted and short. He bangs through the front door in time to hear **Her Scream.**

Cambridge breathes powerfully against her cheek. "Last. Chance. Caitlyn. If you move, I will slice you, then fuck you until you're dead!" He presses down, crushing her back against the unforgiving floor, her chest pressed tight beneath his solid mass. She gasps for air. *Can't breathe.* He moves his upper body then thrusts for her opening. She greedily pulls a breath. He thrusts again. She arches her back, raising a leg high enough to keep him from entering. *Think. Move. Think. I had a gun. Where? Where?* She flails her arms wildly, searching, reaching. He wraps his hand around her throat, "Fuckin whore. Stop fighting!" *Gun. He has a gun.*

Caitlyn reaches around her assailant and pulls his gun from the waistband of his jeans. She presses it against his side and pulls the trigger.

He slumps heavily on top of her, drags the hand holding the knife toward them, and struggles to raise it above her. It is his final act of aggression before another shot rings out.

West rushes down the stairs unsure who's been shot—who's alive.

Her Moan

The dead body of Matthew Cambridge is dragged away from the battered Caitlyn English by Weston James. He assess her wounds, strips to his bare chest, and uses his undershirt to cover the slice to her breast and cut to her thigh, the white cotton quickly turning wet and crimson—a trophy Matthew Cambridge will never see and never bring to his lair at CL-14. West blankets the trembling woman with his jacket.

It smells of outdoor freshness and man— all man—that man, the thought flits somewhere as she slips in and out of consciousness.

West takes space near the warrior woman on the cold, hard, concrete floor, holding her as gingerly as possible. He spends every second willing her to respond to his words, his touch. He is begging her to come around when Marietta police storm the grounds and give her aid.

West rides with Caitlyn and Stanner to the hospital, then sits at their bedsides in ICU. He refused admittance for his own injuries, three broken ribs and a mild concussion, a far less serious grade than the one suffered by Caitlyn. He had a fold-out chair moved near her bed and posted 24-hour guards outside the room, then paid silent vigil for his friend and his woman. His head is hang-dog low when she whispers three days later.

"Cowboy, I sure could use a sip of water."

The bigger than life man fixes wet eyes on the woman who fought the pull of hell to stay this side of living. "Caitlyn," her name catching in emotion.

She tries a smile with her very bruised and swollen lips, squeezes his hand and whispers, "What's a girl gotta do around here to get some water?"

Paying Respects

On an early summer morning, at Beard Park Cemetery located on the outskirts of Syracuse, in the county of Onondaga, New York, Raymond Paul Chase is laid to rest. The Syracuse police detective has been gone for many months. His family and friends have been unable to pay their last respects until today.

That was Ray's fault.

Most of the assembled mourners were called to handle an investigation that Detective Ray Chase didn't finish before his sudden death—an investigation that brought his estranged wife and son back into his life for a handful of days and brought a woman he worried deeply about to the brink of death. Ray's loved ones are standing on a tiny hill beneath a towering, lush elm peering into the open grave of a man who died a hero.

Ray would vehemently disagree.

Caitlyn English was called upon to eulogize Raymond Chase. She holds the request to pay homage as an honor, one that touches her deeply. Before she shares her words, Caitlyn completes Ray's final request. To his chosen few, the ones from whom he sought help handling his final act on Earth, she presents a handwritten note prepared by the deceased detective. One by one she addresses each recipient—one by one they tuck the envelope away into pockets and handbags, choosing to keep Ray's words for private reflection.

When the last wish of the deceased is granted, the mourners join hands and encircle the woman who led the charge on Ray's behalf. The woman who didn't Stay Safe enough—but the woman who survived. In a show of strength and humility Caitlyn English offers words that will be remembered for their simple truths.

"Raymond Chase was a good man, a brave man. A good enough man to know when to walk away and when to return. A brave enough man to stand up against injustice, no matter where he found it. He was a hero who taught the weaker among us to follow in his footsteps—even when those footsteps led us to the pits of Hell. Raymond Chase wanted but one thing when he left this earth." Caitlyn wipes a tear that runs her cheek, pulls a deep breath and whispers,

"He wanted us to Stay Safe."

The End

Please enjoy the teaser for the next
~~~ Twisted Threads ~~~

Stay Safe…

STAY SAFE

~~~ TWISTED THREADS ~~~
WOOD
SHERYLL O'BRIEN

The First of Many.
Homecoming

The petite, blue-eyed, raven-haired coed ran her hand nervously across the ridiculous beaver hat she bought at a university spirit table. "Stupid mascot." She sprinted a good length on the dark road then opened a creaky, old, rusted gate at the back end of her family's farm.

"Nice hat."

"Shit, Matt, you scared the hell out of me."

"Didn't mean to, Marylou." He reached out to touch her. She leaned away. He laughed a bit, "Sure would like to have your beaver on my head again."

She rolled her eyes, and pushed a sigh, "We're not getting back together, and we're definitely not having sex."

"We're not?" He stepped close, reached up and ran his hand across the fur, "Feels good."

She slapped his hand away, "I'm in college. I can't date a high schooler."

**"I don't want to date you.
I only want to rape you."**

ABOUT THE AUTHOR

She is not dead.

Sheryll O'Brien crafts characters without constraints. She tells them who they are, then let's them show her better versions of themselves. She gives them life and they live it beyond her wildest dreams.

Sheryll is a lifelong resident of Worcester, Massachusetts, where she is wife to the most supportive husband ever, and mother of two adult daughters, one who refuses to leave her home and the other who refuses to tell her where she lives. Of most significance, she is MammyGrams to the sweetest six-year-old, Hadley.

Sheryll worked several years in the fundraising community of Worcester County, writing grants for non-profit organizations. She began writing for her own pleasure after surviving brain surgery and breast cancer. Happily, for her fanbase of family and friends——she is not dead.

If you have enjoyed reading my book, I would very much appreciate you taking a few minutes to write a review and post that review on amazon.com and goodreads.com.

The opinion of readers can help prospective readers make a purchasing decision.

To learn more, please visit my website, www.pullingthreadsnovella.com subscribe to my blog for updates on future projects.

I would absolutely love to hear from my readers, you can email me at,

pullingthreadsnovella@gmail.com

www.ingramcontent.com/pod-product-compliance
Lightning Source LLC
Chambersburg PA
CBHW071339020726
47502CB00001B/170